Pr

THE CHALLENGE
"ONE OF ROMANCE'S MOST GIFTED AUTHORS."

Publishers Weekly

THE CHOICE
"I SIMPLY LOVE THIS BOOK."

Joan Wolf

"A WONDERFULLY ROMANTIC AND SPARKLING STORY. The colorful backdrop is perfectly portrayed and the emotional depth will move readers to laugh and perhaps shed a tear or two."

Romantic Times (*Four Stars*)

"TOP-NOTCH . . . told with flair and fraught with sexual tension."

Publishers Weekly

THE CAD

"The very best romance novels are almost like an adrenaline rush: there's the excitement of realizing that you are hooked, the intense focus that comes with being totally engrossed and the sweet, oh-so-satisfied letdown when the last page is turned. *The Cad* gave me all of this and more. . . . THIS ONE GOES STRAIGHT TO THE KEEPER SHELF. . . . WONDERFUL."

Romance Reader

"A REAL TREASURE."

Romantic Times

"TITILLATING, DANGEROUS AND IRRESISTIBLE . . . full of passion and plot twists that I could never have imagined. Brava, Ms. Layton!"

Under the Covers

Other Books by
Edith Layton

THE CAD
THE CHOICE
THE CHALLENGE

EDITH LAYTON

THE CHANCE

HarperTorch
An Imprint of HarperCollinsPublishers

This is a work of fiction. Names, characters, places, and incidents are products of the author's imagination or are used fictitiously and are not to be construed as real. Any resemblance to actual events, locales, organizations, or persons, living or dead, is entirely coincidental.

HARPERTORCH
An Imprint of HarperCollins*Publishers*
10 East 53rd Street
New York, New York 10022-5299

First HarperTorch paperback printing: October 2000

For Jeanne Simpson,
luminous lady of sense and sensibility

One

Only one wedding guest was frowning. He stood, arms crossed on his chest, and watched the other guests celebrating. It was a perfect evening for it. A long, soft midsummer's evening, mild and balmy, the kind made famous by Shakespeare—the kind that England rarely got in reality.

The wedding party had moved from the church to the groom's nearby estate for the reception. It was a glorious one, lasting from daylight into dusk. Musicians sat in leafy arbors and played. Lanterns hung from the trees, twinkling in the boughs like trapped stars. Torches flamed on the lawns, echoing the candle-filled chandeliers inside the house. The guests danced in the ballroom, onto the terrace, and then out on the scythed lawns that rolled to the river's edge and on into the coming night.

The frown didn't suit Lord Raphael Dalton. He

wasn't much past thirty, but had a hard-planed, angular face with strict features, their only saving grace the surprisingly dark lashes that offset his deep blue eyes. He had tried very hard to compensate for his unfortunate red hair, cropping it ruthlessly close in a modish Brutus cut. But even that couldn't make it remotely fashionable. He was spared the pale, freckled skin that often went with such hair, his complexion tan and clear. He was lean, with a wide rack of shoulders, and bore himself as the military man he'd once been. Rafe didn't have a mild appearance; the scowl made him appear harsher.

He wasn't looking at his newly wed host and hostess. Instead, he didn't take his gaze from a dark lady standing on the terrace nearby. He watched her as closely and jealously as a cat at a mousehole.

Or so at least his friend, the earl of Drummond, remarked softly to him.

Rafe's head turned fast. He pinned his friend with a blazing look. "And how'd you know if you hadn't been watching her that closely yourself?" he snapped.

"By watching you, of course. I didn't have to even glance at her. Your eyes were mirrors of her soul," the tall, thin, languid earl answered. He saw Rafe's expression. "And if you hit me here and now," he added softly, "you'll disrupt this lovely wedding party."

Rafe blinked; his shoulders drooped. "Too right," he said, rubbing the back of his neck, "You're right. Damme, don't you get sick of being right, Drum?"

His friend shrugged and hid a smile. "Perfection is

wearisome, I agree. But, Rafe, I thought you were as happy as I to see our friends wed. If you keep frowning like that, people will wonder if you see some problem with their union."

"Problem?" Rafe asked, amazed. "Did you ever see Wycoff so content?" he asked, looking at the groom. "Takes years from his face. And look at his Lucy. It does the heart good."

"Exactly, so stop scowling."

Rafe's harsh expression eased into genuine puzzlement.

"You look murderous."

"Do I?" Rafe's head went up. His cheeks grew warm. "Sorry. My thoughts were far from them. Little could make me happier than to see those two married."

"Little could make you happy indeed," Drum murmured.

Rafe still gazed at his dark lady. Only, the lady Annabelle was not his, and might never be, he reminded himself. Apart from the fact that he was a man women didn't look at twice—nor did he blame them for it—she was still bound heart and soul to another man. A man as unobtainable for her as she was for himself, Rafe thought savagely. The man she still yearned for was a good man, but well matched and married to another good person, so why didn't she cut line and move on? *For the same reason you don't stop wanting her*, he told himself as he stood watching her, helpless to look away. He hadn't expected to see her here, hadn't known she was a distant connection of the groom. She was so wellborn, she was likely related to half the nobles in England. But not to him, and not likely ever to be, and that grieved him.

The lady Annabelle wore a filmy gown of blue. It seemed to match her mood as much as her magnificent eyes. She was lovely. Famously so. Sonnets had been written to her; she was justly considered an Incomparable. Midnight hair, all soft and shining sable curls, midsummer-sky blue eyes, a dainty little nose, alabaster skin. Slender, but with a ripe though petite shape—if there were a list of features a lovely female should possess, a man needed only to consider her to see them all. The sonnet had said that too. And her laughter was like birdsong. *Her infrequent laughter*, Rafe thought, scowling again to see her sad smile as she greeted a friend.

Annabelle was of good birth, an earl's daughter with a tidy fortune. Intelligent and charming. Four and twenty and still unwed, which was shocking. She could have had any man she set her sights on. But the man she'd wanted had wanted another, and she couldn't get over it. Handsome young Damon Ryder had been her near neighbor all her life, she'd grown up wanting him, and whatever Annabelle wanted, she got. Only not this time. He had met another, fallen headlong into love, and never looked back. Everyone said Annabelle had been merry as a grig before the man she loved married elsewhere. Rafe hadn't known her then.

Sometimes he thought, with the pitiless honesty he was afflicted with, that if she were still merry and bright, he mightn't be as attracted to her. He might

have admired her as another man would appreciate
a treasure in a museum, and passed on by. It was her
sorrow that called to him as much as anything. Her
sadness made her accessible. He could do something
for her. He might perhaps heal her. At least he knew
how to protect a woman; he could make a sad lady a
good mate. Now he wanted only to make her smile
again.

He tore his gaze from her and looked at the couple
who so troubled her as they danced. Damon Ryder
was as handsome a male as Lady Annabelle was a
female. A strikingly good-looking, good-hearted fellow. He'd married a spectacular beauty of his own.
His wife, Gilly, was as fair as Annabelle was dark,
and just as lovely. But Gilly was unique. Forthright
as a man, she'd a generous heart and a loyal soul in
that beautiful body. Rafe held her as dear as a sister.
He was as happy for her now as Annabelle was not.

His friend saw the changed direction of his gaze,
and smiled. "It's lucky that Gilly gave our host an
excuse not to travel north to have the reception at his
father and mother's house."

"Well, the bride insisted I be here," Gilly Ryder
laughed. She and her husband had stopped dancing
and overheard him. "And since I said I couldn't
travel far in my 'condition,' his mama had to accept
it. Wycoff blessed me for it, but I'm happy to be an
excuse."

"So don't dance so much, baggage," Drum teased,
"Or she'll guess."

"Ho!" she said. "As if that would stop me. How
much longer shall I be able to dance this close in his

arms? Soon there'll be something coming between us," she said, running a hand over her flat abdomen. "I know, I know," she added, with a bright look at her husband. "That's not something a lady would say."

Damon Ryder grinned at his wife. "I know. Lucky me. Now they've struck up a waltz. So come, let's dance as close as we can while we may."

"That's a lucky fellow indeed," Drum said, watching the pair waltz off together.

"And there's another," Rafe said, watching the viscount Wycoff and his new bride dancing, their gazes locked. Neither was in the first bloom of youth, but both were handsome, more so now that they were radiant with happiness.

"Who would have guessed that Wycoff, of all people—*Wycoff*," Rafe, said, shaking his head, "would be so tamed by love?"

"Anyone, actually," Drum answered.

Rafe fell still. After a moment, he glanced around, looking for his lodestar, the magnet his eyes kept returning to. He saw her standing nearer than he'd known, at the terrace rail—and she looked stricken to the heart. Her hand lay against that heart as she stared, wild-eyed, at Gilly and Damon Ryder.

"Damme! She heard us. She must not have known!" Rafe muttered angrily. "Well, who would? Gilly still looks like a girl—but now she's going to be a mother." *The mother of Annabelle's dream lover's child. Another nail in the coffin of that dream for her,* he thought. He knew too much about dead dreams. He also knew what he had to do, and strode over to

Annabelle before he could think better of it, leaving his friend Drum standing alone in the twilight.

"My lady," Rafe said, bowing, "May I have this dance?"

"I'm sorry, I can't, I—" she said, stumbling over her words, still staring at the Ryders, transfixed.

Rafe didn't bow and move on, as was proper after being rejected. He stayed where he stood and stared down at her. She looked up to see him frowning. "Yes," she said on a broken laugh, "you're quite right. I'm making a spectacle of myself, aren't I?"

"No. I am. Looks like you turned me down and I'm being rude by hanging about anyway," he said. "They'll say I'm rag-mannered. Much I care. I am. But would you care to dance, after all?"

She bowed her head. "I should be honored, my lord."

"Everyone calls me Rafe," he said, giving her his hand.

"So you've said." They stepped into the pattern of a new dance. "Forgive me, I'd forgotten. We've met, haven't we?"

"At the Andersons' party, at Alamacks, the Ryders' wedding," Rafe said, and felt her stiffen as he said "Ryder." They'd met many times after that as well, even danced together a few times. But they'd seldom spoken. He'd lost most of the few pretty words at his command when he met her. It hardly mattered; he doubted she'd listened to him before.

"Yes," she said, looking down. He knew she was avoiding his eye; she never had to watch her feet when she danced. He'd watched her dance often enough to know that. "At their wedding. But I never did understand your connection to them," she said. "Are you related to her? Mrs. Ryder, I mean."

"No, known her a long time, though. I'm friend to the earl of Drummond. He's cousin to the Sinclairs, who fostered Gilly. I'm pleased to call them all friends now."

"And I see you're a man of few words," she said, with a singularly sweet smile that made him almost miss his step.

"I listen better than I speak," he said tersely, minding his step in the dance and with her. She'd never spoken so personally to him. He looked down at her sad little face and felt his heart clench tight. So lovely, so very somber. She gazed up at him, her eyes innocent. Too innocent. He might be enchanted by her, but he knew when he was being manipulated. It felt so good to have her stare at him, he didn't mind.

"Did I hear Mrs. Ryder intimate that she was . . . enceinte?" Annabelle asked ingenuously, as though they both didn't know that she'd heard it clear. "Expecting a babe?" she added, as though the simple soldier that he'd been wouldn't understand any other term. "I don't mean to be rude or bold, or *vulgar*," she added, "but since her husband's a very old friend of mine, I'd love to know so I can plan the perfect gift."

"Aye, she is. Early days. But there'll be a babe by spring."

She breathed in sharply. Then let out a shuddering sigh. When she spoke again, her voice was too bright. She still looked at her slippers as they paced through the dance. "How wonderful!" she exclaimed gaily, "To think, *Damon* a father! I vow that makes me feel ancient. I recall when he was just a boy. Well, we were near neighbors. He likely may have been one of the first things I ever saw when I was a babe myself, our parents were such good friends . . ."

She chattered on as they stepped through the form of the dance. She was too animated. But he recognized and admired bravery. He wished he could tell her so, but couldn't think of the right way to say it to her. Nothing would make her feel better about knowing the love of her life's wife was going to have his baby.

He couldn't let her know he knew she was suffering either. He wished, not for the first or even tenth time, that he had his friend Drum's glib tongue. Or his friend Wycoff's clever way with repartee. Or any one of a dozen other men's easy grace and way with females. He was blunt and to the point. Men admired that. Women were a different matter entirely.

The one thing he needed with this woman was Damon Ryder's face. He didn't have anything remotely resembling that. He could hear her out, though. He could let her know by his persistence that he cared. He could be of service to her. That was what he did best.

"Are you staying in the area after the wedding," he asked when she paused to take a breath, "or going back to London?"

"I'm going home," she said as bluntly as he might have done.

"Too bad," he said. "I'd like to see you again."

Her eyes flew to his. He thought that she might actually be seeing him now. "Would you?" she asked thoughtfully.

I've only followed you like a puppy through a dozen balls and every fete I've been lucky enough to see you at. If you'd ever looked my way, you'd have seen, Rafe thought, and said, because he was weary of only looking and longing, "Yes. I would. I've wanted to for some time. But there's always such a crush around you."

"And you were afraid of crowds?" she laughed.

She was good at flirtation. Rafe knew he was in over his head. "I'm not afraid of much, my lady," he said, and added, on sudden inspiration, "except, maybe, not seeing you again this summer."

"But if you didn't see me again until autumn or winter, it would be as well?" she asked archly. His lips tightened. "No, I'm only jesting," she added quickly. "Thank you, my lord—Rafe."

Annabelle cocked her head to the side and looked at her dancing partner again. She'd seen him before, of course. But now she looked at him closely for the first time.

He had that unfortunate hair. It was hard to see beyond that. Now she tried. He wasn't strictly handsome. But not ill favored either. Lean and fit, too. He had a brusque manner and seemed filled with nervous energy. But he was clean and well dressed and carried himself with an air of confidence and self-possession. He seemed like the kind of man a man would look up to. He had good birth and she supposed some fortune; his friends were highly placed. She was here tonight because her father was connected to the Wycoff family. He was here because he was friends with Lord Wycoff as well as with Damon. And she knew he was smitten with her. Utterly.

Damon and his wife danced by. Annabelle saw them through the side of her eye. She didn't have to; she knew where he was whenever he was in the room. This time she refused to turn her head. She looked at Lord Raphael Dalton instead. "You know," she said, "Mama wanted to stay in London. I was the one to insist on going home, but now I think . . ." He watched her intently. "I think I'll return to London, after all . . . Rafe. You did say you'll be there too?"

The wedding was over, the festivities ended; the guests went back to their homes and lives. But the next day after breakfast, Rafe and Drum still lingered at the inn they'd stopped at.

"Too nice a day to stay cooped up in a coach," Rafe finally said, looking out the window. "I think I'll ride back to London, instead."

"If it was raining hot coals, you'd say that," Drum laughed. "So she gave you the time of day and now you're planning your own wedding feast? Take care, my friend," he said seriously. "Sometimes a woman with a broken heart can only heal herself by breaking others."

"Mine's not that fragile," Rafe said.

"More so than you know, I think," Drum said

slowly. "I'm happy for you, but a bit disappointed. You were going to Italy with me for the rest of the summer, remember?"

Rafe looked stricken.

"No, no," Drum laughed, "I won't hold you to it. I'm not such a fool, or a child. I've been there before. I think I can find my way back myself."

"Thank you for understanding," Rafe said in relief. "Another time, maybe—though to tell the truth, I hope I can't then either." His voice lowered; he seemed embarrassed but determined. "Look, Drum, you know me well—too well. I don't anymore. Or at least, I don't recognize myself when it comes to her. I can take females or leave them, and in truth, if I take them, it's usually only for an hour, and an expensive one at that. I like them well enough. I love what I can do with them. But I've never felt like this about any woman. It's nothing like me."

His friend tapped a spoon on the table. "No, really? And what about Mary Hastings?"

"She was a girl, I was a boy," Rafe said, shrugging one shoulder.

"And Catherine Deveraux?"

"Just flirtation. She married where her family led," Rafe said with another shrug.

"And Maria Sanchez?"

"Her family would have skinned her—and me—if they'd thought she'd even looked at me!" Rafe said, in shock. "Damme, Drum! She visited me in hospital when I was in the Peninsula, that's all. Like many a well-bred señorita did, for the morale of the troops."

"She'd have married you in a heartbeat. Now *you*

look, Rafe. You've never valued yourself, so far as the ladies go."

"And they do," Rafe muttered.

"The point is they don't. It's just you've never looked for more than an hour with any of them—except those you knew wouldn't involve that well-protected heart of yours. The Deveraux chit, Mary, the Sanchez woman, I can think of a dozen more. You wrote them off before you even tried courting them, so of course they sheered off, in time. You've been considered an eligible *parti* by everyone but yourself."

Rafe gave him a grim smile. "Need your wits examined, Drum. You're talking about yourself, though why the female population finds you so enthralling, I don't know. Aside from the fact that you can talk them up sweet. They ignore that great trumpet of a nose and all those bones of yours at one word from you. But me? I'm a simple fellow, at a loss for pretty speeches, and no great lover. I mean in the sense of enthralling them," he added hastily. "Never had any other complaints. Not that they'd dare," he added gloomily. "I look too dangerous for that. And besides, they get what I pay for, just as I do."

"My point exactly," Drum said with satisfaction, "You don't bother with decent women because you don't think they'll be interested. But they are. And why not? You're brave, honest, thoroughly kind and good-hearted."

Rafe threw back his head and laughed. That expression did suit him, softening all the hard planes of his face, making him look almost handsome.

"Aye!" he said. "Just what any maiden prays for in a man—all the attributes of a faithful dog. That's not a dream lover, Drum. Females want the fellows with silky manners and faces to sigh over. And certainly not one with red hair! It's considered ugly as sin and unlucky to boot. I've known that since I was a tot. First fellow I punched was one who called me 'ginger nob.' Not the last, either. I'm not complaining. That might be what showed me I could handle myself in battle and set me on the path to the military. Which I did like. I never said I wasn't a good man, by the way. Only I don't think that's what the ladies look for."

"The smart ones do. But how would you know?" Drum asked, tapping his spoon on the table for emphasis. "You're hanging after a lady who doesn't treat you as well as a dog."

Rafe's smile faded.

"No, listen," Drum said. "You've followed her for weeks now. Then, finally, she sees you, whistles you to her side, and you trot after her. I don't think that's any kind of love on your part. It's boredom complicated by loneliness. Anyone knows weddings are catching. I believe you've caught the dread matrimonial fever. It's as much because you're at loose ends for the first time in your life as anything else."

"Loose ends?" Rafe echoed, surprised.

"With no war for you to fight, my friendly warrior. Not in the field, or on the Continent as a government agent when you couldn't march to the drum anymore. Peace is taking a terrible toll on you, Rafe." Drum smiled. "You've dashed from London to the countryside and back again more times than I can count, looking for something to do. And most of them things you'd never have done a year or two ago. You've gambled and whored, and now, as a last extremity, even taken to going to Society balls and fetes. The gaming and the wenching, I can understand, if not approve. Neither did you, not so long ago. But Society balls? *You?* You're vulnerable now, my friend. That's why I worry about you, and not some chit who plays with men's guts because she hates having lost the one she really wanted."

"You're saying there's something wrong with her?" Rafe said tersely, his hands closing to fists on the table.

"No, perhaps not, at least not permanently," Drum said wearily, passing a long-fingered hand over his eyes. He looked up, piercing his friend with his azure stare. "It's been over a year now since Damon wed Gilly, and all Lady Annabelle's done is flirt, lead suitors on, and then drop them. Who knows when or *if* she'll change her mind and seriously consider another man?"

"She has a constant heart," Rafe said.

"Let's play no more games," Drum said. "You know very well she lost the man she really wanted. Yet you court her even though all know she hasn't changed her mind about that? Before God, Rafe, why would you settle for being second choice?"

"Because I always have been, Drum," Rafe said simply, "you know that."

His friend fell still. "But it isn't right, it never was," Drum eventually said.

Rafe shrugged. "It's what I'm used to. What I can do—what I want to do—is to show her second best can be best for her, in time."

"Have you got that much time?" Drum asked.

"I hope so," Rafe said. "If not, I'll make it so. I don't disbelieve in myself, Drum. I can fight for myself if I must. So I will. She's lonely, she's lost. I can help find her."

"And you said you were bad with speeches?" Drum asked, shaking his head.

"I'm only speaking truth. I never have trouble with that—that's part of my problem. Well, I'm packed and my horse is standing," he said, rising to his feet. "I'm off to London now. Fare thee well in Italy, old friend. Come back soon. Wish me luck?" he asked, offering his hand.

"I suppose I do," Drum sighed, rising and taking his hand. "Though the truth is, I still hope you find a woman who sees you, knows you, and instantly wants no one but you."

"Not too many attractive madwomen about these days," Rafe said as he turned to leave, "but be sure, I'll keep an eye out for one, if it makes you happy."

"No, my friend," Drum said softly as Rafe went out the door, "it's to make you happy. God knows you deserve it. Even if you don't believe it."

two

The town house was on a quiet street near the park, and looked as neat and unpretentious as its owner usually did. But its owner wasn't very neat when he arrived in front of his house just as a soft purple twilight began to blur its familiar outlines. Rafe was dust covered, travel stained, and weary. He'd started out later than planned and made the journey back from his friends' wedding before night, but it had been a long day of hard riding.

He wanted a cool bath and a bracing drink, in whatever order they came in. Or both together, he thought as he rode down the narrow alley behind his town house to the stables he shared with his neighbors. Rafe was glad to hand his horse over to the stableboy who ran to greet him. He gave his horse a pat for services rendered, shouldered the bag he'd slung on the back of his saddle, and made his way back to his own front door. He went up the steps, raised the bronze door knocker, and let it fall. Then stood there, frowning, as time dragged by and no one answered his summons.

It wasn't like his man Peck to be out at this hour, Rafe thought, but the fellow had free will, after all. Peck, his servant from his army days, was his butler, footman, and valet—his entire staff, a fact many of Rafe's friends found amusing. It wasn't a matter of economy. Rafe had more than enough money for his needs and was as free with it as any man. As he felt he had to explain too often to his friends, it was simple efficiency. Peck ran the house. He hired maidservants to come in to keep the place tidy, and he kept the pantry stocked—or at least stocked as much as a bachelor who seldom ate at home needed.

"As to that—Peck can cook up the only meal I require at home," Rafe explained when Drum raised an eyebrow at his paltry staff. "He can fry an egg and toast a bit of bread as well as any man. Don't need footmen either, because I don't need protection in the streets. I could protect others, if it came to that. I run my own errands or have Peck take care of them. As for duties at the door, I can let myself out, and hardly anyone but you fellows come in."

An old army man, Rafe insisted he didn't need a valet either. "I shave myself faster and more efficiently than any valet could. Peck takes care of my clothes, I put them on. I'm not a demmed mannequin. What more does a man need?"

Well, he could use someone to let him into his house after a long absence, Rafe thought with a sigh as he put down his saddlebag and searched through it. He dragged a key from a hidden pouch in the side of the bag and let himself in.

The place was quiet and smelled musty. Rafe frowned. It wasn't like Peck not to keep it aired. By now the lamps in the hall ought to have been lit. Rafe began to worry. He wasn't a fanciful man, but Peck was getting on and London was a dangerous city. He hadn't been home in two weeks, so he supposed the place didn't need sprucing up. But Peck was as neat and methodical as he himself was, and where in hell was Peck at this hour anyway?

"*Halt!*" a quavering voice commanded.

Rafe dropped his bag. He spun around and in one fluid motion sank to his knees and crouched low, the pocket pistol he secreted in his jacket whenever he traveled already in his hand.

A stocky man with a bald head stepped out of the shadows, the musket he held pointed straight at Rafe's heart.

"Halt! I said—or I'll . . ." the man warned—and then paused. "Oh, it's you, m'lord!" he said with relief. Peck lowered the musket. "Gawd!" he went on, passing a shaking hand over his sweating forehead. "That close to blowin' yer head off, I was! And what are you doing here? I mean," Peck said, getting a grip on his diction and himself as Rafe uncoiled to his full height again, "you were off to the wedding and then to Italy with the earl, you said." He looked down at the musket. "Sorry to have put you in the line of fire, m'lord, but you scared me out of ten weeks growth coming in like that."

Now it was Rafe who raised a hand to his forehead. He gave himself a tap with the heel of his hand. "Damme! Where are my wits? The chit stole them along with my fancy," he murmured. "I should have sent word. My plans changed, Peck. The earl's off to Italy on his lonesome. I'm staying on here for the time being. We almost played Trooper and Frog right in my own front hall! Fine thing that would have been. Sorry. I wondered why the lamps weren't lit. I should have thought."

"No, it's me who's sorry, m'lord. I was packing, on my way out, when I heard the door open. I come creeping downstairs wondering who it was. No one was supposed to be here. I was out all day making arrangements for my trip. I only came home to get my bags, then lock the place up tight for the duration."

Rafe's eyebrows went up.

"Uh . . ." Peck said haltingly, "since you were going to be gone, you gave me the month off, if you'll recall? Told me so just before you set off to the countryside for all the wedding festivities. So I was off to visit my sister in Kent, but don't you worry, I'll send her word and have the place set right and tight in two shakes."

"No, don't *you* worry," Rafe said, his brow clearing, "I remember now. You haven't seen her in ages. Time you paid a call, and past it. Off you go, my man. You think I'm such a poor specimen I can't fend for myself here until you get back?"

"But there's your breakfast—and the house to keep up," Peck protested.

"I'll eat at my club. Just send to the employment

service and keep a housemaid coming every Tuesday and Friday, like always," Rafe countered. He began to strip off his gloves, frowning at the filth on them as he made for the staircase to the upper floors and his bedchamber.

"But—your jackets! Your cravats!"

That did give Rafe pause. He'd be calling on Annabelle, and couldn't afford to look shabby. Inspiration struck. "No matter," he said airily. "Give me the name of a tailor or cleaner or what have you, and I'll get them laundered and such. I can dress myself. I always do. Do you think I'm a fop? But before God," he added as he paused on the stair and frowned down at Peck, "one thing I do demand of you, my man."

"And that?" Peck asked warily.

"I'm for the tub now. If I was any dustier, you could plant marigolds on my blasted head. So bring me a bottle of that good sherry we hauled home from Spain. And a glass. On second thought, you can forget the glass."

Rafe woke early the next morning. He washed and began to dress. It took longer than usual. He was glad he'd talked Peck into leaving. The fellow would think he'd lost his mind during his travels if he saw him now. He himself wondered if he had.

Rafe flung off a second ruined neckcloth and frowned at himself in the mirror. Fellows from the dandy set spent hours in front of their looking glasses, discarding neckcloths they didn't think were

perfectly tied, casting them off like trees dropping
leaves in autumn. They weren't the only ones to fuss
over their clothing. A fashionable man dressed his
part in London these days. Poets passed as many
hours over their cravats as they did over their sonnets. Even bucks and bruisers such as the Corinthi-
ans, men who favored athletics over fashion, had a
style of their own and tried to look like others in their
sporting set.

Rafe didn't trouble himself with fashion. His
clothes had to be clean, but he dressed merely to go
out, and chose his attire depending on where that
was to be. That was it. Except this morning. This
morning he was fretting over his appearance like a
mincing fop, he decided, disgusted with himself.

He usually got things right first go. But right and
well done were two different things, he muttered to
himself now. He held his breath as he finally, success-
fully tied his neckcloth, and let his chin drop so he
could stare at his completed ensemble in the glass.

The neckcloth was folded in a casual but correct
fashion, and was crisp and white. His blue jacket and
dark gold waistcoat were fitted close, but he could
move his broad shoulders if he had to. The half boots
on his feet were polished till you could see Welling-
ton's face in them—if he'd been there to see. Tan
breeches were tight knitted and wrinkle-free. He
couldn't help the color of his hair, but it was brushed
and neat, and he'd been careful to give himself an
especially close shave.

Too bad he couldn't shave his eyebrows too, he
mused, staring into the mirror, those two rusty wings

swooping in a frown. Shave them down to the skin, the way he'd heard some eccentric nobleman had done to his redhead son—to erase all trace of the supposedly unlucky, unpopular color. A man could be bald and be more fashionable than a redhead, if only because that was more common. But he'd look stranger without his brows. He sighed. They'd have to do; they were a darker shade of copper than his head, anyway.

He gazed into his own troubled eyes, and then away from that bleak blue stare. He looked like himself and there was no help for it. He'd done all he could. He was an old campaigner. Preparation was done; he was armed and ready. It was time to go into battle. He'd have his breakfast, then pay his morning call—which was the reason for his getting dressed. No, he thought, it was the reason for his getting up today.

Rafe had dressed for a visit to a lady, but all he could see were men. Her salon was filled with them. Lady Annabelle, her beaming mama, the Countess Wylde, and a meek maidservant were the only women in the room. He could hear Annabelle's clear laughter. He could catch glimpses of that lovely face, but only from between her other morning callers as they crowded around her. Some sat, some stood, some lounged against the fireplace or windows to show off their clothing. There were eight other men in the small front room. Finely dressed, socially facile gentlemen. Rafe quelled an impulse to call for his hat and march out again. He stayed where he was, silent and glowering at his own helplessness. The other men were practiced flirts. He could only stand and listen, waiting for an opening. He had something to say.

But no way to say it.

The conversation prattled on. One fellow told a joke, another capped it. A languid lord related an anecdote and laughed at the end, which was the only way anyone could tell it was a joke. An elderly earl told a pointless story, and a young fop praised Annabelle's eyes again. Rafe stirred. It was time to call for his hat and leave. Because even though he was a man who could wait motionless for hours if need be—he didn't see the need anymore. Nothing he could say could match what these men were saying. Most of the conversation was inane, but all of it was acceptable social discourse. He couldn't compete. He didn't have the gift of small talk.

But neither did he want to leave yet. A man couldn't win a battle he didn't fight. Rafe squared his shoulders, braced his legs, and waited.

He positioned himself so he could watch her, and he did, carefully. When he got over the shock of her loveliness, he could observe her. The lady Annabelle was a few years older than most women in the ton who were still available for marriage. This was because of her disappointment in love, but it was singular, and a thing that detracted from her perfection in the eyes of many gentlemen. Not Rafe. He watched her with fascination, as always. She was all delicacy and grace.

She wore a jonquil yellow gown this morning.

Her soft raven curls trembled when she laughed. Her skin was snowy white and clear, her retroussé nose charming, her lips pink and pouting, even when she was not. She was everything dainty, entirely feminine.

Rafe had passed too many years in the sole company of men not to be fascinated by such a wholly alien creature. The thought of putting his hands on that little body aroused him even as it alarmed him. Such fragility made him feel too rough, too big, too clumsy. But he knew about women. He might never have really loved or been loved by any female, but he'd liked many and been fortunate enough to have a few like him. The generous or incautious ones shared their bodies. Others rented them. The tiniest one could accept almost any man, and sometimes, if he was lucky, wear him out as well. This dainty woman held out that promise—and the hope of something much more. Something he'd never known.

He knew people too, too well to be entirely swayed by her physical charms. Unlike many men of his acquaintance, Rafe believed a woman's mind could be as keen, or as dull, as any male's. In his opinion, a person's sex might skew his or her reasoning, but not impair it. A man had to judge accordingly. He'd met women as hard as rocks, survivors of war or their own difficult lives. He'd known hardbitten sergeants with emotions softer than a dewy maid's.

Rafe wasn't entirely unhappy to stand back and let others take the stage. As a spectator, he could assess the lady now. There were things only an onlooker could note. Like a man sitting in a window watching the passersby in a crowded street, he could see things that those who were moving could not.

She was not as charmed as she appeared to be. He caught flashes of impatience in those beautiful blue eyes. A certain calculation as she assessed a suitor. Sometimes there was more than momentary impatience to be seen in those lucent eyes. Sometimes, more often than he liked to see, she looked inward and stilled. That was sorrow, he could swear it. She was vulnerable. She stood in their midst, admired and yet alone. A certain pervasive sadness haunted her. It drew him, it called to him, it made him stay.

And she did notice him. She might not have said more than good morning when he came in, but she kept looking his way. He reasoned that could be because she was a consummate flirt. It didn't matter to him, because that blue gaze found him, if only through the corners of her eyes. She saw him. Often.

She laughed with the other gentlemen. She made a few comments, but didn't speak much more than he did. She hardly had the chance, with all the men vying for her attention. She listened and watched as much as Rafe did too. He could only hope she came to the same conclusions about her callers. They were three parts fool, two parts fop, three parts fribble, and all looking for acceptable matches.

Time crawled by, but it did pass. There was only so much time one could stay at a morning call. One by one, reluctantly, the gentlemen began to make their good-byes. They took Annabelle's little hand and bowed over it. They murmured last compliments, made promises, pledged their devotion, and filed past Rafe to fetch their hats and walking sticks and leave.

Now he could act. Rafe came up to her to say his farewell. He got his first clear look at her, and paused, gazing at her helplessly. He quickly looked to the hand she offered him so she wouldn't see what was so obviously in his eyes.

"Lord Dalton!" she said with pleasure. "Rafe, I mean," she added, showing him a dimple near her lips as she smiled. "You were so silent I thought you'd left without saying good-bye."

"I wouldn't do that," he said.

"Well, I wouldn't blame you if you had. Such a gabble! Thank you for the flowers, by the way."

He'd sent her flowers because he'd danced with her the other night, and wanted her to remember that. But the room was filled with flowers. She'd danced all night.

"You're welcome. Thing is," he said, daring to gaze directly at her eyes, "I'm not much for polite chatter. Well, as you saw. Or rather, didn't hear. I leave the jokes and stories to other fellows. But I make a very good audience. So I wondered if you'd care to drive out with me this afternoon. If you've had enough gabble, I can at least promise you some quiet time in the park. I'm reckoned a good driver, and it's a fine day."

She tilted her head to the side, obviously weighing

him, clearly considering him. "How kind," she said, "but I'm so sorry, I'm promised to Radcliffe this afternoon."

He nodded. "So I thought you might be. Then may I ask if you have escort to the Swanson ball Friday night?"

"Lud! Another party at their house! But yes, I recall I accepted Croft's kind invitation."

He'd heard enough. A man might want to storm a castle. But if he hadn't the right provisions, he couldn't no matter how brave his heart. "Then maybe you'll save me a dance. Good morning, my lady."

"But that drive in the park sounded so good," she said wistfully. "And I heard you were a member of the Four in Hand."

The Four in Hand Club was a prestigious driving club, membership difficult, awarded for skill, not connections or money. He nodded. "I am, and so perhaps you could come driving with me Saturday?"

"Alas, no," she sighed.

He'd heard quite enough. He was besotted, but not a fool, and wouldn't be made one. He knew what he was. If it wasn't enough, he didn't blame her. But he wouldn't make himself less. His face went still. His voice grew cold. "Too bad," he said. "Another time then." He inclined his head in a bow and turned to leave.

"Tomorrow?" she asked suddenly.

He turned again, his surprise clear.

"Don't tell Mama I'm so forward or she'll have my skin," she added with a little grin, looking to where her mother was still sitting. "I don't mean to beg, but as it happens, I am free tomorrow, and so . . . if you are too?"

"I am," he said, trying to tamp down his delight so he wouldn't grin like an idiot. It might be the prestige of being with a member of the Four in Hand, she might be simply bored. But she would be going out with him. It should have been enough, but it wasn't. He had to push his luck and try for more of her company. "At two? Would that be good for you? That way we can take tea, as well. There's a place near the park."

She went still, considering. Had he asked too much? he wondered, waiting.

"Lovely," she said. "I look forward to it. I hope it's a fine day too."

Rafe bowed, went into the hall, clapped on his hat, and strode out into the street. But he didn't see where he was going. He was too excited, and then too busy wondering what sacrifices a man had to make to the gods in order to hold off the rain.

He walked home, counting his assets. He had to prove to himself it was more than luck; she might actually want to spend time with him.

First, he had good birth. He possessed a passable fortune which he'd increased by wise investments. He'd been helped with that by the advice of Drum and Damon Ryder. As to that, he had loyal friends and through them entrée anywhere, even among the best families in England. Rafe's footsteps slowed as he realized there wasn't much else he could think of to recommend him to a lady like Annabelle.

He tried to think of more.

He didn't look like a Greek god, like the man she'd adored, but no female had ever run from him either. He had a strong back, good teeth, clear skin, and could drive a horse to an inch. He was a bruising rider. He didn't drink overmuch. He'd never raised his hand to a female and never would. *Wonderful*, he thought ruthlessly, *next you'll be mentioning that you're kind to animals.*

Naturally then, he mercilessly listed his deficits.

Not a Greek god, no, not by a long shot. He knew his face had all the charm of the side of a cliff. And there was that damnable hair. Not a poet. What had lovely Isabella, his paid companion in Spain, said? Oh yes. When she'd stopped laughing, she'd managed to tell him, "Raphael, *mi amor*. Telling me my hair is so shiny and lustrous, just like a horse, is *not* flattering!"

Rafe smiled now, remembering. But so she had had silky, long, black hair, almost blue-black in the sunlight. It had captivated him. "Flowing black mane" was what he'd actually said, though he conceded that wasn't much better. Isabella had followed the armies. She'd had a merry heart and no morals, and in her short life had had more men than he'd cared to think about. Still, the memory of a woman who had genuinely liked him cheered him now. Because when he'd been wounded and lay all those months in hospital, she'd visited him regularly. And he hadn't even had the keeping of her by then.

The sum of it was that he didn't know what fate and Lady Annabelle had in store for him. But a man had to try his fate or he was less than a man, and there was no sense fretting over it. Stranger things had happened. He had a chance simply because life was all chance. He quickly took the steps to his door and let himself in. He'd change his clothes, go to his club for luncheon, and hunt up Drum, he mused as he went up the stair.

But Drum was on his way to Italy, he remembered. The Ryders were in the countryside now. Their neighbors, his old friend Ewen and his wife, Bridget, were at their estate with their children. London was thin of company in the summertime. But Annabelle was here. That was enough for him.

Rafe whistled as he stripped off his jacket. He washed and then selected a more comfortable jacket. He'd go driving after luncheon, take the team out and put them through their paces, get any tics out of their stride so Annabelle's drive would be perfect. He heard the door knocker echoing through the empty house as he stepped out of his room again.

Maybe Town wasn't so empty after all, he thought as he went to the door. Maybe Drum's gypsy notions had faded and he'd decided to stay in the country.

Rafe swung open the door. And stared. It took a moment for him to recognize the man in his doorway.

A very tall fellow, broad shouldered, but his jacket hung from those wide shoulders. Thick honey blond hair, too long but strangely attractive around that classically handsome face—a too thin face, all cheekbones now. The face once had a deep tan; now it only served to make his skin more sallow. The hazel eyes showed fatigue; his smile was wide but thin. He was a wreck of a man, more so because he'd once been a very handsome fellow.

"*Eric? Eric Ford?* What a surprise!" Rafe said, hastily concealing his shock. The man had served with him in the Peninsula. But then he'd been a healthy young giant, so handsome everyone said his face had saved his life many a time, since no one— not even a Frenchie—would want to put out his light. It would be like defacing a work of art. They'd been friends in those days, and had corresponded since. Rafe went home, but Eric had gone with his army career. India had been his last address. He'd written to say he'd been ill. Rafe hadn't realized the extent of it. He was staggered. It hadn't been that long, yet the man was a shadow of his former self.

"Eric, by God!" Rafe exclaimed, recovering, "Come in, come in. How long has it been?"

The gaunt man on his doorstep shrugged. "A few years, to be sure. Are you sure about us coming in?"

Belatedly Rafe realized there was a woman on the front stair too. She stood in Eric's shadow. Rafe got a fleeting glance of a wan, foreign-looking face with great dark eyes, before she dipped a curtsy to him. But Rafe's gaze didn't linger on her. He saw a pile of hard-worn traveling cases and bags on the steps beside the couple now too. His eyes flew to his old friends'.

Eric shrugged again. "Wrong time, if not the wrong place, eh? When I wrote to say I'd be coming to London, you suggested I stay on here with you. But plans change. Aye, who knows that better than us, eh, Bren?" he asked the woman. "Lucky thing the hack's still there," he said, looking back at the hired hackney at the curb. "Good seeing you, Rafe."

"It won't be if you take one step away!" Rafe threatened, throwing his door wide. "I remember now. My head's been all sixes and sevens these days. You did write. I did invite. By God, Eric, you have not been uninvited. There's plenty of room! Come in, stay as long as you like. My plans changed. That's true. But not towards you or your lovely wife."

"Wife? God forbid. Me and my lovely sister," Eric murmured. "In truth, Rafe, I'd leave on the instant. But at this particular instant, I do believe I need a chair." He laughed weakly. He closed his eyes, swayed, and toppled over.

Three

Rafe carried Eric to a bedchamber, then anxiously watched until his friend regained consciousness.

"Thank you," Eric said, grimacing after he swallowed the brandy he'd asked for as soon as he'd roused from his faint. "Swooning like a girl. Who would have thought it?"

"I would," his sister remarked from a corner of the room, where she was unpacking his kit bag.

"Skipped luncheon," Eric grumbled, ignoring her comment as he held out his glass for Rafe to refill. "As soon as I get some food in me, I'll be fine."

"Need more than food," Rafe said, withholding the decanter. "First you tell me what's toward, then you get another glass. Not before."

"Yes, sir! Captain, sir," Eric said with sarcasm.

"I won't 'Lieutenant' you if you don't 'Captain' me," Rafe said calmly. "That's over. You sold out, as did I. We're equals here. Only not yet. When you can take me in three rounds—which is two and a half rounds more than you'd need if you were fit—we'll be equals."

"Ho!" Eric said hollowly. "No man could batter you down. No matter what shape he was in. You're slender but tough, as firmly set as an oak growing by the water, Rafe."

Rafe's gaze was steady. "Going to tell me the whole of it? Or just fling praises at my head? I'm not going to blush and change the subject. Out with it, man."

Eric sighed and looked down into his glass. "You know I had that leg injury in the Peninsula . . ." He looked up. "By the way, how's the arm?"

"Attached," Rafe said.

"Damn near lost it too, didn't you?"

"Aye, but I had the other to bat them away when they came at me with the saw," Rafe said, frowning. But only because his friend's comment made him remember the ugly scars he bore, scars he was sure would repulse a tender lady—at least at first. *But a man can make love in the dark, or turned the other way. For that matter, he can keep his damned shirt on,* Rafe thought, and added, "My arm's here. As are you. Now, are you going to tell me or not?"

Eric shrugged again and hitched himself up higher on the pillows. "The leg healed. But I think it undermined my health. I used to be stout as the titan I resembled. When I caught that fever in India I was almost put paid for. If Brenna here hadn't shipped out when she heard, and nursed me back—I don't know if I'd be back at all. I'm recuperating, Rafe. But

it was a near thing and it will take a while for me to
be sound again. That's why I'm here. The brat insists
I see a first-class London physician before we head
home. As to that, I think we'll just have enough
money to get back after I do! Not that we're impover-
ished, mind," he added hastily. "It's just that the
sawbones here in London have fees big as their
heads. I only hope their talents merit it."

"Don't worry about it," Rafe said, "You'll have the
finest doctors, I'll see to that. And you'll stay on until
you can pull the horses home."

"I should think not!" Eric said, sitting up and trying to swing his legs over the side of the bed.

Rafe was there before he could put a foot down.
He grabbed his friend's shoulders hard and looked
him in the eye. "White as the pillowcase," Rafe muttered angrily. "Damme, no! Listen, my friend, you
did me a good turn once and I've been waiting a long
time to do you one. I'm not going to let you deprive
me of that. Here you are, and here you stay until
you're better. *All* better. What, should I let a friend
stay in a hotel when I have the whole of this house to
myself? *I* should think not. So get yourself into some
nightclothes. I'll send for the finest physician you
could want."

"We couldn't impose . . ." Eric's sister said anxiously.

"Nor will I!" Eric said.

Rafe cut them off. "You'd be doing me a favor. I'm
alone here. Peck—remember him? He's my valet and
butler now, but he's gone off to visit his sister. I

thought I'd be gone now too. Good thing I changed my plans, at that! The plain truth is, I forgot you were coming. I was going to Italy with my old friend Drum—the earl of Drummond—you must remember him. You were still in the hospital when I left with him, or rather when he hauled me off to play cat and mouse with Bonaparte's supporters on the Continent."

"I envied you that," Eric said with a wan smile, settling back on his banked pillows again.

"Don't blame you," Rafe said. "I'd never have thought trickery in a drawing room could equal riding into battle, but it was just as chancy and dangerous. Suited me down to the ground. Any rate, I just changed my plans about going to Italy with Drum. 'Just' is the word, I changed my mind abruptly." He smiled. "It's what's got my thinking muddled. For good reason. There's this lady. Aye, a lady. Not just a female. Well, the thing of it is that she's here. So here is where I want to be. But she's the only person I know or care to know in London right now. So you're more than welcome. I was getting lonely."

"Lonely?" Eric asked. "With your lady here?"

Rafe's lean cheeks grew warm. "She's not my lady yet. Time will tell."

"Let me tell her a thing or two about you," Eric said.

"You? Never!" Rafe laughed. "One look at you and all I'll see of her will be the back of her head. You have a way with women I've never seen the likes of. Remember that little señorita in . . ." Rafe remembered the man's sister was in the room, and gave a cough of a laugh. "Perhaps now's not the time for such remembering."

"You needn't stop on *my* account," she said. "I've heard it all, and what I haven't heard, I've seen. It *is* remarkable. I had to screen Eric's bed from insects in India, but sick as he was, I vow I had to toss more adoring women out than swat mosquitoes."

Rafe turned his head to look at her. She was an exotic creature, tall and slender, with strongly etched features and dark coloring, making her look more Spanish than English to him. She was not in her first youth, and the dark clothes she wore and the obvious hard traveling she'd done made her seem as tired as her brother. She didn't resemble him in any other way. He had bright hair; hers was smooth and black. Pulled back from her face, it threw her well-defined features into bold relief, making her exhaustion evident. Skin the color of camellias was further shadowed with fatigue. Her eyes were large, dark, and almond shaped, her nose aquiline. Her mouth was sculpted with a bowed upper lip and plush lower one, curved so she always seemed to wear a half smile. Perhaps she did; her voice was deep, soft, and tinged with amused irony.

"Yes," she said, her lips curved into a real smile, "hard to believe we're brother and sister, isn't it? Everyone thinks I'm his Spanish bride, or an Indian one, picked up in his travels. He *will* go to exotic places."

"She's Welsh as Llewellen himself," Eric said, "on her mama's side, at least. Bren's my half sister. Seven years younger and a world removed from me, in her heritage. My stepmama claims descent from the old princes of Wales, and has books to prove it. The looks as well. My mother was golden as the sun, like my father. He likes to say my stepmama's luminous as the moon. She is. That's Bren and me—different as day from night." He smiled at his dark sister. "But I bless her. The family raised a row when she insisted on shipping out to find me after I got sick. I did too. Much good it did when she'd got her mind made up. Her maid up and quit two weeks after she arrived in India. Her Indian maidservant quit when we said we were going back to England. But Bren stuck it out and got me home. I'm a lucky man."

"You always had luck with womenfok," Rafe said. "Mothers and sister as well as every other one, I see." He took out his pocket watch. "I've things to do. Must send a note to my physician and get him to come here. Then get you a nurse—"

"That you will not," Eric thundered. "I can do for myself, thank you."

"*If* you don't do too much," his sister said too sweetly.

"We'll see how it goes," Rafe said, rising to his feet. "In the meanwhile, make yourselves comfortable. There's a connecting room you can use," he told Eric's sister. "You might want to open a window and air it out, but it's ready for company. Always is. If you need anything else, I'll be downstairs, getting things together. Dinner at nine? I'll send to a restaurant for it. If you don't feel strong enough, we'll have it right up here."

"I'll be downstairs," Eric said.

"Perhaps," his sister said.

Rafe smiled and left the room.

After their host stepped out of the room, Brenna walked to her brother's bedside and gazed at him steadily. "Ought we to stay on here, Eric?" she asked.

"I think we must," he answered. "I'm weak as a kitten. Do you mind? And if we have to stay on anywhere in London, this is the best place right now. To tell a truth I wouldn't breathe to Rafe, I'm not sure I could make it to a hotel tonight. Tomorrow, perhaps. And if we have to, we'll go to one then. But I don't think we will have to. I think Rafe really did forget his invitation. He's not a liar. Or at least, not a good one."

He forced a grin. "Don't look so worried. I don't think I'm getting the fever again, I'm just so damnably drained from our travels. I think we must stop here awhile, Bren. I hope it won't be long, and Rafe's a good fellow, you'll see. Honest to a fault, perhaps. And brusque in his manner, unfortunately. He always was. It doesn't matter to men. You mustn't take it amiss either. He's got a heart of gold."

"So we'll stay until you're stronger," she said simply. "As for your friend Lord Dalton, I think he's telling the truth too. I'm not put off by how blunt he is, I rather like it. Insincere flattery is what makes me nervous. Not plain truth. Anyway, you're right. I can see he's a very good man indeed."

. . . *But taken, of course*, she sighed to herself as she turned back to finish her brother's unpacking, *as the*

good ones always are. No wonder. He was so very
handsome, that vivid coloring, that strong, determined face, a soldier's body and a gentleman's
grace. She knew from Eric's stories what a brave and
stalwart friend he was. As for his good heart? It was
plain to see from his actions as well as in his face.
Now, there was a face a man could depend on. A
woman as well. But he'd hardly looked at her. It was
more than the fact that she was far from her best
right now. His heart was taken, and he was the sort
of man who didn't trifle.

Wasn't that always the way? she thought
gloomily. Eric said she was too choosy. But it was
only that there were so few to choose from. She bent
to her unpacking with a sad smile. The best ones
were always taken—or had been lost.

Rafe woke at dawn, sitting straight up in bed as
though he'd heard the call to battle. This was just as
crucial to him; today he was taking Annabelle for a
drive.

He got out of bed, washed, shaved, and then
sorted through his wardrobe, looking for something
casual yet expensive, elegant yet . . . *Like a man on the
dawn of the day of battle? Ha! More like a girl on the
evening of her first ball*, he told himself in disgust
when he realized what he was doing. He closed his
wardrobe door smartly. She'd take him as he was or
not at all. Any rate, he thought, pulling a clean shirt
over his head, even if it was to be not at all, at least he
had a good friend to pass the time with until he met

with her. That would settle his nerves. Eric and his sister had arrived with perfect timing, and he was very glad of it.

Last night they'd sat up laughing and reminiscing, only stopping when Brenna firmly told them it was time for Eric to sleep. Rafe had noted his growing pallor too, and helped her get him to his bedchamber. She'd sat by the fireside all evening with them, doing mending, but keeping an eye on her brother. She'd seemed to know just when to ask a question, and just when to be still. She'd laughed so honestly at their stories, they'd soon indulged in their nostalgia. *Sufficiently edited,* of course, Rafe thought with amusement.

Eric and his sister appeared at the breakfast table downstairs, just as Eric had vowed he would. They were good company and made Rafe realize how much he hated eating alone. He was relieved to see his friend looked somewhat better. Faint color tinged Eric's hollow cheeks, and he ate a decent breakfast. Brenna looked rested too, her face no longer drawn. They laughed together again, and talked a good deal more. The morning passed quickly.

But as the hours went on, Rafe became more distracted. His guests couldn't help noticing it. They fell still when he checked his watch once too often. Rafe saw it, and his face heated, more so when he realized they could see it. Another curse of his coloring.

"Caught me fair and square," he said, shaking his head. "It's nearly time for me to leave. Will you two be all right here on your own? I'm taking my lady driving this afternoon, and then to tea. The doctor will be here after his usual hours, he said. Well, I admitted it was no emergency. That won't be until nearly seven. I'll be back by then. If you need him, I've left a note with his direction on my desk. I don't expect anyone else to call—hardly anyone even knows I'm in Town. So there's nothing for you two to do but rest. Anything more I can do now, before I go?"

"You've done enough!" Eric said. "I'm going to sleep away the rest of the day, I think. And let Bren wash her hair, or do her fingertips, or whatever it is females do when they have time for themselves. Lord knows she deserves weeks of such time."

"I'll have them," she said simply. "Have a good afternoon," she told Rafe. "We'll fend for ourselves, and do fine. As will you. You look very well. Any lady would be honored to have you as escort."

But would the lady of his choice? Rafe wondered as he thanked her, bowed, and left the pair so he could find out.

Four

She wore celestial blue to match her eyes. Her straw bonnet had blue flowers twined through it to further make the point.

Lady Annabelle has the finest eyes in London Town
They sparkle so, the other girls frown.

One of her admirers had written that. It was only true, Rafe thought as he helped her up into his open phaeton.

"You look lovely," he said when he'd got himself settled in the driver's seat, his heart thumping as loudly as if he'd just climbed up the tallest fire ladder in London.

"Why, thank you," she said with a charming smile, making him wish he'd said something clever enough to deserve it.

"We're in luck," he said. "The weather's held. I thought a ride through the park? And then to Hammond's? They set a fine tea, I heard, and it's close to the park. Or would you prefer Gunter's?"

She bobbed her head. "Oh, Hammond's, to be sure. I love their teas. But we must stop back here to collect a chaperon on the way, you know. It's got nothing to do with you, Rafe. I can ride out with you in an open carriage—and a very attractive one it is too, I might add. But go to tea? Never. Any little thing starts tongues clacking in Town, and taking my tea alone with such a dashing fellow would have all the hens chirping. Why, they'd have us married before you could blink!"

"Let's go straight there now, alone," he said, grinning.

She laughed, pleased. "So you say now. But my dear sir, you hardly know me."

"Then let's remedy that," he said, and shook the reins. His horses responded, his heartbeat slowed, his wits returned. If he was doing something, he performed well. He was, after all, a man of action. He drove toward the park.

The noise of the city drowned out any opportunity to talk. Raucous street sellers' cries, horse wagons rumbling over the cobbles—the general clamor kept them silent until they drove through the gates of the park.

"You first," she said, as soon as the sounds of the city faded enough for them to talk. "I'd like to know more about you. Tell me about yourself if you please."

"Not much to tell," he said, and heard how gruff and boorish that sounded. Besides, it wasn't true. He didn't like talking about himself, that was all. "My family home's in the South, by the sea. Arrow Court's been there since England itself, I think. My parents are still there. My brother's the heir. I had a choice of the army or navy or church. Can you see me in a cassock? But the cavalry suited me fine."

"Indeed?" she asked vivaciously. "Where did you serve?"

She sat up straight and gazed at him with every evidence of fascinated interest as he spoke. She was interested. But not in his conversation. She could listen with half an ear as he went on. The other half of her attention could focus on studying him. He wasn't a loquacious fellow, she thought, but no man could resist talking about himself. The wars were only recently over. She had dozens of suitors who had served in some capacity; men loved to talk about their army days. It gave her time to assess him.

Her mother was right, she thought as she watched him guide his horses. He was attractive, she supposed, in his way. Too bad that wasn't the way she wanted a man to look. It wasn't just his ridiculous hair. Damon Ryder was her ideal; no man in England was as handsome. She'd thought so the moment she'd first seen him. That was almost the first time she'd focused her eyes. And what a sight he'd been, from boyhood on—her ideal. She'd never made any other plans for her life. She was to be his wife. The phantom children she'd imagined all her life had all borne his stamp. He was meant for her. It was understood. Except by him. Her parents had thought so; she'd thought so. He hadn't.

It still hurt with a pain that didn't dull with time, but only grew sharper when she thought of her life to come. He'd been married almost a year. But what was a scant year compared to all the years of her life? It had changed her in ways she couldn't yet fathom. They said she'd grown ice around her heart. She hadn't. She would have felt the cold. Worse, she felt nothing. Except this distance between herself and the world now, as though there were an invisible film between it and her. She could observe everything, but it seemed nothing could touch her anymore. That was good. The feeling of unreality was not.

Many men wanted her. She still only wanted Damon. But she'd make do. She'd have to.

But with this man? Damon looked like a Greek statue come to life. Rafe looked like a man. But Damon had a wife now. A wife who was going to bear him a baby soon. Annabelle shifted on the hard, high seat and looked for more than she could see in Rafe. It was time for her to marry. She needed a man to help her bury her hurt so no one could see it or pity her for it anymore. She knew she could never bury her heart's desire, but she could and would lay away her heart instead. Marriage was necessary. Her suitors claimed to have love enough for both of them. They had better, she thought.

Rafe was neat and clean, precise to a shade, she decided. Still—thinking of shades—his hair! Such a pity. That ghastly color! It blazed copper in the sunlight. It did look oddly well with his eyes, though.

Good eyes, at least, she thought. Clear and stark, blue as new ice. A strong face, long, strong hands. He guided the horses well, he—

He turned to look at her, pinning her with that bright, direct stare. She blinked. He'd stopped talking. What had he been talking about?

He laughed at her expression. "You have to watch what you ask for. Didn't mean to put you to sleep with my stories. Turnabout's fair play. Now you tell me about yourself—and mind you don't put me to sleep, because then who'll drive my team?"

She laughed with him, pleased and surprised. Who'd have thought such a strict face could be made so attractive by just one genuine smile? Her interest in him nudged up a notch. He was eligible, amiable, wealthy enough for her papa's standards, and acceptable to her mama. Not a brilliant match. But not a disastrous one either. Lord Raphael Dalton showed definite possibilities. And he was smitten. She intended him to remain so. The Season hadn't started and she'd promised herself one more before she made her decision. But he definitely showed promise.

It was easy for her to talk about herself. She told him about how odd and lonely it was to have been an only child. She laughed about how very sad it was to have been so coddled, and pretended to be so grateful for his sympathy. She pouted and prattled and watched to see his reactions, a little startled to see boredom definitely beginning to glaze over those perceptive eyes of his. So she spoke about London and the plays she'd seen and her opinions of them, and saw him pay attention again.

Interesting, she thought. Definitely another point in his favor.

"Speaking of plays and the theater," she said slowly, "are you going to be in Town for the rest of the summer?"

"Likely," he said, watching the road in front of them. "And you?"

"Oh, definitely," she answered, tilting him a look from under her long lashes. "I was terribly bored before, but suddenly I find London so very interesting again."

His head turned; he gave her all his attention.

She looked at her gloves. "One can never get tired of London, I suppose," she went on innocently. And then looked up and smiled at him saucily so he'd know she knew very well just how ambiguous that sounded.

"Certainly are a lot of things to do in London," he said, "most of them better to do with a friend. I had an invitation to a masquerade at Vauxhall for next week. But my friend Drum up and left me for the Continent. All my other friends are rusticating. If you like, we can go together—if you're free."

"I would like," she said pertly, then sighed, "If I'm free . . . I'd have to see my appointment book when we get home. Can you wait until then for an answer?"

"Of course," he said. "It isn't until next week, after all. Do you like Vauxhall, by the way? I find the food paltry, but the place is good enough for spectacles in the summertime."

He didn't press her for an answer, beg or tease or mention it again. She was startled. Then even more interested.

After an hour Rafe turned the horses back again. He drove back to her town house and jumped lightly down to tell the footman at her door that they'd returned. Annabelle was again pleased. Many men would have only flipped a coin to a passing boy and sent word to her door. But perhaps, she mused, he was only trying to show off that limber frame of his. She didn't blame him; it was an asset and he probably knew it. He was certainly well put together. Not perfect in every dimension, like Damon. He was rangier, leaner. But certainly fit and agile.

Rafe waited at the door for Annabelle's chaperon to join them. Annabelle's mama, the countess, resplendent in purple, finally came out, alone, and greeted him. He bowed, looked behind her for a maidservant, and saw none. The front door closed and the countess walked on toward the carriage. Then Rafe realized no one else was coming.

She was the chaperon who was going to go to tea with them? Rafe's eyes widened a fraction. This was a high honor.

He gave the countess his hand and led her to his carriage. He helped her up to the seat. She thanked him and settled herself between him and her daughter. But her eyes flew to Annabelle's. Annabelle gave her a tiny smile and a tinier nod. Her mama's eyes widened too then, with sudden interest.

Rafe noted it. He clucked to his team and the carriage moved smartly down the street. "So, to Hammond's, ladies?" he asked, his spirits rising.

Before Annabelle could answer, her mama did. "Yes indeed. But I heard your town house is not far from it. *Do* point it out as we go by, would you? Vulgar curiosity, I know," she said in a way that implied she knew she could never be vulgar no matter what she said, "but one likes to know where all one's friends live, doesn't one?" Annabelle's face flushed. Rafe suppressed a grin. He really was being inspected top to bottom. Ordinarily he'd have been annoyed with such a request. But Annabelle's mama? She could check his back teeth if she wished. Asking to see where a fellow lived was like asking for a glimpse at his bank account. Anyone could drive past a man's house without letting him know about it. She wanted him to know.

"Certainly," he said, his spirits rising even higher. He turned his team westward. "It's only a few streets out of our way."

Annabelle flushed pinker. She grew even more rosy when they came to his street, and her mother asked so many questions Rafe had to slow the horses to point out his house.

"Should you like to see it?" he offered casually. "My man's away at the moment, and I've a friend stopping with me, but I've just got back from a trip and haven't been able to muss it up much."

"If it's a problem, we'll stop by another time," Annabelle said. "Mama will understand."

"It's no problem," Rafe said. The thought of her in his house was enormously gratifying.

"But we wouldn't want to impose," Annabelle protested.

"You couldn't," he said, turning to her and losing the train of his thought as he found himself getting lost in her wide-eyed gaze. He shook himself, concealing it by shaking the reins to hurry the horses. The only problem he could see was the usual when a female clapped eyes on Eric. But Eric had said he'd be sleeping. And he'd been sick.

"Good!!" Annabelle's mama cried. "I hadn't wanted to be indelicate, but—one needs to visit the facilities, one finds."

"And they're inside all the houses on this street," Rafe said honestly. "Got hot water on the second floor as well."

"Oh, do tell?" the countess said avidly. "We do not where we are staying. How charming."

He let the ladies off in front of his house, drove around back to the stables, and hurried to the front steps where he'd left them. But they were nowhere in sight. Frowning, he tried the door. It was unlocked. He pushed it open.

And wished he hadn't.

Annabelle and her mama were stopped stock still on the threshold. A woman stood in the hall facing them. She was boldly illuminated by the afternoon sunlight pouring through the transom over the door. She wore a man's long crimson dressing gown. Her unbound raven hair was wet and shining; it lay like wet black silk, clinging to her shoulders, making the front of the gown damp as it fell in a glistening cascade to her breasts. Her clearly defined, outlined, upthrust breasts. She was obviously wearing little else, because she was barefoot. She clutched the gown closed at her neck. Her eyes were dark and bright, opened wide in shock. Her cheeks were crimson. It became that exotic face very well, making it vivid and voluptuous. Her mouth was opened in surprise.

But not half so wide as Lady Annabelle's or her mama's.

Five

"Impossible," Brenna said. She said it softly but firmly. She kept her hands in her lap so no one could see their fine trembling.

Her brother closed his eyes, laid his head on the back of his chair, and counted to thirty again.

Rafe paused in his pacing round the room. "Not impossible," he said as firmly as she had. "Necessary."

"Not necessary," she said, and then laughed. It sounded genuine. Her brother opened one eye. "My lord," she added as Rafe stared.

"Rafe," he muttered.

"Very well then," she went on, "Rafe. You *are* a man of few words. And you've been saying the same ones over and over again. Now I ask you to listen, please. I'll count off my reasons for not accepting your proposal as carefully as my dear brother is counting to control his temper. *One*, it was my fault, and there is no way you should be penalized for it. It was a stupid mistake. I shouldn't have gone to the door. But you had no servants, and you said you weren't expecting anyone. I thought you were locked out and wanted one of us to open it. Yes, I'd just gotten out of the bath, but no, I would *not* wake Eric, he needs his rest.

"*Two*, I didn't think you'd be so smitten by the sight of me in Eric's dressing gown—I lost mine in transit, so I had to borrow his—that you'd forget yourself and overstep the bounds of host by making advances. I'm hardly a temptress." She laughed again, as though that were a ridiculous thought.

Rafe stared at her. He would have thought it was too, before. Before he'd got a look at her in the sunlight after she'd had a day to rest. Last night she'd looked drab and wan. This morning, slightly better. This afternoon in that dressing gown? Maybe it was just because he'd seen her through Annabelle's eyes, but she'd looked like the "expensive trollop" Annabelle's mother had proclaimed her before she'd pulled her daughter out the door.

Now, with the high color of embarrassment staining her cheeks as a cosmetic, his friend's sister's face was vivid, startlingly attractive, and undeniably sensual looking. He didn't know how he could have missed it before. Those sloe eyes, those shapely, smiling, cherry red lips, that slender, curving body . . . She'd pulled her wet hair back into a sleek knot,

Spanish style, on top of her head. It glistened blue-black in the sunlight, accenting that full mouth, that seductive face of hers. She looked dangerously exotic, capable of enacting a man's most intense sexual fantasies.

. . . If she weren't Eric's sister, Rafe thought quickly, suppressing the dangerous thought. Eric wouldn't have a slattern for a sister. Or if he did, he wouldn't bring her to a friend's house with him. Or at least he'd have warned him. There was honor among friends. Whatever his half sister was, Eric was honorable. That was enough for Rafe. And who better than he to know looks were no measure of a person? He'd lived through a war and brought most of his friends out of it alive. His hair hadn't been unlucky for anyone but himself.

"So *three*," Brenna continued, "I was caught in what might seem to be an embarrassing situation."

"*Seem?*" her brother said dryly. "Yes, like the sea seems wet."

She ignored him. "And *four*, and finally," she went on, her low, throaty voice making her words sound very final indeed, "I'll go home and it will be forgotten. I'm sorry if it made your lady angry with you, Rafe, but I'll explain it to her and mend matters. She seems like an intelligent woman."

"Intelligent and observant are two different things. Damme—" Rafe paused. "Excuse me, but I'm a little upset at the turn of matters, Miss Ford."

"Brenna," Brenna said softly.

"Annabelle and her mama are reasonable females,

I'm sure," Rafe said, ignoring her, "but what else were they to think? Dam—by Go—dash it all," Rafe said in frustration. "Forgive my soldier's hasty tongue, but I'm not used to the company of women. There—that's it exactly. How are they to know that? You looked at home here, you looked alone, and to all intents and purposes—except for mine—you were. It was my mistake as much as yours, because . . ."

He bit his tongue. He couldn't tell her that he'd entirely forgotten her presence in his house in the presence of his lady, though it was true. So he went on to an even more bitter truth.

"Because it was my fault as well. For barging in without letting you know we were coming. And for being too boggled to think fast. I tried to save your name. I wasted precious seconds wondering if I should claim you were a servant or such."

"When I was half-dressed and in a man's dressing gown?" Brenna asked.

"A servant?" Eric said with amusement. "London *has* changed since I was here last. Tell me, what was she supposed to be servicing?"

Rafe glared at him. "We are henceforth engaged, Miss Ford," he told Brenna formally.

"We are not," she said firmly. "You'll tell her the truth."

"I did. You heard. It made them fly faster," Rafe muttered. "I never saw females move that fast, out the door and down the street like a shot. I had to send a stable lad after them with the carriage to get them home. It was the least I could do. The best I could do too. *I* couldn't go thundering after her. She made it clear she didn't want me near."

"But she was upset, and no wonder," Brenna said. "It was an easy thing to misunderstand. I *wasn't* properly dressed. And how could she consider what *you* were saying, the way her mama was screeching?"

"I heard it upstairs," Eric mused. "I was dreaming I was at the opera, and woke up to hear the soprano going sour."

"So," Brenna told Rafe as calmly as she could, remembering that shrilling, "you tell her again. I'll visit and tell her too. We'll get Eric to put in a word if we have to. No woman can resist him. Then we'll be gone and the thing will have blown over."

"*If* they don't talk about it to others," Eric put in, "and I can't think of a female who wouldn't."

"A female who wanted to mend fences wouldn't, and I can't believe she doesn't want that," Brenna told her brother. Seeing Rafe's glum look, she added, "They won't gossip about it if he talks to her soon enough. And besides, they don't know who I am, do they? Rafe explained I was his old friend's sister, but I don't remember him using any names."

"I learned some discretion in my work on the Continent," Rafe said. "Names are too precious to give away lightly in time of war."

"Love and war both," Eric said with a small smile. "So. I concede you might be able to talk it away. Then if we leave as quickly as we arrived, it might mend all."

"You're not ready to travel," Rafe said stubbornly.

But Brenna saw a hint of hope light up those bright eyes of his.

"Damned if I'm not able to go," Eric said. "I'll say worse if you keep me here," he added at Rafe's quick look of censure.

"You'll say nothing if you're dead," Rafe said angrily, "and if you're not healthy enough to travel and you do, I'll kill you myself."

He heard what he'd said and his angry expression vanished. His lips quirked. Eric laughed and Brenna smiled.

"We'll see what the doctor says," Brenna said, "and then we'll talk more."

Rafe nodded.

"Fair enough," Eric said.

"There," Brenna said, with a calm she didn't feel. Because the words Rafe's lady's mama had flung at her were still echoing in her head. "Trollop," "slut," and then with a flourish, *"whore!"* the lady had cried before she'd stormed out the door. It would take a lot of talking to soothe that woman's feathers. But they would. Then she'd leave this all behind.

She glanced at Rafe. Today he was dressed in tones of blue. The color accentuated his eyes and actually complemented his hair, which was growing a little overlong for him. But it suited him better that way, she mused. The vibrant color added to the sense of vitality and urgency about the man. He stood tall and straight, poised for action. Brenna was used to army men, those who preened in their uniforms, those who became invisible without it. This was a fellow who would radiate confidence and command whatever he wore. He pulled out his watch and consulted it, and Brenna felt a small pang because she *would* be leaving this all behind her.

"I'll go see what's keeping that physician," Rafe said, and then paused. He shook his fiery head. "Charming of me, eh? No, I'm not trying to get you out sooner," he told Eric. "It's just that I must have something to do."

"I remember," Eric said, chuckling. "You haven't changed. I thought the inactivity in hospital would finish you faster than any battle could. So go find yourself an errand or two. Matters will be that much closer to being settled when you get back. I'll keep the angry mamas out until you return."

"Need some fresh milk too," Rafe said. "You like it in your tea, right? Anything you require, Miss Ford?"

"A little peace, a little quiet. Could you bring me a bag of that?" she asked whimsically.

"My going out now will give it to you," he said, bent his head in a semblance of a bow, and strode out of the room.

"Hotspur," Brenna whispered when he'd left.

"That Shakespearean hothead?" Eric asked with laughter in his voice. "No. Don't be fooled, Bren. Rafe's hasty, but not unthinking. He's never been rash. It's just that he thinks better when he's in motion. We always said it was a good thing it was his arm that got damaged, not his leg. I don't know how he'd have borne it. He said it wouldn't have mattered if it had been his legs, he'd just walk on his hands." Eric smiled. "He's a good man, Bren. You could do worse, much worse."

"Yes," she agreed, "I could marry him. But he's very much in love with his lovely Lady Annabelle. If you'd seen his face when she saw me . . . You're wrong. Marrying him would be the worst thing I could possibly do."

"So if you leave him to his lady, what about your reputation?" Eric said, watching her closely.

She shrugged. "I put paid to that when I went to nurse you, didn't I? 'Unladylike,' 'bold,' and 'too forward,' were just a few of the things they said then. Much I cared. Much I care now."

"Because Father gave you his blessing at the end," Eric said. "You have a whim of iron, as he wrote to tell me. But to return home unmarried, after this? If it gets out, there'll be fresh gossip. Take care. This could put paid to your future hopes. You do want to wed and have babes of your own, don't you?"

" 'Of my own'?" she asked quizzically. "Are there any others forthcoming? Are you considering marriage then, my dear?"

"No, not in this decade, at least. But you don't want to spend your life as a dutiful daughter or housekeeper for a bachelor brother, do you? You're only three and twenty, puss, and still prettier than most women in England."

"Not pretty," she corrected him. "Lady Annabelle is pretty. I am never that."

"Handsome then," he said.

"Thank you," she said, "just what a woman wishes to be told."

"Need flowers, child?" he asked. "Didn't get enough thrown at your head on the way here? There

wasn't a sailor on the ship who didn't want to woo
you. I couldn't close my eyes for a minute—not that
the wreck I've become frightened anyone. But I had
my pistol at hand."

"Your scowl was enough to terrify anyone," she
reassured him. "You've just lost a few pounds, but
we'll put them on you again. You're looking better
already." It was true. Her golden giant of a brother
had frightened her badly when she'd met him in the
hospital. He'd been almost unrecognizable, waxen
and gaunt, his skin yellow, his eyes dim. She'd wondered if he'd ever leave the place alive. But she'd
stayed and cared for him, and he'd rallied enough to
go home with her. The trip to England had been difficult for him. He was still too thin and weary, but even
so, he looked healthier than he had in weeks, and she
silently blessed Raphael Dalton for his safe harbor.

"As for me?" Brenna said. "My dear, sweet,
deluded Eric, it wasn't 'handsome' the men were
pursuing, and they weren't exactly 'wooing' in the
sense you think. I'm too much of a lady to say what
they were after, but I'm cursed with an appearance
that promises more than 'handsome' does."

"Blessed, more like," he said, closing his eyes again.
"You'll understand when the right fellow appears."

He has, twice, she thought.

It was as if her brother heard the thought, because
he quickly added, "It's the future I'm thinking about.
Yes, you've got looks, Bren. More than you've a right
to, the way you take care of yourself. But time's
passing."

"Thank you for reminding me," she said sweetly. "But no and no. Fair's fair, Eric. Your friend Rafe is being gallant. But he doesn't want or need me."

He nodded. There was nothing more to say, and besides, he was suddenly too weary to say another thing. Too sad about it, too. After all, she was right. Rafe didn't want or need her—and he'd noticed she didn't say she didn't want Rafe.

"My lady's not receiving visitors this morning," Annabelle's butler told Rafe after scanning the visiting card Rafe handed him.

"Right," Rafe said. "Understood. But tell me if it's just this visitor she can't receive."

"I couldn't say, m'lord," the butler answered.

"That bad, eh?" Rafe asked. He'd been prepared for this. He reached into his pocket and took out a note, and a golden coin. He gave both to the butler. The coin disappeared into the butler's own pocket immediately. Then he stared at the note.

"See that Lady Annabelle gets that, would you?" Rafe said.

The butler nodded. "But I might say? The lady's mama is more agitated than the lady Annabelle is. And her papa has refused to listen to the fuss at all."

Well, he wouldn't, would he? Rafe thought. *Not a subject he'd want to get into, considering the ladybird he's been with for the past twenty years.* "Then please take her the note," Rafe said.

It was a simple message. It said,

*I'll be back tomorrow morning. If you think the
thing through, you'll realize it was as innocent as I
said. I'd hardly be fool enough to invite you in otherwise, would I? In hopes of your understanding, and
apologizing for any difficulties, I remain*

> *Yr Svt,*
> *Dalton*

He was not yet at the point of signing a note to her
"Rafe." He hoped to be, soon. "I'll be back tomorrow.
I'd be grateful if you'd let the lady Annabelle know
that. Good morning."

"Good morning, m'lord," the butler said, gently
closing the door in Rafe's face.

Rafe walked away, deep in thought. She'd see
him tomorrow, or the next day or the next. He
didn't give up easily. He couldn't. He wasn't guilty
of what she'd thought. Someday they'd laugh about
this. He wished he could smile now. *So close,* he'd
been that close to beginning his courtship in
earnest. Now he had to start over again. He picked
up his head and his pace and strode on. He could
do that. He was very good at campaigning, and
impervious to insult. After all, he'd plenty of experience with both.

He made a few stops on his way home, although
it took him a roundabout route. He placed an order
at a nearby restaurant, stopped a milkmaid he
passed in the street and left an order with her. Then
he visited an employment agency several streets
away. It was late afternoon when he got back to his

own house again. He went up the stair to Eric's room and halted at the door.

"Ah, Lord Dalton," the doctor said, straightening from where he'd been bent over Eric's bed. "No, don't worry," he added at Rafe's startled expression, "our patient hasn't suffered a relapse. I found time to see him earlier than I'd thought. In fact, he's doing very well. These tropical fevers take the heart out of a man, but now he's back on English soil, I predict a rapid recovery. If he gets rest, of course, good nourishment, and takes his medicines."

"He wants to travel on this week," Rafe said, his brow furrowed.

"Impossible," the doctor said, snapping his case shut.

Rafe nodded. "As I thought. Thank you. I'll see it is impossible."

Eric sat up against his pillows. "We're leaving, Rafe. I'm getting better. Didn't you hear the man?"

"I heard. You didn't," Rafe said. "You're staying, if I have to sit on you."

"You'll have to do more than that to get me to stay on. There's no reason for me to sponge on you any longer," Eric argued. "I can travel home. It's only a matter of days."

"No. Until the doctor says you can walk home if you want to, you stay on here. And there's an end to it. I've already made all the arrangements. I hired on a valet for the both of us and a housekeeper for the look of things. A footman too. And a cook. I'm sending a note to my family to ask the name of a respectable female relative to come stay on here for the duration too."

"You don't need all that help, at least not for my sake," Eric insisted, "because I'm leaving. And your respectable female won't stay that way long if she's all alone in the house here with you—and that's what she'll be in a day, I promise you."

"Now, look—" Rafe said angrily. He didn't get a chance to finish. Brenna's calm voice cut him off. He hadn't seen her; she'd been sitting in the shadows. Now she rose and walked over to the physician.

"Doctor," she said in her gentle, soothing voice, her dark eyes on his, "forgive me for interrupting, but these two have their horns locked over this. Can we two work out a compromise, do you think? If my brother travels in slow stages, in a well-sprung coach, with me watching over him all the way, being sure he takes all your medicines on schedule, won't that do as well? After all, as you can see, he's fretting himself to pieces just lying here day after day."

"Day after one day!" Rafe said in annoyance.

But neither Brenna nor the doctor paid any attention to him. She smiled at the fascinated physician and went on, "Dear sir, what do you think if we make the trip in three days rather than two? Or four, if we must. He can rest as well in a comfortable coach as he can in a bed, can't he? Better, perhaps, because if he thinks he's got his way, he'll be able to relax and sleep. He can't do that here, if he's fussing, can he? We'll find a middle ground. If we don't go until the end of the week, will that suit?"

"Why, yes, my dear, if you put it that way, I suppose he can," the physician said, his eyes on Brenna's soft smile.

"Damme, but—" Rafe said, and stopped as the physician spun around and glared at him.

"My lord!" the doctor said. "There's a lady in the room."

"A clever one," Eric said, and grinned.

"Thank you, Doctor," Brenna said, ignoring her brother. "And that way, too, I can pay a call and see if I can mend matters here before we leave." But now her eyes were on Rafe, and the question in them was for him.

He nodded, grudgingly. "All right. Can't see it will hurt. But if things go wrong, you're to turn right around and come back."

Brenna nodded back at him. He hadn't said if he meant their trip back home or her visit to Lady Annabelle. She decided he meant both, and she agreed. Both ventures were gambles, after all.

Six

"I t was kind of you to see me," Brenna told her hostess after she was shown into the salon by a footman.

"Mama would have my head for it," Annabelle said simply. "But she's out now. If you don't take long, you can avoid her. I'd suggest avoiding her . . . Miss . . . Ford," she said, reading from the card Brenna had left, as though she hadn't already committed it to heart.

"Thank you, I'll be brief," Brenna said, holding her head high, hating the fact that she'd had to give her name, but knowing there was no other way to have been admitted. "May I sit?"

"Oh, do," Annabelle said carelessly, as if she didn't know what a deliberate insult it was to make her visitor ask.

Brenna sat, gingerly, and took a deep breath. She

looked around, trying to regain her composure. It was a lovely room, done up in the latest style with yellow and blue wallpapers in a Chinese theme, matching green draperies, and graceful, expensive furniture, all in the Eastern motif. The lady who sat posed on a long yellow satin settee was no less lovely, graceful, and expensive.

They were both dark-haired women. The resemblance, Brenna thought gloomily, ended there.

Her hostess was dressed in a golden silk morning gown trimmed with white. She had beautiful blue eyes in a no-less-lovely face. She was altogether dainty, curved, milk white and ebony, a little Dresden figure of a lady. Except for her expression. She sat at her ease and eyed her visitor openly, with undisguised distaste.

The lady was so perfectly set in her parlor, she made Brenna feel too big, rawboned and shabby, although she knew she wasn't. She might have her faults, but she knew very well they were none of those things. She had no idea that her hostess agreed.

Annabelle watched her visitor with concealed chagrin. Her mama spent so much time and money getting this room perfectly right. It had been, until now. The one thing it had lacked, it seemed, was this slender, graceful woman. She completed it. She wore a simple green walking dress, but her looks were as exotic as the distant lands everything in the room came from. Even her faint perfume was spiced rather than sugary.

It made Annabelle doubt her own attractions

again. She'd thought only Damon's beautiful wife could cause her this kind of confused pain.

But everything she'd seen of this woman so far was shocking and disturbing. She been roaming about a bachelor's house, half-dressed, or half-naked, depending on how one looked at it. And the look of her! Fresh from a bath and scented like a harem. Rafe had tried to say she was simply his friend's sister. *A friend's sister! Dressed or undressed like that!* Even so, if she'd tried to trap him into a proposal that day, she was an unprincipled monster. If it was a lie and she was simply his mistress, it was almost as upsetting. Apart from causing doubts about her own appeal, Annabelle wasn't used to dealing with that class of woman. The evidence seemed clear that her visitor was not her equal, in class, mind, or principles.

For once, Annabelle wasn't sure how to deal with a social situation. But if she was interested in any future with Rafe, she had to. It rankled.

"Rafe says you're not his mistress," Annabelle said suddenly.

Brenna's face paled. There was no attempt to sugarcoat the thing, or broach it gently. This was insult, not even thinly disguised. She rose to her feet.

"Oh, bother. Sit down, if you please," Annabelle said, annoyed with her own clumsiness. "If I meant to insult you, I'd do better than that. It's just that we've no time for trivialities and it's hardly the place for them. Did you want to discuss the weather or fashion before we spoke about it? We haven't the time. Rafe's a blunt man. I'll be no less so. Is what he says true? And can you prove it?"

"Absolutely true," Brenna said, sinking to her chair again. "I'd never met him before we arrived at his house two days ago. He'd even forgot he'd invited us. My brother, Eric, served with him in the Peninsula. They met in a hospital there, when Rafe was wounded," she added to the faint crease of puzzlement she saw on her hostess's otherwise unlined brow.

"Oh, yes," Annabelle said, though she hadn't known Rafe had been wounded.

"Eric collapsed," Brenna went on. "We'd just returned from India where he'd been gravely ill, you see. Rafe insisted we stay on with him until Eric could be seen by a good physician."

" 'Rafe'?" Annabelle asked, her little nose going up as she tried to look down it at Brenna.

Brenna's face flushed. Her chin went up too. "He insisted I call him that, as my brother does. But you're quite right. 'Lord Dalton,' I should say."

"So you should," Annabelle said, "but that at least rings true. He's very careless with his name."

"I'm not," Brenna said, her voice firmer, because she was done playing cat and mouse with this woman. She had something to say; she'd say it and be gone. "Nor am I careless in any other way with him. I've come to tell you that. I've got no reason to lie. We'll be gone from his house, and London, by week's end. It would be a pity if a simple mistake on my part ended your relationship with him."

Brenna looked down at her hands in her lap. "Yes, I certainly ought to have remembered I needed a chaperon if we were going to stay in a bachelor's house with him. I shouldn't have answered the door in my dishabille either. But I didn't even consider it." She glanced up at Annabelle again, and a rueful smile touched her lips. "I thought I'd open the door and dash upstairs again. That's how seductive I felt I looked. I'd taken a bath. I thought it was him at the door needing to be let in. Foolish and careless, I know. But that's all it was, and it was only because I was so preoccupied with my brother's health that I didn't think."

Annabelle saw how her visitor's face lit from within when she smiled. Anyone could see how a man might be attracted—but her story rang true. She tapped a fingernail on the arm of her settee. "As I said, can you prove it?"

Brenna laughed, startling her hostess. It was a full, throaty laugh, as earthy as it was genuine. "My dear lady," she said, "no, of course not. But consider the facts. I'd never met him before. I've been in India for the past four months. We arrived in London the day before. Do you think Lord Dalton is so irresistible that I landed on his doorstep and went straight to his bed? With my own brother in the house? Lord Dalton is attractive, but I'm not mad."

Annabelle studied Brenna, watching her eyes. The woman was calm, but she couldn't conceal the fires that sprang up in those dark sloe eyes of hers. "Is he attractive then, do you think?" Annabelle asked honestly, unable to stop herself. "Odd, I like him well enough, but I'd not thought it. Or is red hair a new passion in the East?"

Brenna sobered. "I'm not from the East. Or that far east, at least. We're from Shropshire. But I do think he's attractive. And it means nothing, because I've no relationship with him whatsoever. My feeling for him is gratitude for his kindness to Eric. And you may believe that or not, my lady. I'm going home in days and will likely never see him again. I just thought it would be a pity if you did the same, since he has a care for you, it seems." But her voice clearly implied she couldn't understand that.

She rose to her feet again. "Thank you for your time. I hope you consider what I said. I'd feel guilty if I were the cause of any grief for Lord Dalton, after he did such a good turn for us. Good day."

Annabelle didn't get up. It was another studied insult. Brenna went to the door, her hands gripped tightly on her recticule.

"It will take some time and talking to make my mama see the light," Annabelle said. "If, indeed, it turns out to be light and not just a will-o'-the-wisp. But I find myself believing you, and so she may come round—in time."

"So it will be forgotten?" Brenna asked eagerly.

"If you leave, and if it's true," Annabelle answered thoughtfully. "I tend to think it is. It's unlikely you two were secret lovers. Or that you were his mistress. It's doubtful that such is your usual occupation either, as mama insists. But you can see the problem, can't you? After all, you so looked the part the other day."

Brenna's jaw set tight. She forced a light laugh. "And not today? The less I dress, the better I look? Thank you for the compliment. It's usually only the gentlemen who see that."

Annabelle flushed. She watched her visitor leave. Only when she heard the front door close did she relax. "Well, what did you think?" she asked as the door to the connecting room opened.

"She's not his lover," her mama said. "If she'd a claim, she'd have made it. I asked Lady Claire, who knows everything, and Mrs. Teller, who makes up everything she doesn't know. Neither of them had heard of any such liaison. Dalton's had his share of ladybirds, but everyone knows their names, and no one ever heard of any dark, foreign-looking chit. She comes from Shropshire? The Fords, from Shropshire? I don't know them. I'll have my Betty ask her friends to find which of them come from there. Servants know every scrap of gossip. We'll discover all, don't you worry.

"But whatever the wench's past, and she looks as though she must have one—did you hear that laugh?" the countess asked, diverted. "A courtesan's, mark my words. Be that as it may, I doubt she has a past with Dalton. The dates don't agree, for one thing. For another, as he said, he's too clever to have asked us in if they had been lovers. He'd hardly have forgot she was there if they were. She'll be gone at week's end. The rest is up to you. He'll be ready to do anything for you if you take him back now."

"He'd be ready anyway," Annabelle said. "But she likes him. She'd have him if she could," she mused.

"Well, why not? There's an income," Lady Wylde said. "Good family. Good friends and entrée any-where. But you could do better."

"And I could do worse," her daughter said, think-ing of all the things her visitor hadn't said, things she'd read in her eyes when she'd spoken about Rafe. Things she herself hadn't seen in him, but only sensed. Things that made her too uneasy to dwell on now. "But Lud!" she sighed. "That hair! Still . . . that's why God made razors. All right. I'll give it a week more, at least. Then if she's left as she said she will—we'll have him in for tea. Not too soon, though. There's no sense rushing things. The Season hasn't even started yet. He'll keep."

"Like mullet on ice," her mama said, and laughed. "I've been speaking to the servants too much!"

Annabelle didn't laugh. Her lovely eyes nar-rowed. She raised a finger. "Yes. Exactly. Good point. Let's not keep this to ourselves, Mama. We can't. You've been asking around about her. They'll won-der why. Who knows who might discover the real answer? Let's nip it in the bud by letting the story out to show we don't care. If I do decide to have him, it won't do for it to look as though I was his second choice, even for a night."

"As if there were a chance of that!"

"But I've been a second choice before," Annabelle said.

Her mama's laughter stilled.

"And I've been the object of gossip before as well," Annabelle went on, a note of pain she was unaware of in her voice. "I won't have it again. Let me clearly be the wronged party this time. Why not? It might have been innocent on her part—but it might not have been. We can't give her the benefit of the doubt. Doubt gives too many easy answers to gossipmongers. The woman set a trap. It wasn't his fault. We were clever enough to realize it and absolve him. There it is, and so we'll say."

"Why, just so," her mama said. "Isn't that what I've been saying?"

Annabelle smiled. Life hadn't treated her well, but her mama always did. But now Life might have just decided to make it up to her. If not by getting her the man she wanted with all her heart, then at least by giving her one who'd devote himself to her with all his heart. She'd see. She had all the time in the world—or at least until the end of this Season—to pick a husband. Many things could happen in that time. She might even take Dalton. He needed a closer look. She deserved someone who doted on her after all the disappointment she'd had. And it wasn't as if no one else wanted him, after all.

Brenna drove back to Rafe's house, her thoughts on where she'd just been. She laid her cheek against the carriage's window glass to cool it, because her face still burned with embarrassment. It had been a demeaning interview. But necessary for Annabelle and herself. No wonder Rafe was fascinated by the lady. Her reluctant hostess had been beautiful, elegant, and yet seemed strangely vulnerable. She'd also been rude, even crude at times, and thoroughly vindictive. But she'd a right to be. *She must love him very much,* Brenna thought sadly. *Well, but who would not?*

"You took my knight," Brenna said with interest.

Rafe sat back from the chessboard. "I did. Don't see why you're shocked. It was indefensible."

"She's more than shocked," Eric commented from a chair by the fireside, "she's staggered. She usually beats men at the game. They're so busy flirting they never see how clever she is."

"A blatant lie," Brenna said calmly, though her eyes sparkled in the firelight. "It's just that gentlemen don't think we females can reason, and so while they humor us by playing chess with us, they don't expect to lose. That's when they do. Lord Dalton took me seriously. That makes him a good opponent."

"Thank you," Rafe said.

"And I didn't lose yet," she added.

"You will," Rafe said. "I see where you're going, and you won't get there. I'm an old soldier, Bren. I take every opponent seriously. Maybe if I'd only fought on battlefields, I wouldn't. But some of our most clever foes were female, and they fought in ballrooms and in bedr—other places," he said quickly. "Dam—drat, but you're such a good companion, I forget your sex when we talk too!"

Some of the sparkle went out of Brenna's eyes; she looked down at the chessboard with concentration.

"Don't leash your tongue on my behalf," she murmured. "I've spent the past three months visiting an army hospital. I've heard it all."

"I advise you to try to forget that, Bren," Eric said. "The world isn't like our friend Rafe. He appreciates loyalty. But there are too many who'll think worse of you because of it. It was folly for you to leave home and hearth and race across the world on your own to see to me. I said it then, I'll say it now. I wish you hadn't, though I admit if you had not, I might not be here to wish it." His smile was sad. "She chivied the nurses, Rafe. You should have seen her, just like a little border collie, nipping at their heels. She yapped at them too, if she had to."

"I do not yap," Brenna said.

"She was relentless," Eric went on, ignoring her. "Brought me doctors when I needed them, water and food and comfort too. She came when she got word of my illness and stayed until she got me well. I didn't dare die. She didn't even get a chance to see the country. She didn't miss a day by my bedside and hurried me home as soon as I left it for fear the climate would get me sick again. But though I appreciate it, I rue it, Bren, and you know it."

She shrugged. "I had a maidservant with me at all times. I stayed in a respectable home, with your friend's wife and sister. I traveled from England with an older female as escort, though she was the most tedious creature on the planet, didn't I? I did everything according to the rules."

Eric shook his golden head. "You left home, alone.

Well, at least without a husband. And you came back without one. At your age? It isn't done."

"Mama couldn't go," she said simply, "Nor could Papa or anyone else. What, was I to leave you there alone? I was the right one to go because I *was* free. And there's an end to it."

"I wish it was," Eric said. "I know you did it for me. But I'm sorry for it. And now *this*!"

"Playing chess with Lord Dalton is such a scandal?" she asked, a slight smile tilting her mouth.

"In most circles," Rafe said, straight-faced.

She looked up at him and smiled.

"If what happened gets out . . ." Eric said.

"It won't," both Brenna and Rafe answered together. They grinned at each other. Rafe gestured, inviting Brenna to speak.

"I spoke with Annabelle. She agreed," Brenna said. "If we leave, as scheduled, there'll be no talk, and it will be forgotten. Except I'll remember it to the day I die. When I opened the door and saw their faces! The time I found that snake in my slippers was a party by contrast!"

"And when I came in and saw all your faces," Rafe said, and laughed. "You looked like you'd been shot. They looked like they'd found you dead."

"No," Brenna said. "At least they might have been sorry for me then. *Might*, I say. Because in that dressing gown— Eric, why couldn't you have had a nice blue one? But crimson! Crimson silk, with red dragons all over it too. Your lady friends have terrible taste."

"Thieves can't be choosers," Eric said without sympathy. "Should have worn your own."

"I lost it," she said, "and if I hadn't, it might have been even worse."

"Really?" Rafe asked with exaggerated interest, "Now, what could yours have looked like?"

The firelight couldn't account for the high color that bloomed on Brenna's cheekbones as she bent to the chessboard again. She touched a pawn with one finger, as though contemplating her next move. Rafe's mock leer vanished. Brenna had long, slim fingers, but now he noticed their nails were bitten down to the quick. It surprised him. She was a perfect lady, and a lady's hands were always well cared for. She lifted her hand from the piece as though she saw the direction of his glance, and curled her fingers under so her nails were unseen, the way she usually held them. It made him feel curiously protective. He wanted to tell her it made no difference to him, and knew he couldn't, and it didn't matter anyway.

"Must you leave so soon?" he asked. "I mean," he added, when her head came up and she stared, "we've had such fun together."

"Much fun you'd have if we stayed!" she said, amazed.

"I know," he said. "I wasn't thinking. It's just that I want everything. Listen," he turned in his chair and looked at Eric. "*If* I win my lady—if we wed—matters will mend in time. I don't want to lose contact with you. I feel badly enough that you have to leave before it's time. If I'd my way, I'd have you stay here weeks, you know."

"I know," Eric said.

"We've got the coach hired and readied. We're packed," Brenna said. "We only need the doctor's blessing, a few more vials of his miraculous medicine, and we're off. But we thank you for your hospitality, we really do."

"You will write to me and let me know how things are going?" Rafe asked.

She didn't answer right away. She looked at him for a long moment. Rafe couldn't read her expression. The study was lit by gaslight jets high on the walls, but because of that, the light was uneven. It had seemed cozy to Rafe until now.

He'd been happy to have Eric's company again. Eric had been a good friend and a boon companion when they'd been in the hospital together in Spain. Rafe hadn't expected much of him when they'd met. Eric's handsome face and towering physique made him appear overconfident; the effect was that of a lazy lion. He had every reason to be vain, but Rafe soon discovered he wasn't. He was simply sure of himself. A man grew to know the very fiber of a fellow when he saw how he bore adversity. Eric's wound had given him that, in spades. He'd borne it well. Rafe found him to be generous, considerate, and plucky to the bone.

Eric's sister was a delight to while the time away with too. Steady, but possessed of a keen sense of humor, she constantly showed new and enchanting facets of her personality. Rafe found himself looking forward to their time together the last few nights. They spent the time talking, playing cards, singing while Brenna played the piano, and making up silly games to amuse Eric.

Rafe was always more comfortable around women in the evenings anyway. The dimmed light dulled his cursed hair, making him more like other men. The firelight might mock that, but it touched the edges of everyone's hair with flame. Even Brenna's inky hair had a crimson aura tonight.

But now the room suddenly seemed to hold secrets in the long shadows and dim corners. Brenna sat at the edge of the light that illuminated their chessboard. The expression in her dark eyes was lost in shadow. He could only see the strong, high bones in her face, and then the way her smile started, and shifted.

"Of course," she finally said. "We'll write. We expect you to write and tell us of your engagement too, you know," she added. She bent her head to the chessboard again. "Your move," she said.

"Send back a message to let me know you're safely home!" Rafe said as the coach prepared to leave the front of his house.

Eric sat at the coach window. The early sunlight gave his face a warm peach glow. He smiled, and for a moment looked whole and hale again. The physician said he was making a remarkable recovery. Rafe shifted his booted feet. It still felt wrong to send him away so soon. He frowned at how very wrong it felt.

"Don't scowl," Eric said. "I'll be fine. I hope we meet again, under better circumstances. And happier ones. Send me word so I can dance at your wedding. Good-bye, old friend!"

Rafe couldn't see much of Brenna's face behind her brother's, but he could hear her low, carrying voice. "We'll write. Good luck," she called, "and thank you!"

The coachman snapped the whip, the coach rolled away from the curb, and Rafe stood watching as it went up the street, rounded the corner, and vanished from sight. He waited another moment, finding himself curiously reluctant to go back into his house.

He wasn't the only one to feel bad about the departure.

"Aye, well, there goes this position," Rafe heard the footman he'd hired say to his newly hired butler as he stepped into his house. "We'd best pack and get back to the agency, eh?"

"Best not," Rafe said, startling them. "I find I like the service. Stay on until my man gets back next month and then we'll see. Looks good for a fellow to have a staff, and I'm tired of running errands. Cook's good too," he told the footman. "Speaking of service, I've a note for you to deliver. But I've got to write it first. Hold. I'll be back."

He strode into his study, picked up a piece of paper and a pen. He put two hands on the desk and bent over the blank sheet of paper, thinking. Then he sat, dipped the pen in ink and wrote.

My dear Lady Annabelle,
All is clear. They're gone.

> *Yr Dvtd Svt,*
> *Dalton*

Rafe frowned. Not what he wanted to say. Too rough, too curt, too much like the man he was. Not at all like the man he wanted to be for her. He thought a moment, then picked up the pen again and added a line.

And they won't be back.

He frowned ferociously when he read that. But it was only true, at least for now, and a man had to do whatever he could to win. He picked up the note and strode out to find the footman to deliver it for him.

Seven

Rafe had only climbed to the high driver's seat of his curricle, not the top of a mountain. But he felt the same feeling of breathless triumph when he got there. Triumph—and light-headedness. Because she was there waiting for him. And she smiled at him. The sunlight spun blue rainbows in Annabelle's soft curls, and showed her complexion white as rice, smooth as milk. Her eyes were blue as cornflowers and she smelled of roses. He clucked to the horses to get them moving, and worried that any words he would say would sound the same as that cluck. But he spoke anyway; he was never a man to run away from a challenge.

"I'm glad you reconsidered," he said carefully. "About seeing me again, that is."

"Why, so am I," Annabelle said.

"It's been ten days."

"Have you been counting?" she laughed.

"Yes," he said seriously.

She was, for the first time in a very long while, at a loss for words. He didn't flirt. It was hard for her to know where to go with a fellow like him. She liked to flirt and prattle and play with words. He had a fine, wry sense of humor; she knew that. But he was very serious about her. She wasn't quite ready for that. But neither was she ready to give him up. She changed the subject.

"I spent *my* time shopping," she said, opening her parasol. "London's scarce of company, but the summer's coming to a close and soon there'll be so many balls and entertainments! Mama won't hear of me wearing anything I wore last Season. A waste of time and money, to my way of thinking, but she's obstinate."

"She'll meet us at teatime?" he asked.

"Oh, yes, all's forgiven. But what a shocking young woman you harbored! Careless and thoughtless. I can't blame Mama for jumping to the most awful conclusions. I did too. But as my mama reminded me, a man's not responsible for one's friends, so how can he be responsible for a friend's sister?"

"She's not shocking at all," Rafe said sternly, his eyes on his team, "or thoughtless. In fact, it happened because her thoughts were all on her brother."

"Yes," Annabelle said, sliding a look at him. " 'Provincial' would be a better word. Oh—let's not talk about it anymore," she added, seeing how grim his face had become.

"Right. So why don't we talk about what you'll wear to dinner at Vauxhall next Saturday? If you go with me?"

She laughed, genuinely amused. One minute she decided he was so severe and cold she couldn't imagine why she was even thinking of something permanent with him. The next, he said something so winning she wondered why she didn't snabble him up. He'd never replace Damon in her affections. No man could. But he was just unique enough to intrigue her. She'd been numb so long. At least he interested her, and that was something. And he adored her. That was everything now.

"Dinner, at Vauxhall?" she murmured, spinning her parasol on her shoulder. "Isn't it a little late in the day to ask me that?"

"If it is, then I won't."

Not quite so adoring then? She liked that even better.

"It isn't," she said. "Should I wear blue?"

He turned to look at her. "Wear anything," he said. "All I'll see is you."

She blinked. It was like receiving a sonnet from any other man. "Blue, then," she said, with a smile.

They took tea with Annabelle's mama. It was awkward. Rafe couldn't be at ease with the countess. Annabelle obviously got her looks from her papa; she seemed to have her personality from him too. Lady Wylde was a squab of a woman, but there was nothing small about her presence. She dominated the conversation even when she was silent, her shrewd eyes following their expressions—as well as everyone's in the tearoom.

So Rafe concentrated on Annabelle. He watched her pour his tea with pleasure. It gave him a curious thrill to see her doing something for him, and she did it with grace and charm. Her hands were like little butterflies, like those of Japanese ladies in illustrations he'd seen. Small white hands—but he was brought up short when he saw the neat, pale arcs of her smooth oval nails.

They reminded him of another woman's nails, short, chewed nails on hands she'd kept hidden, except when she played the piano. Then they couldn't be concealed. He'd noticed them again the last night she'd stayed with him, when she'd played and they'd sung together. Strange to see such a calm, well-bred woman with such ravaged nails. Her hands had looked functional and competent on the keys, though. He remembered the music and the laughter, and wondered how she was doing.

Annabelle made a little jest. She heard her mama's laughter, but not Rafe's. She looked up from the teapot to see his expression. That clear blue gaze was on her hands. But not its focus. He was seeing something else, something far away. That was strange. And interesting. Just last night her mama said she thought Annabelle only wanted him because she wasn't sure if she could have him.

"Possibly," she'd answered, truthfully.

"But you can, you know," her mama had said.

Possibly, she thought again now, and asked, "Milk?

Or is it too hot? The tea," she added, smiling, when he recalled himself and his guilty gaze flew to her.

"It's fine, thank you," he said.

So it was. But it was over too soon. At least, it was for Rafe.

There were long days to get through until Saturday, Rafe thought after he left Annabelle. Days in which he couldn't see her, because he'd asked. She'd be busy every night and day until then. At least, she said she was. He wasn't surprised. She was a popular young woman. And they both knew if she saw him more often, everyone would assume they were about to be engaged. She wasn't ready to make that decision yet. He didn't blame her.

Three days seemed long to him now, but he knew it wasn't the eternity it felt like. He'd find ways to entertain himself; he always had. Still, he saw the sun lowering and his spirits sank too. There was dinner to get through tonight. Good as his new cook was, Rafe discovered he now hated the thought of eating alone. When company left a house, it always seemed emptier than it had been before they came. Eric and his sister had filled the place with their laughter and talk. Rafe handed his curricle over to a stableboy and found his footsteps lagging as he walked to his front door.

His closest friends were gone from town; even his newer friends had just loped off home to Shropshire . . . Well, but he belonged to clubs, didn't he? he

thought, brightening. Or at least he had, once upon a
time. He was sure he'd sent in his subscription dues.
If he hadn't, he was equally sure they'd welcome him
again. Let his new servants dine on his dinner at
home; he'd go find something to divert himself.

He considered his options. He didn't want to talk
horses and driving all through dinner, so that let out
the Four in Hand Club. Nor did he want to discuss
politics all night, so he'd avoid White's and Brook's.
He'd stay away from Boodle's too. Gambling was
exciting, but his mind wasn't on it, so that was out.
Only a fool wagered when his head was elsewhere.
And he'd just discovered his heart was connected to
his head.

He and Drum had spent many happy hours at the
Roxburghe. But their dinners went on for hours and
he wasn't in the mood for five courses, not to mention seven bottles of wine. Getting drunk would only
make him maudlin. He didn't want sex either, or at
least, he did, but the sexual encounter he wanted was
impossible now, and he wouldn't settle for less. So
the finest brothels in Town were out. That meant
missing a chance to meet up with some of his old
army friends too.

Rafe scowled. The unexpected visit from Eric had
spoiled him. The long and short of it was, he wanted
to spend time with someone he knew. He'd spent so
much of his life on the Continent in the past years,
there was little chance of that . . . He stopped in mid-
step, and grinned. Simple. The Traveler's Club.
Someone was always arriving in London and stop-

ping off there before going on home. There was always someone ready to ship out to some foreign port waiting for his ship to leave too. He'd surely find a familiar face there.

Rafe found it hard to concentrate on what his dinner companions were saying. It wasn't just because they were dull. John Farkas and Lord Roman were interesting fellows, but one had just come back from Egypt and was filled with memories of it, and the other was just heading out for America and was preoccupied with plans for that. Rafe's old schoolmate the Viscount Hazelton had led a fascinating life, but he was besotted with some female and hadn't a sensible word to say for himself tonight. Rafe couldn't have heard it if he did. The men at the next table had too many.

The dining room at the Traveler's Club was emptying; dinner was over. The four men at the next table stayed there and gossiped. Only they called it 'reminiscing.' Gossip was for women.

Their voices carried in the half-filled room.

"Remember Huntley's little vixen?" one of the men at the next table said loudly, drowning out the conversation at Rafe's.

"Aye," one of his companions, a beefy fellow with a ringing voice, answered. "She went to Freddie Bell, then Copley. I had the keeping of her once myself. What that trull couldn't do wasn't worth doing! Could put her ankles behind her ears. Never saw the like of it. Wasn't so much good, mind you, as it was special. Off-putting at first, to be sure, but definitely special. Never forget it, at any rate."

Rafe's companions gave up all pretense of talking and grinned at each other.

"Aye, she was something," the beefy fellow went on with drunken sentimentality. "Whatever became of her?"

"Off to the Continent," one of his friends said with a shrug. "Austria, someone said. Maybe you'll meet up with her again there."

"Ho, she must be at least thirty now," the thickset fellow roared. "Too old for sport, for certain! Probably can't get an ankle up on a chap's bum now! But Freddie Bell! What a cutup he was, to be sure! And what about his sister? That dun-haired chit. You know, the long-toothed one. *Celeste,* aye, that was it! 'The belle from hell,' remember? Never think it to look at her, but who didn't get a leg over that one, eh? Not a female in Town couldn't learn a thing or two from her either, eh? Eh?"

The words rang out in the sudden hush that fell over the rest of the room. Gentlemen did not discuss other gentlemen's sisters no matter how drunk they got.

"Sisters are the very devil," one of the other men at the noisy table complained. "Get too close, and you have to march down the aisle. Stay too far, and you insult the brother. One of the reasons why I travel so much." He looked up blearily and finally noticed the silence in the room. "Say, none of you chaps have a sister, do you?" he asked the men at his table. "If so, tell me now, and I'm gone from here, I swear it!"

"Mine are married, thank God," a tall gentleman sitting next to him said, "but speaking of sisters—did you hear about the mess Dalton got himself into with the fair Annabelle because of one?"

"Dalton? He back in England?" the fat fellow asked, looking up from his glass.

"Yes, and in hot water already," the tall gentleman drawled, so eager to tell his tale he didn't notice the frantic looks his suddenly alert companions, facing Rafe's table, were darting at him. "See, he was entertaining some army man he knew in the old days— name of Ford, from Shropshire, I heard. Any event, seems Dalton left this Ford fellow and his sister at his home one day while he was squiring about the fair Annabelle and her dragon of a mama. There's almost a match there—at least I've got a golden boy on it in the betting book. Why are you all wigwagging at me? I could have put down more, but I'm no flat. The lady's known to change her mind.

"Well, anyway, Dalton invites the dragon and the lady to his house to have a look at it—they're sizing him up, y'see. They open the door—and there's the friend's sister! Naked as the dawn, wearing nothing but her hair, and she flips that back to show them *all*! And there was a lot to see—they say she's built like Venus on a clamshell."

He sat back, misconstruing their stunned expressions. "She tried to trap him, see? Didn't wash," he said, seeming disappointed about that. "Lady Annabelle is fair in mind and body. She forgave Dalton—after he turfed the slut out, of course, and . . . Oh."

He'd finally turned to see what his three companions were gaping white-faced at behind him.

Rafe loomed there. "Interesting," Rafe said, "but a lie."

"Are you calling me a liar, sir?" the tall gentleman asked.

"If you tell that story, yes," Rafe said, glowering down at him.

"I'm no liar. I tell what I heard," the man said.

"You heard wrong," Rafe said.

"*Apologize*, man," one of the man's table-mates hissed to him.

"For telling truth?" he answered. "I think not. What are you going to do about it, Dalton?"

Rafe's fists knotted. The tall man saw it and flinched. But he remained firmly seated. He forced a laugh. "A brawl in a gentlemen's club, Dalton? Oh, good! The best way to be sure the slut's name gets bandied about."

Rafe's face grew dark.

"So what are you going to do?" the tall man asked again. "Challenge me?"

"If you wish," Rafe said through clenched teeth, "Though I'd rather settle it in the court of fives and have it out with fists. That way I won't have to leave the country after I exterminate you, as I'd have to if my sword or pistol settled the thing."

The tall gentleman rose to his full height. He had a long, lean body, a perpetual sneer, and a malicious expression in his slitted eyes. That and the obvious dissipation in his face ruined what might once have been exceptional good looks. "I don't mind leaving after I win," he said with a smirk. "I'm on my way to the Continent as it is. There's a little matter of a claim of paternity. Some slut seeks a husband and is trying to play me for a fool. I'm off until she comes to her senses, or finds another victim. I won't apologize. So. I take it you're issuing a challenge? Or are you afraid to try me?"

Rafe's friends leapt to their feet. "Walk away, Rafe!" John Farkas cried. "The man's three parts drunk and two parts fool."

"That's five parts, won't wash," the beefy man at the table said after much thought.

"They're drowned in drink," the Viscount Hazelton told Rafe, putting an arm round his tensed shoulders. "There's no sense to it, Rafe. Save your pistol for true villainy."

"Would you unman me?" the tall man asked with cold amusement. "I'm none the worse for a bottle of wine. Nor do I fear meeting my lord Dalton," he jeered. "I spoke the truth as I heard it and I have no reason to disbelieve it. If he wishes to try to silence me for it—he may try."

Rafe bowed. "I'm at your command, my lord Liar."

The tall gentleman stiffened. He took a step closer to Rafe, saw his eyes, and stopped short. "The name is Dearborne," he said instead. "Name the place and time—I'll be there. Be sure to name the mortician too, because I intend to be thorough."

"If you prefer to leave England in a box, it's your

choice," Rafe said as coldly. "Julian," he asked his friend, "will you second me?"

The viscount looked miserable. "If I must, of course."

"So," Dearborne said triumphantly, "as *I'm* the one challenged—you all just heard him, didn't you?—*I* choose the weapons. I prefer swords. Still care to meet me?"

Rafe gave a terse nod.

"Indeed?" Dearborne asked silkily. "I chose swords because skill's more interesting than aim, and more difficult—*especially* for a fellow who almost lost his arm in the wars, as I heard you did." He laughed. "And I've studied fencing with the great Angelo. Yes," he gloated. "So. May I suggest you apologize to me now?"

"You may," Rafe said. "If you've lost your mind. Tell me, who did you study with? Harry?"

Dearborne was taken aback. "Harry Angelo, yes. The greatest swordsman in England."

"I think even he'd dispute that," Rafe said. "His father was the best. I studied with him at Eton when I was a boy. He was an old man then, but there was none better. I polished up that training later with his son, Henry, Harry's brother."

Lord Dearborne's high color, even reinforced by port as it was, began to fade.

"Yes," Rafe went on, "and Henry was superintendent of sword exercise in the army. A fellow's arm gets rusty if he don't keep at it, so then I kept training with a friend of mine, Henry's other brother, Edward. A professional soldier and the army's instructor of the sword. Demons with swords, every one of the Angelos," he mused. "I fenced with Harry once too. His brothers could beat him hollow."

"But your arm . . ." his friend Hazelton said anxiously.

"Yes, your arm," Dearborne said with regained confidence. "Surely you have to take that into account."

"Which arm?" Rafe asked. "I trained myself to use both. *So*," he said mockingly, "arrange things with Hazelton here—or apologize. It's up to you. Just admit you lied. As you usually do."

Dearborne snarled; his fist shot out. Rafe shifted his weight, dodged the blow, and countered by catching Dearborne square on the chin with a fist. As the man's head snapped back, Rafe followed it with his fist, hitting him in the nose. A quick blow to the stomach made Dearborne grunt; another sharp rap to the head made him stagger. One more hit to the chin put him down. And out.

Dearborne lay on the floor, groaning and bleeding copiously from his nose.

"That was for the lady in question," Rafe said, straightening his sleeves, "and for an old friend, and others probably too numerous to mention." He looked down at Dearborne. "Won't waste good shot or dull a fine blade on you. Better be on the next ship out, though, or I'll see to the finishing touches in some other way." He stepped over Dearborne. "I'll pay for cleaning the carpet," Rafe told a spellbound waiter as he walked out of the dining room.

Hazelton strode alongside him. "He said he didn't

want to use fists, then struck without warning. But you were ready for his treachery!" he said with admiration.

"I'm always ready for treachery," Rafe said, grimacing.

"Have you hurt yourself?" his friend asked worriedly, noting Rafe's pained expression as he tried to rotate his shoulder. "I thought you said you could use either arm."

"I can," Rafe said, wincing. "That doesn't mean I should."

When Rafe went out to dinner that night, he winced again. Not because of the pain in his arm. He saw the looks he was getting. Admiration. Awe. Even envy. He tried to concentrate on his cutlet.

"It's the way of the world," Hazelton laughed when he saw how Rafe hunched over his dinner plate, scowling at his blameless veal. "London's buzzing. Dearborne's off to the Continent with his nose in a sling and his name in the dirt. There's not a man here who doesn't applaud you for it. Scandal-mongering was one of Dearborne's more endearing traits."

"I wish they'd forget it," Rafe said wholeheartedly. "The sooner they do, the sooner they'll forget the reason for it."

"They already have," his friend said.

Rafe shook his head. Part of what had saved his life in the past was knowing when there'd be trouble

ahead. He felt it in his aching bones now. Not for the
first time, he wished Drum were there. He'd never
have to explain a thing to him, and they'd worked
together against bad odds before. He had a sinking
feeling the business wasn't done.

Dinner passed easily enough. The looks Rafe got,
the glad greetings from relative strangers, the way
others came up to his table to greet him, the whispers
in his wake, annoyed him. But they weren't dangerous. What he overheard as he left the room was.

Two drunken bucks were waiting in the hall for
their hats when they saw Rafe come to collect his.
They'd gamed in the back room, and drunk even
more than they'd gambled. Now they were weaving
out of the club to look for better sport. They found it.

"I say!" one said loudly. "There's Dalton. Can't be
another with that flaming head. He's the ginger-top
who took down ol' Dearborne! Good show!"

"Good show? I s'pose." the other sneered. "But
futile, in my humble 'pinion. A fellow's a fool to fight
over a slut's good name. She'll only dip it in the dirt
a'gain, mark my words. She must have been dicked
in the nob as well as being a whore. Imagine ...
tryin' to cut the beauteous Annabelle out! Took off
her clothes, did she? Ho! The creature could have
shucked down to her bones and she wouldn't have a
chance of showing up the fair Annabelle!"

Rafe's head shot up.

His friend rolled his eyes. "Ignore them," Hazelton said.

But Rafe had already stalked over to the pair. "I

would not repeat that," he told them in a deadly soft voice. "One, it's not true. Two, it makes me very angry to hear untruths."

"Oh, goin' to fight me too?" the heavier of the two asked with a smarmy smile. "Well, sorry, m'lord. I'm a better man than Dearborne in every way. If you want to test me, do it." He started unbuttoning his jacket.

"Gentlemen," Hazelton said, "this can be resolved in neater fashion at a later date."

"Nothing neater than my right fist," the man said as he flung off his jacket. He rolled up his sleeves and assumed a stance, two fists raised. "Let's settle it here and now. Or do you need a day to get your courage up?"

"No need," Rafe said with resignation. "I don't want to brawl," he said over his shoulder to his friend, "but I can't let this go on. There's already talk. Maybe this will put an end to it." He put up his fists.

The other man made a feint toward him. Rafe danced back, but kept his eyes on him, measuring his face, his pose, his reach.

"I didn't invite you to the waltz," the man jeered.

Rafe nodded. Then his fist shot forward. The sound of it connecting with the man's jaw was loud as a pistol shot. The sound the fellow made when he hit the marble floor was worse.

"I've just discovered something else," Rafe told Hazelton through clenched teeth as he took his hat from a frozen faced footman. "A man can't die of pain, no matter how he may want to. Damme," he said, as he tried to flex his shoulder, "I don't know if I can survive this Season."

"Or if any of the gossips will," his friend sighed.

The coach rattled on down the long, rutted road to Shropshire. Brenna looked out the dusty window. Shadows were making the hedgerows turn purple and brown, the fields beyond them growing misty lavender with oncoming night.

She glanced into the corner of the dim coach. Her brother lay back against the leather squabs. She knew he wasn't sleeping. She'd seen him shift his long frame a few too many times in the past half hour. "We have to stop now," she said.

He opened his eyes. "I feel fine. Let's go on."

She couldn't make out his expression, but she couldn't hear the usual rich, deep timbre in his voice either.

"No," she said firmly. "You may have the constitution of an ox, my dear, but I don't. My teeth are half rattled out of my mouth. My kidneys have made the acquaintance of my lights and liver—they're all a jumble now. And I'd give several fortunes—if I had them—to use the convenience a lady may not mention. Please, may we stop for the night now?"

He chuckled, low. "Witch," he said fondly, "you know I can't resist that. I doubt you're even weary, or that you have to use that . . . convenience. Still, yes, of course, tell the coachmen we'll stop."

When the coach pulled up into an inn yard a few

miles down the road, he held her hand to help her out. As she emerged from the coach, Eric saw her face clear in the lantern light. "You *are* tired," he said, instantly remorseful, "Forgive me, I wasn't thinking."

"No need for forgiveness," she answered. "You were right, I'm not really weary. The thing is, I *was* thinking. And not good thoughts. Lud! I made a mess of matters, didn't I?" Her eyes, dark as the coming night, sought his. "Do you think I can ever go back?"

He pressed her hand. "It'll be forgotten in a day," he told her softly. "London never has more than seven-day wonders."

But she'd never forget Lord Raphael Dalton, Brenna thought sadly. Because she'd been trying to do just that, without success. Not in seven days, or even years, perhaps. He stuck in her mind, in all his red-haired glory. She couldn't shake him loose; she'd tried for days now. Such a fine, forthright, upright man, a good man, brave and honest, and such men were so few and far between. Few in London, none perhaps where she was going. She'd soon be so far from him, and was getting further away in time and distance every hour she went on. Because when those seven days were up, Rafe would be wed, or as good as, wouldn't he? And she was going home now. *Much that mattered*. He hadn't seen her even when she was there.

"Yes, it'll be over soon and the incident forgotten by one and all," she told her brother, mustering a smile. "You're right, of course."

"I wish I were wrong this time," he said, examining her face.

She bowed her head. He knew her too well.

Eight

R afe's scowl could have curdled milk, but he stood still and suffering as he let his new butler tie his neckcloth for him. There was nothing else he could do, after all. His right arm was in a sling. He grimaced when the butler stepped back and he had a look at himself in the mirror.

He tore his eyes from his own reflection and saw the butler's nervous face. "Nothing you've done." Good job, actually," he said. His eyes returned to the glass. It *was* a good job. His cravat was perfection, he was shaved smooth, and his hair was tamed. His fashionable tight-fitted jacket hung right, even with the sling.

But even the application of a leech hadn't improved his face much. The swelling over his left eye had gone down some, but the skin was still discolored. He raised his head. And the long bruise on his jawbone still looked terrible, though the purple had faded to green . . .

"An application of some maquillage, my lord?" the butler offered tentatively, seeing the direction of his gaze. "An application of a simple cosmetic paste? My last employer suffered from a bad complexion. It did wonders for him, smoothing his skin and hiding defects. You haven't got the same problem, of course—but tonight? A dab here or there, perhaps?"

"So I can look healthy as a poxy whore? No, thank you. But thank you," Rafe added hastily. "You've done wonders, best that can be done. But I won't paint. A man can't brawl and come out looking like a poet. It will have to do."

He touched his jaw. That bruise had come from the incident in the alley outside Watier's after he'd heard what that idiot lordling at the faro table had said about Brenna Ford. The eye had been given to him by the fool at Gentleman Jackson's who'd been telling a filthy joke about her. He'd given back two for one in each case, though, he thought with little satisfaction. The sling was the price he paid for each victory. The arm wasn't as ready to protect as he was.

He had a more serious engagement with John Stiles still to come. It had been arranged after he heard the filthy thing Stiles had said about Brenna. But Rafe doubted that fatal dawn would ever come. Last he heard, Stiles was making hasty plans for a long sea voyage.

But there were dozens of other tongues wagging in London, and all about the same thing—Brenna Ford, the scheming wench who had stripped to her skin and tried to entrap him in marriage to spite Annabelle. And that was the nicer version of the rumor. He didn't know how the story had got out or how it had reached such proportions. Worst of all, they had her name.

Rafe stalked from the room, avoiding the mirror. He was tired of looking at his bruises. It didn't matter. He had worse ones on his conscience. He'd prowled the house half the day, and most of the night, pacing and thinking, trying to find a solution. He couldn't challenge all London. But he couldn't let it go on.

He was halfway down the stair when he heard voices at his front door. So, Stiles hadn't fled after all. He'd sent his second to arrange matters. Rafe took the stairs quickly, his teeth clenched tight. The only question was whether to wait until his arm was fully healed or try to get the thing over with quickly. Stiles was a fair shot, after all, and—

"*Drum!*" Rafe said, coming to a halt at the bottom of the stair when he saw who was standing in his front hall.

"Himself," Drum acknowledged. "So the rumors I heard were true," he said with interest, noting the sling and then studying his friend's battered face.

"What rumors? By God, forget that, what are you doing here!"

"Good to see you too," Drum said, stripping off his gloves. "Yes, thank you, I *would* like a brandy and a chair by the fireside after my hard travels. No, no, don't get yourself into a taking, only joking—but I would like that, you know."

"It's yours," Rafe said, leading him to the study. "Tell me what you're doing here in your own sweet time."

"Thank you," Drum said, accepting the glass of liquor Rafe quickly poured from a decanter.

He settled himself in a chair by the hearth and raised his glass to Rafe. "Ah! The spirit to put the spirit back in a man," he sighed after a sip. "I've been riding hard." He saw Rafe's expression and gave him a crooked smile. "Not *that* hard, no, not all the way from Italy. Well, the long and short is, I never got there. I didn't get lost, except in the diversions Old Hightower had to offer at his place in France. You remember his house isn't far from the coast. He still lives in grand style and loves to keep the place well stocked with company and good food, and it's still always open to wandering Englishmen. It was so comfortable there I decided to stay awhile before moving on."

He took another sip and grimaced. It wasn't because of the liquor. "Then our old friend Dearborne arrived," he said, "and I heard rumors about you. I came back to see if they were true. If only half of them were, it occurred to me that you might need my advice and counsel—not to mention," he added, looking at Rafe's arm in a sling, "a good right hand."

Rafe nodded. "What did Dearborne say?"

"What I've heard the rest of London saying since I got back this morning. Only he was saying it more colorfully. He'll have difficulty saying it in future, though. I broke his jaw."

"Really?" Rafe asked, diverted.

"Yes, inevitable after I told him what I'd do if he didn't stop his tongue himself. He showed steel—a dagger—when my back was turned to him. Turns out he's ambidextrous. It's fitting that a two-faced man would be, don't you think? Poetic, almost."

"Careful," Rafe said with a smile. "You know I am too."

"Only because you practiced long and hard when you got that arm of yours shattered," Drum said blandly. "It never came naturally to you. It does to him. The lucky thing is that he's not half as fast as he thinks he is with either hand. Be that as it may, Rafe— what the devil is going on? Is it true?" he asked, looking at his friend seriously. "I mean, the talk about the wench who showed her all to your lady and tried to stake a claim on you? And what are you trying to do? Make war against half the males in England? Because if it's true, there's nothing you can do."

"It's not true," Rafe said, running his good hand through his cropped hair. "She's no wench. Nor did she do that. Her name's Brenna Ford—she's Eric Ford's sister."

"I knew who she was. But she didn't do it?" Drum asked, his glass paused halfway to his lips.

"No. She's every bit as sound as Eric is. She's younger than he is, but very mature in her manner. Charming—intelligent too. A sensible woman, a calm, steady, respectable female who has no blame in this." Rafe rose and began pacing. He began telling Drum the story, and frowned, because it seemed even worse as he told it.

"I know I was a fool," Rafe said with frustrated

rage, "but I forgot I needed a chaperon if I was going to invite a young woman to stay here. But I didn't think of Eric's sister in that way, and neither did she act that way toward me."

" 'That way'?" Drum asked bemusedly.

"As a woman." Rafe shook his head. "Which she is, no matter how I thought of her. Damme, but as you know too well, I wasn't thinking of anything but Annabelle. The whole thing happened because of that. The Fords had done some hard traveling, so the day after they got here, I let them alone to rest and recuperate. Meanwhile I took Annabelle and her mama to tea. Nothing would do but the mama come see this place. Well, seems she's considering me," he said, unable to keep the pride from his voice. "I left them at the door while I stabled my team. They raised the door knocker. Bren—I mean, Brenna Ford—thought it was me."

Drum's eyebrow went up at how easily Rafe had used the woman's pet name.

"Thinking I was locked out, she opened the door," Rafe said.

"Bad, but not lethal," Drum commented, sipping his whiskey, watching Rafe carefully.

"Lethal," Rafe sighed. "She'd just taken a bath. She was dressed!" he said quickly as Drum's azure eyes went wide. "But only in her brother's dressing gown. It was crimson. With dragons on it," he added darkly. "Her hair was down, and wet. It's long, and very black, exotic looking. And she smelled of bath salts and jasmine."

"Interesting," Drum said, "but worse, yes."

"I offered for her, of course."

"Annabelle?"

"No, Bren," Rafe said.

"Of course," Drum said casually, but his eyes were very wide now.

"She refused. Several times. Said it would blow over. They went home. But now all London's filthying her name."

"So what's to do?"

"I think—and believe me, Drum, I've been thinking of little else—but I really think I have to go to the Fords and see how it's affecting them."

"She may be right, it may blow over," Drum mused.

"Yes. For me. Especially if I keep courting Annabelle. But maybe not for Bren and Eric. I've done what I can, aside from protecting her name by main force. I've tried to shine up mine too. I hired on enough servants to service a castle. I don't go anywhere your maiden aunt wouldn't have tea. But the gossip keeps spreading. I can weather it—rumor has it that I'm the wronged party, after all. But what about her? They're proud as the devil, the pair of them. I had to fight to get them to let me call a physician for Eric, and there he was, white as the sheet on the bed he was lying on. You'd never believe how sick he looked. And still, I had to insist.

"So I know they'd never tell me if they were social lepers by now," Rafe said in frustration. "No, I have no choice. I have to see how the wind is blowing in Shropshire myself. *If* the slander hasn't reached that far, *if* it does blow over before it gets there, then I'll come right back and resume my courtship of Annabelle. That's going well," he added with pleased amazement. "If not?" He shrugged, his face going suddenly blank. "I'll bite the bullet and wed Eric's sister. She's a good sort, Drum. She doesn't deserve this."

"Nor do you," Drum said thoughtfully. "Well, it's a better plan than continuing to pound every male in Town into the ground, or at least all who have the story—and that's all of them. I'll go with you, if I may?"

"I'd like that. Thank you. Tomorrow? Or do you want time to rest?"

"Oh, it's far too diverting. Tomorrow, of course."

"I just have to write a note to Annabelle. We were to go to Vauxhall Saturday," Rafe said.

Drum looked up at the sound of his friend's voice. He'd seen Rafe suffering too many times during the long years he'd known him. He seldom saw it so naked in his face.

"Just as well I miss that appointment," Rafe said curtly, seeing the quick sympathy spring to his friend's eyes. He ran a hand along his jaw. "My face looks like sausage. Feels like it too. It'll be healed by the time we get to Tidbury, though. Lord! Tidbury instead of Vauxhall Gardens," he said with wonder. "Trying to mend a wrong done to a respectable female instead of wooing the fairest one in England. Life's full of surprises."

He frowned. "I'll go write that note to Annabelle now so it can be delivered first thing. We'll leave at dawn," he said, and turned on his heel, leaving Drum to his thoughts by the fireside.

Annabelle flung down the note the footman delivered to her. She'd felt the blood drain from her face as she'd read it. Her mama snatched it up and read it quickly.

"Dalton's gone? On 'sudden urgent matters?' Where?" her mama asked.

"Oh, who cares? That puts paid to *his* pretensions," Annabelle said too airily, turning aside as though to catch sight of her reflection in the mirror, but keeping her eyes down so her mama couldn't see into them. "I certainly won't cancel our plans just because of my lord Dalton, thank you very much. I told everyone I was going to Vauxhall Saturday evening, and go I shall. I can get Williams, or Mr. Oaks, or Lord Carling, to take me instead."

"Of course you can, my dear," her mama said. "And any number of other gentlemen besides. I'm sure he didn't mean any insult. He's mad for you. It must be urgent family matters or some such."

"Maybe," Annabelle said. "It had better be," she murmured. She turned a sunny face back to her mother. "Nevertheless, I'll send a note straight back telling him not to bother visiting me again when he returns. He'll know leaving a lady in the lurch isn't done. At least, not *this* lady. I can't smile and pretend it doesn't matter, Mama. It does. What will he think of me if I accept a broken appointment as though I was afraid to make a fuss in case he wouldn't make one with me again? Oh, don't worry. If I choose, I can mend matters. I've done it before, haven't I?" she asked on a laugh that broke, startling her.

She cleared her throat. "I don't know that I *will* forgive him again. We'll see. But who shall we get to replace him?" she asked gaily, as though it didn't matter. "Oaks has a way with a jest, but Carling is *such* a good dancer."

Her mother gave opinions on each suitor. Annabelle hardly listened. There was a lump in her chest and a weight on her heart. It wasn't that she'd decided on Dalton, but she'd been considering him seriously, if only because he'd made her aware of herself again. His attentions were more than flattering; they'd become necessary to her good opinion of herself. Now this? It was only the intimation of trouble. But she was no stranger to trouble.

She was the most beautiful girl in London—or so everyone said. She was called an Incomparable. She wasn't stupid or shallow either. She was educated, accomplished. She wasn't just an ornament. She *felt* things, she thought, fighting tears. Other women her age who cared less and had less had nonetheless married long since, some happily. So why was she so unlucky in her choice of men?

The one man she'd wanted, the one she was sure would be her heart's mate, had never seriously looked beyond her face or tried to read her heart. Everyone had said their marriage was inevitable, given they were so well matched, old neighbors and easy friends, and he was always so kind to her. But he hadn't desired her for his wife. Every other man she'd ever met had.

She never thought she'd settle for less than the perfection Damon Ryder had seemed to be. But she'd unbent enough to consider Rafe Dalton. He was smitten, persistent. But with an occasional edge that made him more interesting than her other suitors. Cursed by his hair, his blunt features and manner, he was altogether inferior to her Damon. But precisely because of that, she knew he'd be eternally grateful to her for marrying him. It made perfect sense. It made her feel powerful and safe. Surely he'd be the last man on earth to hurt her. And yet, now *he* toyed with her affections? How *dare* he?

Annabelle danced away to look into her wardrobe so her mother couldn't see her face. To be spurned once was devastating. Twice would be almost a comedy—if it didn't hurt so much.

The earl of Drummond arrived at his friend's town house shortly after dawn the next day. He was admitted, then left to cool his heels in the study. His friend was still in his dressing gown when he came downstairs to greet him. "I thought you'd want to leave early, so as to get the journey done before evening falls," Drum said, eyeing his friend's sleep-tousled hair.

"So I did," Rafe said, "but I can't. I decided to stop on the way and pay a brief morning call on Annabelle before I do."

"To say farewell? You do have some sensibilities after all." Drum joked.

"Very few," Rafe assured him, "But this isn't even that. She sent me a note in answer to mine. She doesn't understand. She's furious about my canceling plans for Vauxhall, I suppose. Says she doesn't want to see me again. Can't blame her, but I can have a word with her before I go, to smooth matters. A note's no way to change plans. I should have realized it before I sent it. I'm no hand with the ladies, Drum," he said with a wan smile. "I don't want to make a misstep now."

Drum looked sober. "If you don't mind some advice?"

"Feel free."

"Well, I wonder if you should even try to explain. How do you propose to do it? It might muddy the waters further if you say you're going to see Brenna Ford. Annabelle may jump to worse conclusions."

"I won't lie," Rafe said seriously. "Not just because I'm bad at it. I don't like to lie. Lies have a way of catching up with a man. But there's nothing wrong with sidestepping the thing. I'm just going to tell her I have to leave town, I'll be back soon as I can be. And that I'm sincerely sorry if I inconvenienced her, because that would be the last thing on earth I'd want to do. Should that do it?"

"It should. But if she asks for the specifics?"

Rafe shrugged. "I'll tell her. I'll ask her to trust me. After all, I'm not going behind her back. A liar would. Surely that should reassure her?"

Drum nodded. "So it should. All right. Now, since

I only had time to swallow a few eggs and a loaf of bread before I left my house—what do you have to offer to keep me nourished while you get dressed?"

Rafe laughed. "Still got that locust appetite? Well, one good thing this mess has got me is a fine chef. My breakfast is yours. But eat quickly, I dress fast, even with one wing. And leave a crumb for me, will you?"

A few hours later, they set out on two horses, riding side by side.

"You sure you can ride with one arm in a sling?" Drum asked before they mounted up.

"It's almost healed. Besides," Rafe said, patting his roan gelding, "Blaze knows me better than most men do. I'll be fine. I need speed, and he can give that to me."

But they made slow work of traveling a few streets. It might be one of the finer districts in London, but the streets were crowded with carts and wagons making deliveries, carriages of ladies and gentlemen, and scores of well-dressed horsemen on their way to pay morning calls too.

After too long a time for Rafe's nerves, he stopped in front of Annabelle's town house. He slipped down from the saddle, brushed off his immaculate coat and breeches, and at the last moment remembered to smooth back his hair. Then, refusing to look back to where Drum sat his horse, grinning like a gargoyle, he rapidly took the steps up to the front door.

The butler recognized him and looked, for a moment, disconcerted.

"I've come to see Lady Annabelle," Rafe said, stepping forward to go in the door.

The butler blocked him. "I must see if she's in, my lord," he said, avoiding Rafe's amazed eyes.

It was the correct time for a morning call. More than that, it was ridiculous that a butler had to see if his own mistress was in. Much more. It was an insult. But Rafe nodded, stepped back, and waited as the butler closed the door. He didn't look back to see what Drum's expression was now.

A few minutes later, the door opened again. The butler looked even more dour. "She is not in, my lord," he said.

The rims of Rafe's ears felt hot. His head went up. "I see. And tomorrow?"

"I will see, if you'll be so kind as to wait?"

This time the butler left the door ajar. Rafe heard voices raised in conversation and the boom of masculine laughter from inside the house. Annabelle was entertaining callers this morning. He felt his face grow hot. If it were any other female on the planet, he'd leave and never come back. But it was Annabelle. And he had perhaps insulted her. He waited.

The butler made his stately way into the salon, through the ranks of his young mistress's usual clot of gentlemen callers. He approached Annabelle. She looked away from the gentleman who'd been telling her an amusing story. He always knew all the latest gossip, but what her butler had to say now might be more important.

She'd been presented a card a moment before.
She'd crushed it in her hand, dropped it back on the
butler's silver salver, and told him she wasn't
receiving Lord Dalton. If he was back so soon, it
meant Rafe wasn't accepting that. She felt a faint
thrill of delight. She turned inquiring eyes to her
butler.

"The gentleman asks if you'll receive him tomorrow," the butler said softly.

"Oho!" the gentleman who'd been chatting with
her laughed. "I wonder who's in your bad graces.
Tell me what he did so I can be sure never to do it."

"It's no one," she said airily, not wanting to give
him a hint of who it might be, in case she decided to
see Rafe again.

"Poor wretch!" he said avidly, looking past the
butler's shoulder trying to see if the rejected fellow
was standing in the hall.

"And if he inquires as to the next day?" the butler
persisted.

"Oh, tell him I'm not available then, or the day
after that, or the next either," Annabelle said pettishly.

" 'Tomorrow and tomorrow and tomorrow'?" her
gentleman caller quoted happily. "Lud! poor fellow!"

"Just so, tomorrow and tomorrow and tomorrow."
Annabelle laughed nervously, wanting the moment
over, before he could see who was waiting. "Tell him
that."

The butler walked heavily back to the door to
relay the message. Rafe didn't blink when he heard
it. He nodded, turned, and went down the stair like

any gentleman after a morning call, not like one who'd just been deeply insulted.

He was upset, not destroyed, Rafe told himself. After all, this outcome had a certain sad symmetry, not to mention certainty. He'd aspired to something beyond his reach. He'd failed. He'd go on. He always had. He tried to ignore the way his face was burning, and how useless, pointless, and shamed he felt.

Drum looked at his face and picked up the reins without a word.

It wasn't until they were well out of London, at lunch at an inn on the main road, that the subject was brought up again.

"You didn't ask," Rafe said suddenly, putting his glass of ale down on the table and fixing Drum with a bright blue stare. "And I know you're usually curious as a cat. All right. Here it is. She refused to see me. In fact, she said she didn't want to see me 'tomorrow and tomorrow and tomorrow.' Poetic. And definitive. So be it. She won't. I suppose I do have some sensibilities, after all. I was raised a gentleman, but I'm just a man who aimed too high. I was bound to fall. Better sooner than later."

"Bedamned to that!" Drum said, his own eyes kindling, "You can look high as you like, Rafe. Never doubt it."

"Look, yes, achieve, no. Have done," he said. "It makes what I might have to do that much easier."

"You really mean to marry the Ford woman?" Drum asked in astonishment. "No need to be so rash! This thing with Annabelle may pass, you know."

"No. It was inevitable. Any rate, whatever I

decide, I can go on with a clear mind. There's no impediment now."

But not with a clear heart, Rafe thought, and changed the subject before the pity in Drum's eyes made him feel even more unhappy. Though he wondered if that was possible.

Nine

I t was a small village, set in a valley off a winding road that meandered off a main road travelers only found by leaving the highway. There was a green in the center of town, with a pond and a string of ducks to ornament it. There was an ancient church in need of repair to match the ruins of the castle on the hillside. Five merchants had stores on its two streets, and there also was a smith, and a tavern in an inn with rooms to let that seldom were.

But Brenna was dressed for a stroll through Regent's Park, not just a stroll through the heart of Tidbury. She wore a pink walking dress and a fashionable bonnet, as though she expected to meet the best of London Society, not just the few neighbors she might chance to see. She carried a straw basket and held herself as though it were filled with spun-glass eggs, not the card of pins she'd just bought.

"Lord! I could crack nuts on the back of your neck, child," her brother said in a low, laughing voice as they strolled along the main and only street. "These are our friends—relax."

The pretty bonnet turned toward him. It was a coal scuttle style, so he could only get a glimpse of her profile. It was enough to show him she wasn't smiling. Her usually upturned lips were held in a tight, straight line.

"Daisy looked upset this morning when she got back from the village," Brenna said.

Her brother frowned. She was too breathless after such a short walk. It had to be nervousness changing her voice.

"I asked her what it was," Brenna went on. "She said 'nothing.' So I knew it had to do with me, or us. I can't help wondering if she'd heard anything about—" Brenna ducked that proud head and watched her feet "—Rafe, and that incident. I know that's foolish and highly unlikely. Still, I told her to tell me whatever it was. All she said was, 'There's folk whose mouths run on wheels, and there's an end to it, miss.' So what am I to think?"

"That I'd wring the necks of those whose mouths said anything cruel about you, that's what," Eric answered. "I'm getting better every day, so I could. And it's more than highly unlikely that a word about what happened in London has been said—it's impossible. There's no way a soul could know about Rafe or the 'incident.' If people are staring at you, it's because nothing as exciting as you has happened here since the Conquest. Think about it. You've been gone a long time. You've been all the way to India. Most of them haven't even been to London. And you're dressed for a visit to the Palace instead of the seamstress. You look very fine today, you know. So relax. Your secret's safe."

She nodded. Still, her silence showed him she didn't believe him. They strolled on. The smith dipped his head in a greeting as they passed. But he didn't take his eyes off Brenna as they did. Brenna felt a vague disquiet. It grew when Mrs. Hubble and her friend Mrs. Kent nodded to Eric, stared at Brenna, and looked away. When Brenna saw John Taylor, she let out a breath she didn't know she was holding. John was an old friend.

"Eric!" John said with every evidence of pleasure as he rushed up to take Eric's hand. "Good to see you. We'd heard such frightening things about your health. But here you are big as life, and filled with vigor, I see. Jane will be so happy to hear it. I didn't come to visit—well, but I just heard you were home. It's only been a few days, hasn't it? Please call on us. I'd stay longer, but I promised Jane I'd bring the post double quick. Don't want her to box my ears. Take care, and visit soon. Hello, Miss Ford," he said with difficulty, as an afterthought, glancing away from her. He tipped his hat and paced off down the street before she could answer.

Brenna turned a frightened face to her brother. "*John?* Saying hello that way? 'Miss Ford'? And not looking at me? Oh, Eric!"

Eric stared after their old friend. "Talk about

someone whose tongue runs on wheels," he said thoughtfully. "But he's newly wed, and you know what a bossy creature Jane is. It means nothing."

It meant something when the vicar saw them. He started to smile, stopped, fumbled with his watch, and did a poor acting job of pretending to consult it. After making an exaggerated face at his watch, he turned in the other direction and hurried away.

Now Eric frowned. "He's always been a fool and a coward, with the moral fiber of a lily, even when we were at school. But just because of that, I think I'll have a word with him. Go on to the dress shop as you'd planned. I'll meet you there."

The bell over the door to the shop jingled as Brenna stepped in. It was a tiny shop; there was no way Brenna could step out again when she saw who was already in there. The two women started when they saw her. Miss Timmons, the dressmaker, had a mouth full of pins, so she couldn't speak. But her eyes grew round.

Jenny Slack made a more rapid recovery. She was a thin woman Brenna's own age, well on her way to inheriting her mother's cottage as well as her reputation as town gossip. "Brenna Ford!" she said with delight. "Back from London."

"Back from India, actually, by way of London," Brenna said, "Hello Jenny, how have you been?"

"As ever," Jenny said, her eyes running up and down Brenna, evaluating her with lightning speed. "But *you!* Oh my dear. How *brave* you are," she cried, her thin hands fluttering to take Brenna's in their icy clasp. "How *good* to see you safely home after all your travails. No matter what anyone says, you *are* a brave creature, when all's said."

"India wasn't that dangerous," Brenna said, glad of something normal to talk about. Normal, and good. Though she'd never admit it to Eric, she thought what she'd done was amazing and valiant too. "There's infection and disease, and the weather *is* horrible," she went on, "and the people sadly oppressed. But the army takes care of its own, and at least we have Eric back now. So it was all worth it."

"But who was talking about *India*?" Jenny said, amazed. She dropped her voice, and patted Brenna's hand. "I mean, after that loss you suffered."

Brenna took her hand from Jenny's cold clasp and backed a step away. "Thomas fell in Spain, Jenny," she said softly. "That was many years ago."

"Yes, who could forget such a tragedy? You two were *so* well suited, *so* in love," she sighed. "Everyone could see it. Then you lost him. We wondered how you'd *ever* recover. Then to lose your *other* fiancé in India just months ago! And under such *dreadful* circumstances. Poor girl. Oh, we all heard about that, be sure," Jenny said avidly, noting the stunned look on Brenna's face. "You wrote to say it was a mutual understanding that ended it, and so your parents said. But *we* knew how hard it must have been for you, poor dear. Terrance Smith had a cousin there, you see, and he wrote and told us *all*."

Brenna took another step back, but finding the door already open behind her, halted.

"Oh, Eric!" Jenny said gaily, looking over Brenna's

shoulder. "I was just telling Brenna how brave a girl she is. To come back after *all* that has happened since she left us. That incident in India with the faithless officer was simply *appalling*. Poor girl! As for after that—*I*, for one, do not care a fig for what others say," she said, snapping her bony fingers. "There must have been a good reason for the *horribly* embarrassing thing that happened. No disrespect to your sex, Eric, or to my dear husband's, but it's usually the gentleman who is to blame, when all's said."

"To blame for what?" Eric said in a dangerously soft voice.

"For the scandalous incident at Lord Raphael Dalton's home in London, to be sure," Jenny said, amazed. "Why, was there *another*?"

"No, you couldn't wring her scrawny neck," Brenna said on a broken laugh as she and Eric rode home again. "There's laws against it. She's always been a horror. And she never forgave you for not noticing her when she was eligible, so there's the reason she faced me with the gossip. At that," Brenna said, lifting her chin, because there was no one around to see her face now but her brother, "I'm glad she did. Now, at least, I know."

"Know now that you have to accept him? Good, at least for that," Eric said. His hands were tight on the reins, though their old horse didn't need any on them, since he'd know the way home blindfolded and would only bolt if he saw dinner in front of him.

"*That?* No. Never," Brenna said wearily. "I meant

at least I know it's out, and so now I can deal with it. First off, though, how can we keep it from Mama and Papa?"

"We can't," Eric said through tight lips.

"We must," Brenna argued. "We can't have Papa charging into London looking to horsewhip Rafe. Papa forgets his age, and all sense, when it comes to insults. There's no insult involved here."

"You have to marry him, child," Eric said gently, looking down at her, seeing her hands clenched in her lap in spite of the calmness of her voice. "Rafe's a good man and will do the right thing."

"Which is to marry the woman he loves," Brenna said stubbornly "All right. *I'll* have to explain it to Mama and Papa then. They'll see reason. They love me."

"And I don't?"

"Too much to see that I could never be happy knowing I wrecked a good man's hopes for happiness," Brenna said. "Now, let's not argue. You'll see."

He soon did, and it gave him small satisfaction to have been so right. After they got home and sat down to tea, Brenna broached the subject to her parents.

"Have done. You didn't do anything wrong," her father told Brenna in his booming voice when she was done explaining. Colonel Alexander Ford was tall, blond, and handsome as his first wife had been, and their son, Eric, was. His hair had more silver than gold now, and age had gentled his power. But his voice still held it.

"But the talk in the village—" Brenna began.

"Bedamned to the talk!" her father said, pounding

the table for emphasis. The tea service hopped in place. Brenna's mama shot her husband a reproachful look. He looked as sheepish as such a big man could, and mopped up some spilled tea with his napkin. "You say you don't want him? That's enough for me," he told Brenna gruffly. "It was an honest mistake. It would be a worse one to go on with it. I won't have you sacrificing yourself to some fool just for the sake of our reputation."

She looked stricken.

"Just so," Brenna's mama said. She was a small, dark woman, still lovely, though well into her middle years. Even so, Maura Ford was many years younger than her husband. Alexander Ford's first wife had followed the drum, moving with her soldier husband whenever duty called. She'd been a golden lioness of a woman who'd died of a fever, tragically young. Everyone said Colonel Ford was a lucky man to have got such an adorable pixie to heal his heart after she passed away. Eric and Brenna knew he was.

They also said Brenna Ford got her dark good looks from her Welsh mama, her stature from her Viking of a papa, and the devil's own stubbornness from the pair of them. Long retired, Alexander Ford claimed the sparks set off by his two dark ladies kept him young. They maintained it was his stubbornness, refusing to grow old. He said he didn't dare with them around.

"He really offered you marriage?" Brenna's mama asked her now.

"He'd better have," her father said in a menacing rumble.

"He offered it constantly," Eric said.

Brenna nodded.

"And you turned him down every time?" her mama said. "Well then, good. Gossip is temporary. It only lasts a few years, or decades. Marriage is forever—if you're lucky," she said with a fond look at her husband. "But how terrible to have to live all your life with a man who's ill bred, or boorish, or vulgar. Men can be difficult even if you love them." She smiled at her husband. "But if you didn't? How dreadful to have to suffer such a husband's attentions. Even worse, to carry the spawn of such a beast under your heart for months, and then raise it!"

She gave a theatrical shudder. "That's too much to sentence you to for such a little crime. Why, you only cast doubt on your reputation, and ours. And your brother's, of course. But Eric's such a handsome rogue, he could still have his pick of excellent matches . . ." She paused, and went on a little more sadly, "Well, he still has a choice of suitable ones, at least. So don't worry. Eric will make his way somehow. He would even if you'd killed the fellow instead of just setting all England to talking about how you tried to snare him."

It was a terrible thing to say.

Eric's gaze shot to his father's—and saw the hidden light in his eyes. He recognized the expression in his stepmama's eyes as well. He relaxed. *So*, he thought. They'd already heard the gossip. The two were at it again. As always, every decision they made in front of their children had been previously agreed upon. Eric's own eyes kindled with laughter.

But Brenna was watching her mama with horror.

"You did the right thing, Bren," her mama said resolutely, "whatever the cost to the family."

"I just don't understand why Eric would bring her into the orbit of such a villain," her husband said, frowning at his son.

Eric hid his amusement under the cover of flustered guilt. "I didn't think—I didn't mean to leave her to his sole protection. But I was ill and I—"

"It's not his fault," Brenna said quickly. "None of it. And Rafe—Lord Dalton, that is—is *not* boorish or ill bred or whatever else you said. Just the opposite. I've seldom met a nicer man. He's generous and kind, and good company too. You'd like him, Papa," she said earnestly. "He was a fine officer and is a true gentleman. You'd like his manner, Mama. He's charming without trying to be. In fact, there's nothing hypocritical about him. He doesn't pose or posture. He's no slave to fashion, though he always looks just as he should. He's noble, a thoroughly good man."

Her voice grew sad, and softer. "That's just it. He's too good a man to do such a thing to. I can't accept his offer of marriage. He loves another," she said, and stopped talking. She found something interesting to stare at on the floor.

Eric's mirth fled. His father's smile flattened. The light in Brenna's mama's eyes was doused.

"Oh," Maura Ford said, "I see. Well, then. We'll just have to ride it out together then, won't we?"

After all, it went unsaid, they'd done it before.

Brenna nodded because she couldn't trust herself

to speak. She excused herself from the room and went to pace the gardens. Her parents and brother looked after her, helplessly.

They couldn't help her when she lost her first love either. Thomas Powers had been a soldier too. Young, only four years older than her seventeen-year-old self, he'd pledged his love within two months of meeting her. Tom had been a gangling youth, but he'd looked splendid in his uniform. Brenna couldn't remember now what they'd talked about to make them laugh so much together. She couldn't recall what they'd had in common either, because it hadn't mattered to them. They were drawn to each other, absolutely. He was one of Eric's company, a good lad from a good family, and though she'd never had her Season, and he'd only danced with a few eligible girls, both families were delighted. Both tall and dark, uncommonly good and attractive children, they looked and thought alike. They seemed to have been made for each other.

They never got a chance to prove it. They were engaged five months before he went off to fight in Spain. He never returned. She never quite regained her good standing in the community. They were young and eager, and though they were careful, their courtship looked too ardent. She'd have been pitied, not scorned, if he'd shipped out sooner.

The problem was, they loved each other and were both too inexperienced at love and too young for their years. They wanted each other. But they were raised to be good, and that kept them from fulfilling that love before marriage.

And so all everyone saw was that desperate yearning.

He'd pass her in company and touch her shoulder; one finger trailing across her skin was enough to ignite both their passions. She'd glance at him and her heart was in her eyes, and his eyes would follow her everywhere. They'd brush each other's fingers, touch each other's sleeves. They'd be locked in each other's arms every chance they got to be alone. But they never got to be strictly alone for long, and so, of course, those stolen embraces were seen.

She remembered frustrating, fervent caresses, long, moist kisses; it was a romance filled with longing and longer sighs. They scorched the earth that separated them when their glances locked across a room. And so everyone thought they knew what they were sighing for.

Three nights before he left, they met alone, and arranged it so it could be for a long time. He said he was going to a nearby town to buy some last-minute necessities. She said she was going to a friend's house. Neither of them had ever lied to their families before. Half the trembling when they met in the abandoned barn was because of that. The other half, their overwhelming desire.

He had the top of her gown down to her waist in minutes; their writhing in the straw got the hem of her skirt up to meet it. His jacket was off, his shirt opened, the fall on his breeches too. Then they stopped, as the enormity of what they were about to do occurred to both of them. Tom rolled over on his back, one long hand on his hot forehead, the other covering himself.

Brenna sat up and raised herself on her arms over him. "What?" she asked, "What is it?"

"*It* is," he said on a hoarse chuckle. "Too soon, too late. Oh, Bren, I ought to have married you weeks ago, as you wanted. But then . . ." He turned aside so he could sit up and not touch her. He put his head in his trembling hands. "I thought it was wrong to wed you and bed you, and maybe leave you with a child if I was going off to war. It would be even worse now."

"I can follow you," she said eagerly, as she'd said all the times before when they'd talked about this.

"You can," he said, "but you won't. Listen, Bren," he said, as he rose to his knees and tucked his shirt in, "I'm not from a military family. I don't want my wife following the drum. I want you home, here, safely waiting for my return. It's the only way I'd feel safe enough to do my duty with a clear head. I'll come back to you. Then we'll make love day and night. But not now. It would be wrong."

That stopped her like a bucket of icy water, dousing her overheated passions. *Wrong*, she understood. She was a good girl. Still, she'd have gladly done something wrong for him. But not on her own. Thrumming with unfulfilled desire, torn by conflicting ones, she rested her head on his shoulder. Then she straightened her gown and strolled hand in hand with him back to the gig, and they drove home. He left three days later. And never returned.

She waited, patiently, hoarding his letters, marking off each day on the calendar, only becoming puzzled as the weeks wore on by how everyone in town kept stealing keenly interested peeks at her. The style of the day meant a girl's gown was tied under her breasts, and fell from there. A lot could be hidden if a slender girl had high, upstanding breasts. Brenna did. But she didn't understand what they were looking for until she overheard some girls chatting one day as she went to the lady's withdrawing room at a local party.

"Well, it's been seven months, and there's nothing to show, so you owe me a thimble and three sheets of pins," one said.

"Maybe she carries small," another said.

"I think she carries not at all," another put in. "Lucky thing. And with all the work that Tom put in! Brenna's escaped and so you must pay up. She's not with child."

It should have ended the matter and restored her reputation. It didn't. Because after all her carrying on with him, he never returned to make her an honest woman in their eyes, or any other way. He couldn't. He fell in battle the year after he left England.

The townsfolk felt bad when they heard the news. But years later the gossip was still there behind the politely smiling lips of Brenna's former friends and all her neighbors They never knew how she grieved because she hadn't gone back into his arms that last time and stayed there no matter how wrong it would have been. She felt it was more wrong that he'd died so young without showing her what might have been.

They didn't know that, and wouldn't have believed it if she'd told them. They'd the evidence of their own eyes, after all. They'd seen how the two had been together and imagined how they'd acted when no one else was there. The girls knew what they'd have done if they were in her place. The men grew warm just thinking what they'd have done in his. And so if the girls in town thought less of her for it, Brenna found, after her period of mourning, that the young men expected more. She sent them on their way with a flea in their ear—and sometimes with a slap on their smug faces. They went on to marry other girls.

Her parents sent her to an aunt in London to see if she could find a beau. She was a soldier's daughter and a soldier's sister, and had almost taken a soldier to wed. She sneered at the dandies and fops, and wrote begging to come home. They took her back because they couldn't bear to see her sad. She refused to have another Season until Eric came home. But Eric went on to India after the war was over. And one day Brenna woke to realize she was two and twenty, and still unwed.

So, much as she wanted to help her brother, Brenna wasn't that unhappy to leave home and travel halfway across the world to do it. Her parents protested, but not as much as she'd thought they would. They wanted her wed. Her brother had friends. She'd loved a soldier once. They knew she had a warm and loving heart, and could find another.

She did.

Spencer Fry was Eric's friend. He wasn't exceptionally handsome, rich, or clever. But he had a warm smile and a competent way about him. Thickset and medium height, he was one of those men who seemed ready to do what needed to be done. Brenna needed a guiding light. He provided it. Her days were spent in the hospital with Eric. He was so ill she dared not stray far from there. Her evenings were passed quietly at home with Spencer's sister and her husband. Brenna got to see little of India, and less of other men. But she saw Spencer every day. She came to rely on his advice and comfort, and looked forward to evenings when he'd walk out with her. His kiss didn't move her, but his laughter did, and she knew she'd come to a safe harbor.

They'd come to an understanding. Brenna hadn't known he'd come to another sort of one with an officer's wayward daughter before she'd met him. When the woman had told him their child was coming, he'd gone to Brenna to apologize and say a sorrowing farewell. Because he loved only her, he'd said. But he'd been trapped, and there was no help for it.

Well, so one woman's lover denied her out of honor, and she was left alone forever, Brenna thought as she paced her parents' garden's paths. And another woman acted without honor, gave all to a man she wanted as a lover, and won him forever.

There was no justice in the world, and she'd stop looking for it. *Folly to have even thought of anything with Lord Raphael Dalton!* But he'd attracted her as no man had since Thomas. He'd all of Spencer's manner and competence, and so very much more. *And the most beautiful lady in London as his love, you fool,* she thought, and stalked through her parents' garden, angry at herself and the world, and what passed for love in it.

Ten

"Ah, the bustling metropolis, at last," Drum commented, glancing around as he and Rafe rode side by side down the main street of the little village, "Do you think they have an inn? Or shall we have to camp on the green?"

"There's an inn," Rafe, said, looking ahead. "Not much. But we won't be here long."

"You intend to sweep her up on your saddle like a Saracen invader, and ride back to London?" Drum asked with interest.

"If I have to."

There saw no postboy or ostler, so they tied their horses outside the inn and entered it. The place was empty. Their boots rang out on the bare wood floors. They looked around, waiting for the landlord to appear. The place was timbered in Tudor style, and was cool and dim. It smelled, not unpleasantly, of ale and age and old woodsmoke. The ceiling was low; the common room took up most of the downstairs and was furnished with bare wood tables and chairs. The hearth was huge and cold, because it was still daylight, and summertime. But the walls were whitewashed and pristine, there wasn't any dust or dirt to be seen, and not a cobweb hung from the exposed dark oak beams.

The innkeeper came out from a door in the back. When he saw strangers he seemed shocked. He instantly recovered, bowing as low as though to a pair of princes, not just two well-dressed, but road-weary travelers.

Overjoyed at the prospect of overnight guests, and such well set up ones too, the innkeeper immediately invited them to stay in his two best rooms. "They're at the top of the stairs. Go right up and get yourselves settled, gents. Then come down and I'll pour you a pint. It looks empty now—well, 'tis! But most folk in the village gather here at the end of the day to have the same."

"We will, and thank you," Rafe said.

"Dinner, as well? You don't have to mingle with the village folk—we've a private parlor," his host added, after another look at the quality of his new guests' clothing.

"Dinner, of course," Rafe said. "We've come a long way and will do justice to it. The common room will do fine for us."

* * *

". . . Because there's no better way to get a lay of the land," Rafe told Drum as they were unbuckling their saddlebags and cases from the horses a few minutes later.

"Reconnoitering," Drum said. "Wise. It may be we won't have to see the fair lady. After all," he added as Rafe stared at him, "if there's no gossip here about what happened in London, what's the point?"

Rafe stopped in his tracks, his saddlebag hanging from one hand. He frowned, began to speak, stopped, and began again. "Thought you wanted to see Eric again. I know I'd like to know how he's faring."

"Indeed, but you could learn that from local chatter too. Rafe, my friend," Drum said, seeing Rafe's perplexity, "your heart's pure as running water, but don't you see? If you come visiting the lady, that in itself might start gossip you want to stem. I vote we stay the night, hear what we can, and then if there are no problems, go back to London so you can resume your life again." He laughed at Rafe's expression. "You've changed from the old days! You'd be rotting in a French prison if you'd thought like this then. Don't you see? You've accepted your awful fate too well. You've convinced yourself to sacrifice, but you don't see a possible escape route opening in front of you."

Rafe nodded. "You've got a point," he said, considering it. Could it be true that he might so easily go free? The thought took an enormous weight off his mind. But it left a curiously heavy one in his heart. It sounded too easy, and his had never been the easy way. Was it possible to learn everything in one night? Even if he repaired things with Annabelle, could he ever really be sure he hadn't damaged Brenna for the rest of her life?

Rafe shouldered his traveling bag as he did his responsibilities, and so went very slowly up the stair.

Twilight cast long shadows over the fields outside the Inn. Late summer crickets pumped their reedy songs twice as hard because they felt the autumn closing in. Inside, the buzz of conversation drowned out the night sounds. The landlord had laid a fire against the damp; the heady scents of the dinner the two newly arrived guests just finished still hung in the air.

At least a dozen men of all ages and a few older women sat at their ease, nursing their tankards. Although they didn't do more than take occasional sideways glances at the two strange, clearly fashionable gentlemen sitting apart at a table near a window, it was obvious they were wildly curious about them. When the local patrons had come in, they'd stopped and stared at the pair of them. But since the two gents seemed content to sit and drink the way everyone else was doing, their presence was, if not forgotten, then at least ignored as the evening wore on.

Voices in the room lifted as time went by and tankards were refilled. The talk was all about crops and rents and weather.

"Nothing for it," Rafe said in a low voice after an

hour went by with nothing more exciting that the price of grain and the lack of rain being discussed. "Going to have to infiltrate. Buy a few pints for the house, ask a question or two."

"Wait," Drum said, as quietly. "It's better to wait for them to forget us completely and get round to gossip. They will. What else is there to discuss in backwaters like this?"

"You think London's different?" Rafe asked. "That's all they do there. That's what brought me here," he added bitterly. But he sat back and waited.

He didn't have to wait long. Soon someone asked someone else about the harvest ball to come at the squire's manse. Before long the patrons of the inn were all talking about it, wondering who was going to go with whom. That naturally led to talk of courtships, coming marriages, and possible unions. Before much longer they were all laughing over the fact that Annie Grimes was at last going to lead Young Tully to the altar in the spring. Then, speaking of unions, a man asked if anyone had heard anything new about the Ford girl. Rafe's head came up.

"Haven't heard a word," an older woman said, "but mind you, early days yet."

"Aye," one man cackled. "I'll wager you're watching her waist even keener than when she was engaged to that soldier boy."

"Pity, that," the woman said. Many present shook their heads. "So well suited, the pair of them."

"So well suited?" the old man cackled again. "Aye, and almost showed exactly *how* whenever they was

together. Always fondling or kissing, forever eyeing
and ogling. Their looks could boil water."

"Young love," a woman said sagely.

"Young lust," a man laughed.

"Whatever," the woman said. "There's a great sorrow for a lass to bear."

"Others bore more," a man said with some griev-
ance. "What of me, eh? With our Bill gone down with
his ship? Aye, and you, John Thatcher, with your son
lost in France?"

"Or the Smythes and the Fletchers, and their
brave lads gone?" Thatcher said sadly. "We've all
suffered."

"Or me, with my dear Sonny, never returned?"
one old woman said. They all fell silent.

"Well," the landlord's wife said in more sprightly
tones, trying to change an awkward subject, "Brenna
got over that in time, didn't she? But then, poor girl,
to lose another lover—the new one she found in
India! The girl lives under a dark star, and there's
truth!"

"Lost her mind too, waltzing off to India on her
lonesome. Scandalous!" the old woman muttered.

"Looking for trouble," another agreed.

"And she come home to find it," a man said into
his tankard as he drained it. He thumped it down on
the table and went on with relish, "Imagine! What
she done in London! Strippin' down to her particu-
lars like that! Just to cut out another lass and steal her
man away? Shameful, says I, no excuse for it. Plenty
as has lost loved ones, right here, there is. Do you see

such carryin' on from them? There's some takes any excuse to do what they wants. Brenna Ford's a slut and it's a shame and a scandal, says I."

Rafe began to slowly rise, hands clenched. A hard hand grasped his arm tight, holding him down.

"Hold," Drum whispered urgently. "Say one word and you damn her utterly. Throw one punch and her name is lost forever, no matter what else you plan to do for her. Think, man! Be invisible. Remember? You're on your feet? Use the motion to scratch your arse or signal the landlord for more ale, but don't react to a thing you hear. Have you forgotten all? The lady's doings may not be as important to England as Napoleon's were, but you must use the same tactics now."

Rafe turned a blazing stare on him. Then he closed his eyes for a heartbeat. When he opened them again, all expression was wiped from his face. He raised a hand to call the innkeeper, and slowly sank back to his chair again. "*Damme!*" he whispered, and fell still.

The conversation in the room was becoming more animated.

"See such from you?" a man scoffed at the one who'd spoken. "Stripping yourself to your skin? There'd be a treat. If you're planning to do it, Clyde, kindly let us know, so we can run!"

This caused much merriment. And made Clyde angrier.

"I didn't scandalize myself," he said fiercely. "Brenna Ford did that, thank you very much. I heared she ripped off every stitch on her and stood bold as brass before a room full of swells, come to call on the poor gent. With his fiancé at his side! Well, what was *that* poor lass to think, and her the Toast of the Town, at that? Madly in love with the lord, to boot. A beauty, I heared, and no mistake! She wept, and ran, is what she done. And there's our Brenna, smiling, naked as the day she was whelped. Hoping as to snare him, she was. But she give them an eyeful for nothing, for I heared he sent her away a second after. That's why she's up at the Hall now, silent as a nun, in disgrace!"

"Well, I'm that surprised," another man said, "For I've known Brenna since she were a tot, and never thought to see the day. She's always been modest, clever as she could hold together, and as good a neighbor as one could want."

"Grief turns some lasses' heads," another commented sagely.

"Well, there's much we don't know, and that's certain," an old man said, shaking his head.

"It's the loss of two men what turned her," the angry fellow said, putting down his empty tankard. "She had two men, lost 'em both. That's what done it. A woman gets a taste for some things and can't do without, don't you know, and she'll do anything to have it again."

There was an outcry at that.

"Ho! You wish it were so, Clyde," one man called.

"And how would you know?" another jeered.

"Mind your tongue in front of ladies," one old woman shouted, as another cried, "Fie! For shame!"

"Brenna Ford?" A smooth, cultured voice asked. It was raised just high enough to be heard, and just low enough to make the others fall still to listen harder. Everyone in the room turned to look at the two strange gentlemen in the window, and stared at the tall, thin one who had spoken.

"Your pardon," Drum went on, "but did I hear you say, 'Brenna Ford'? Would that be Lieutenant Eric Ford's sister, by any chance?"

Nothing could be heard in the room but the crackling of the logs in the fire.

"Aye," one cautious fellow finally said, " 'tis she."

"Oh my!" Drum said with exaggerated shock. "Then the tale certainly lost something in its travels . . . or rather, gained something, I should say. Hasn't it?" he asked his friend. Heads swiveled to look at the hard-faced redheaded gentleman with the chillingly blue eyes. "Mistress Ford was in London lately, that's true," Drum continued, "as was I. But what *I* heard, and I know most of the persons involved, was that she and her brother were houseguests of a friend of theirs. A former army officer. A nobleman of some note and reputation, but alas! A fellow with a killing temper, in more ways than one."

There wasn't a sound in the room as the mellifluous voice, tinged with amusement, went on. "I know the gentleman you were talking about. But he was *not* engaged to be wed to anyone, and is not. What *I* heard, and in itself it's a shocking story, is that the mother of a lady he knew met Miss Ford and took exception to her loveliness. Well, but one has cause to believe she had plans for her own daughter. The woman sadly has few scruples but many ambitions, and she wanted the gentleman for her own son-in-law. Thinking Miss Ford had captured my lord's interest, she spread a tale or two about her after Miss Ford left Town. But *nothing* like what I've heard tonight, I assure you!"

Rafe didn't take his eyes from the crowd as Drum went on.

"She just implied that Miss Ford was casting out lures to the gentleman, which I know for a fact was not true. But even that would only involve the fluttering of eyelashes and waving of fans and such. Nothing half so lurid as what I've heard here tonight. Have you ever heard the like?" he asked his friend with interest.

"Never," Rafe barked, casting a look around the room that made the patrons of the inn shrink back in their chairs.

"Well, there you are," Drum said. "Good heavens! How the tale has grown! I hope Lieutenant Ford doesn't hear of it. He's recovering, so there wouldn't be much he could do about it—immediately. But his friend, the London gentleman! He'd be outraged— an easy thing for him to be, by the way. He's an accomplished swordsman, a crack shot, and a prime one with his fists. He was mentioned in the war dispatches many times and finds the constraints of peacetime . . . inconvenient, and so is as often mentioned in the clubs for his duels. The truth is, he's a warrior to his fingertips. He's killed his man a half dozen times. Those he can't challenge, he thrashes. The fellow has a shocking temper."

Rafe frowned at Drum. Drum smiled sweetly and continued, "So if he felt an innocent lady, and a friend of his at that, was being so viley traduced! It would go hard with him. Wouldn't it?" he asked Rafe with a sweet smile.

"Ah," Rafe said, understanding. "Yes. Very hard," he said, glowering at the others in the room.

"I shudder at the thought!" Drum agreed dramatically. "He wouldn't go after the lady who started the tale, of course. He *is* a gentleman. But I fear he'd slay the nearest man at hand, or anyone he'd heard said such a thing. How could he hear it, you ask? Well, we're friends, you see. The irony of it is, we're here now to visit Eric Ford, to see how he's faring in his convalescence. We thought we'd make a week of it. The hunting is good hereabouts, we heard?"

"Naught but rabbits, sir," one quavering voice put in after a long moment of silence had fallen over the room.

"Pheasants," ventured another.

"And ducks," someone said from the back of the room.

"Well, good," Drum said, rising to his feet and stretching his long limbs. "Ah, this fresh country air. Makes a fellow sleepy. Much as I'd like to stay and chat, I fear it's to bed for us, if we want to visit the Fords first thing in the morning."

Drum stood too. He looked across the room at Clyde. "The Fords are friends of mine," he said in a clear, cold, carrying voice. "I'll be visiting them now and again. I'd hate to hear a lady's name bandied about by those who don't know what they're talking about."

The crickets outside and the fire in the hearth were

the loudest sounds in the room as the two gentlemen climbed the stair to their rooms.

"See?" Rafe said with bitter triumph when he reached the door to his room.

Drum nodded. "But see how effectively we silenced them?"

"For now. Made me look like a loon, though. I've a temper, but I'm not a madman. Why didn't you simply speak truth?"

"Because Reason never stopped gossip," Drum said blithely, "But terror does."

"Do you plan to live here for the rest of your life and keep terrorizing them?" Rafe scowled. "It's worse than I thought. I've got to marry her."

"Don't be so quick to be a human sacrifice," Drum said. "Didn't you hear them? Where there's smoke, my dear friend, there's often fire. And it seems the lady has a fair share of that. They said she'd already lost two lovers."

"They also said she stripped herself naked in my hall. I'd like to have seen that," Rafe said scornfully.

"I thought that was something you didn't want to see," Drum said as he opened his door. "She may be innocent in this, but I think you might consider the other things they mentioned."

"That she was fond of the lad she was going to marry?" Rafe asked. "You'd expect her to be distant from him? That she went to India and was jilted? What of it? I met her, Drum. My life's depended on my estimate of a fellow's mettle in the past. I pride myself on my ability to judge men. Are women so much different?"

"Oh, very much," Drum laughed. "But that's not for us to argue tonight. Go to bed. Tomorrow we'll see how the land lies. Gossip can only do harm if it's listened to. Let's find out what the Fords have heard. It may be this is nothing but thunder that will blow over, leaving it to rain somewhere else, in someone else's life."

Eleven

It was an old, rambling rose brick house, U-shaped in the Elizabethan style of the days when it was built. The fields around it were filled with blue cornflowers, asters, goldenrod, and marigold. The gardens were brimming with late roses, red on one side of the house, white on the other, because everyone knew how unlucky it was to have the two growing together. It was a comfortable looking place for all its size, as it lay dreaming amidst flowers and grasses.

There wasn't a sign of life as the two gentlemen rode up the drive to the front door. The crunching of the horses' hooves on the gravel alerted someone, because a youth came running from the stables in back, buttoning his jacket as he ran. He halted and stared up at the two men.

"Is your master or mistress about?" Rafe asked.

"They're visiting," the lad said, looking at them with interest. "But Lieutenant Eric and his sister be walking in the gardens. Want me to fetch him? Or do you want to go in?" he asked belatedly. "The butler's there."

"We'll just join the lieutenant," Rafe said, dismounting. He handed the boy his reins. "In the back, you said?"

The boy nodded, fascinated by the pair of elegant gentlemen.

"They don't seem to get much company," Drum commented to Rafe as they walked down the crushed shell path that led to the gardens in back of the house.

"Or no one's coming to visit them these days," Rafe muttered.

The knot garden was empty; the lawn beyond only held rooks and robins. They strolled toward a pond they could see glittering in the sunshine beyond that. As they came to a gentle rise in the land, they finally saw two figures standing by an old willow that was dipping its green fingers into the pond.

Drum recognized Eric Ford by his height, broad shoulders, and bright gold hair. His gaze arrowed to the slender lady Eric stood with. She wore a gown blue as the water behind her, and her sleek midnight hair was so dark it shone with hints of blue in the sunlight. She looked up and saw her visitors.

Rafe stopped. He straightened his shoulders. "There she is," he muttered to Drum.

"Rafe! And Drum!" Eric shouted. "This is a surprise!"

His sister said nothing. She only stared at Rafe as though he were visiting from the dead.

"*That's* your 'Bren'?" Drum asked, for once shocked out of his usual urbanity.

Rafe didn't answer. He only strode forward, then stopped a foot from Brenna and stared at her.

Drum stared as well. *This was Rafe's "calm, sensible, steady, respectable woman"?* he thought in astonishment. The calm, steady, and sensible parts remained to be seen. She might be respectable too. But it would take work on her part to remain so. She was exotic as a houri and just as erotic looking. She didn't notice Drum staring because she only had eyes for Rafe. Drum saw the eagerness leap into those raven depths before she quickly concealed her delight, and then her dismay.

Rafe looked as if he'd just suffered a blow to the head. Drum felt it too. Annabelle was tasty, and no mistake. She was a comfit, a confection, a charming, dainty, little, extravagantly expensive pastry. But Brenna Ford? The woman was a heady liquor, a feast of spices, with a sensual pull strong as the full-moon tide in an estuary. Of course Annabelle was jealous and her mama vindictive. He'd invented the story of their spite for the locals, but saw he hadn't had to. It could only be true. That was why Rafe was so conflicted! Drum turned his head to look at his friend. Rafe was still staring.

No wonder! Drum thought. *To lose the anticipated treat of a sweetmeat and discover yourself with such a full plate anyway? Oh my poor Rafe! What a delicious predicament you've got yourself in.*

Rafe knew he should speak now, at least to introduce Drum, but couldn't frame a word.

He was surprised at how glad he was to see Brenna. She'd become a friend in a very little time. It was more than that. It was broad daylight; she was fully and properly dressed. But she looked every bit as sensual as she had that shocking morning in London that had sealed their fate. The reality of the future he would face with her hit him hard.

He didn't like having his hand forced. He wasn't sure he was ready to give it to anyone but the woman he'd lost. But he couldn't have that woman, and this one had been slandered through no fault of her own. And she was a friend's sister. There was the fact that she was bright and good-hearted. And there was no denying this insistent attraction. But she wasn't a choice so much as a duty, and he had to come to terms with that.

He could do worse. She *would* do worse without him. That in itself should be enough for him. She needed him. That was something he could address himself to. He straightened his shoulders. He could bear this burden. He might not get what he'd wanted most, but he was used to that. A man had obligations that transcended his own needs. He always had, and now it looked as though he always would.

His heart had been heavy as he'd traveled to see her. But the shameful secret he was reminded of now was that at the mere thought of her, other parts of his anatomy had grown heavy too. Not with sorrow. The truth was, he'd felt a languor; a deep and abiding expectation had risen in his loins whenever he'd thought of who he was riding to see. It startled and bemused him.

At the inn last night, they'd said she'd been engaged to be wed. They'd joked about her past. He didn't doubt she had one. It explained much. She fairly radiated sensuality. So she wasn't a virgin. She'd loved before. She was beautiful, she was of age, she'd been engaged. He could understand it. He didn't expect a virgin bride anyway; he'd never been first in anything, and it wasn't a concern of his so long as she'd be faithful in future.

Not for a minute did he believe she'd tried to trap him. For one thing, there was no way she could have known who was at the door that morning. Even if she'd heard of Annabelle, she'd never seen her, and could hardly have nipped into the bath, flung a robe over herself, and appeared at the door so quickly. For another, and more important, why would she want to? Why would she want *him*?

He didn't know her very well. But in truth, and he was ruthlessly truthful with himself, he didn't know Annabelle that well either, did he? He'd make the best of it. He was relentlessly practical. He'd had to be. His heart might have been cracked, but a man could put his heart away and make a good marriage anyway. There would be compensations. His were obvious. She had a good mind in a fine body, and he was a man who knew how to divorce his mind from his body. He'd do the best he could for her in turn.

He realized he'd been standing stock-still staring at her for far too long. "I came to see how you were faring," he blurted.

"I feel much better, better every day, thank you," Eric said in amusement. "Kind of you to come so far to ask."

Rafe shot him a glance "One look at you told me that."

"Oh, did you look at me?" Eric asked sweetly. "Brenna, here's the earl of Drummond, the 'Drum' I told you so much about. We met in Spain."

Drum bowed to Brenna. "So pleased to meet you, Miss Ford. How are you, Lieutenant? I hear you had a bad time of it in India. But I thought you'd your fill of the army when we left you in Spain."

"I should have," Eric said ruefully. "I ought to have left when Rafe did. But I thought India might be interesting. It was worse than Spain for me. There was no war on, but I found an enemy. The fever. In Spain I could at least see what my problem was. A gash or a gunshot's visible. But fever's an invisible wound. It made me nervous, I admit."

"Speaking of invisible wounds..." Drum said slowly, with a significant look at Rafe.

"Has the gossip reached you?" Rafe asked Brenna, never taking his eyes from her pale face. "I mean, there was some in London." He paused. "Some" was a lie and he was uncomfortable with lies. "I came to be sure it wasn't affecting you here," he said quickly.

"I've heard nothing," she said as quickly.

Eric's golden eyebrows swooped down in a frown. "*Brenna!*" he exclaimed.

Dusky rose appeared high on her cheekbones. She picked up her chin and stared at her brother. "Well, nothing to trouble Rafe. And I haven't exactly *heard* anything. It's more like knowing something's being said," she said defiantly. "Anyway, it will pass."

Her brother shook his head. Rafe did too. Brenna looked from one to the other and smiled a tight smile.

"It's like being at a convention of noddy dolls, isn't it?" she asked Drum. She held her head high. "So there's gossip. And so what? I've endured it before. I will again." She saw Rafe's expression. "I was engaged to be wed once upon a time," she told him tersely. "I lost my fiancé in the wars. I seemed to have lost my reputation then too. We were young and fond. People assumed we were more than that. Small villages often hold small minds. But I regained my reputation in time. As I will again. I had a beau, in India. He shied off. I came home to a less-than-palatable reputation because of it. That will pass too."

"Not this time," Rafe said. "This time I'm part of the problem."

"No," she said firmly. "I told you, you shouldn't be punished for my mistake. I did a foolish thing. You did nothing but try to be a true friend to Eric. You will *not* be penalized for it, my lord. Never think it for a moment."

"I ought to have arranged things more carefully," Rafe said tersely. "I invited you to my home without making the right preparations. I was the one who left you open to insult. Never think I'll allow you to suffer for my mistake!"

They squared off against each other.

"Don't be foolish," Brenna said, staring up at him, her eyes darkened with emotion. "You're a gentleman and a kind one. But I am not your responsibility, sir."

"You were, and I mishandled it," Rafe said adamantly. He knew his responsibility now too, knew she was making a sacrifice, but also knew whose sacrifice it had to be. "I can't let it go."

"Oh, can you not? I believe you will have to," she said through clenched teeth. Men and their honor! She'd had enough of it. She wouldn't let him ruin his life for the sake of a few rattling tongues. The man was prepared to give up his love for the sake of her honor? He was too decent for that, and so was she. They weren't in London now. This was her home, and her life. She'd manage it herself. "Why, look at the time!" she exclaimed with patently false surprise. "Teatime, unless I miss my guess. Will you join us, gentlemen?"

"You don't have a watch," Rafe said curtly.

"I do have a sundial," she said, gesturing to the garden behind her without looking back at it. "So will you join us?"

"I will," Rafe said, "and we'll talk this over some more."

"I think not," she said, and marched back toward the house.

"I believe we will," Rafe said, falling in step beside her.

Drum strolled behind the pair, with Eric. "This," he told Eric in a soft voice, "should be interesting."

"Oh yes," Eric agreed, "You see, I know Brenna too."

Twelve

Rafe and Drum acted like guests with nothing on their minds but a visit, and wound up fighting an old battle all through tea.

"I suppose I might as well have been talking about the Fall of Troy, not a fort in a backwoods in the New World," Colonel Ford finally said as he sat back and surveyed the table he'd turned into a battlefield, where napkins had become forts, spoons were cannon, cups and saucers opposing forces. "It seems like yesterday to me. I was barely into manhood, and look at me now. Still, the American wars must seem like nothing to you who fought on French and Spanish soil."

"War is never nothing, sir," Rafe said. "I found your experiences fascinating."

"Agreed," Drum said.

"Warfare hasn't changed that much," Rafe said. "It won't until we find a better way to resolve disputes or invent ways to end them faster. It's still a matter of a man and his weapons. And his nerves when he confronts the enemy—or himself alone in the night."

"Well said," Drum mused. "Though I didn't fight on any battlefield, it seems that way to me."

"You fought our enemies on just as dangerous ground," Rafe said. "He fought with his wits," he explained to his host, "and saved thousands, not just his own skin. Though he risked that often enough."

"A spy?" the colonel asked with interest.

" 'Agent' is the word they prefer," his son said with a smile, remembering what he'd been told when he'd met Drum in Spain.

"Just so," Drum said. "But now, as for that battle on the night of seventy-seven, sir, might I ask—"

"You may not," Maura Ford put in quickly. "I deprive my guests nothing, but it's too beautiful an afternoon to waste fighting old wars. After dinner when you gentlemen are snug with your port, you may rake up old conflicts. You *are* staying to dinner?"

"We'd be delighted," Drum said.

"If you're sure it's no trouble?" Rafe asked, after a look at Brenna's thunderstruck expression.

"It isn't. Never mind my sister. She was weaned on sour apples," Eric commented.

Brenna colored. "We'd be pleased to have you to dinner," she said haughtily. "You've traveled a long way. It would be rude to send you back without at least a dinner to show for your trouble."

Eric bent so his mouth was near his sister's ear. "We've been charmingly civilized, feeling our way," he whispered, "but now it's your turn. Time to face him, Bren. I suggest you and Rafe take yourselves outside and have the thing out now."

"Thank you for a lovely afternoon," Drum said, rising. "We'll be back for dinner."

"Miss Ford," Rafe said as he stood, "if I may have a word with you, before I go?"

"Of course," she said with a jerky nod. Head high, she left the room with him.

"Nice lad," Colonel Ford commented.

"Very," his wife said wistfully, watching her red-headed guest walk from the room at her daughter's side. "Bright yet unpretentious, with excellent manners."

"Salt of the earth," the colonel said. His wife and son paused. That was his highest praise.

"Yes, Drummond's a good fellow," Eric teased.

His father shot him a glance from under frowning brows. "You know who we mean. Think he'll mend matters as he ought?"

"Alexander!" his wife gasped. "You promised you wouldn't say anything to Lord Dalton until Eric has a chance to discover his intent!"

"I won't," the colonel grumbled. "Just wanted to know if the fellow would think of doing the right thing on his own."

"He didn't do anything wrong," she protested.

"I think the difficulty lies in the fact that he *is* trying to do the right thing," Eric said sadly. "But you know Brenna."

"Ah," her mother and father said at the same time. With equal sorrow. Because they did.

"The idea's ridiculous," Brenna said. "Just ridiculous," she muttered as if to herself, though he was right beside her.

They sat on a stone bench in the garden, beneath a towering weeping beech tree. She seemed composed. But Rafe saw her hands knotted in her handkerchief in her lap, those hands with their poor ragged nails that made his heart clench every time he saw them.

Much about her spoke to him on levels he didn't comprehend. He gazed at her and tried to understand this powerful attraction he felt for her. He hadn't forgotten Annabelle; he never could or would. But whatever chance he'd had with her was gone. A man had to know when to stop campaigning, war or peacetime, or lose more than his life. Without honor, a life wasn't worth much.

But what would his life be now? He knew what he had to do. He wished he knew the woman he had to do it with half so well.

He looked at Brenna as she sat in the sunlight. She wasn't the most beautiful female he'd ever seen. But she was possibly the most erotically appealing one. There was something powerful in her reserve, in the supple lines of that body she tried to hold so aloof, those small, high breasts, that swanlike neck. Her presence made a man's nostrils flare like a stallion's when a mare approached. Whatever it was, it was certainly in those eyes of hers, the curved mouth she kept in a prim line now. He couldn't help but think of all the fine textures of the female form when he saw her, of warm, smooth, satiny skin, sliding limbs, the moist, secret, silken places hidden within a woman's warm and welcoming body.

Was her reputation in the village well earned? But he'd no other choice but to court her. Besides, he had to trust his perceptions or lose belief in himself forever. And he'd run out of time. His senses applauded that conclusion, even if his sensibilities didn't. It was all he could do not to snatch her up in his arms to find the truth of it. Could his mind accept her as readily as his body wished to? Would his heart ever find room for her at all? But a man could distance his mind and body from his heart, he thought with sad cynicism. He'd still be a virgin if that weren't so.

He braced himself. Now he had to speak with more persuasion than he usually did. He'd lost Annabelle, but she wouldn't suffer. If he lost this poor lady, she would, and he'd the strangest feeling that he would too.

"Not ridiculous," he answered her now, "necessary. I've ruined your reputation. A woman can have looks, brain, and good family. All of which you do. But without her reputation, she has nothing. I've taken that from you. I'm merely suggesting I give it back."

"*Merely?*" she asked, appalled. Her eyes were wide and dark as she fixed them on him. "Are you mad? There's nothing 'merely' about it. You settle your fate so easily? It means your whole future, man!" She tried to calm herself, and held up one hand so he wouldn't speak before she could. "It means your entire life," she said, "your . . . everything. Think about it. Marriage may not mean that much to you."

"It does," he said.

"But if it does—to throw away future chances . . . Or is it that you don't expect to be faithful? Because if you don't, I hasten to assure you marriage means fidelity to me, if not to you."

"It means it to me too," he said.

"And children . . ." She fought for words to explain it.

"Them too," he said.

"But—but you *have* a lady you love." She saw his eyes grow cold. "I never meant to presume," she said hastily. "It's just that I heard . . ."

"You heard right," he said simply. "And you may presume as much as you want. I presume to settle your entire future, don't I? Now, as for the lady . . ." He took a breath. "No sense pretending she doesn't exist. But I don't—at least not so far as she's concerned now. I called on her before I left London. She refused to see me. And won't in future. 'Not today,' her butler said, "nor tomorrow or tomorrow or tomorrow.' "

"Well, after what she saw, and the way her mama feels, it will take time—" Brenna began to say.

"No," Rafe said, cutting her off. "No, in fact, it shouldn't take that much time. I didn't do anything."

He rose, paced a step, and faced her. He was all in tones of brown today; it suited him, she thought. The color subdued the red in his hair, turned it to chestnut and made the blue in his eyes flare. He was fit and trim, all polished bronze. She'd always thought army men were taller, stronger, kinder, and more sensible than other men, as her father and brother were. Dragoons had to be taller, that was true. The rest she knew was her own prejudice, but dear Lord! Raphael Dalton was a superior sort of man. She listened carefully, hardly daring to believe what he was saying.

"I don't give myself airs. Anyone can tell you I don't think much of myself either. But I have some opinion of my worth. Even if I didn't, it seems to me a man's a fool to pursue a woman who doesn't believe in him. I expect a male friend to trust me. I expect no less from a female. I fancied her. That's true. I had a lady in mind. I no longer do. Now I'm proposing marriage to you.

"I can see advantages for you in it, " he added, when she didn't speak, but only sat staring at him. "I've funds. Plenty. I invested wisely. My brother will inherit, but I've a name too. A town house in London, a small estate in Kent. I don't get drunk. Or gamble above small stakes. I've a terrible temper, that's true. But don't worry, it's only shown in words to females. I'll try to rein that in too. I offer you my name. Your brother's my friend. I can be a friend to you, and will try to be a good husband too. We can make something of this, Bren.

"Now, if you've another man in mind or foresee a better offer, I'll understand. If you don't, I think I must insist. Come, I'm no Adonis, I know. I'm a closemouthed fellow with more faults than merits, if it comes to that. But I'm trustworthy, all say. I'm a better bargain than spinsterhood, aren't I? Well, if you don't think so, then please tell me why."

" 'A better bargain than spinsterhood'?" she said, stung, sitting up straight. "I assure you I don't have to marry. I could do many things, I promise you."

"Yes," he said impatiently, "so many occupations open to a female who can't marry. You could watch other people's children, as an aunt or a schoolmistress. Wouldn't it be better to watch your own? You could do charitable work and . . . Damme, I'm making mincemeat of this. But I mean the best for you."

"And for you?" she asked sadly.

"I'll be well pleased," he said. "You want me to write sonnets? I'm not that sort of man. I think you'd make me a good wife. I need to settle down sooner or later. Why not sooner? When there's a need for it? Why not you?"

He looked serious, and frustrated. Very somber too, she thought. And why not? He was bargaining his life away for the sake of friendship. He was such a good man, and so very attractive. And so muddle-headed. She'd been impressed with him in London; she was nearly overwhelmed by him now. She suddenly knew she'd never get an offer from a better man. It almost broke her heart to refuse him. But she was convinced it would eventually break his if she accepted. Her father had taught her honor too. She rose to her feet and faced him, head high.

"You offer me everything but love," she said, "and I fear I must have that."

"Oh," he said, tilting his head to the side. "But I can give you that too."

Before she could ask him how, he moved. He took her in his arms. Before she could protest, he bent his head to hers and she felt his lips on hers. *So soft*, she thought in surprise, *so gentle*, she thought in astonishment. So sweet and warm and good.

His kiss was courteous. Then less so as she relaxed against him. He opened his mouth against hers and she felt the touch of his tongue against her own. She caught her breath, then sighed at the sweet, dark thrill of it. His hand skimmed along the curve of her waist, to her breast, to her throat, in gentle inquiry. She answered by pressing closer. Long-suppressed yearnings sizzled along her spine and spread to every starved intimate part of her body. Her breasts peaked against his chest. She loved the strength she sensed behind his gentle touch, by the very scent of him, clean linen and sunshine. She put a hand on his hard chest to distance herself, but was lost when she felt the rapid beating of his heart underneath it.

He tenderly cupped her cheek in one big hand. Her eyelids fluttered open. He looked down at her with something intent and unreadable in his blazing blue eyes. Then he kissed her again, more thoroughly than before.

When he drew away, she felt his breath hitch in his chest under her hand when he spoke. "Your answer, Bren?" he asked.

She gazed at him solemnly. "Is that love, Rafe? I think it was something else."

"It's a beginning," he said. "And so?"

"You can't pretend to love me," she said, hoping he'd lie, hoping he'd tell her a truth she didn't dare believe.

He didn't. "No," he said. "I don't pretend. But I do know it's the right thing to do for both of us. We respect each other. As you see, we can find pleasure in each other. You're doomed to years of disgrace if you don't, and even if you can live with that, I can't."

"You don't want to know more about me?" she asked defiantly. "Even if you didn't hear the gossip, you heard what I said. I was engaged to be wed once, and almost was again."

"Are you telling me you've had lovers?"

"No," she said, "I'm telling you the truth."

"You loved them?"

"I loved my fiancé," she said. "I was attracted to Spencer's kindness at a time when I needed a friend. There have been no other men in my life."

"I thought as much," he said calmly. "So you were engaged to marry. And so? You're four and twenty, and very lovely. I don't expect you lived under a hedge. I'm almost a decade older. I doubt you expect innocence of me. The only thing I need to know is if you love someone now. I can't expect you to have honored a pledge to me when you didn't know me. I'd expect it in future, though."

"Well, of course!" she gasped. "I said I'd never be unfaithful!"

"Good," he said. "Then it's done."

"What's done?"

"You've agreed."

"I didn't mean that," she protested.

He looked down into her eyes. "Didn't you?"

His gaze was clear, so candid, she had to look away. "You could do better," she said weakly, giving him a last chance to be free.

He bent his head and kissed her again. This time when he drew his mouth away she could feel a fine tremor in that strong frame pressed so intimately to hers. His voice was rougher when he spoke. "I could? No, I think not."

"But this," she said, as she bowed her head on his shoulder and felt the heat of his body against her cheek, "this is not love, Rafe."

"It will do," he said, and tilted her head up so he could kiss her again.

They walked back to the house, hand in hand. Drum stood in the drive talking to Eric as he waited for Rafe to ride back to the inn with him. The two men saw the couple's linked hands, and smiled.

"It's done then?" Eric asked.

Rafe nodded. Brenna cast her glance down.

"It's well done," Eric said, taking Rafe's hand.

Drum took Brenna's hand as Eric congratulated Rafe. "My best wishes," he said. "Rafe's a very lucky fellow."

There was sincerity in his searching azure gaze. "You can hardly know that," she said, "but thank you."

"Clichés are the rule in these situations," Drum said, "but anyone can tell you I loathe them. I merely speak truth. Just please be kind to him," he added with one of his ironic smiles. "He has heart and courage in plenty, and has needed them all his life. Kindness, however, is not a thing he looks for or has much experience of."

"If I were kind," she murmured, biting her lip, "I'd refuse him, I think. You know all," she said in a rush, looking up at him with entreaty. "Is it fair for me to go on with this?"

"Fair?" Rafe asked. She spun around. He'd stopped talking to Eric, and heard what she'd said. "Fair?" he laughed. "All's fair in love and war."

She gazed at him, hoping something in his expression would tell her which one of those things this marriage of theirs was to be. His face gave away nothing. Then he took her hand again and led her into the house to tell her parents the happy news.

Thirteen

Dinner was over. Rafe and Brenna had the drawing room to themselves, the privilege of an engaged couple. They sat together by the fireside, Rafe with long legs crossed and one arm draped casually over the back of the settee. He was at ease. Or at least as much at ease as Brenna had ever seen him. Only one boot was tapping the floor.

He'd spent the day since they'd announced their engagement writing letters to get everything in order for their wedding. They were still discussing plans.

"No sense in a long engagement," he said.

"A hasty wedding will give rise to more talk," Brenna said.

One of his brows went up. "Could there be more talk, you think?"

She inspected her hands where they lay folded in her lap.

"The banns take three weeks—we'll take three more," Rafe went on. "That'll be time enough to take down some eyebrows, if you're worried about that."

She was. "Why such haste?"

"Why such reluctance?" he countered.

"I'm giving you time to change your mind," she said seriously.

"My mind seldom changes. It's one of my worst faults. What's yours?" he asked suddenly.

"My what?" she asked, startled.

"Your worst fault."

"Oh," she said. "I'd guess—my impetuousness. No—my wanting to do the opposite of what I'm told. I don't always, you know. But I want to. No, that's not bad enough." Her forefinger found its way to her lips. She chewed the end of it as she thought. "My pride! That's it. There's a big fault. Eric's right. I'd rather suffer in silence than let anyone know I'm hurt, and so sometimes I think I'm insulted when no one meant anything by it. But how am I to know that if I'm off sulking somewhere? And I do that too."

He reached out and gently took her hand. His other hand soothed the back of it so she couldn't curl her fingers. "Sulking? Feeling hurt? Tolerable faults," he said, looking at her hand, "not terrible ones."

Her color rose. "Well," she said, "there's another. I chew my fingers. I suppose that's one."

"No," he said seriously, "chewing other people's fingers would be a fault. Your own? Merely a habit."

She looked up and saw his smile. She laughed. "I don't suppose you consider poking fun at people a fault of yours?"

"A virtue," he said lazily, moving his other arm from the back of the settee, letting his fingers trail lightly along her shoulder.

She shivered. He bent his head and brushed the top of her forehead with his lips. He lowered his head—and she moved away, with a curious little twitching movement.

"No, please, none of *that*, not now," she said, shaking her head. "I know what *that's* like. I don't know you. Tell me more."

"Do you know what that's like with me?" he mused. "Not half, I'd say. But I'd say that, wouldn't I? All right. About me. I'm a simple man, Bren. What you behold is what I am."

"Your family then?"

"Oh, as for that. Much more to talk about. I've an estimable older brother. The perfect heir. As unlike me as you can get without taking a boat. Blond and fair—in looks at least. Learned and poetic. A gentleman of parts—half horseman, half scholar, and all smooth and polished. My mama dotes on him. My father's proud of him."

"And you?" she asked.

"We don't get along." He saw her expression, and laughed. "No, we don't come to blows. We just don't understand each other. We don't have to. He's got the title and will get the estate. I have my own devices. There's no love lost between us, but don't worry, there's no hate either. We're brothers. And there's an end to it. I've written my family to tell them of the marriage. I think you'll be impressed by them. I know they will be by you."

"No other family?" she asked, eager to get off the subject of what they'd think of her.

"I had two sisters. Neither survived infancy. I had an uncle. He left me the estate in Kent and the town house. There's another handful of uncles and aunts, a few dozen cousins we see at affairs of state. We're not a close-knit family. That's all until my brother marries, and that won't be until he meets a paragon. Until you and I add to the clan, of course."

She looked away, flustered.

"There is that, Bren," he said softly, his fingers touching the back of her neck, "more of *that*, yes. I do want children. I'd be lying if I didn't tell you how much I look forward to the getting of them with you."

Other men had said more about their desire for her. She didn't remember if she'd ever felt it more. He was short-spoken, but his words struck to the heart in their brevity, clarity, and obvious sincerity.

He kissed her then. It was a few minutes until her hands left his shoulders and went to his chest to keep her distance. He retreated at her touch. But his question was clear in his eyes.

"I don't know you yet," she said, as shocked by her response to him as to his obvious reaction to her. "We really don't know each other that well, do we?"

He nodded. He crossed his arms on his chest. "Right," he said. "Forgive me. Believe it or not, I'm new at this. That is to say, I've known women, but not like lovers. No, that's not true either. I mean, I've women friends, and I've known lovers, but I've little experience with joining the two. Damme. Not the thing to say, right?"

"The perfect thing to say," she said, laughing.

"Right," he said, pleased by her amusement. "Well, then. To know me. To know you. You begin. Your favorite color? Your favorite dinner? And then your favorite song and story. And when you're done, may we kiss again?"

Rafe and Drum stayed on for almost a month, every minute filled with things to do. They enjoyed themselves, as did Eric and his father. They found the hours passed quickly as they rode, hunted, and reminisced together. Brenna couldn't complain; she was caught up in a whirlwind of plans for her wedding.

When Rafe and Brenna spoke together, it was usually about those plans. They talked of other things too, in the first flurry of getting to know each other. Most were trivial, most said in company, and mostly to make everyone laugh. But some more important things were asked, and answered, when they were alone each night, at last.

"No," Rafe finally told Bren, as they sat before the fire in the salon late one night. "Listen, and hear me this time please. I'm not pining for Annabelle. Or constantly thinking of her either. Only you're doing that. And it's time to be done with it, Bren. It's over. I've made my peace with it. So should you. No more hinting or trying to bring up the subject in new and clever ways. I'm not saying I didn't care for her. I did. But a man who carries a light in his heart when there's no fuel for it burns himself up from the inside out. I've seen it happen. I wouldn't let it consume me."

"It's the sort of thing one can't prevent," she said sadly.

He went still. This was a thing she never spoke about. "Is that how it is with you? When you think of what might have been?"

She shrugged. "You mean when I think of Thomas, my fiancé? No, not in the way you mean. I did love him," she said honestly. "He was young and carefree, and so was I. We'd such plans! When he died I didn't think I could ever love again. More than that, I felt so sorry for him, so guilty I was still here and he wasn't. So guilty that I hadn't . . ." She paused and lowered her lashes. "Hadn't loved him even more."

"Your family was right not to send you after him," Rafe said. "He was right to insist you didn't accompany him too. A man has his comforts when his woman follows the drum to be near him, but there's little comfort in it for her. She worries more and grows old before her time. That's another thing I've seen too much of. Army wives wait and fret. They live in tents or rented houses too near the battlefields. They live half a life there, waiting for word of their men, or brief, unsatisfying visits from them. It's not fair."

She nodded. "So he said, and so it had to be. But I still regret it. It doesn't consume me in the way you mean. Not anymore. Time heals that, I suppose. But I thought I was done with thoughts of marrying. I didn't like the men I met in London and didn't want to be introduced to any stray men anxious relatives can always be counted on to produce. They usually have some terrible defect—but a 'good heart,' the relatives assure you. That heart invariably comes in a wretched package."

They laughed over that. "And the local fellows?" Rafe asked.

"They marry early. Those who didn't, or who became free after, didn't interest me. I had my family. They mean everything to me. Because of that, I went to India to see to Eric when he got sick. Someone had to be with him, someone to see things got done. How could we leave him alone in a foreign land, unable to care for himself? Even my parents had to agree, though Lord knows we fought about it."

She shook her head. Rafe's nostrils flared, scenting the spiced patchouli in her hair. Tonight she'd tied the sleek black mass of it so two soft black wings framed her face on either side; they swayed like billowing curtains in the breeze when she moved her head.

"I knew traveling so far by myself would end any plans for marriage, at least with any local men," she went on with a sigh. "A woman can follow her husband, but a single woman traveling across continents on her own? It was considered a fast, daring thing to do. I suppose it was. But it was a thing I had to do. When Eric began to get better, I had a chance to look around. The first thing I saw was his friend Spencer. He showed me such kindness. He offered me more. A chance for a family, a future of my own. I didn't love him, but I did care for him. He said that was enough. I thought it might be."

"What happened?" Rafe asked quietly. "You don't have to tell me—no, damme, Bren, but I think you do! After all, I don't have any secrets—at least ones of the heart—from you."

She laid a hand on top of his. His hand turned and swallowed hers up in a firm, warm clasp.

"Yes, you do deserve to know. It's just that it's so embarrassing." She looked into the fire. "It turned out that all the while he was courting me, he was courting another friend's sister, much less properly. When he told her he had to break it off, she told him she was carrying his child. That was an end to us. Because he did the right thing. They married, immediately. He was an honorable man. And so there you are."

"*Honorable!*" Rafe said, his eyes blazing. "I don't think so! An honorable fellow doesn't fool around with a friend's sister and then break it off when another more desirable female swims into view. It's a wonder Eric didn't remove his head for him. I would have."

"Well," Bren said, her curved mouth tilting into a true smile, "She *was* bird-witted, and fubsy-faced, and shaped rather sadly . . ."

"So he was well served." Rafe laughed in relief. "I see you're not grieving over the loss of him. Nor should you."

"No. I discovered that though I was shocked, I wasn't destroyed. But people felt so sorry for me I could hardly bear it."

"I'll be faithful to you," he said, his hand touching her cheek. "I can't promise that will bring you great joy. But I can promise I'll try to see it does."

He took her into his arms; she went gladly, needing the solid warmth of him now. She got far more.

They kissed. He already kept his word, she thought dazedly. Because his embrace brought her wild joy, a savage, vaunting desire, so intense it worried her. She didn't love him as she had Thomas. She didn't know him half so well. She'd felt thrilling things in Tom's arms. But she and Tom had both been so young and new to their own bodies, and eager to share them. This man knew her needs better than she did.

She was constantly astonished such a plain-spoken fellow could be so skilled and careful in his lovemaking. He'd given up pursuit of his love for her sake. He might be trying to make the best of a bad bargain, but he was making it a peerless one for her. She knew men could make love without love, but she had no idea they could do it so thoroughly. It shamed and embarrassed her that she could respond so utterly. It couldn't help delighting her too. His touch was gentle but sure. His mouth was knowing; he led her on to heights she'd never considered.

He also knew when to stop, and lately that was before she was ready to. He was so genuinely good, wonderfully attractive, and safe. *Safe?* she thought distantly, as his hand cupped her breast and she caught her shivering breath. Never that. And yet, always that.

She forgot her train of thought as he gently tugged the top of her gown down and his warm opened lips found her breast. He was a man of few words. But he could carry on a long and patient conversation of caresses, building the tension until she was half-mad beneath his hands. She gasped now as his lips closed over the taut tip of her breast. Her head went back;

his mouth left her breast to breathe fiery, silent secrets against her neck. She held on to his hard shoulders and shivered, and squirmed against him.

They sought more, and in a few fevered moments almost found it. But they both drew back at the same moment, shattered, unsatisfied, but old and wise enough to know this was no place to know more.

He sat back. "Not in your drawing room," he said ruefully. "That would be taking advantage of your family's hospitality."

"Not my hospitality?" she asked on a shaken laugh as she dragged her gown up again.

"No," he said simply, taking her hands in his. "I'd never take advantage of you. I take what you want to give me, Bren. Nothing more. But nothing less. I do look forward to your taking advantage of me, though," he added with a smile.

She smiled back at him. He reached out and tucked a bit of her hair back. "It won't be long," he said softly. "But too long for my control. That's why I'm going back to London tomorrow."

She stopped smiling.

"I think it's better if we part for a while now," he said, and added more gently, "I've things to do. And I don't want to take advantage of anything here. It would never do for the colonel to find me doing what I most want to do. And Eric's growing so strong now, I don't dare!" He grinned.

But she didn't smile back at him. Another man had left her here, and never returned.

He must have remembered that. "I'll be back," he

said. "Never doubt it. I'm a man of my word. I live by it. And I will live. I promise."

After their journey back to London, Rafe and Drum sat in Rafe's study and shared a glass, a toast to Rafe's future.

"She's a fine woman. You do better than you know, I think," Drum said as he put down his glass, "but not better than you deserve. I'll leave you now. We can meet for dinner or luncheon or whatever you wish. Just send me word. If not, I'll see you on the trip back to Tidbury—unless you need me before that?"

"Thank you," Rafe said. "I can't ask more. I'm sorry I took up so much of your time as it is. I'm sure you had more important things to do."

"Actually," Drum said with a faint smile, "I had not."

Rafe looked at him curiously. "I've known you these many years. I just realized that the more I think I know about you, the less I really do. You're a secretive fellow for all your outgoing ways. No wonder you were such a good agent for His Majesty. Your comings and goings were always a mystery to me— and why you remain my friend, even more of one."

Drum laughed. "Why? You say you're a simple man, Rafe, but you always find yourself in the midst of the most interesting situations. Beyond that? You're a good friend and a true one, and a man of rare good sense. As for things you don't know—I'd list how valuable you are to your friends as foremost among them. I'll stop giving you reasons now because I've got too many things to do and can't spend hours listing them. Give you good day, my friend. I'll be here at the appointed hour."

Rafe saw him out. He went back into his study to write notes. First the letter to his family. He'd already written to tell them of the coming wedding, but now he needed to take care of the specifics. Brenna's mama had written to invite them to stay with her. But now he could let them know he could arrange for rooms at the inn if they preferred.

He got a sniff of his sleeve as he picked up a sheet of paper from his desk. A bath, definitely, a bath after all his hard riding. First, though, a note for Peck, due home any hour. Because he might not be there when Peck got back, and didn't want the old fellow shocked to bits by all the new staff that had invaded the house. After his bath, Rafe decided, he'd have to be off to a jeweler to get Bren a bride present, and a ring. Then a trip to his tailor for a suit of clothes to suit a new groom.

Then dinner. And early to bed, at last. Because he had dozens of other errands to run before he was ready to ride back to Tidbury. As well as decisions to make. Would they come here after their honeymoon, or go to his parents' estate, or to his own country estate? Speaking of honeymoons . . . there was none arranged. Where to go? Not abroad; they'd discussed that. They were both weary of foreign travel and sea voyages for a while.

She'd left the decision to him. Harrogate? Too

stodgy. Perhaps Bath? Bren would like that. Or maybe the Lake District? No, autumn was drawing in; it would be too cold . . . But then he'd have to warm her, wouldn't he? Rafe mused, with a smile. The Lake District sounded fine to him. He'd have to find a booking agent.

Rafe was walking down Bond Street, almost sauntering. He was pleased with the ruby and diamond necklace he'd got Bren, thinking how it would suit that long white neck, that ebony hair, when he heard his name called. He looked up. And stopped still.

"Lud!" a familiar voice filled with teasing laughter exclaimed, "I didn't think you'd cut me dead, sir. But you almost did. I was shocked—until I realized you wouldn't have noticed a wild horse charging at you. Good afternoon, Lord Dalton," Annabelle said, dipping a pretty curtsy. "How have you been? I haven't seen you anywhere lately."

He stared at her. She was hard to look at, she shone so brightly in the sunlight. She was literally dazzling in her perfection today. All in white, she wore a silvery shawl over her gown; a matching bonnet was decorated with a large and showy white blossom over one ear. It suited her dark curls; they feathered around her forehead, showing her alabaster skin and prettily blushed cheeks, making her eyes bluer. Those eyes were regarding him with fond amusement.

"I've been out of London," he said haltingly. "But I didn't think you'd notice, or care."

"Oh, notice, certainly," she laughed, "but care? That's not for a lady to say to a gentleman. I was just remarking on your absence the other day, wasn't I, Marie?" she asked the maidservant who stood next to her. "I'm delighted to have almost literally run into you, my lord," she added teasingly. "It will save me sending you an invitation. I'm having a grand soiree at my house, a ball, in point of fact. It's in three weeks, but I wanted to make sure you'll be there."

Rafe frowned. She was charming, she was friendly. Why? Was it some kind of revenge she'd got up for him? It couldn't be anything else. He didn't like such games; in any event, he couldn't play one now. He'd lost her; he'd resolved to live with it. If he didn't look at her too long, he could. He bowed. "I thank you, my lady, but I won't be able to attend. I'll be getting married, or at least on my honeymoon by then."

All the laughter left her face, along with the light in it. The faint color drained from her cheeks. Her eyes widened; she swayed on her feet. Rafe sprang forward and seized her, holding her upright. She was tiny, he realized as he held her close, fragile and small boned; it was her personality that made her appear more substantial. And she was still redolent of roses, as he remembered.

Her maid fluttered ineffectively. Annabelle's eyes were closed; she took deep but ragged breaths. Rafe looked around, wondering if he'd have to carry her somewhere to recover. Passersby were stopping and staring at them. He felt her body grow rigid under his hands. He let go of her instantly, afraid his blundering attempt at comfort might cause her more harm. He stepped back. She stood on her own and stared at him, her eyes enormous.

Her head went up. "Your pardon," she said in a shaky voice, "but I'm surprised. It is not the habit of gentlemen to court one woman while engaged to another. At least, I thought it wasn't."

"I wasn't engaged when I was in London," he said. And then, bluntly, because he couldn't find the words to frame it, he added, "And you said you never wanted to see me again."

She frowned.

"That day I last called," he said, "you said you didn't want to see me then, nor 'tomorrow or tomorrow or tomorrow.' "

She frowned in incomprehension.

"Your butler told me." He waited for her answer.

She didn't have one. But she had to speak. Through the corners of her eyes she could see well-dressed passersby looking at her. Everyone could see her disgrace, everyone could watch her being discarded now, Annabelle thought in horror. She clasped her hands, trying to collect herself, thinking as fast as she could with her mind all awhirl.

Had she said that? she thought, aghast. Had she actually quoted Shakespeare to say such a rude thing to a gentleman whose only sin was in having to leave Town? She'd refused to admit him that day, she remembered. But she'd merely wanted to punish him for that nonsense with that slut, and that old, gossipy Baron Barlow was there listening, positively salivating at the scent of gossip and she . . .

Now she remembered, and felt a cold chill. Her stomach twisted, her cheeks grew hot. *She had said that.*

But she'd been angry with him then. She did that kind of thing when she was vexed. She'd forgotten it a minute after it was done. She always begged forgiveness for her rash behavior once time passed. She would have this time too—when she saw him again. Then she'd have remembered the incident, if not the exact wording of it. She would have run into him again, at a party, the theater, in the street, as now, and explained, apologized, laughed him out of any resentment of it. But he'd been gone almost a month and she hadn't had a chance.

She'd missed him. Missed his straightforward speaking, his odd sense of humor, his utter devotion to her too. She couldn't tell him that. She damned the moment she'd told her butler to tell him the other. She didn't love him. But now she'd never know if she could. She was alone again, abandoned again, deserted for another woman again—and by him! By her second choice. This plain, blunt, simple man who had adored her. And no longer did.

Annabelle felt easy tears rush to her eyes. She grew angry so she wouldn't give in to self-pity and let the tears flow. *How dare he?* She didn't know why she'd even entertained his suit, she thought—though she knew, and grew angrier because of it. She felt sick and guilty and furious with herself and him. He'd dealt her a terrible blow. She struck back.

" 'Tomorrow and tomorrow and tomorrow'?" she forced herself to ask quizzically. "My word! I'm hardly so poetic."

"But your butler said—"

"And you believed him?" she asked, widening her eyes.

Now it was he who stood shocked. "You didn't?"

"Oh, my dear sir," she laughed, her hand on her heart, "would I want anyone to think I'm a bluestocking? It's that rascally butler of ours, depend on it. His every off night is spent at a playhouse. Such a dramatic fellow—the post arrives and he announces it like a war! No wonder you jumped to such a conclusion. I wondered where you'd got to. Now I understand. Too late, I see. Oh!" Her smile faded. "How rude of me. Who is the lady you've turned to—I mean, the lady you've honored with your attentions—if I may ask?"

"I am to marry Miss Ford," he said coldly, his face expressionless. Some strong emotion was behind his words. He gave her a jerky bow. "So I'll have to miss your soiree. Good afternoon, my lady."

She watched him walk away. He stalked down the street, his long stride as distinctive as that ridiculous copper-colored hair. Her anger was already turning to guilt. She wanted to call him back, to explain. She raised a gloved hand—and lowered it. She couldn't. Because it was a terrible thing to have said to him, however she came to it, and besides, it was too late. And she'd had enough pain.

"My goodness!" she remarked to her maid in a high, artificial voice. "What a scrap of gossip, to be sure. He's marrying the creature. What a clever piece she must be."

Fourteen

Instinct took Rafe home. He couldn't watch his step or notice his direction; his heart and mind were in turmoil. He walked past his footman and butler and wordlessly went straight to his study, closed the door behind him, and sat at his desk with his head in his hands.

She hadn't rejected him.

But he was committed.

She'd been hurt by him. She'd cared for him, after all. She'd almost fainted when she'd heard his news. He remembered how she'd felt in his arms, so light and delicate, warm and womanly. She'd been as close to him as he'd dreamed she'd someday be. But never how he'd hoped it would be. He felt like he'd stepped on something small and fragile. He'd only wanted to protect her. But he'd wounded her.

He felt as though he suffered a wound himself.

His stomach churned; it was hollow and cold. He felt like a fool and a villain. It was only justice. He'd hurt her, twice. The first time when she'd seen another woman, a strange half-dressed woman, looking so at home in his house. The second time just now, when he'd told her he'd chosen that other woman as his wife. He'd lost Annabelle twice too. Once by stupidly believing an exaggeration on the part of a servant. Again when he'd acted on it. He closed his eyes, but saw only the same truth. He couldn't make it up to her because now he was pledged elsewhere.

To Brenna.

Rafe thought of inky hair and perfume that set his senses reeling. Of a sweet face and a melodious voice. Of laughter, and longing, about what he'd promised and what he needed. And then, as always, foremost, about other people's needs, which always must come before his own.

What was it he'd said not so long ago? An honorable man didn't fool with a woman and then break it off when another more desirable female swam into view? He'd spoken too soon about something he didn't understand. Because here was a situation in which he'd done that, all unknowing, and whatever he did now, someone would be hurt. Whatever he did do, he couldn't compound his error by repeating it.

He tried to reason coldly and clearly, as he had other times when his life had been at stake. Even if she hadn't so crassly dismissed him, Annabelle had been by no means his. He knew that very well. He lacked the looks and charm she'd sought in a husband before. She had dozens of suitors to heal her heart—a heart that might never have been given into his care. Brenna had no suitor but him. She had a family he respected. He genuinely liked her; she seemed to like him. She was a strong-minded woman; he doubted he'd have been able to persuade her if her emotions hadn't been even a little involved. And when she brought those emotions into play, she made his head spin.

He'd given his word.

He raised his head at last and knew what he must do. He'd known from the first. All the rest was rationale. He was a man of his word, and that word, once given, was his bond. That was that, and there it was. There was little sense in dwelling on it; there was time enough for regrets.

It was over; it was time to begin. He couldn't grieve. Or at least, he refused to. He would go on with it; he'd make the best of it. There really was nothing else he could do. He pinched the bridge of his nose and absently reached for the stack of messages on his desk, a pile that had grown tall during his absence from London. Work was always his solace and his weapon against despair. He unfolded the top letter, the last delivered, and scanned it, his mind half on the words and half on his decision. He read it. Once. And then again, as his mind and eyes focused.

He crumpled the paper in one hard fist. Then he laid it on the desktop and smoothed it, so he could read it again.

. . . and so we fear we cannot attend the wedding. Your brother and I will stay with your mama, of

course. It is only an upset of the stomach she's taken,
but we can scarcely ask her to travel now, can we?
We will meet your bride as soon as you are able to
bring her to us. Congratulations.

Yr Father,
Lynwood

Rafe's fists and stomach knotted. Another of his
mama's many fleeting ailments that beset her when
she didn't care to stir herself. Or another charade of
one. It hardly mattered. His father, as always,
sounded as amused as annoyed with it. They were
not coming, in any event. Not coming to their own
son's wedding. He tried to excuse it. It was, after all,
late notice. It was far. *It was their own son's wedding*.
He grimaced, wondering how he'd explain it to
Brenna and her family and how they'd feel about it,
so that he wouldn't concentrate on his own feelings.

Those feelings were disappointment, pain, and the
old sour ache of helpless regret. Nothing new, he
thought as he reached for the next letter and raised it
as if it weighed a ton, nothing new in any of this,
actually.

Outriders rode the gentlemen's two horses behind
their coach; the gentlemen's valets rode up with the
coachman. Rafe and Drum sat inside. An unusual,
uneasy silence lay between the two friends. For once,
it was Drum whose fingers were tapping, who sat
straight as a ramrod, whose whole lean frame

seemed to thrum with unexpressed energy. Rafe sat looking out the window.

"Out with it," Rafe finally said to the reflection in the window. He turned his head to look at his friend straight on. "You haven't said three words together since we left London. That's not like you. We haven't spoken since we parted company over a week past. I know you've been out and about the town. You must have had some adventures, and you can easily talk the knot off a log when you've a notion. You don't. Why?"

Drum looked even more uneasy. Rafe remembered, for the first time in a very long time, that he was the older by a few years. It had never been noticeable. Drum had been sent ahead in school, but fit in with the older boys because his intelligence as well as his worldly cynicism had been marked even at that early age. That long, lean face and lanky frame had helped make him seem an equal. But now he looked young and strangely vulnerable. His face was stripped of the usual calm, ironic amusement with which he viewed the world.

"All right," Drum finally said. "I heard something in Town." He spoke quickly, watching Rafe closely. "It surprised me. More, for the first time in a long time, I was shocked. I discount gossip or at least half of it. Still, I can't help feeling the half I allowed might be true—if only because I heard it from so many sources. And it's bad. We're on our way to your wedding to Brenna Ford. Yet I heard you were seen embracing Lady Annabelle in public, in plain daylight, on Bond Street, just the other day."

Rafe frowned. Then laughed, harshly. "Aye, it's true."

Drum cocked his head. "No, that's not the whole of it, is it?"

"No," Rafe said, "not half. It's worse than that."

"Do you want to talk about it?"

"No, but I will," Rafe said.

"I've always attributed the highest, most honorable standards to you," Drum added, his eyes nakedly troubled now. "It's not fair to burden another man with your own conscience, I know. But I've always seen you as a man of absolute morality and rare judgment. Before God, Rafe, I can't see you as an adulterer, a cheat or liar. You may not have lain with the lady while promised to another, but this is very bad, even so."

"So it would seem," Rafe said. "But bad as it is, it's not what it seems."

Drum let out a breath. Rafe could see the expression in that long face lighten. "Yes, of course. Care to tell me?"

"Simple, too simple," Rafe said. "I met her in the street. Rather, she roused me from my thoughts by greeting me as though she'd never turned me away in the first place. That surprised me. She twitted me for not having called on her, then immediately asked me to some ball she was going to hold at her house. She was all teasing, dimples and light. I was off balance. I couldn't understand her change of heart. I didn't believe it either. I thought it was some cruelty to pay me back for the gossip about Bren. So I just told her straight off that I couldn't come because I was to be married that week. She was shocked."

"I can imagine," Drum drawled.

"No, more than that, by God, Drum, she was going to faint. Went white as a sheet and lost her balance. I sprang to her assistance. I had to hold her upright." He paused. "Likely that's what was seen. I grant, it may have looked otherwise—no, damme! It couldn't! What sort of an oaf would grab a female in the street and snatch her up in an embrace?"

"An ardent lover," Drum said. "A man half out of his mind with love and thwarted lust."

"No!" Rafe said, his eyes widening.

"Yes, I'm afraid they're saying that," Drum said sympathetically, "And I fear, I do most sincerely fear, that it's the lady herself who's doing most of the saying."

"To save face," Rafe said dully, nodding. "It does make sense."

"It's damnable, Rafe," Drum said angrily. "She may well have been looking to gild her own reputation, but she had no right to make mincemeat of yours."

"No," Rafe said, shaking his head, "I'm to blame. I misread everything. She's young, she's unworldly, she's used to getting her way. Then she didn't—spectacularly, when she lost Damon to Gilly. I pursued her without much hope. I sheared off when it seemed I was right about how she couldn't possibly want me. Now I have to believe she was actually considering my suit."

Rafe paused, his face still, but his old friend could

recognize emotions under that calm surface; he saw pity and grief intermingled in those stark blue eyes.

"Can you imagine how she must have felt when I bluntly told her I was lost to her too?" Rafe asked helplessly. "Don't blame her. I don't. I think she's had enough of disappointment. So she spread a tale about me to save face. What of it? She acted in haste and regrets at her leisure."

"And you?" Drum asked quietly. "Shall you do the same?"

Rafe's head went up. He fixed Drum with a killing stare. Then his shoulders relaxed. "No," he said, "never think it. I'm going to marry Brenna. And that's what will be. I don't look back."

"It's not too late," Drum said. "Don't compound a mistake. If your heart's in Annabelle's pocket, don't give your hand to Brenna Ford. That way, two—no, three—of you will repent at leisure."

"So knowledgeable about love, are you?" Rafe asked with unusual sarcasm.

"No, to the contrary. I know nothing of it except what I've seen. But I've seen more tragedies come of it than joy. Which is why I'm presumptuous enough to ask you to consider it carefully."

"I have. I am. I did. I said I'd marry Brenna. I will. Now," Rafe said, rising and thumping on the carriage roof with his fist, "this riding like a gent is fine, but not for me. I'm going out to ride. I'll take Blaze over now and give him real exercise. Myself as well. And you?"

"Oh. Yes, it's a fine day," Drum said, because he knew Rafe well, and knew the conversation was over, even if the questions hadn't been answered. He wouldn't ask more because he didn't know if he really wanted those answers now. Or even if there were any real answers at all.

Brenna's mama looked at the gown Brenna was trying on for her trousseau. It was rosy as sunrise, with white sleeves. It fit perfectly, made Brenna's skin glow, setting off her ink black hair beautifully. "Wonderful," she told her daughter in satisfaction. "That's the last of them. Now we have everything but the groom."

She heard her own words in the silence that followed them.

"But what about the flowers?" she hastily added. "From the garden, the wood, or the hothouse, do you think? Asters? Gardenias? Or roses? Roses, I think, don't you? The weather's so mild I think we can count on lovely roses even this late."

"And we can count on Rafe," Brenna said firmly. "He said he'd be here, and he will be. Mama, don't worry. He's a very good man. He'll be here, and this wedding will be. I think it really will be third time lucky for me. Because I'm older than I was with poor Thomas. And I care for Rafe in so many ways that I didn't for Spencer. This time I know my mind, my heart, and even my body."

"Brenna!" her mama said.

Brenna grinned. "Oh, I beg your pardon. I forgot you don't know about such things."

Her mama laughed. "It's only that I always forget

it's time you did, my dear." She wore a smile, but her gaze was serious and searching. She hesitated. Brenna breathed a small, sad sigh. With all they'd discussed, there was one subject they hadn't touched on since Thomas died. Mama, like everyone else she knew, probably wondered how far she and Thomas had gone to pledge their so obvious love for each other. There was nothing she could or would say about it now, as then. Her memories of Tom were her own.

But her mama surprised her. She took her hands. "It's not a betrayal, Brenna. What you and Rafe will share is part of marriage. You deserve to enjoy that part of it. Tom would have thought so too. Rafe's a good man. I like him, Eric swears by him, your father's thrilled. But the fact that you desire him— *that* makes me happy. Desire and the fulfillment of it is a very good thing in marriage. More than that. It can bring you two together heart and mind, and heal many a foolish argument or silly mistake. It's a solace and a comfort in times of trouble, as well as being such a source of joy. I'm sorry for women who have to do without it, and so glad you've found it with Rafe."

"Well, no, I haven't found all of it—not yet," Brenna said. "But don't worry, it's a thing I look forward to."

"Good!"

"Mama!" Brenna said, pretending shock to make her mother blush.

But it made her happy too. In fact, she thought after her mama left the room, it was a thing she found difficult not to think about. Rafe wasn't the most handsome man she'd ever seen. His face, when all was said, was as simple and straightforward as he was. He had even features, strong white teeth, and clear blue eyes, but there was nothing to make maidens sigh in it. He made her sigh, though. His body was strong and straight, well muscled and lean; he dressed it for function, in clean, neat clothing. Everything about him was economical. His conversation too. He was a man's man. *And this lucky woman's man*, she thought.

In spite of what she'd told her mama, she sometimes had a hard time believing in that luck. There were times since he'd left, in the nights, and on the days when she went to the village and saw all the speculative looks she got, when she wondered if he really was coming back. Or if Fate or some bizarre twist of Fortune would keep her groom from her at the last, as had happened to her before.

Because this time she didn't know if she could bear it. This time she was more in love than she'd ever been before. It wasn't a marriage of convenience for her. She wouldn't deceive herself. She'd been half in love with him when she'd left London. His kindness, his kisses, and his company had taken her all the rest of the way. If she had to marry any man, she was glad it was Rafe, because she'd never marry because she had to. She loved him, utterly. She couldn't like the way they'd been thrown together. But she could never regret it. Unless he did. Where was he?

The wedding was in one week's time. He was due

back. He was not there yet. And now, at last, in spite of all her efforts, doubts began to creep past the threshold of certainty.

She folded her new gown carefully, then quickly dressed again. Idle hands made for idle thoughts. There were things to do. Guests would be arriving. His parents were coming; she'd much to do. Doing her errands would banish doubt. Until the night.

When she got downstairs she saw her parents and Eric in a huddle near a huge box in the front hall. They were speaking softly and secretly, and looked up at Brenna with guilty expressions that told her they'd been talking about her. She'd seen it before. She missed her step and almost stumbled. She gripped the stair rail with whitened knuckles and abruptly stopped.

"It's a wedding gift," Eric said quickly, seeing her sudden terror. "From Rafe's parents. We were just wondering why they sent it on instead of bringing it themselves."

"I think they decided to send it ahead because their coach is filled with clothing," her mama said. "They must mean to stay on a while here."

Her father held out the note that had come with the package. Brenna crossed the room quickly, took the note, opened and read it. She looked up and managed a wavering smile. "Well," she told them in too cheery tones, "it seems they can't come, after all. His mama is taken ill, she says. An upset stomach. She invites us to stay with them after the wedding."

"Oh," her mama said.

"Well, but if the woman's sickly, there's good reason to stay home," the colonel said gruffly. "But the brother?"

"Rafe says there's little affection between them," Brenna said abruptly, folding the note again.

"His father can hardly leave his mama behind," her mother said nervously, seeing Brenna's distress.

"They're unthinking, not deliberately rude," Eric agreed, his eyes on his sister. "It's in keeping with the little Rafe let slip about them. He read me some of their letters when we were in hospital. A man could die of frostbite from them, whatever his wounds. Never think they disapprove of you, Bren. The problem is more likely that they don't care who he marries. There'd be no reason for them to disapprove of you. They had no bride in mind for him. We have sufficient name for them. All their concern is for his brother."

"Well, we'll be Rafe's family from now on," his mother said stoutly, "so we'll scarcely miss them."

"It's their loss, all round," her husband said.

Brenna smiled at the way they rallied round her, determined now to give her family—and his own, in time—to Rafe.

But as the appointed day for his return wore on and Rafe didn't appear, Brenna's manner grew more absent, her smile more strained.

Her brother intercepted her on one of her many inconsequential busywork errands. "Bren," Eric said gently, "stop teasing yourself. You're looking for the worm in the apple, aren't you? There is none."

She nodded. She wanted to believe him and wished she could.

* * *

He arrived at sunset. The horses and coach came up the drive with a clatter. Rafe sprang down from his horse, tossed the reins to a grinning stableboy, and took the shallow steps to the Fords' front door two at a time.

She should have waited in the drawing room, like a lady. She could have had them call her down from her room, so he wouldn't guess how worried she'd been. But Brenna heard the commotion and went flying out the door, and almost ran straight into him.

He was taken aback. He seemed, for a moment, hesitant. Then he opened his arms and took her in his embrace and, in spite of everyone watching, kissed her.

The Fords stood in their doorway, smiling.

But the earl of Drummond, from high on his horse, looked down, and looked concerned. Until Eric hailed him. Then, as if remembering where he was and who was watching, he smiled too.

Fifteen

I t was a time for celebration, a riotously funny dinner party, filled with jests and bright conversation.
The earl of Drummond could lighten any gathering
when he put his mind to it, and he did. He knew just
what to say to make men laugh and just how to say a
thing to a lady to make her smile. Rafe was very
grateful to his friend.

He didn't realize Drum also knew how to draw
him out, making his candid and wry observations an
integral part of the fun. Brenna laughed, and joked,
and glowed with pleasure. Her father and brother
and Rafe—all the men in her life—were together,
liked each other, and were very like each other too.
She exchanged many grins with her mama. This was
right. This was the way it ought to be, should have
been, and with continued luck, would remain.

When dinner was over and they rose from the table, Rafe surprised them all.

"No port for me right now, no snuff or smoke, thank you. I'd like a few words with my bride-to-be," he told the others. "So if we may have some privacy?"

He said it gently; he wore a smile when he did. It was only habit that made Brenna's heart catch. There had been too many surprises in her life. She'd been told bad news too often to take any departure from the norm easily. Especially this close to her scheduled wedding.

She rose slowly to her feet. Her father and brother grinned knowingly; her mother wore a fond and reminiscent smile. But Brenna saw Rafe's friend Drum shoot him a sharp look, and her fears grew. Rafe caught up her hand and led her from the room. That hand was icy cold in his. Her dark eyes searched his expression when they got to the drawing room and he closed the door behind him.

He gathered her in his arms and kissed her.

She was surprised, then beguiled. As the touch of his mouth on hers increased, she put her arms round his shoulders and eagerly answered his growing urgency. They clung to each other. Though their kiss was sweet, they both felt its desperation, and drew apart at the same time with the same searching questions in their eyes.

She spoke first. "I didn't know if you were really coming back," she admitted.

He paused. Because for a time there he hadn't

known either, and the guilt of it ate at him. His voice
was gruff when he spoke. "I promised I would."

"Well, but . . . promises," she said with a little
shrug.

He took her shoulders in his hands and held her,
his gaze on hers. "I keep my word."

"So I see," she said, curiously unsatisfied, uneasy
with something she didn't understand. "What is it
you wanted to talk about?"

He dropped his hands. "My parents aren't able to
come to the wedding."

"I know, they sent word, and a wedding gift."
She saw his expression. "She hasn't gotten sicker,
has she?"

"Mama? No, don't worry. She gets just sick
enough to avoid exerting herself." He paced a step
away, then back. He looked at her, shocked again at
how he'd forgotten how vividly lovely she was. She
was that, and clever, well-bred, and entirely blameless. He wanted to let her know that. He wanted to
let the world know that. And he needed his parents
to see how well he'd done.

"They don't put much value on me," he said.
"Maybe they do, but they put more on their own
comforts. But they do ask to meet you. We didn't
make firm plans for our honeymoon. Would you
mind if I took you to meet them after the wedding?"

"No, of course not," she said. "I want to meet them
too." She also wanted to understand how they could
so offend their son, perhaps to help change that.
"That's fine. I've never been so far south. Odd, I've
crossed the ocean, yet never seen much of England."

He nodded, relieved. "It's often like that. Well. Then. Good. Oh. I got you this, in London," he said, reaching into his jacket. He withdrew a jeweler's case and handed it to her.

She hesitated, then snapped it open. And gasped. A skein of brilliant red rubies burned against the dark cloth of the case; each was surrounded by a sparkling maze of diamonds that twinkled like shards of starlight even in the dim lamp-glow. She stared at it.

"Here, let me," he said, taking the necklace from the case and holding it in the air in front of her.

Her hair was upswept tonight, so she only had to step into the circle of his arms and bend her neck. She felt his fingers brush against her skin and, as he worked on the clasp, felt his breath against the small hairs at the back of her neck, and shivered. "There," he said, standing back, pleased. "Take a look."

She walked to the pier mirror on the wall and gazed at herself. Her hand went to touch the shining glory that hung like an enchanted spiderweb against her breast. She snatched her hand away when she saw her blunt fingers with their bitten nails. She felt like a washerwoman daring to touch a bit of exquisite lace. This was a dainty lady's necklace, delicate, intricate, more suited to Annabelle than herself. Had he been thinking of Annabelle even as he bought her a bride's gift?

"The rubies suit you," he said with satisfaction. "They match your lips. I saw bigger ones, but they looked too heavy. These are bright, particularly fine, I thought. The diamonds are to make the thing look even lighter. They go well with your hair too. The salesman said rubies can look ponderous if you're not careful. I got you a ring to match," he added when she didn't speak.

He held out a smaller box to her, but she could hardly see it because of the way the sudden tears made her eyes swim.

"Bren!" he said, taking her into his arms. She buried her face against his jacket, but she couldn't hide her emotion from him. He bent his head. "Weeping?" he asked softly. "Don't. Glad I didn't give you that tiara to match now. Would have overset you entirely. Bren, Bren," he said, craning his neck trying to get a look at her face. "Is it that you like them, or don't?"

She managed a chuckle.

"I don't have the family baubles," he said, rubbing her back, trying to ease her unexpected display of emotion. "They go to my brother. They wouldn't suit you anyway, old cabochon cuts of stones in settings heavy as lead. And when his son marries, his wife has to give them back, for his bride to wear. These are yours, entirely. Forever. Why are you still crying?"

"Because they're beautiful."

"Oh," he said. His hands stilled. "I should have got ugly ones?"

She laughed. She raised her head. He kissed her.

And then they'd nothing more to say aloud for a long while.

There was a party the night before the wedding.

Tidbury hadn't seen such glittering guests in all its

history, not even that time bluff Prince Hal had stopped for the night at the inn a few centuries before. He'd only had a bishop, some generals, and courtiers with him. The Fords had glittering members of the ton at their home tonight. How Prince Hal's entourage had dressed and spoken was long forgotten. The residents of Tidbury lucky enough to have been invited vowed they'd never forget these guests. Brenna knew she never would.

She was introduced to attractive men and women, all of them poised and dressed to perfection. It was apparent they were Rafe's good friends. They were kind to her, but it was plain as the nose on her face that they knew the gossip about why this marriage was going forth. Who didn't? And so, however charming they were to her, it was clear they were inspecting her carefully, if covertly. She didn't like it. But she didn't blame them.

A radiant lady all in silvery silk, with tiger gold eyes and flaxen hair, glamorous as a fairy queen, put a little hand on Brenna's sleeve a moment after they met. "You *are* beautiful!" she crowed. "Just as they said! You look so exotic, so Eastern, like an Arabian princess, though that devilish handsome brother of yours says you're native as far back as the Druids, and related to Welsh royals no less! But not a bit high in the instep, or haughty with it, he said. Well, so I can see for myself. Oh. I don't mean to presume, but what's on my mind is on my tongue—at least that's what my husband always says."

"So I do, for all that changes it," her husband replied. He was such an astonishingly handsome gentleman that Brenna blinked. "Which is good," he went on, with a fond look at his wife, "because I don't want it changed. How else would I know what mischief you were up to? But, Miss Ford," he added to Brenna, "my wife is only right. You're every bit as lovely as we'd heard."

"Well, she is," his wife said. "But I think, after all, that compliments are unfair," she added, seeing Brenna's expression. "She can hardly agree or disagree, can she?"

"Ho," Rafe said with a smile, "the queen of disagreement herself speaks! So it must be true. Brenna, these are old friends, Gilly and Damon Ryder."

"And we're older ones," a tall, dangerous looking fellow, dressed immaculately in the latest fashion, said. He bowed. "Ewen Sinclair, Viscount Sinclair," he said, introducing himself, and then more proudly, "and my wife, the lady Bridget."

Brenna ducked a bow. The viscountess was lovely, her face unforgettably charming in spite of the thin scar on it. The scar, in fact, only called attention to her loveliness.

"Sinclair. Bridget," Rafe said with a smile. "Glad you could make it."

"There was no way we wouldn't," the viscountess said, surprised.

"There is one way," her husband laughed. "We had to miss Gilly's wedding, remember?"

"How is the little terror?" Drum asked.

"Terror, *huh!*" Gilly Ryder said. "As if she didn't have your heart in her collection too!"

"Well, so she does," Drum admitted. "It's only

tragic that I gave it, along with my undying devotion, to the wench—and she doesn't have three teeth in her pretty little head yet."

"Four, this morning," the viscountess laughed.

"As to that," Rafe said, "too bad Wycoff and Lucy can't come. They're good friends too," he told Brenna. "Just married as well. I'd have liked you to meet them. You will, in time. Sorry they won't be here, but not for the reason for it. It's good that there'll soon be another in that family too."

Brenna was glad of the flurry of conversation that followed that announcement. Rafe's family hadn't come. But it was clear that these elegant people constituted a family of his own choosing, and more, that they genuinely cared for him.

She hadn't known he had so many firm friends of high rank. It made him seem even more unobtainable. She was going to wed him in a day. Did they think she'd cheated to do it? Charming as they were, did they look at her and see a phantom Lady Annabelle by her side, compare them, and find her wanting?

By the time they turned their attention back to her, Brenna was locked in embarrassed silence. It was good the musicians struck up a country dance. It saved her from trying to find something to say. The musicians earned their keep. She didn't have to talk very much again that night. She could dance with her guests, mind her steps, and wait for the waltzes. Rafe claimed every one. Then he could hold her and she could look into his eyes and forget the past and the future, and revel in the present with him.

* * *

The bride dressed with trembling hands. With all she knew, there was much she didn't know. It was a huge step she was taking.

"Don't worry," she answered her brother's worried look when he came to escort her downstairs, "I'm sure. Terrified, yes. But I'm sure of what I'm doing."

"It's only that. . ." he paused. "Bren, seems I'm the one who couldn't sleep last night. I had those famous prenuptial nerves. We've been pushing you to this. But you don't have to do anything if your whole heart and soul isn't in it. Don't let Society make up your mind. Or us, either. This is belated, but it's never too late. We'll support you in whatever you decide to do. Whatever I said in the past—don't let me influence you overmuch. I think Rafe's a fine fellow. But I'm a man, and so I might not know what a woman wants in a man."

"You? Admitting that?" she teased. "No," she said more seriously, "I'm sure. I can't like the circumstances. You're right about that. But I can't help liking him either."

" 'Liking'?" he asked with a troubled look at her.

She ducked her head. She looked poised, finished, elegant, lovely. Red roses to match her new necklace and the vivid rust of her new velvet gown were fixed like a crown in her glossy black hair. But when she looked down, the shining white part in her hair showed how human and vulnerable she was. Eric frowned, even more concerned.

She looked up at her brother again, her eyes sincere. "I confess to feeling much more than that," she told him softly. "But I liked him immediately. And I think the liking will make all the rest grow, and last a long, long time."

He smiled. "Yes," was all he said. But when they got downstairs, the first thing he did was to look to his father and nod. His father relaxed, at last, and took his daughter's hand to bring her to the church.

It was a simple country wedding, but the sun shone on it. The guests were all in their best, the bride and groom uncommonly attractive, even for their wedding day. The groom was all in shades of brown and tan. His bright bronze hair and the bride's russet gown matched the autumn blossoms she carried and complemented those that bedecked the ancient church. She went down the aisle, showing none of the apprehensions in her heart.

They met at the altar, Rafe all smiles, Brenna all blushes.

The congregation smiled upon them. Not all the gossip was banished. But not all had to be spoken today. Much was self-evident. The groom's family wasn't there. The bride once sat in this very church with another lad who everyone knew was her chosen groom. The very reason for this wedding had been noted and much discussed. But not today, since some of the guests clearly remembered a certain redheaded gentleman's threats made at the inn in town on that evening not so long ago.

And so all the guests forgot the past as the wedding went forth, because weddings were about futures. And, too, the bride had a strapping brother and a fierce father, and the groom looked fit and dangerous, and everyone knew what they said about redheads and tempers.

As the bride and groom stood in front of the church, waiting for the carriage to take them to the wedding breakfast, Rafe said his good-byes along with the congratulations he accepted. He'd be gone after breakfast and wanted to be sure the right words were said when they could be.

"Thank you, Drum," he told his groomsman sincerely, clasping his hand. "You've been a true friend. I'll never forget it."

"Forget it," Drum laughed. "You've better things to think about now."

"Good luck," Eric said as he took Rafe's hand. "I can't think of a better man for her, and I'm happy for both of you."

"Now I've two sons," Brenna's mama told Rafe tearfully.

"And a fine new one at that," the colonel said gruffly, a hand on his son-in-law's shoulder.

Brenna had said her good-bye to her family the night before, which was good. Because she was too nervous to remember her name right now.

Then the happy couple and the guests repaired to the bride's home, where they drank champagne in sweet fruit nectars, dined on eggs and fish, meat, fowl, and fantastical aspics, pastries, cakes, fruits and breads, jams and honey. It was supposed to be a breakfast reception, but it lasted on through the afternoon. When all the toasts and jokes and promises were made, and made again, the bridal couple at last made their final farewells.

They left the house to discover Rafe's coach had acquired a blanket of flowers; the four horses that pulled it wore blossoms twined in their manes and tails. Peck, dressed for a state wedding in clothes from the last century, sat up with the coachman, his seamed face further wrinkled in smiles. The bridal couple entered the carriage in a shower of rice and petals. The groom tossed coins and blossoms back at the company. The coachman cracked his whip. The horses started, and the bridal couple were borne away.

"Well, that's done," Rafe said when they'd gone down the road and around a corner and so far out of sight of Brenna's home that all she could wave at were hedgerows. But she was still leaning half out of the window, waving.

She plopped back in her seat, wearing a broad grin. She turned and looked at her new husband, and every one of his reservations—and he'd had some at the last—vanished. They hadn't spoken a private word since they'd been pronounced man and wife. He didn't want to breathe one now. There were more important things to do, things that transcended words.

She looked deliciously disheveled. The wind had tossed her hair half out of its pins; it was a glossy, shining mass that lay on her white shoulders—or shoulder. That lovely russet gown had slipped down on one side. Her tiara of roses was listing from its moorings. Roses spilled from it; crimson petals tumbled in those glorious black tresses. Her cheeks were blushed, that smiling mouth was the color of pomegranates, and her dark, tilted eyes were filled with excitement. He saw camellia skin on that bared shoulder, he saw the rapid rise and fall of pointed, upthrust breasts.

He felt a rising excitement. *His* now. His wife, his bedmate, his chance at last to make the best of their bargain. Whatever he'd gained or lost, whatever lay ahead, they had at least that. He smiled back at her, luxuriant lust suffusing him as he put out a hand to her.

"Sush a wedding!" she said.

He paused.

"I never saw sush. Didn't my mama do us proud, Rafe, didn't she?" she caroled.

Now he remembered all the toasts she'd drunk, each one striking her as a little more hilarious than the last. He suspected much. Before he could ask more, the coach jolted, and she fell into his arms in a froth of giggles. She flung her arms about his neck and planted an enthusiastic kiss on his chin, because she missed his mouth. He sighed.

"Bren," he said, but she stopped his mouth with a more expertly aimed kiss.

It was dark and delicious. She opened her mouth beneath his; she wriggled into his arms. And hiccuped. And giggled. He tasted Brenna, and wine.

He moved away just far enough to take her close but keep her head on his chest. Safe from everything he yearned to do.

"You've had a lot to drink," he said.

"Yesh," she agreed solemnly. He could feel her head as she nodded agreement against his shirtfront.

"Let me see," he said thoughtfully. "Drum toasted us, as did your brother and your father. Your neighbor the squire did too, for a long time. Then his son did. And the vicar. And all my friends, of course. Did you refill your cup for each one?"

She giggled. He felt her nose, cold as a pup's and damp as one too, against his chest as she swung her head back and forth. "I don' remember. But I confesh I was very, very anxioush, Rafe. Very, very, very . . . anxioush." She raised her head and looked him in the eyes, her own dark with sorrow. "I didn't know if you were coming back. I almost expected to hear you'd married Annabelle. She's so lovely, Rafe," she grieved, "so beautiful, and delicate, and—and all. I'm so sorry you had to marry me."

"I'm not," he said.

"So you say," she said wisely, "because you are a true gent, Rafe, an officher and a gent, and so say all. Rafe?" she said oddly, before he could deny it. "I never get carriage-sick. Never, never, never," she said, swinging her head until a few more roses came tumbling down. "But it's bumping so! And I had some of that pudding, and some of that turkey and some of that fish . . . Do you think we could stop the carriage? Please?"

The carriage immediately halted by the side of the road. And Rafe's new bride showed him she had indeed had some of the turkey, pudding, and fish, and much more.

"I'm sorry," she moaned as he helped her into the carriage again.

"Don't be. I'm not, except for your sake," he said as she settled back in the coach. "Your stomach must hurt. I imagine you feel like the devil. It will pass. Lord knows everything else did," he chuckled. "Lie back and close your eyes."

She tried, then bobbed up like a cork in water, her eyes enormous and frightened. "That makes things spin more!"

"Let them spin—they'll stop. Close your eyes."

"If I do," she said fervently, "I'll surely die."

You'll live," he assured her. "You won't want to, but you will."

"I'm so embarrassed," she sniffled. "What you must think of me."

"I think you drank too much, too early, and too fast."

She groaned. "But if I close my eyes, I'll get sick again."

"No," he said, gathering her up in his arms and holding her against his heart, "there's nothing more to lose. Rest."

And so there is nothing more to lose, he thought as the carriage moved on and he heard her breathing become slower and more regular. The interior of the coach smelled like the back alley of a bad wineshop on a late night. His bride was tearstained, and her gown was otherwise stained too; it was a good thing he'd seen and scented many worse things in his life. He pulled back his head and peered down at her. Disheveled was enticing. Unkempt was not. He settled her against his chest, and lay back against the leather squabs of the coach. His sigh made her head rise and fall on his chest.

He'd made up his mind and acted upon it, and one of the things he'd used to convince himself was anticipation of the pleasures of his wedding night. Clearly that would have to wait. But he was used to waiting, and disappointment. It hardly mattered. There was time. All the time in the world now. It was done.

He closed his eyes to hide their expression even from the coming twilight. It was done.

Sixteen

Brenna woke. And groaned. Not from the stab of pain she felt when the sunlight hit her eyes, or the residual nausea when she raised her head to try to squint at it. But because everything came back to her as relentlessly clear as the morning sunlight that drenched the room.

She sat up—and cowered down beneath the coverlets again. She was naked! Her eyes darted around the room. She was alone. She groaned again, drew her knees up, and put her head on her arms, curling up on herself like a cooked prawn. Alone, on her wedding morning. After having been left alone on her wedding night.

She didn't blame him. She'd been sick, drunken, and outrageous. She dimly remembered being abjectly sorry, and telling him so. She clearly remembered his kindness, his tucking her under the covers, his amused but sympathetic voice assuring her the room wasn't rocking, and if it was, it would stop, and that she wasn't likely to perish from one bout of drinking, no matter what she thought. But she might die of embarrassment, she thought glumly now.

She looked around the room again. She hadn't seen it too well last night. She hadn't seen anything too well then. It was obviously an old inn she was in, with a gently sloping roof and a tilted wooden floor. A many-paned window, thick as bottle glass and crazed with age, magnified the brilliant morning sunlight. She could hear doves cooing. The curtains were white, the counterpane on the bed printed with a charming pink and white floral pattern to match. Her bed was high, overstuffed with soft feathers, the linens smooth and clean. A snug private room, a rural retreat, it would have been perfect for lovers.

She wondered where he was. And where the convenience was.

There was no sign of life except for the murmuring of the doves; the walls were too thick to let in any sounds from the inn itself. A pitcher and basin stood on the dresser by the bed. Brenna licked her lips, and could swear she felt her tongue clack. She poured a glass and gratefully drank it down. She grimaced at the taste and hastily used another glass to gargle and wash out her mouth. Then she poked one long leg out from the covers and, guilty as a sneak thief, slowly inched out of bed in search of her clothing, and the convenience, in whatever order they appeared. She refused to think about how she'd gotten out of her fine gown. She might be innocent of the actual act, but knew that drunk as she'd been, she'd have known if they'd done anything remotely approaching that . . . or at least, so she hoped.

She'd reached the wardrobe at the side of the room when the door swung open. She gasped. She thought Rafe did too. He stood in the doorway, his blue eyes blazed with sudden light as he looked at her. He was fully dressed, neat as a pin in russet and gold, his bronze hair damp from a morning bath. She smelled soap even from where she stood—or rather, crouched. She didn't have enough hands to cover everything, even though she bent double. He pulled the door closed behind him without taking his eyes from her. They stared at each other.

He was at her side a moment later. She was covered from his view a second after. Because he took her in his arms and held her close. She could feel his heartbeat against her own breast.

But she is magnificent! Rafe thought in amazed shock and delight. Her hair was as tousled as a black haystack, full of witch-knots. Her face was pale, her eyes even more tilted because they were still swollen with sleep and the aftereffects of her indulgence. But he thought she looked enchanting, literally. Because he was bewitched to silent, sudden, overwhelming lust at the sight of her naked body. Now he was brought beyond that by the feel of her in his arms.

Her face enthralled him, her body dazzled him. Long, lean, with subtle curves at waist and hip, her bottom round and high, breasts arced high over her narrow waist, her pubic thatch a sable triangle blazoned on her creamy skin. Everything about her was smooth and sleek, and looked delicious.

He lowered his head to her glossy hair. It felt like satin against his lips, and was still scented faintly of patchouli. He disregarded the other scents she'd added during their wild ride last night. His mouth traveled along her cheek, tasting the flushed warmth of her face. He splayed his hands over that silken, heart-shaped bottom and drew her closer. The feeling was electric. He caught his breath and brought his mouth to hers.

She drew back and looked up at him with a troubled gaze. "I taste terrible, even to myself!" she protested.

"Do you?" he muttered, as one hand traveled up, following the swelling lines of her body. "Do you?" he whispered, as he felt himself rise hard against her flat belly. "Do you think I care?" he asked roughly as he felt her nipple pucker and point into the palm of his questing hand.

She opened her mouth against his. If there was any bad taste left, it was lost in the shock of the harsh taste of devastating need, of intense liquid heat, of deep and dark yearning. She gasped against his mouth, she sighed as his tongue answered her, she pressed herself against him and shivered.

A step would take them back to the bed. It did. She lay looking up at him, her eyes wide with surprise, dark with desire. He laughed softly as he gazed at her hungrily. Leaning his weight on one hand, he tried to unwind his high, binding neckcloth with the other as he bent to her. But the linen was wound too tightly; Peck, damn him, had done his job too well. He abandoned the effort as he tried to shrug out of his jacket. The tight fit of it threatened to make a satire of his desire as he struggled to free himself. But the fall on his breeches was easy enough, he thought in triumph as he hastily undid it and rose over her as she lay looking at him with amazement and . . .

. . . And he was about to take his new bride like a back-street whore in the streets of Seville at a quarter past midnight on a rainy night, quickly, carelessly, and for his own immediate release.

He reared back. He turned from her and sat on the bed beside her, breathing hard, collecting his wits. No matter how eager she was, this was a thing he wanted done right, slowly, luxuriously, with time to play and learn. This first time between them couldn't be a hasty tup. And, too, he'd arranged to travel on within the hour. Take her from a quick coupling and parade her under the eyes of Peck, the coachmen and outriders? She deserved more courtesy. And he, who never thought he deserved anything, found he wanted more. He wanted time to savor this new treasure he'd found—and to be sure she did too.

"Lord, Bren, but you bewitch me," he said gruffly, "but we have to go." He rose from the bed and began to put his clothes in order.

She lay back and watched him, hardly comprehending why the fire he'd kindled in her had been so quickly doused. She was still dazed. It had been an intense moment. She'd wanted to hide, then wanted to go to him, then wanted so much more, she'd astonished herself. Her stomach began to clench and ache from unrequited desire. She felt cold with fear and shame. Again, a man she'd wanted had turned from her at the last.

She sat up, holding the coverlet to her neck. "How did I get undressed last night?" she whispered. She'd been very tipsy. She had the sudden horrible notion that more had happened after all; perhaps he was repulsed by something she'd done then?

He glanced at her and laughed. "It wasn't me, if that's what you're thinking. I wouldn't do anything while you were so besotted. I have my faults, but I have standards. You decided you were too warm. The only thing I did was make sure you didn't take off your gown on the way up to the room."

He came back to the bed and laid a hand on her cheek, his voice gentled. He stroked a thumb along her high cheekbone, "I went to get you some water, and as I did you shucked yourself out of the gown and burrowed under the covers quick as a wink. I never saw a thing. I never heard such an apologetic sot either," he added. "You couldn't stop saying you were sorry. There's no need. I didn't do anything, but neither did you. Wine's the culprit."

"But just now," she said, her eyes searching his, "why didn't— I mean, you stopped. Was it anything I did?"

"Yes. You made me forget my manners. When we love, I want it to be better than that," he said, wishing he knew how to explain it better, because she looked hurt. Probably because he'd been such a boor, he thought savagely. She might have experience, but not with a man who forgot all delicacy. "Damme, what you must think of me! Poor girl," he said sincerely. "I haven't turned into a swine simply because you married me, I promise you that.

"So," he said abruptly, because the look in her eyes was too tempting and the way her hair fell on her naked shoulders made his palms itch. "Best get dressed. You may not feel like eating now, but I'll wager a sniff of the biscuits they're baking downstairs will change your mind. The Jericho is out back, down the path at the foot of the garden. A deuced inconvenient place for a convenience, if you ask me. But it's a fine morning and they keep the place clean and sweet smelling. I'll have them send up some hot water for you. I've spoken for a private dining parlor for our breakfast. It's to the right of the stair. See you there when you're ready then.

"We're got hard traveling ahead if we want to reach the next inn by nightfall," he added, looking back at her as he paused in the doorway. "We could stop earlier on, but if we pick up the pace, we can stop at the Swan. It's a fine place, good food and an excellent reputation. I think you'll like it—it was always a favorite of mine. Then we'll be close enough to my parents' so that we can sleep late and still get there before night falls again."

"Fine," she said to his back as he went out the door. Though it wasn't. She didn't care about inns. Now she worried about this marriage and her own perceptions. Could she have been wrong? Could the circumstances have affected her more than she'd admitted? She'd painted him as a patient, courteous lover. So he'd seemed to her all through their brief courtship. But just now he'd almost completed the act of love in a moment, with only a moment's notice. He hadn't seduced her, courting in slow stages, luring her with many kisses and caresses, as Thomas had. He'd been eager and uncomplicated in his desire, his wooing as hard and elemental as he was. He'd almost taken her in a rush, not even bothering to undress.

And she'd wanted him anyway.

She didn't understand herself. Or him. Because at the last minute he hadn't wanted her, after all.

Rafe dismounted from Blaze and helped Brenna from the coach when they stopped, near noon. He'd ridden beside it, to give her privacy and time to recover from her doubtless aching head. His gaze traveled over her. He was worried; she was pale.

"We can stop here," he offered. "The inn looks comfortable. You can sleep the afternoon away. We'll go on in the morning."

"No, I can nap in the coach. I feel fine," she assured him. "Even if I didn't—I confess I don't like traveling. Maybe it's because I had to do so much when I went to India. I'd rather do it the way I take bad-tasting medicine, fast—to get it over with. Don't you agree?"

His cheeks heated. Was she making a sly reference to his lovemaking? He deserved it. "Fine," he said. "Luncheon, and then onward."

They made a good lunch, and drove on.

He rode outside, wondering if she'd forgive him, and how soon he could get her undressed again after they reached the Swan.

She sat in the coach and wondered if he'd come to her bed again. And how quickly he'd consummate their marriage, and if she could find the nerve to tell him to linger. And if he could.

But that wasn't why she could find nothing to say when she got to their bedchamber at the Swan. They arrived there as twilight fell over the moors they'd traveled. Even the darkness couldn't conceal the state of the room.

Rafe picked up a lamp from a table and held it high. His head went up. "Faugh!" he said. "This place is a sty!"

Brenna didn't disagree. Though a pig wouldn't tolerate the place.

It smelled stale, of mildew and old clothes left in the rain. The floor was stained and unswept, the rag rug on it simply a rag, the windows cloudy with ancient grime. The wavering light showed a mouse-hole in the wall at floor level. There were thready cobwebs on the sooty reaches of the low, timbered ceiling. She touched the bedcoverings with one gloved finger.

"Don't!" Rafe said. "Who knows what will jump out! No wonder there was no one in the common room," he snarled, "and Peck and the coachman had to stable the team themselves!"

He took her hand and led her down the creaking steps to the front hall, and banged a fist on the reception desk.

"Where's the owner? Send Jenkins to me!" Rafe demanded when the innkeeper slouched out of the taproom.

"Jenkins? Ha! That villain, he sold out to me three years past," the landlord complained. "I been running the place ever since. He never told me about the new road coming, did he? The new road gets all the coaches now."

Three years? Brenna thought, looking at Rafe in surprise. It had been three years since he'd been home?

Rafe checked. "New road?" he asked.

"Aye, fifteen miles to the east, it lies. Straight as a ribbon, and paved a treat. Well, you're free to go as you see fit, my lord," the landlord went on with a sly grin. "The next inn you'll come to is the White Rabbit—only three hours east from here, if you're lucky."

"Damn!" Rafe growled. "It's already dark! We can go on," he said, turning to Brenna, "but if the road from here to there is as potted and rutted as the one we just came from, I can't like taking the horses over it in the dark."

"And a west wind be blowing," the landlord said, smirking. "Rain be coming on afore midnight, or sooner."

"I leave it to you," Rafe asked Brenna. "Shall we stay or chance the night?"

"Whatever you think best," she said simply. *But if we stay, do I dare take off my clothes tonight?* she wondered.

She needn't have. Rafe forbade it.

"God knows what you could catch if you took off so much as a stocking! As it is . . ." He stared at the bed with loathing. "Good thing I've slept in worse places. Not many. But some."

In the end he produced a horse blanket from the carriage and spread it over the bed, laid his greatcoat over that, and cautioning Brenna to leave every scrap of her clothing on, saw to it that she lay down on top of his coat. He took off his jacket and lay beside her.

The silence in the room was enormous. "I don't think I should blow out the light," he told her after a moment, when the silence became less enormous as they heard faint skittering and scratching in the walls.

They were still again. But then Rafe heard another sound, and his heart contracted. He turned his head. Brenna lay on her side, facing away from him. Her shoulders were quivering. He rose on one elbow and looked at her with apprehension, ready to pick her up, pack all up, and ride off into the night if it would make her stop weeping. He put a hand on her shoulder and bent so he could see her face.

"You wretch!" he exclaimed, when she gave up trying to hold her merriment in and burst out laughing.

"Oh Rafe," she said after she subsided to giggles against his neck, "what a farce of a honeymoon this has been! First I get drunk as a sailor. Then we stop overnight in a cess-pond!"

He kissed her. He quickly drew back, so as not to tempt himself further. "At least we begin in laughter, Bren. That's not bad, is it?" he asked seriously.

"No," she said, curling into his embrace with a sigh, "not so bad, Rafe. Not at all."

"We'll do better, I promise," he told her.

"That won't be difficult," she said.

He smiled and lay down to sleep beside Brenna, his arms around her. She was a good companion, he thought gratefully, a good sport, better than he deserved after the way their marriage had gone so far. He couldn't imagine what a cosseted lady like Annabelle would have made of such a shabby start to her honeymoon . . . *nor will I*, he thought, snapping awake with a frown. Even if he couldn't keep Annabelle entirely from his mind, he had to keep thoughts of her out of his marriage bed. He sternly forbade himself to think about her while he lay so tightly snugged against this woman, his wife.

Brenna used his shoulder as her pillow. When she fell into a deeper slumber, she murmured in her sleep and laid her head on his chest, one hand on his heart. He breathed in the warm, spicy scent of her, strangely moved at how she slept so trustingly in his embrace, even in this terrible place.

Not so bad, he thought bemusedly, relaxing again. Not what he'd wanted, but he seldom got that. But this was not bad at all.

Seventeen

Neither slept much. Rafe woke at dawn and slipped from the room, not knowing Brenna was awake, feigning sleep because she didn't know what to say. It was strange waking with a man in her bed. Stranger realizing he was her husband now and wondering who should make the next move, and realizing no move could be made in this filthy place.

They made a hasty breakfast. Neither said much. Brenna saw Rafe was preoccupied and edgy. She was as well. They were back on the road at first light.

They dined more leisurely when they got to the new road and stopped at an inn for luncheon. The food was excellent, the facilities clean, and the servants efficient and charming.

Feeling comfortably full and refreshed, Brenna put her head back against the padded leather squabs of the coach when they started out again. She watched Rafe riding alongside, seeing the straight and proud way he unconsciously bore himself. He had one hand on Blaze's reins; the other rested in a fist at his hip. He rode with his head high, alert, although at the same time languid, confident, and at ease. He looked like some ancient lord surveying his newly conquered land. Brenna's eyelids grew heavy; she nodded off to sleep, smiling at the thought of Rafe as a victorious medieval hero. She woke when the coach abruptly stopped. Rafe opened the door, bringing in a gust of fresh, salt-smelling air. She sat up and smiled at him.

"Oh, I woke you?" he asked, noting her tousled hair and sleep-blushed cheeks. "Sorry."

"No, no," she said hastily, her hands going to her hair to tidy it. "I just dropped off for a moment. Mmm, is that the sea I smell?" she asked, raising her nose.

"Yes. We're very near. That's why I came in. Thought I'd point out a few things to you as we get closer to my parents' home."

"We're almost there?" she asked nervously.

"Yes," he said. "Have a look. Since we turned off the main road a half hour past, we're getting closer to the sea."

She gazed out, surprised that she could see a long distance now. They'd traveled through forests and passed bleak moors. This was neither desolate or overgrown. There were low hedgerows bordering the road. Beyond them, the land was gently curved and hilly, and she could see a glint of what had to be the sea.

"There aren't any cliffs here," Rafe commented,

"at least not like the ones to the west, or on the north coast. Arrow Court sits on a rise and dominates the village, but it isn't one of your brooding castles on a hill. We'll get to the harbor in a bit. Just thought you'd want to see the town as we ride through."

"I would," she said, sitting up and looking out the window as the coach started up again.

The road crested a hill, then she could see the sunlight glinting off the water. The ocean lay ahead, an endless expanse of slate blue with a gilded path where the sun was lowering in the west. It was all she could do not to clap her hands. "It's beautiful!" she cried.

"Yes," Rafe said, leaning past her so he could see what she did, scenting her perfume and feeling the warmth of her. His elbow was near her breast; her cheek was almost touching his. He cleared his throat and tried to ignore it. "Tide's in. A very different story when it's out. Then all you can smell is fish and seaweed. The Court faces the open water, so it's usually wild and fresh smelling."

"How lovely it must have been to grow up near the sea," Brenna said wistfully. "How you must have enjoyed it."

"Yes," Rafe said abruptly, sitting back. "I could see how easy it would be to sail away when I grew up." He realized how that sounded and added, "I might have joined the navy when I was a boy, but by the time I'd grown I'd had my fill of water and wanted something different. Well, at any rate," he said as the coach entered the little town, "as you'll see from all the nets drying, the people in town are mostly fisherfolk."

"Fisherfolk . . . and smugglers?" she asked impishly.

"No," he said, "not here. Moonlighters worked other places along the shore, by moors or cliffs where they had better places to hide. Gangs like the Gubbins and the Hawkhursts ruled this coast. They kept their trade their own. Any rate, even that's history. It's a dying practice. Peace is bringing peace to the coasts of England as much as her armies. There isn't much point to smuggling what you can buy as cheaply and less dangerously."

"You sound sad about it."

He smiled. "I am. Or would have been if it had happened when I was a boy. I was always looking for smugglers' dens. It was just the sort of thing for a boy seeking adventure and escape."

Brenna gazed out at the little town. She understood about the adventure, but didn't see what a boy would want to escape from here. The village was charming. It hugged the shoreline, its ancient stone cottages crowding up to the one road that ran through it. The narrow streets were cobbled with speckled sea stones to match those that made up the cottages. But every house was well kept; there wasn't a one that lacked flowers in the dooryard, even this late in the year. Roses flourished in the tiny gardens out front of the houses; bright blossoms blushed in window boxes and pots.

Gulls wheeled and cried overhead; she could see tall masts bobbing at anchor in the harbor at the end of the main street. Brenna could also see the villagers, congregating out of doors, enjoying the closing of the day. They sat on their front steps, or stood chatting in the street, watching the coach curiously as it passed, obviously loath to go inside on such a lovely late afternoon.

There was much to appreciate. Spectacular views of the wide and open sea could be seen at the end of every alley and between the neat cottages, and the outlook from the snug, semicircular harbor was astonishing.

There was something else bright that Brenna noticed as the coach made its slow way over the cobbles and through the town. She saw it in a fisherman mending his net, a woman gossiping in a dooryard, in a small cluster of children playing at the side of the road. Brenna giggled. It wasn't just reflections from the setting sun. Fully a quarter of the townspeople she saw had bright halos. Some were red as roosters, some brass, others bronze. Their hair was as burnished as the sunset.

"I can certainly see you come from here!' she laughed, turning to Rafe. "Is it rust in the water supply? Or a common ancestor?"

He didn't smile. "The latter," he said curtly. "Well, we should be at the Court in minutes. Don't worry," he added, looking up and mistaking her surprise at his tone for alarm at their destination. "You'll do fine. They'll like you—at least, as well as they like anyone. They've got nothing to complain about in you. In fact," he said with a gruff laugh, "that's probably going to be the only thing that displeases them."

Brenna had seen bigger manor houses and palaces, but though Arrow Court had obviously begun as a fortress, it was now a gentleman's castle. A long, winding drive led to the Court, allowing visitors to be impressed with it at several angles before they arrived there. A shallow rectangle of a reflecting pool lay in front of the house, mirroring it. Brenna didn't think it deserved that second look. Made of gray stone, over the ages the house had turned skeleton white, bleached by the sun and salt in the constant scouring sea wind. It was U-shaped with two wings at either side, the entrance in the middle, protected from the salt breeze. Brenna didn't like it; she thought it looked like a sphinx with the drive between its paws.

The coach stopped; Peck leaped down. He flung open the door for his master. Rafe stepped out of the coach, and hesitated. He looked up at the many windows glittering in the westering sun. Then he turned abruptly and gave his hand to Brenna. He smiled at her expression.

"Courage," he said as she stepped out. "What they think doesn't matter. At least not to me. Remember that."

But it seemed to her he spoke to himself as well.

* * *

A butler showed them in. "Greetings, my lord. It's good to see you again," he said to Rafe, bowing, proper as a stranger's servant.

Rafe nodded. "My lady and I have traveled far today, Atkins," he said brusquely as he stripped off his riding gloves. "Ready my room if you please. Tell my parents we're arrived, and see to my man's comforts, would you?"

Brenna felt uneasy as the butler bowed yet again and silently showed them into the salon. Rafe was friendly to everyone, but he was cool and diffident in his own family home. She glanced around as they went to the salon, getting glimpses of the house. It was formally furnished and very beautiful. The salon was a long room facing the ocean. The walls and furniture, several shades of green, muted the bright last light reflecting from the sun falling into the sea. But the man who ambled into the room after they got there brought the sunlight with him in his hair.

He was as well dressed as the most meticulous gentlemen in London. Tall and slender, he had a smooth, pale, and flawlessly handsome face. His hair was straight, fine, and lemon blond; longer than fashion dictated, it moved against his lean face as he walked. He glanced at Rafe, then stared at Brenna.

"But she's beautiful, brother!" he said. "However did you manage that?"

"Luck," Rafe said abruptly. "Bren, this is my brother, Grant. The Viscount Grant. Brother, this is Brenna, my bride. Where's Mama? And Father?"

"I see exposure to beauty hasn't softened your tongue, brother," Grant said, still staring at Brenna. "A pity. My dear, let me welcome you to Arrow Court. Was it a difficult journey?"

"No, it wasn't. It's a pleasure to meet you. How do you do?" Brenna said, putting out her hand.

"Better, now you've arrived," he said, taking her hand, holding it too long as he smiled down at her.

There was too much in what he said and the way he said it, Brenna thought. He was pitilessly handsome and probably used to females swooning over him. But that didn't make it right for him to hold her hand so long, look at her so lingeringly, or speak to his brother's new wife in such a sly, seductive way. She didn't like it. Her own brother was equally fair. Though she'd seen Eric use his looks to his advantage sometimes, his vanity was always laced with rueful humor. Grant's vanity was obviously part of his personality.

"Thank you," she said calmly, taking back her hand with deliberation. She glanced around. "What a lovely room."

"Oh, the place has its points," Grant said as he stared at her. "I'd be happy to show you them."

"Thank you, my lord," she said simply, her chin rising, "but I'd rather Rafe did the honors. That way, you see, I can hear his memories along with gathering my own impressions. I think I'd find that more entertaining."

He smiled. It was not an attractive one. "You have a champion, Rafe. How amusing."

"She has a brother who makes you look like a troll," Rafe said, "so you might as well cut line."

"How charming!" a light voice called out. "The boys are at it again."

Brenna looked up to see Rafe's parents approaching. She swallowed hard. *Poor Rafe,* she thought fleetingly as she dropped to a curtsy. His family seemed to have stepped down from a portrait on the wall, they were that perfect, beautiful and cold.

His mama was as fair as his brother; if there was gray in her hair, the thistledown lightness of it concealed it. Her face bore only a few lines; her exquisitely gowned figure was still fine for a woman of middle years. She had blazing blue eyes and long lashes she used to good effect. But her mouth was unsmiling as she studied her new daughter-in-law. Her husband, Rafe's father, the marquess, must have been a distant cousin; he looked as similar to his wife as only a relative might be. He was also the image of what Rafe's brother would be in a few decades. A little leaner, a bit grayer, but that immaculate face had settled into harsher lines, which gave it more character and less true beauty. They were three cut of a cloth. Rafe was nothing like.

Rafe was tall, and so were they. But they had fair hair and his was ruddy. He was slender where they were willowy, and his lean frame looked more hardened than refined. His features were even and good, but never as perfectly sculpted as any of theirs. He in no way resembled them, except for his eyes. They were as starkly, brilliantly blue as his mother's. In that alone he bested both his father and brother. They merely had dark blue eyes.

"Welcome," Rafe's father said, giving Brenna his hand as she rose. "Well, not only did you bring new blood to the family, I see you've added new color to our ranks too," he remarked to Rafe, though he glanced at his wife. "She's lovely. And looks nothing like you in the least," he told his wife, smiling.

"Her coloring actually enhances yours, Mama," Grant said. "How clever of Rafe, to be sure."

"No. How lucky, as I said," Rafe said. "Sorry you couldn't attend the wedding, Mama. You look quite recovered now."

"Don't say it with such rue!" his mama laughed. "I was too ill to go a step, and my dear husband wouldn't abandon me to the quacks. I am so sorry we could not be there for the happy day, my dear," she told Brenna without a shred of regret in her voice. "Though why Grant refused to stir, I do not know."

Grant's head went up. "I thought you approved," he said through a smile made of gritted teeth. "You acted like it was your deathbed, Mama. I feared taking a step would give you a fit, not to mention a fever."

"Indeed?" his mama said lightly. "I hadn't realized. Such devotion amazes me. I am indeed a lucky woman."

"I'd little choice in the matter, knowing that you'd never let me hear the end of it if I left you," her husband commented. "But your children are naturally devoted. Only see. One son stays at your bedside as loyally as a lapdog, even though the physician decided it was not more than a touch of wind. And your other neglects his honeymoon in order to bring his bride for your immediate inspection and approval."

The marchioness blanched at the word *wind*. Grant grew whiter at his father's mocking words. Rafe's face remained impassive. His father smiled. *All this spiteful teasing in front of their new daughter-in-law?* Brenna thought in astonished anger. Her hands closed to fists and she felt her nails, reduced as they were, cutting into her palms. *This nest of scorpions produced Rafe?*

Dinner upset Brenna even more. Rafe's family managed to shock her into silence. Rafe didn't say much either, except to grunt answers when asked a direct question. That wasn't often, or near often enough for a son who'd been absent for years and had just brought home a new wife, Brenna thought with indignation. Instead, his family made themselves the center of attention, performing for their visitor's benefit—or distress. They joked and teased. But the teasing had a hard and cutting edge, with everyone a victim except for the speaker at the moment.

"It's their manner of courtship," Rafe told Brenna, as her eyes widened again at something humorous and cutting the marquess said to his wife, and she slashed back at him wittily.

"They're terribly amusing," she managed to say.

"Yes. *Terribly*'s the right word," Rafe muttered.

Brenna learned much about the family as she listened, appalled. The marquess was indolent, selfish, cold, and inattentive to his family. His wife was flighty, vain, and two-faced. Their eldest son was jealous, trivial, and spent too much money on himself and his many unworthy flirts. Or at least, that was the gist of their jokes at each other's expense.

But when they said things to imply Rafe was secretive, rough mannered, and unattractive, Brenna rose to the bait and leapt to his defense.

The second time she did it, Rafe put his hand over hers. "There's no point to it," he breathed softly, as his mama laughed at a clever rejoinder Grant came up with. "You only play the game."

She realized it as he said it, and nodded. So it was a game, one that accompanied dinner from the soup to the fish, growing nastier and more pointed as the meat and poultry were borne out of the kitchen by straight-faced servants. By the time desserts were brought in, the trio's smiles were like snarls, but the terrible joking went on. Brenna wondered that anyone could eat in such a climate. It seemed to whet their appetites. Even Rafe ate and drank stolidly as he listened. She was the only one who couldn't.

"Ah, our new daughter is watching her figure," the marchioness commented when she saw yet another full plate being taken from in front of Brenna.

"It's so she can be sure we gentlemen will watch it," Grant said, with a wolfish grin.

"You'd think a fellow with pretensions to polish could come up with something more original," his father drawled. "But I agree."

"They say Byron dined on vinegar and potatoes to turn the trick. Shall we order up some for you, my dear?" the marchioness asked Brenna sweetly.

"But she is perfection!" Grant said. "She has no need to starve herself as some older ladies have to do."

"Yes, but even we don't exert ourselves to such lengths. We leave that to you gentlemen," his mama snapped.

"Come, Rafe, have you ordered her to whittle herself down to nothing?" his father asked.

"No," Rafe said.

"But look at her plate," Grant mused. "Untouched."

Brenna knew there was too much untouched that they didn't imagine—yet. She couldn't let the subject go on. At the very least, she realized her appetite and weight would be the theme of many future jests if she didn't throw them off the track. She smiled, though her hands knotted in her lap. "I usually have such a ravenous appetite!" she protested. "And the food looks delicious. But even the scent puts me off. I don't know—since I woke this morning, I've been feeling oddly bilious. And yesterday morning as well!" she remarked with much feigned surprise, blinking her eyes. "Remember?" she asked Rafe innocently.

He blinked, then grinned. He reached for one of her hands and took it in his own. "How could I forget?" he asked. "I may not be an oil painting, but few women have woken, looked at me, and then cast up their accounts!"

There was a silence at the table. The obvious rude rejoinders the others could have made froze on their lips.

The marquess was the first to recover. "Good God!

Don't tell us you're about to make my dear lady a grandmama! How charming, Sylvie. How sweet for you to so soon become a dear old lady. Who would have guessed? Surely not you. Shall we call you 'Gamma' from now on? And order up some lace caps for you while we're at it? Or would you prefer a kerchief for your graying locks?"

"Or would you care for a walking stick?" she shot back at her husband. "I can see it now—the old man of Arrow Court, hobbling out to sit on the lawns to watch all his many grandchildren playing at his arthritic feet."

"A chased silver walking stick, at least, one hopes," Grant commented with a chuckle.

"And with Rafe's dear old perennial-bachelor brother standing nearby," his father said, "still wondering why he never found the perfect mate he said he was always searching for."

Brenna didn't have to fake the blush she felt rising to her cheeks. "Oh my! I didn't mean I'm expecting a babe," she blurted. "It's far too soon for that!" She pretended flustered shock at such an interpretation of her words, realizing the idea of such an early pregnancy was sure to be misconstrued, resulting in even worse taunts from this family. "An inn we stopped at on the way here, the Swan, had terrible food," she said. "I still haven't recovered."

"Oh, the Swan?" the marchioness said with relief. "How bad of Rafe to take you there! But isn't that just like him? He learned nothing here. He hasn't a hint how to suit a lady's needs."

"Whereas I have one, my dear?" her husband asked. "Why, thank you—that's not your usual song."

"In your expertise about inns, yes," she shot back. "We weren't discussing a lady's other needs."

"How refreshing. A new topic," Grant said. "Am I to hope we've quite exhausted your complaints about those other needs?"

"But we can't discuss your needs, my boy," his father said with a sweet smile. "We can scarcely keep up with them, can we?"

They forgot Brenna as they made fierce fun of each other. Brenna looked at Rafe, the pity and the question clear in her eyes. His hand tightened over hers. "Later," he said. "I'll tell you later."

But first she had to endure the ordeal of a private interview in the salon with her new mother-in-law as the gentlemen shared their port in the dining room, as was the custom.

The lady had a lot to say about her family. Any attempt to absolve Rafe was ignored, so Brenna sat back and listened to her mother-in-law prattle on about the deficiencies of men in general. Suddenly the marchioness stopped, as though struck by a thought. She looked at Brenna and asked confidentially, "My dear, don't misunderstand, please, but I must know! Is there Spanish blood in your family? Or Moorish? Even some Gypsy who enticed an ancestor along the way? I mean some distant ancestor, of course. Because you look so—foreign."

"There are those who think Wales is another country entirely," Brenna said, laughing. "My papa often says so, because his Viking ancestors didn't venture that far west. My mama can trace her family back to Llewellen and claims she's a princess, many times removed. You must meet her; she's very tolerant of foreigners too. She believes the English are alien because they're latecomers to her homeland, you see."

Her mother-in-law didn't ask her another personal question. Still, Brenna was relieved when Rafe came into the room. After a few moments, he rose and stretched out a hand to her.

"Come," he said gently, looking into her eyes. "I'll take you for a stroll in the moonlight before bed, my bride."

It was such a loverlike thing to say that Brenna colored up and stared at him, amazed. She rose as though sleepwalking and took his hand. His parents and brother were mute as statues as he led her out of the salon, down the hall, and out the door.

The moon was indeed full and bright. It cast the white house into ghostly relief; the long drive shone out of the dark like a white ribbon in the silvery, shadowed night. The wind blew soft, scented of brine. They strolled, the only sound the gravel crunching under their feet, crickets thrumming in the fields, and the wind in the tops of trees that grew beside the path.

He stopped beneath an ancient oak and let go of her hand. The moonlight made his hair the color of any man's. Without the distraction of its hue, Brenna could at last see the stark attraction of his hard masculine face. Moonlight was her best light too; she knew it. She'd been told her hair and skin tones suited her as well as the moon fit the night sky. She lifted her face, parted her lips, held her breath, and waited for his next move.

But he wasn't looking at her. He was gazing over her head, back at the house, his lips tightened. "Sorry to make such a mooncalf of myself, and a spectacle of you," he said bitterly. "The one thing they fear is emotion. It was the only way to get you out of there. There's no sense going back until they've gone to their rooms. We're a tempting target for them. Come, it's a bright night, as light as dawn. I'll take you on a walk, show you some things as long as we're already here."

"Oh," she said, hesitating, swallowing her disappointment and embarrassment for what she had thought. "Fine . . . as long as we're already here."

He paused. "I never asked. Are you afraid of the dark?"

"No," she said sincerely. "Of many things. But not that."

"Good," he said, catching up her hand again. "I thought I'd take you in the morning, but a man must seize the time he's given. That's now. Come, I'll take you to a tomb and introduce you to a ghost. It will explain much."

Eighteen

The mausoleum stood alone on the hillside, facing the sea. It was made of the same stone as the Court, but the solitary tomb was not the same style. It was a perfect square, squat and functional.

"The man who sleeps here built both this and the Court," Rafe explained as he unlocked the gate that enclosed the mausoleum. "Ancestors added the wings on the house, windows and porticoes and such. The Griffin would have scorned them. Sir Griffith of Arrow Court, the founder of our line," he explained. "They called him 'the Griffin.' He was a warrior. It was safety he built for, not pride."

He paused because Brenna did. "Are you afraid? He was buried here centuries ago. It's just him and his lady. The others preferred the churchyard. I suppose he wanted to be near the Court, to protect it for eternity. We don't have to go in, you know. I just wanted to show you the place when I told you about him, and my family, and me. But it's not necessary to go inside. We can stay here. Or go back to the house if you want."

He seldom talked so quickly. Brenna straightened her spine. She didn't like the idea of going into a house of death at any time, much less in the dark of night. But it was obviously important to Rafe. So it was to her. She laughed. It sounded lost and lonely. She lowered her voice when she spoke again, to suit the emptiness of the night. "I'm not afraid," she said, "only puzzled . . . There *is* a lamp inside?"

Now he laughed. "Yes, and I've brought a tinder-box. Come, there are no ghosts here that aren't in the main house. Or my life."

He unlocked the door to the mausoleum. He lowered his head and stepped inside. A moment later Brenna saw a leap of light as he lit some lamps. She felt foolish after she took his hand and stepped over the doorsill. It was comfortable inside, with nothing of death or despair to be seen. It smelled of the sea and the pines that dotted the hillside. The light, from two braziers on the walls, was a warm wash of red-gold, illuminating the place. It turned the white stone walls and floors rosy as dawn.

There wasn't much inside the spare little house. There were two small, high windows and a small altar with two ancient stone caskets on either side. Both bore carved gray effigies, warmed to mottled copper by the leaping light. The stone lady lay on her stony pillow, her arms crossed on her granite breast. The warrior lay in the same pose, in full armor, his pennants and banners carved all around him, his faithful stone dog guarding his pointed stone toes. It was hard to read their features; they'd been carved by ancient craftsmen, and the years had blunted whatever details there might have been.

"The Griffin," Rafe said, indicating the warrior's casket he paced around. "Here he lies, where he lived after he won this place. 'A faire and juste Knight,' as it says here. So they all say, even to this day. He won at the lists, at the jousts, at the quintain. But he was no parlor knight. He didn't spend as much time here as he wished. The king sent him abroad to Crusade for his honor. He did. So. Here he is—the founder of the Court, and my bane."

Brenna's head shot up. She stopped examining the tomb and stared at Rafe.

"Yes, well," he said, pacing. "The thing of it is, Bren, that I'm not his get. Or probably not. It's the not knowing that keeps my parents' relationship so nicely honed and sharp. My coming here makes it worse for them, I think. At least, I can't believe they'd still live together if they ate away at each other like this every day."

"Some people—some couples—they like the cut and thrust of argument," Brenna said. "I know it's not the same, but back at home there's a farmer and his wife who delight in embarrassing each other, in telling everyone how bad the other is. Mrs. Cuddy will complain to anyone that her husband never bathes. He tells everyone she's cold as ice, and her cooking jeopardizes his life. And you should hear what he says when he's in his cups! But Lord help anyone who tells them something bad about the other! It's just the way they are."

Rafe kept pacing. She spoke faster. "Mr. Cuddy once told my father it spiced up his life—"

"Possibly, possibly," Rafe muttered. "At times it seems so here too. But the truth is . . ." He leaned against the Griffin's sepulcher and fixed Brenna with a solemn blue stare. The torchlight leaped, showing the tense set of his face as he spoke.

"Mama is flirtatious," he said with a shrug. "Always was. It was her trademark in her youth, and enchanted everyone, including my father. They were distant cousins whose parents urged the match. They weren't sure. But when they met again as adults, they married in haste. They were mad for each other. Still, they battled from the first. Everyone says so. Even Grant remembers it. I wasn't yet born when one day after a terrible fight my father picked up and moved to London. She stayed here, plotting revenge, as she told my father she would."

He levered himself up and began pacing again, his head down. "We had a neighbor, to the west. A wild young man, a ladies' man, petticoat-mad. He cut a swath through the women in London, keeping opera dancers, debauching servants, cuckolding husbands. He kept busy by gambling away his fortune when he wasn't seducing females. Pockets to let, he was finally called home by his furious father. Once here, he proceeded to do the same, of course."

Brenna had never heard him tell such a long story. Or with such frustration and sadness in his voice.

"Mama was beautiful and flirtatious. The young

man was reckless and bold. It was natural they'd meet. What they did after that is the problem. We don't know. But my father heard of the friendship." He looked up at Brenna and gave her a rueful grin. "She wrote to tell him of it, actually. He came home, vanquished the enemy, just as the Griffin would have done in his day. Maybe not. No head rolled. But at least he succeeded in evicting his rival. The young man rode away, off to the Continent this time. Where he died at the hand of another jealous husband, in Calais, I think it was. At any rate, he didn't get far in France. But the thing of it is that he may well have done here."

"Well, but—" Brenna began, seeking words to offer him solace.

He cut her off. "The young man was a redhead, Bren. Fire in the Thatch, they called him. Hotheaded, hot-blooded, and indisputably redheaded. Like me. And unlike my father, my mother, or my brother. Or either of the two infants she bore my father before me, who died in infancy. I was the last child she had. My birth ended her ability to bear more. I've always wondered how much more my birth forced her to bear."

He shook his head. "My mama's a creative liar, and always was. So her protests of innocence impress no one. Did she betray my father? Was it only with a kiss? Or more? Or me? There's no way to know. But that's why I've always known I was the seed of their discord. Or rather, that redheaded young man was." He laughed, "And of half the folk in the village as well, as you saw."

He looked at her fully, his face stark. "If I knew for certain that I was a bastard, Bren, I'd never have offered for you, or any woman. But the thing of it is, I don't know. And never shall. Are you angry I didn't tell you sooner?"

"I'm angry that you think it would matter!"

He frowned. "Of course it does. It colored my whole life—and that's not just a pun," he added with a tic of a smile. "The minute I was born and they saw my head, they hoped it was a trick of the firelight. Then they hoped it was only baby hair and would change to gold as my brother's had. Then they knew it wouldn't and my fate was sealed. So I was told. And so, I promise you, I was made to know. I've always been an intruder here. My friends saw it. I knew it. I couldn't wait to leave. I didn't love school, but it was better than here. As was the army. Any place where I could be judged for myself was better. So don't tell me it doesn't matter."

"It doesn't," she said simply. "Not to me. I don't care. If that redheaded rogue was indeed your papa, you certainly didn't inherit more than your hair from him. You're not a ladies' man. You're not a gambler or a cheat."

"Perhaps because I knew he was?" he asked quizzically.

"Maybe, but if we all could subdue our desires so easily, what a better world this would be. You're a warrior, Rafe," she said firmly, because she knew truth when she spoke it. "It's in your blood. Whoever fathered you, it's clear that the Griffin is more in your line than anyone else in your family!"

He stared at her.

"Well, but look at me," she said angrily. "Dark as a Moor, or a Gypsy, and so your mama was pleased to tell me. All my life I've been told I was exotic, not very British, and who knows what! And the men! Gentleman and commoner both. Always looking at me as though they expected me to do wonderfully improper things with them because I looked so erotic. I mean, exotic," she said, her cheeks flushing darkly. "Yes, well, there it is," she said indignantly, her eyes flashing in the firelight like the Gypsy she'd been called. "I know about my reputation in my own village. Half of it's because I was once engaged, true. But most of it's because of my looks. So what are looks, after all?"

"You look like others in your family, Bren," he said. "I'd wager on it. What about your ancestor-loving mama? You're her image."

"Well . . ." she said, stumped, because it was true.

"But as for the 'erotic' part," he said, with a slow smile, "oh, I do agree. Definitely. I can't wait to show you the truth in that too."

He came to her and looked down at her. He touched her hair, marveling at the tints of red the crimson firelight wove in it. "The torchlight makes us twins," he mused. He cupped her cheek in one large hand. "I can't wait to make us man and wife."

It had been a difficult night. He wondered if she was as appalled as he was by his family, as shamed as he was by his confession of doubts as to his paternity. For a fleeting moment he thought of what Annabelle's reaction to this wild night would have been. He wondered if he'd have told her about the circumstances of his birth at all. He had the ridiculous but uneasy notion she might have even enjoyed his family's bright, barbed quips. Brenna had clearly been dismayed. But she'd borne up under it. He was proud of her, awed by her spirit, humbled by her defense of him. And again, lured and intrigued by her sensuality.

He grazed her lips with a featherlight kiss, almost an inquiry. She put her arms around his neck in answer, and smiled, her upturned lips trembling with suppressed emotion.

She felt his need, and knew it transcended that of his body now. He gripped her closer and kissed her as though he would devour her if he could. She clung to him, seeking the center of the storm of emotions she was feeling. She found it, and more, and cast her inhibitions to the winds. She answered his tongue with her own as her hands linked around his neck and she pressed her body against his.

He raised his head at last and took a deep breath. He moved away an inch, merely holding her in the circle of his arms. She could feel a fine trembling in those arms.

"Bren, my love," he said in a shaken voice, "any more of that and we'd attempt something here that ought not to be done in a fellow's final resting place . . . though I don't know that the Griffin wouldn't love it. He was just that bold . . ." His smile vanished. "As was my mama's redheaded lover," he added bitterly. He shook his head as though to clear his vision. "Come," he said, taking her hand. "Enough of the past. Let's begin our future."

He put out the lights, locked the door and the gate. Hand in hand they paced back to the house in the stillness of the night. The silence between them was not an easy one. It was filled with growing passion. They both knew what they were walking back to find, at last.

Brenna exulted. He'd said "my love"! It might only have been a common endearment, said without thinking. But it was the first she'd ever heard from him. It was enough. He'd married her in haste, as his parents had wed. Not because they'd been mad for each other, as he said his parents had been. But maybe just because of that, their friendship had time to grow. She knew their passion had. She didn't care whose son he was. She only wanted to know whose love he was. Now, tonight, at last, Brenna thought, her entire body tingling from just feeling her hand in his, it might come to pass that he'd forget his dainty lady, and only want and love her.

They entered the house and walked quickly, wordlessly, through the hall—and almost into Grant, who stepped out of the salon and greeted them.

"Well, so what did the Griffin have to say for himself?" Grant asked pleasantly. "Too bad we don't have any amusing family legends about him greeting new members of the family as a test of their worthiness. But he is a jolly old soul, isn't he?"

Grant's pale face was flushed. His eyes glittered; his breath was redolent of brandy. Rafe faced him, keeping Brenna's hand tight in his.

"Yes, too bad," Rafe said tersely. "No amusing legends, no test of worthiness. But they wouldn't involve me, would they? Not being a member of the family, after all."

Grant's eyes widened. He whistled and put a hand up, palm out, as though in alarm, although keeping a careful grip on his brandy snifter with the other. "So! You told her. You revealed more than the Griffin's skeleton, did you? Well, what of it? Only an otherworldly test could prove a thing, and Griffin won't give it. So the only proof, if there is any, is in the tomb—here or in Calais. Or in the vault of dear Mama's memory. And that, as we both know, changes to suit the breeze. I don't think even she herself knows anymore."

"She knows her sons have no business discussing it," his mother said angrily, stepping out of the salon to confront them.

"But who better, my dear?" her husband purred as he followed.

"Indeed," Grant said with a tight smile, "who better? Who else had to constantly hear about his brave, bold younger brother and how much heart and courage the fellow had. So unlike himself. And so very unlike his father . . . or like him—who knows?"

Rafe frowned. " 'His brave, bold brother'? I never heard that."

"Oh, but his father did," the marquess drawled. "I mean, of course, I did."

"I merely commented on his war record, now and again," the marchioness said stiffly, glowering at her husband. "What you choose to construe is your own problem."

"We chose to construe all that was unsaid every

time you read the war dispatches aloud at the table," Grant said with a fixed smile that had no humor in it. "Which was every morning. We chose to construe it from all that was said every afternoon and evening too, whenever the subject of courage, or honor, or worth came up. How charming for us to know how you valued it. Especially since you obviously only discovered it in your second son."

"How charming it would have been if I'd known!" Rafe said, his eyes bright.

"I wasn't discussing you," his mother snapped, "so much as the lack of those qualities elsewhere in your family."

"In which family, my dear?" her husband asked silkily.

Brenna gasped. Rafe heard the tiny sound and turned to her.

"I'm very tired," she said in a tiny voice. "Would you mind if I went to bed?" She didn't belong here. She did, she supposed, but didn't want to. These people fed on each other. She couldn't listen to them as they crowded around Rafe like jackals and stripped him to those poor disputed bones of his.

"Right," Rafe said, nodding. "You've traveled hard today. Excuse us. We're to bed. Good night."

"Ah yes. It's not that long since your wedding night," Grant said, his eyes traveling up Brenna's tensed form and down again.

The implication was clear. So was the intent in Rafe's expression. He glowered at his brother. Grant blinked and stepped back. Rafe nodded again. "Good night," he said firmly.

"Good night," his mama replied with a thin smile, derision in her tone. "I hope you sleep well. I've put you in the bridal chamber."

Rafe took Brenna's hand and led her up the stair. They were both acutely aware of the others standing in the hall, their gazes following them. When they reached the upper hall, they heard laughter coming from the hallway below.

"They weren't angry at each other," Rafe said to Brenna's look of shocked surprise. "Or at least, no more than usual. They'll slice each other up and down awhile longer. Then Grant will ride off to the village to whatever poor idiot female he has in keeping right now. My parents will be stimulated enough to go to their bedchambers together, close as new lovers. I've seen it. It's how it is with them. Don't let it bother you."

"But it bothers you," she protested.

"But I'm used to it," he said, as he showed her into the bedchamber and closed the door hard behind them.

Brenna saw the tight set of his shoulders, the way he'd grown silent, how he prowled the room unseeing, his expression too carefully blank. She glanced around the bedchamber. It was all in shades of peach, gold, and green, with an ornate ceiling in the style of the Adam brothers. Fat naked cherubs chased each other through rosy clouds there, cavorting around an overly endowed Venus receiving the attentions of an obviously ardent Mars. It was clearly a bridal suite, and very handsomely furnished. She wished she were anywhere but there.

His family might be elsewhere, but she could almost feel their leering cruelty. After the way his mama had spoken to her and his brother had looked at her, Brenna felt assigning them this chamber was a mocking comment on her sensual looks and hasty wedding. They lived far from London and obviously hadn't heard all the rumors, and she was heartily grateful for that. She looked at the high bed heaped with silken coverlets and slowly removed an earbob, wondering what to do next. Much as she wanted to know her new husband, she suddenly felt a pang of despair at the thought of sharing the act of love with him here. Because surely anything to do with love would be corrupted here.

Rafe paced. He finally turned a despondent face to Brenna. "Right," he said. "You're right. I can't be used to it."

"That's good," she said. "That's very good."

"Right. Well," he breathed, "I'll change in the dressing room. It's late." He strode to a door and then turned. "Bren? I know I've been bucketing you around the countryside since you told the vicar you'd have me. I'll wager you regret it now. First a filthy inn, then this place, which makes you feel dirty in another way. It means more traveling—but I'd like to leave again, as soon as we decently can. Say in another day or two, so as not to give them more to talk about? If they want to see us again, they'll have our direction. Do you agree? I don't think anything good can come of us staying longer."

"Oh, Rafe," she said on a sigh of relief, "yes. Please."

He smiled and left her. She undressed quickly, washed from the pitcher and bowl on the dresser. Then, after hesitating for only a second, she braided her hair in a long, shining night braid. If he wanted it loosed, he could do it himself. If she did, it would look too much like she wanted him to. She no longer knew what she wanted, except to comfort him. She wasn't sure how to do that here.

She drew on a nightdress as fast as she could, glad she'd refused to take a maid with her on this strange honeymoon. Leaving the lamps burning, she slid into bed and lay back, as relaxed as the stone lady she'd seen in the tomb.

It was a while before Rafe appeared again. She was surprised to see he hadn't undressed. He'd removed his jacket but not his shirt, his boots but not his breeches. He padded over to her in his stocking feet and stood by the bed. He chuckled and shook his fiery head.

"You look like a nun, not a Gypsy, tonight," he said, eyeing her plaited hair, white shift, and white face. "Go to sleep. I'll lie beside you. But only that, tonight. I'll leave on my britches and keep a coverlet between us. Even though you look as eager to love as to have a tooth drawn, I'm afraid that's eager enough for me. Just the sight of you is enough for me," he muttered. "But not here."

He sat on the side of the bed. "Bren," he said, and she heard a new note of pain in his voice, "I'm not sure that's right. But I do know it's not right to even pretend love in this place. Gads!" he said, raking a hand through his hair. "I don't doubt they've got someone at the keyhole! No," he said wearily. "They've more taste and cunning than that. They just make me feel as though they had."

He bent, touched her lips with his, and whispered, "I want you. Never doubt. But I don't want us tainted by them. In any way."

Her breast rose and fell in a deep sigh. She smiled up at him. "Yes," she said, "thank you. I feel that way too."

"But don't smile at me like that. I have my limits," he said.

She didn't know if he was joking or not. He tucked her under the coverlets and then lay beside her and took her in his arms. She could hardly feel the outline of his body, but she could feel the tension in it. He settled her head on his shoulder and stroked her hair. "Sleep," he whispered. After a few moments of her senses twanging like harp strings, she relaxed.

In the end, they slept in each other's arms like weary children.

And woke feeling closer to each other than either had ever felt to any man or woman. Though they hadn't shared their bodies, they knew they'd shared something even more intimate. They couldn't say it, since neither of them was sure what exactly it was. They could only, each in his or her private heart, hope it was enough to see them through the next days.

Nineteen

"The Griffin?" Grant said when Brenna asked about him the next day. "Half of what you hear of his exploits is true. It must be. He's folklore as well as family. Everyone hereabouts sings his praises still. A hard man to live up to. I've always wondered if that's what sent you to the army, brother."

Rafe snorted. "Of course. I wanted to learn to tilt and joust too. Just as well. The French were keen jousters, you know. Thank God for my training or I'd have taken more than saber cuts in Spain. I'd have fallen in all my armor, on the wrong end of a lance."

Brenna grinned. She'd come to appreciate Rafe's humor, to see that his bluntness concealed a lively sense of the ridiculous.

She rode with the two brothers this morning. There was a heavy gray mist, but it was clear enough to see the property Grant was showing them. Now they sat their horses on a cliff-top, trying to see the rolling sea beneath. All they saw was more fog rolling in.

"No," Rafe added seriously, "I wasn't trying to ape the Griffin. The army suited me. If only because I wasn't cut out for the church and, as second son, I had little other choice."

"You acquitted yourself well," Grant said. "You won honors and respect, and almost lost your life while you were at it. You've still got the use of your arm, I see. That's good. Whatever my sins, brother, I did worry about your recovering that."

Rafe flexed his shoulder and winced. "Yes, I kept it. Days like this, I'm not so sure I should have insisted on it." He glanced at Brenna. "It's a rare old sight. You should see it," he said wryly. "Rather, you shouldn't. Scars from one end to the other. But it's still attached, and it works, though with difficulty on days like this."

Grant turned his head; one eyebrow rose as he looked at Rafe. Rafe's eyes widened, then he looked at the sea with fierce concentration. Brenna frowned, not understanding their silent conversation. She replayed the one they'd just had in her head—and felt herself blush. *It's a rare old sight. You should see it. Rather, you shouldn't,* Rafe had said.

Rafe had essentially said she'd never seen his naked body! *Well, but perhaps he doesn't undress when he makes love. He didn't when we almost did the other night,* she thought, *which is a pity, but perhaps gentlemen don't. How am I to know?* Her spirits lifted. *And so who is to know what Rafe does in his marriage bed if I don't? Certainly not his brother. Not if I don't make a fuss over it, at least.* She put her chin up. The subject was turning as unsettling as the weather was.

"The mist's getting awfully solid," she said, to change the subject. "Do you think we could continue this tour when the sun comes out again?"

"Next month?" Grant jested. "Of course. You're right, it's starting to rain. Let's get out of the weather."

They rode back to the stables. Rafe excused himself so he could see Blaze was properly rubbed down and stabled. "Peck is good with the lad, but he's off to the village, they say. I know I treat Blaze like a prince," he said, "but he treated me like one in his time, and deserves it. I'll join you shortly."

Grant walked back to the house with Brenna. She gathered up her hem to keep it from the mud, and gathered up all her courage at the same time. She was hoping to leave tomorrow, which meant she might not see Rafe's brother alone again for a long while, if ever. Hard as it was to ask him a personal question, his parents were impossible to talk to. She seized the opportunity to ask him the thing that had been troubling her since she'd woken that morning.

She paused as they reached the steps to the front door, and spoke before they went up them. "Grant?" she asked. "There's a thing I wonder if you could tell me. This redheaded man Rafe told me about—the one . . . you know. The one there were so many rumors about. What did he look like? I mean—apart from the hair?"

Grant halted. He looked down at her, amusement

and respect intermingled in his expression. "Brave girl! You mean young Rufus? The redhead? Mama's flirt? The baronet's wicked son?"

She hadn't known the name, but she nodded.

"Well, he wasn't Rafe's double, if that's what you're thinking," he answered. "I was only six, but that much I can tell you. In fact, he was a strange type to be such a lady's delight. I thought him merely amusing. He was that, very much so. Even in his looks. I think he was as successful as he was with women simply because they didn't expect him to be such a rogue.

"As to how he looked to me?" Grant asked, pausing, one boot on the stair. "Any grown man is tall to a boy, but he was particularly so, lanky and loose limbed with it. The most conspicuous thing I recall, the thing everyone remembers, is his color, of course. He was like a setting sun—a blaze of orange hair. His complexion was high too, what you could see of it beneath all those tan freckles. His eyes? I see that question on your lips. Sorry, I don't remember. But it's been discussed. Hazel, they say. Not Rafe's color. That would have been too easy."

"Nothing's easy for Rafe, is it?" she asked sadly.

"Nothing's easy for anyone here." His voice was unexpectedly harsh. He heard it himself and looked for a moment ill at ease. It was such a strange expression for him that it caught Brenna off guard. That in itself made her distrust him. This wasn't a man who was often unprepared. His handsome face was always cool and composed. It was quickly so again.

"I don't hate Rafe, you know," he said. "Or even

dislike him. It's merely that it's difficult to know him
now. I had little opportunity to do so before. I was
away at school when he was born. I saw him when I
visited here. But the years are a gulf. And the family
is not close . . ." He chuckled. "The sea is not dry," he
murmured. "But in truth, I envy him. Not just
because of you, my dear," he added, with a mock flirtatious glance at her. "Acquit me! I had to say it,
didn't I? No, I suppose I envied him for his brilliant
war record, as well as for how he neatly found ways
to keep away from here all these years. And because
Mama did speak as though he was her favorite, and
was constantly lauding him. And I feel sorry for him
because she never did when he was here."

"And your father?" Brenna dared to ask while he
was in this strange confiding mood, with none of his
sharp edges showing.

"My father?" He shrugged, in a gesture very like
Rafe's. "Who knows? He's a man of fewer words
than Rafe. And those usually spoken with irony.
Gods! But the fellow loves irony," he said, his eyes
going distant, his mouth curling with distaste. "What
he does say is usually addressed to Mama. When he
concerns himself with us, it is to amuse himself, I
think. Otherwise he only speaks in order to engage
my mother in one of their constant double-edged
personal dialogues."

His eyes focused; he looked at her again. "You
wonder why I stay on here. I don't. I tried London. I
tried the Continent. I came home. I will doubtless
leave again. Both of their sons are rolling stones, I
think. Perhaps Rafe has found his resting place now.

Gads! I didn't mean that to sound that way," he laughed. "But as for Rafe, understand me well. I do *not* hate him."

"But you admit things are hard for him?"

"Of course," he said too lightly.

"I mean, *especially* for him," she said with a touch of anger.

"Well," he said more seriously, looking down at her, all humor fled, "you can change that, can't you? If not the past, then the future, surely?"

She paused. Then she nodded, more pleased with him than she'd been since they'd met. "I can try."

But she was thinking of changing everything, if she could.

Brenna left Grant in the hall and went to her room to change her clothes. The mist had saturated everything; her riding habit was as damp as a used handkerchief, and any breeze made her shiver. There had been blowing mists outdoors; the ancient house had drafts wafting down its long corridors. No wonder Rafe's old wounds ached!

Brenna stripped off her clothes and toweled herself ruddy. She put on a warm gown, threw a shawl over her shoulders, and immediately sat at the desk in the corner of the room.

Rafe came into the room soon after. He paused, seeing her seated, writing.

She looked up. "A note to Mama," she said, "to tell her how I am, and how things are going."

"You think that's wise? If you've got time to write

her a note on the third day of your marriage, what is she to think?"

"That I'm a good daughter, because I promised her I would," she explained. "I wrote to her every day in India. It keeps us closer. And now I've a particular, somewhat delicate question to ask her that I don't think anyone else can answer."

He froze. "*Circumstance* has kept us apart," Rafe said with some difficulty, "I thought you understood."

Her head went up. So did the heat in her cheeks. "*Men!*" she finally laughed. "No, not about *that*. No, something Grant said about your ancestor set me thinking."

"Which ancestor?" Rafe asked.

She put down her pen. "The most recent one. The redheaded man you think might have been your father. I would never betray a confidence," she said quickly, "but you said everyone in the village knows. Do you mind if Mama does?"

"No," he said, though he looked cornered, on edge, on guard.

"Well, then," she said briskly, "who better to know about ancestors than my mama? If a warrior came within five feet of her family five hundred years ago, she knows of him, I promise you. And not only her ancestors. She's a historian, in her own way. I thought to write and tell her about the Griffin, as well as young Rufus."

Rafe's eyes glittered, but she went on. She'd learned from her father that things not named were more terrifying than things you knew. She thought it might be that way with things that embarrassed you too. "Something Grant said—about colors—is nagging at me. He said Rufus was carrot topped. But you're not. Your color's russet. May I tell her everything and ask her about that?"

He relaxed. "Russet? Carrot? You ask if you may split hairs . . . literally?" he asked with a smile as the truth of the old adage in his case occurred to him. "Why bother? If there was any proof, I would've been disowned years ago. Or absolved. Don't worry about me. I've lived with it long enough to accept it. But if it troubles you, do as you will."

"I'd like her opinion. So may I?"

"Of course," he said. "Now, if you don't mind, I'll change my clothes. I smell like Blaze and feel like a landed fish. I'd forgot how it is here when the sun is gone."

She bent to her letter again. So far as she was concerned, the sun never shone here; it was a place of mists and ghosts, and cruel memory. *Only another day*, she told herself, and wrote on, hoping the letter might pave the way to a brighter one.

The day they left Arrow Court was a bright one for Brenna, even though storm clouds raced in from the sea. Rain dashed against the coach window, blurring her last look back at the Court as she and Rafe drove away.

The sulking mists had been blown away. A freshening wind from the west kicked up; an autumn squall was coming. Rafe's parents had warned them of the coming storm. "Then we'd better hurry and get on our way," he'd said, refusing their offer of another night. "It's a popular inn. They won't hold our rooms if we're late."

Now they were in the coach, leaving. Brenna's spirits soared.

"I hope the roads don't turn to mud," Rafe said, looking at the sky. "I'm sorry I rushed you out, but I thought you wanted to leave."

"No," she said, "I *yearned* to."

"Thank you for your courage and understanding," he said seriously. "It can't have been easy. Damme! What a honeymoon I took you on. I'll make it up to you. Where would you like to go now? Where do you want to be?"

"I'd like to be in one place, with you," she said. "You name it, and that will be my place."

He looked a little stunned. Then he brought her gloved hand to his lips. "Thank you," he said sincerely.

Twenty

They got to the inn just before night fell. It was everything the Swan hadn't been.

Their room was large, the bed enormous, piled high with clean coverlets and pillows. The walls were thick, the windowpanes solid. Brenna could hear the wind tearing up the world outside, but it was snug here, and the firelight cast warm russet reflections on everything. There was no dirt or vermin, and thinking of that, no evil relatives either. Brenna sighed with relief.

"Weary?" Rafe asked, as he came up behind her. "Well, rest. We'll set out when the weather clears and not a moment before. There's no hurry anymore, Bren."

She nodded. That was true. They were going to London. But then? The world, and in particular their world, was a long, open road before them. Years stretched ahead. She crossed her arms over her breast, hugging herself. She'd no idea of what those years would hold. Her feeling of contentment vanished. Now, suddenly, she realized she was in this place with a man, a relative stranger, who'd share all those years with her. And her body as well. She'd wanted him as husband; she had him now. But the whole adventure of their meeting and marrying seemed rash and bizarre, now that she'd stopped traveling and could think.

"Don't," he said, coming up behind her and putting his arms over hers, holding her so she rested against his chest. "Don't worry. I can see it in your eyes," he said to her questioning look as she turned her head to see him. "Such telling eyes you have, Bren. You could never speak again and yet say everything with them, I think. Yes. It was a rare muddle we got ourselves in. Now we can sort it out. Don't worry. We will."

She nodded, and stirred. He released her instantly.

"Yes. Well," he said with resignation. "So. I see we have to start anew, do we?"

He was still as a statue watching her, the firelight casting him in bronze. There was weariness in his face, a certain sorrow that called to her, if only because she knew how hard he tried to conceal it. *Poor Rafe*, she thought. *He'd plenty of practice at that, hadn't he? All his life, in fact.*

It wasn't just pity that stirred her now. There was that. But there was also a long-denied hunger and curiosity, and a need to let him know she wanted to comfort him and needed him to comfort her too.

"Rafe?" she said softly. "We need to start. Anew or not. Don't you think?"

He studied her a long moment. "I'd like to," he said, but didn't move.

She smiled, tremulously. "Yes," she said, lowering her gaze, "I mean *that*."

She wondered if she'd die of embarrassment, or hurt, when he still didn't make a move toward her. It wasn't a filthy room, she thought frantically, nor was his family there. Was it that Annabelle's spirit was still haunting him? Or . . .

He closed the space between them in a second. He swooped her into his arms and hugged her hard. He laughed, his eyes sparkling. "Damme, Bren! But you are a one! There I was, worrying what to say, how to broach it. I'm not good with words and didn't dare make a move. How could I? I've brought you nothing but confusion since we met . . ."

He stopped speaking and looked down at her eyes. They were wide and dark and deep. But he saw no refusal in them, only a searching question. Her lips were parted. Those lovely upturned lips. He kissed her, and answered her question. And stopped worrying.

He smiled all the while he shrugged out of his jacket, never taking his eyes from her. He put his hands over hers as she fumbled with the ties on her gown. "No," he whispered. "My job."

He kissed each inch of skin that came into his view as he slid her gown off. Her hands tried to seek his skin through his shirt. But it was a fact of life that she wore less than he did, and so she soon stood naked in the firelight before him, while he still wore shirt, breeches, and boots.

So he does keep his clothes on, she thought sadly, her hands going up to cover herself. He smiled at her belated display of modesty. "I feel like some kind of slave girl," she murmured in embarrassment, suddenly struck by the inequality of their positions.

But so she looked to him, like some temptress from an erotic tale of a lucky traveler's encounter with a harem girl, as she stood clothed only in her inky tresses and golden firelight. Her breasts were high and dusky peaked, those peaks taut from the cool of the room, or her excitement as she saw his eyes go to them. One of her hands tried to cover the dark triangle between her long and shapely legs, emphasizing it. His gaze roved over her. Her waist curved, as did her hips; she had a gently rounded curve of a belly. She was a symphony of sensuous shapes.

He wanted to tell her so. He wanted to tell her she was no one's slave, he was instead slave to his desire, humbled because her passion matched his own. Overwhelming lust stopped his tongue. "No slave, no more than I am," he could only murmur, trying to say it all.

He broke from his reverie and took her in his arms. His mouth found hers, his tongue touched hers, his hands discovered her, then clutched her closer. When she hung her arms round his neck, his hands were free to learn her again.

Impatient, he picked her up and took her to their bed. He left her only long enough to tug his boots off, and then, with a muttered oath, left off undressing himself to return to her. She was waiting for him, in every way.

Her mouth was hot under his; she squirmed at his every touch, and he touched her everywhere, rejoicing in the feel of her and her incredible response to him. His body ached for her; actual pain suffused him. Even that was delicious. Somehow he found the time, between tasting the dark wine of her lips and the nutmeg spice at the tips of her breasts, to drag off his neckcloth and pull off his shirt and his breeches.

But he had to keep stopping to return to the feast of her body. She smelled of rare flowers, salt, sea, and heated female skin. Soon that skin was as damp as his; his hands slid as they caressed her. Soon after, he found the entry beneath that dark apex was slick, ready for much more than his questing touch. He could scarcely believe his luck.

She was everything her looks had promised, eager, knowing, welcoming, ardent. So very ardent that she made him forget his resolve to take his time. He felt like a starving man permitted at a feast. It was not so much greed as overwhelming need—his, and hers, he'd swear it. Lost in her taste, brought to a fever by her touch, and brought to unbearable excitement by her blessed eagerness, he found there was no more time to play at love. There was only time to groan at the sorrow at having to leave off that delicious play and catch his breath at the thought of what lay ahead. Only time to whisper his intent and delight, and rise over her. And then only a last second to sigh at the incredible wonder of it before he joined his lips and his body to hers at last.

Then there was only time to realize, as she stiffened beneath him, that something that had been hindering his advance had suddenly given way as he gripped her bottom and drove into her. There was no longer time to help her share the incredible ecstasy of what he was doing or to pause because he was bringing her pain. He was a man with absolute control, but it was much too late to stop. The way was clear; he surged into her again and again because his body demanded it. But there was alarm mingled with his rapture when he reached his moment at last.

He dropped his head to her shoulder, shuddering with relief, and appalled. He rose up on his elbows again.

"Bren," he said, seeing the blank shock in her eyes, "I didn't know! By God, you didn't tell me. I'm sorry, but you never said!" She closed her eyes and he saw tears at their corners. "Bren," he whispered, "I didn't know. I thought . . ."

"You thought my morals matched my looks," she said dully.

He took a breath. "But you—you never said otherwise."

She didn't answer. He realized it hadn't been her responsibility to tell him. It had been his to believe the best of her. He levered himself up and looked down at her and himself. He winced, and felt his stomach knot. Blood was part of his stock and trade; he was immune to the sight of it. Not this blood. There wasn't much, but it was far too much. It was hers. He'd never thought of sex as a medical matter. He should have. It made him feel even worse.

"Did I hurt you?" he asked, dreading her answer.

"No . . . a little, I suppose," she said. The burning pain had subsided to a dull ache, and it wasn't just physical now.

She closed her eyes and turned her face aside so he wouldn't see her disappointment, and sorrow. She was dazed, disturbed, and growing angry—with herself. Why had she been so rash, so eager?

He heard it in her voice. "I'm sorry. If I'd thought, I'd have been able to make it easier." *Maybe*, he thought; he didn't know. He'd never thought about it.

He covered himself and went quickly to the wash-basin, poured water on a cloth, and returned to her, wordlessly. He'd taken her as a man would take an expensive whore, with enthusiastic lust and no expectation of encountering innocence or resistance. He knew; he'd done it in his time. He'd never known a virgin. If he'd imagined she was one, he'd have prepared her for hours before he'd tried her.

He'd have, by God, he thought in shame; he'd at least have fought himself and not let passion strip him of grace as well as reason. He'd mistaken natural generosity for eager experience, and felt like a clod, a fool, a man who had misused a rare gift. Mostly, as usual, he felt unworthy. He handed her the cloth. "Use this. Or shall I?"

She sat quickly and drew herself up into a knot of arms and knees. "I'm sorry," she said. "I'm making a muddle of this, aren't I?"

"You?" he asked. "By God!"

He put the cloth aside. He perched a hip on the bed and put an arm around her. "I'm not good with words. Not much good with actions either, am I?" he asked bitterly. "Bren. Look. You felt so good, you were so willing, I didn't think. I never knew a maiden. Or thought one would be interested in such as me. I can be gentle. I want to be. Please, don't be angry, or give up on me."

She peeked out from the curtain of her hair. "I'm not angry with you."

"You should be."

She sniffed. "It's as much my fault. I mean, I was crazed too, wasn't I? And everyone thought that since I was engaged—and since I never told you otherwise . . . But I didn't know it would hurt!"

He scowled. "It won't again. Look, can we mend this?"

She looked at him warily.

"Not right away," he assured her, as he stood again. "I'll just go wash up now. But you'll see. No more pain, Bren. Never again. Only pleasure in the future, I promise. And not until you want it."

When he returned to her, she'd washed, put on her night shift, and burrowed under the coverlets.

He shed his robe, slipped beneath the covers, and drew her into his arms. She laid her head on his chest. She was stirred by the feel of that naked chest against her cheek. And saddened too. *So,* she thought with little satisfaction, *he doesn't wear clothes to bed, at least.* Well, that was something; it did feel good. But it wasn't enough. She'd wanted so much, and gotten so little. She'd gotten the pleasure of knowing she gave him pleasure, and that was something, she supposed. But for herself? The prelude to love had been thrilling, but the actuality had been only a painful and bewildering scramble, almost violent and certainly not sweet. No wonder men were so interested in females. No wonder women made them marry before they let them make love. She gulped down her sudden self-pity. His arm tightened around her.

He smelled of firewood and shaving soap. Silken hair covered the hard muscles that lay beneath her ear; it tickled. The pain he'd caused had stopped, subsiding to a dull ache that yet held a curious throbbing that was almost pain. It grew as she thought about how close he was to her. She moved her head and heard the rapidly accelerating beat of his heart. She put her hand over it and felt his body react. It reminded her of how even the sturdiest steed would twitch and shudder at the merest touch of a fly on its sleek hide.

"Your heart is beating so fast," she murmured.

"For you," he whispered, his warm palm on her back, "it beats only for you. No more for now. Except for sleep."

But she couldn't sleep with him so near and so obviously awake. She heard it in his heartbeat; she felt it in his breathing.

"Bren?"

She picked up her head and gazed at him.

"Oh, Lord, but you make it hard for me," he breathed.

She startled; her eyes went wide.

So did his. He heard what he'd said, and silently

cursed his clumsy tongue. This was no time for a warm jest. But surely she hadn't understood that other coarser meaning? He dared not stir lest she know how very much true that other meaning was.

"Do I?" she giggled, then looked, then dropped her head again and smothered her laughter against his chest. "So I do," she gasped.

Now *he* startled.

"I lived with the army," she said, smiling at his reaction. "I heard many things."

"Little wretch," he said tenderly, stroking her back, vastly relieved that she could and would laugh with him, even now. "That's not what I meant."

"Wasn't it?"

His hand stilled. "Maybe not ... You don't mind?"

"I don't. I'm flattered."

"And interested?" he asked, and held his breath.

She considered it. Surely women were not such fools as to endure pain for nothing but someone else's satisfaction? Perhaps she should wait until tomorrow, though? But he was so near, and so dear to her. The longer she waited, the more nervous she'd be. And he might not understand. Her mama always said the moon should never set on a married couple's quarrel. This wasn't one, but it was certainly a misunderstanding. Or was it? She was curious. There was so much that hadn't been realized, his mere presence promised so much more, and he'd said there could be more ... and he'd never lied to her. That decided her.

The end of her night braid tickled his chest as she

nodded. He ran a hand through the braid, loosening the silken burden, spilling it across his body until he could hardly breathe for the cool, perfumed splendor of it against his skin.

"Bren?" he asked. "May I do now what I ought to have done then? Slowly, and carefully?"

She swallowed hard. She nodded again, "I'd like that."

"You will," he vowed.

This time he didn't help her remove her night shift until she was trying to tear it off herself. He threw the covers back when their kisses and embraces made their temperatures soar higher. Last time they'd made love in a blur. This time she saw him entirely, and reveled in it. His body was strong, she knew. She knew it was shapely; his tight-fitted clothes couldn't conceal it. But she hadn't known his skin would be so unblemished, the hair upon it ruddy as his astonishing sex which rose against his flat, ridged, muscular abdomen.

He saw the direction of her gaze and how her eyes widened. He paused, amused and pleased. Then he saw how she looked away in embarrassment.

"It's not a thing I can help. It's not a thing I want to," he whispered. "It's how men are. It's my body's way of showing appreciation of you. God knows I do."

"As I do you," she whispered back to him, and looked her fill this time.

She was utterly enthralled with him. But her expression changed when he rose over her to take her in his arms.

"Oh!" she couldn't help blurting when she saw his shoulder.

"Yes," he said, rearing back, all thoughts of dalliance interrupted. "Ugly. I'm sorry."

She couldn't deny it was a startling sight in contrast to his well-formed body. A welter of thick scars, the shoulder still showed stitches hastily and inexpertly set, the musculature itself redefined by the terrible wound that had sliced down his arm. But she could refuse his bitter apology.

"Why should you be sorry?" she asked, touching a bulge of scar tissue. "I've seen worse. You should see Eric's leg! Makes this look like a fine tapestry."

He gazed at her, astonished.

"Oh!" she said in chagrin. "And here I was angry because you didn't think I was a maid! How could you, when I talk about men's bodies like a . . . trull from the tail of the army!"

"I've always wanted a trull," he breathed against her neck. "Would you be my own trull, please?"

She laughed. And lay back where he gently placed her, and sighed as his lips found her breast. This part of lovemaking was wondrous. She relaxed, then arched her back and stifled a surprised moan as his mouth slowly traced tingling fire down to her stomach too. She was a little embarrassed, then beguiled by the strange tickling sensations he aroused. It went beyond laughter to something beyond her imaginings. So much so that she wasn't prepared for the natural end to the path he so leisurely took. Suddenly, thoroughly astounded, she froze and locked her long legs shut.

Rafe stopped too. It wasn't easy. He raised his head with difficulty, because he was very excited. He'd had lovers. He'd shared pleasure. He knew what women liked; he'd done much and heard more. Now he was afire to do even more with this delicious, exotic, responsive woman—his wife! But he'd never had to prove the joys of love before. He realized he had to proceed carefully. His mind told him that. His mind had little to do with his craving.

"It's all right," he said huskily. "If you still don't like it in another minute, I'll stop. But I think it will please you if you let me."

She considered it.

He knew he had won.

He kissed her lips before she could answer. When he felt her relax again, he went on, blazing a trail down the same inexorable, incredible, thrilling path. She didn't stop him again. She couldn't even think to do it by then. She never wanted him to stop again.

They had their honeymoon, and reveled in it.

She loved his plain speaking and elaborate lovemaking. She was enchanted by his gentleness, his patience, and the way he could lose his patience and bring her to exaltation even so. This thing they had together was wondrous, and best of all for her, it was obvious that they shared it.

He taught her much, showing her how to please him and herself, rejoicing in her lack of false modesty, her acceptance of her own desires as well as his. She taught him how a woman's unfettered, honest giving could make even such a pleasing act better than he'd ever known, changing it from something delicious to a thing approaching glory.

They were extremely pleased with themselves and each other. It was a true honeymoon for both of them. But it only lasted days.

She got her monthly courses. For the first time since they'd come to the inn, she spent a day in bed with a hot water bottle, not his warm hand, covering her abdomen. He went out riding to give her the chance to recover. Apart, they shared the same disturbing thought. They both wondered about the reality they'd left behind and had to face again. Sooner or later they had to leave their idyll at this little wayside inn and get on with building a life, facing down rumor, establishing themselves in the world. They'd gained a rare understanding of each other's passions. There hadn't been time to build more yet. They had, after all, not really known each other that long. There was much more to learn and do.

"Soon as you feel better then," Rafe said a few days later when she asked him about their return to London.

"I feel fine. It's almost over," she said, blushing.

"Is *it*?" he asked with a grin.

"You know what I mean. But I'll miss this place," she said wistfully, looking around the room where they'd shared so much.

"We'll take the best part of it with us."

"The bed?" she asked, pretending shock.

"If you wish, that too," he said, amused, "my lusty bride."

"Is that bad?" she asked. "I mean, it's not very ladylike of me."

"What nonsense. It's very good. Do you want even more praise?"

She laughed. He was very generous with his praise. For a short-spoken man, he talked a lot while at the act of love. But when he went down to see Peck to ask when they could leave, her smile slipped away. Because when she thought about it she realized all he'd ever praised had been her breasts and her belly, her mouth and her rump, and other body parts he enjoyed. That and her willingness to share them with him, and learn more about his own body and its responses.

It was praise. But it wasn't what she was waiting to hear. There hadn't been a word of love apart from easy endearments in the act of love. She wondered if she ever would hear any. He was, after all, a blunt man. She put the thought away. No sense being greedy. If she'd wanted poetry, she'd wait the rest of her life. She had Rafe. It was a good bargain and a fine beginning.

Her hands paused on the traveling case she'd opened. *A good bargain and a fine beginning?* It was so much more. Why was she denying it? She'd been delighted to marry him, convinced she'd tumbled into love with him. She hadn't known the half of it. Now she was, with no exaggeration, plainly and simply and utterly mad about him. But better if he didn't know that—or at least not until he said he was in a similar state . . . She bit her lip. This was *Rafe*, after all. So, she decided, if he didn't confess to a similar state, then she wouldn't. At least, not until she got some hint that he was in that general vicinity.

But thinking of vicinities, she realized they'd soon be in London.

And the woman he'd loved and wanted to marry was still there.

It was a rainy morning in London. The lady Annabelle sat in her bed, drank her morning cup of bitter chocolate, and skimmed the newspaper. Her father always left it for her after he'd gone to his club. Her gentlemen callers loved to spout the latest gossip to her because she seemed so impressed by their knowledge. The truth was, she preferred to know things firsthand, and was interested in more than gossip. But she put her cup down on the tray when her eyes fell on an item in the social listings.

Her face paled.

"Anything wrong, my lady?" her maid asked, seeing her sudden distress. "Anyone died?"

"No—yes, in a way. It doesn't signify," Annabelle murmured. "Lay out something bright for me to wear," she said absently. "It's such a gloomy day."

It was worse that that. *He'd actually gone and married her! Dalton had wed the scheming, lying cheat who'd stolen him away.*

Annabelle closed her eyes in pain. The more because she realized nothing could have forced him to it but his sense of honor. She believed he hadn't actually compromised the wench. So it must have

been her own spreading of gossip that had driven
him to it.

She wasn't used to blaming herself. It hurt more
than his betrayal. *Betrayal?* He'd promised her nothing; she didn't know if she'd have married him if he
had. But she'd considered him, and she'd only considered one other as her possible husband—and now
she'd lost each to less worthy women. *What did those
women do that she didn't? What did they know that she
did not?*

"Annabelle?" her mother asked as she hurried
into the room. "What's this? Your maid tells me
you've had a weak spell? Because someone died?"

"The silly goose!" Annabelle laughed with difficulty. "No, nothing like. I was just reading the paper,
births, deaths, marriages, and such. Speaking of
which, see here," she said in a tight voice. "Dalton
actually *married* that slut of his!"

Her mother scanned the paper, thinking rapidly.
She ached for her daughter and knew she shouldn't
say it. "Such a hasty wedding," she said instead.
"Needs must when the devil drives, I suppose. He was
mad for you—never doubt it. Doubtless there will be
an heir beforetime. Or she told him there would be."

"I doubt it. I believe him. He is honorable,"
Annabelle said.

"Honorable?" her mother scoffed. "He's a *man*.
Even the best of them will take what's free, even if it
isn't the finest. She lured him. He couldn't help himself. She was the dishonorable one."

It made sense, Annabelle thought. And it was

much too painful to keep thinking she'd caused this terrible thing because of her flippant, too hasty tongue. Anger and hurt, guilt, and an overwhelming sense of futility made her gratefully accept it. "Poor fellow," she murmured half to herself, "to be so cheated. But what good is it to know? It's done."

"Not quite," her mama said. "She shouldn't go unpunished."

"What?" Annabelle asked on a shaky laugh. "Are you going to challenge her to a duel, Mama? Hire someone to slay her? Be sensible. She's a clever slut—she won a good man. It's a tragedy for him, but there's nothing you can do now."

"At least we can let people know the truth," her mama said. "So she'll never be able to hold her head up in polite society again. She wanted respectability as much as his name, I'll wager. Who knows whose child she was carrying, appearing out of nowhere, coming from foreign parts like that?"

Annabelle sat still; she hadn't thought of that. *Poor Rafe,* she thought with growing delight. "But they're gone now," she said hastily, "so how can it matter what we say?"

"They have to come back to London sometime."

Annabelle thought about it. "Poor Rafe," she finally said aloud, this time with tremendous relief. Talking about her failed courtship with him would be like a crusade now. Not a defeat.

Twenty-one

"This is one of the finest streets in all of London," the housing agent said proudly as Brenna looked around the salon in the town house he'd taken them to.

"Maybe," she said glumly, noting the small windows and low ceilings, "but we're not going to live in the street. Though it might be better if we were. At least there'd be light there."

"Dark as a cave," Rafe agreed. "Got anything with sunlight?" he asked the agent.

"In the afternoon this room is flooded with sunlight," the man said quickly. "It's late morning, my lord."

"But it will feel this close even in the afternoon," Brenna said. "You know," she told Rafe, "it's not necessary for us to move at all. We'll do very nicely in your house."

"So you've said," Rafe said, "but a new family needs a new house."

Her face flushed. He was right. They might become a family soon enough. They'd only been married a short time, but essential biology made his reasoning valid. Exceptional desire made it even more so. But she didn't like this house. "Well then," she went on doggedly, "I don't think this place gives us that much more room. It has more bedchambers, but they seem cramped, and this room ought to be the biggest and—"

"And it's not for us," Rafe told the agent. "Anything else to show us this morning?"

"There's a charming house facing the park," the agent said.

"I don't think so," Rafe said. "Facing the park means facing the crowds going there."

"Shrubbery has been planted," the agent argued. "Nothing can be seen from the front windows but greenery."

"And nothing can be heard but carts, wagons, and horsemen going by. No," Rafe said. "Maybe we'd better look elsewhere with another firm, one that knows London as well as I do."

"There's a *most* distinguished property on the square," the agent said hastily, "not two streets from here."

Rafe hesitated. That was where Annabelle lived. But it was one of the finest districts. He thought fast. For all its size, London was a small town for the fashionable. If he wanted to avoid Annabelle, he'd have to move to the country. And why shouldn't Brenna have the same advantages he'd have given Annabelle?

Brenna and the agent waited for his answer. Rafe nodded. "Yes, we'll see it. When?"

"This afternoon? After luncheon?"

"Give me the address. We'll meet you there," Rafe said.

"That's probably his best listing," Rafe told Brenna as they strolled down the street after the agent left them. "It's the third property he offered, and so the one he really wants us to see. The first they take you to is so dismal you get discouraged. The second almost fits the bill. The third's perfect, of course. And higher priced than the others. A clever trader does that with all sorts of goods, not just houses. Damon Ryder told me that, and if it's anything to do with money, he's usually right. I think we'll find our house this afternoon."

"But why bother?" Brenna said. "Rafe, it's not necessary yet. Certainly not for me. I can be happy in your town house until we really need more room."

"You deserve more."

"But I don't want to be an expensive wife."

He stopped and stared down at her, his expression amazed. "But you are," he said. "Two eggs at breakfast, *and* a muffin as well? I'll be in the workhouse before you know it."

She smiled. He put his hand over the hand she'd placed on his arm and went on down the street with her again. "Bren, I've funds," he said more seriously.

"I like spending them on something worthwhile. You. Me. Our future."

It was a cool day, but the sun was bright. But nothing could be warmer and brighter than the cockles of Brenna's heart. He'd wed her out of honor, but he paid great honor to her, and had since their wedding day. She allowed herself to think one day he'd realize what had looked like cruel circumstance had turned out to be the best luck in disguise. It had been from the first for her.

Everything about him continued to delight her. His unique looks, that vivid coloring, his military bearing, his quick understanding. Other women might find him gruff, but she knew army men and realized it was only a facade to disguise how tender he really was. She grieved for his low opinion of himself, but thought it might account for his unflagging kindness to others. She appreciated his sly sense of humor and that absolute sense of honor. The way he made love, the courtesy he showed her in everything . . .

If he'd ever loved another woman, she saw no sign of it now. He wasn't a secretive man; she must have won him over completely! She smiled up at him, feeling proud, content, and incredibly blessed.

Today she thought he looked particularly fine. It was cool, but Rafe, claiming his blood was hot, seldom wore a cape or coat. He didn't need to cover himself; he was a fine figure of a gentleman. He wore a high beaver hat, a dark blue jacket, a gray and blue waistcoat, and biscuit-colored breeches.

By happy chance, her own costume matched his.

Her gown was periwinkle, her pelisse a darker blue. Her bonnet was biscuit colored and had a brave blue feather in it. Peck must have picked out Rafe's clothes after having a look at what she'd had on this morning. She and Rafe shared a bed, but they had separate dressing rooms, and she'd gotten dressed first.

She knew a fashionable lady should have a maid. But she wasn't used to being fashionable, and hesitated to add another to her intimate household just yet. Peck was different. He was Rafe's old army companion as much as his valet, and the soul of discretion.

"Rafe!" a voice called, interrupting her thoughts. "My lady Brenna!"

A tall, dark gentleman with a long, clever face and a distinctive nose strode toward them.

"Drum!" Rafe said with pleasure. "Well met!"

The two friends shook hands. Brenna ducked a bow as Drum took her hand and looked at her keenly. His azure eyes lit up as he studied her. "Marriage suits you," he said with pleasure. "Though nothing could make you lovelier, my lady. You have a glow. This rascal looks positively jolly. I almost didn't recognize him."

"Maybe you need spectacles," Rafe said. "One look at my hair would clear up the matter. Happiness doesn't change that. But you're right. I am happy. A remarkable lady, this wife of mine." He gazed at Brenna fondly. He only recalled himself when he realized Drum was watching him with a slowly growing grin.

"And what a wife she is!" he told Drum, in mock

complaint. "Frugal as a parson. As demanding as a nun. She doesn't want to inconvenience me enough to move from my bachelor quarters. I practically had to drag her out this morning to see houses . . . Wait! The very man! You're a knowing one. I want Bren to have a home she can be proud of. I can tell what looks good, but maybe not what's a good address and likely to remain so. Tell me which districts we should avoid."

"Note what a pessimist it is," Drum remarked to Brenna. "He doesn't ask where to look, only where not to. Your work's cut out for you, my dear. You've got him smiling. Now you've got to get him to believe good things are likely to keep happening. As for good districts—this is one. But it's best nearer the square, I'd say. That's where the fashionable promenade, but not close enough to get in your way."

"As I thought," Rafe said, nodding. "It's where we're going after luncheon. Join us?"

Drum hesitated.

"We don't coo or cuddle, I promise," Rafe added. "We're an old married pair now. It's almost three weeks. Well, at least it's been twenty days, and we're fit for company. Unless Bren here loses her head and throws herself at me. She does do that, you know. Watches me meekly, then something snaps and she lunges for me. Shocking."

Brenna pretended to try to snatch her hand from his. Her spirits soared even higher. He'd counted the days just as she had!

"I'll come along," Drum said, "*if* she promises to restrain herself—I'm easily embarrassed. I can catch you up on what's been happening here. You can tell me about your travels."

"We went home," Rafe said, his smile vanishing. "To Arrow Court. But didn't stay above three days."

Drum fell into step beside him, his expression altering too. "Yes, well, that makes sense," he said thoughtfully.

"Introduced her to the Griffin too," Rafe said.

"It's a ritual," Drum told Brenna. "I met him when I stayed with Rafe on school holiday. He terrified and fascinated me. He obviously inspired Rafe."

"That's too bad," Brenna said, "because if he hadn't, just think of the other career Rafe could have had, as a second son. If it weren't for the influence of such a fierce ancestor, imagine what a humble, peaceable, placid vicar Rafe could have been—he might even have been made a bishop!"

They laughed at that. They laughed and talked all through their luncheon. The earl of Drummond was one of Rafe's oldest friends, and Brenna was delighted to see how easily he led Rafe into reminiscing. She learned more about Rafe's past at luncheon than she'd done since she'd met Rafe's parents. He didn't easily talk about himself, but Drum knew how to draw him out.

"We met at school," Drum explained, "with little in common. I was ferociously homesick and furious at having been exiled. Rafe was delighted to be there. But we discovered common cause."

"Misbehavior," Rafe laughed. "This fellow was the most inventive boy there. He knew how to get into mischief immediately. That always takes one's mind off miseries."

"And this one," Drum said, "never refused a dare. He set high standards for me."

Brenna didn't learn much of Drum's background. She could easily believe he'd been a superior spy. He knew how to turn the conversation away from himself with laughter or questions, or plain artifice. But for all his secrets, she could easily see how much Rafe valued him. That was enough for her—until Drum went along with them to see the third house the agent had to show. Then she could have happily strangled him.

"Tolerable," Drum drawled after they'd toured the house. Brenna's head shot up. She loved the place, light and airy, with high ceilings and wide windows and modern conveniences, such as gaslight and indoor plumbing even on the second floor. It had a graceful garden in back, with the stable conveniently to the side. She couldn't wait to tell Rafe how perfect it was.

But Rafe heard Drum's vague assessment and nodded agreement. "Exactly," he said, in bored tones. "Tolerable. What else have you to show us?" he asked the agent.

He didn't even ask my opinion! Brenna was hurt and confused. They left the house after making another appointment with the agent, and began to stroll back down the street. Head down, she held her tongue until she could control her emotions enough to speak. Which was as well. Because as soon as they left the agent, Drum began to chuckle.

"Your face!" he told Brenna. He relented. "My dear lady, it's every bit as lovely a house as you so obviously think it is."

"But you can't let the fellow see that, Bren," Rafe told her gently. "He was raising the price in his head every time he showed you a new feature of the place! You lit up like the sun, beaming so much he was almost rubbing his hands together. No, 'tolerable' is the best you can say—while the seller's in the room. I thought I'd make him an offer tomorrow. If you want. You do, right?"

"I love it," she breathed.

"Good," he said. "I'm going to offer half of what's asked."

Drum smiled. "He'll take a quarter over that."

Rafe agreed, "I think so too. Happy?" he asked Bren.

"I am," she said, "though like your offer, that's only a fraction of what I feel!"

Their laughter caused the fashionable on the avenue to stare. One lady, halted in traffic, looked out her carrriage window. She stared, then made her coachman stop. She stepped down from her carriage and waited for them to come abreast of her. When they did, she wore a glittering smile to match her sparkling eyes.

"Rafe!" the lady Annabelle said with pleasure. "So good to see you again. You naughty fellow! You quite disappeared from London and never showed up at the ball!"

A red cape the shade of heart's blood protected Annabelle from the cool breeze. Brenna loved red but seldom wore it because she thought it made her look too wanton. It was charming on Annabelle. It made her seem an adult version of Little Red Riding Cloak from the children's story, at once innocent and elegant, and startlingly lovely. The vivid color and her ebony curls peeking out from her hood showed by contrast how dazzlingly white and flawless her complexion was. It also made her eyes look blue as a jay's feathers. That bluebell gaze was only on Rafe.

He stopped. He bowed and seemed to search for words to answer her. When he did, his voice was brusque. "I'm sorry," he said. "I thought I'd told you I was to be wed."

"Oh my dear!" she laughed. "But that's not dead, is it? Engaged men do go to parties. Even wedded ones do!"

"Well, that's what I am now," he said. "Here is my wife, my lady Brenna. Bren, you know Lady Annabelle, don't you?" It was only a social nicety, a thing he'd plucked from the air in order to have something to say. A tic of a wince shattered the impassivity of his expression, as he belatedly realized how inappropriate a thing it was to remind them of.

Annabelle seemed too shocked by the introduction to notice that. "*Wife?*" she gasped, her hand going to her mouth as though she'd uttered a vulgar word. "Oh!" she said faintly. "I didn't know—that is—" her voice faltered "—I hadn't heard. Surely it was only yesterday that we met right here in London and you told me of your plans? But *married*, so *quickly*?"

Every rude thing anyone could have made of their hasty wedding was in that question. Brenna went a shade paler.

"One doesn't think of such haste in such matters," Annabelle went on. "I thought 'engagement'—a wedding in the spring . . . How foolish of me." She attempted a laugh, but it came out weak and unconvincing. "I only thought of what *I* would have done. Congratulations, my lord. Best wishes, my lady. What an extraordinary thing! Where was it? The wedding, I mean to say. Not here in London, surely?"

"At my home," Brenna said.

"In Tidbury," Drum put in smoothly, watching Annabelle, "as charming a village as I've ever seen. I was there, as were the Ryders." He saw a flare in the depths of Annabelle's eyes, and gave an almost imperceptible nod, as though to himself. His voice became cooler. "It was a country wedding, but a well-attended one. I'm surprised you didn't see notice of it in the papers."

"Really? One hardly has time to read. It *is* the peak of the Season, my lord," Annabelle said, her voice tight.

"The Sinclairs were there as well," Drum went on, "among others you know, of course."

"Of course," Annabelle said, but now her pretty little chin went up. "Well, sir," she said, turning her attention to Rafe, "now you're back, the mere fact of your wedding does not let you off my hook," she teased. "I mean to say I'm having another party next week! Yes, at the height of the Season. I'm bound to repay all the invitations I've gotten. A soiree merely.

Not a ball. But there'll be dancing. You will come, surely. You *do* want to introduce your bride to everyone, don't you?"

"That's up to Bren," Rafe said.

Brenna knew him better now. But when he wore no expression and used that voice, she didn't know his mind at all. She saw how he kept looking at Annabelle. *Well, a man would look at a woman he was talking to,* she told herself. *But what is he thinking?*

"Whatever you wish," Brenna told him, wishing she knew what that was—and not wanting to know, all at the same time.

"I think it's a good idea," Rafe said abruptly. "After all, we may soon be neighbors."

It was hard to judge whose face grew paler, Annabelle's or Brenna's. But Annabelle spoke first.

"Why, how lovely. I'm deeply flattered," she said, with an arch smile at Rafe, and a tilt of her chin as she smirked at Brenna.

Rafe and Brenna sat in silence in front of the hearth in Rafe's study that evening before dinner. She wrote, he read. It wasn't a companionable silence for Brenna. She put down her pen. The note home helped somewhat, but she couldn't dispel her doubts. She glanced at her husband. That bright head was bent over the correspondence he was reading. They'd said few words since they'd met Annabelle, and those few were uncomfortable for both of them.

"I didn't choose to see the house because of her,"

he'd told her gruffly as they were walking home, after they'd left Annabelle and Drum. "I admit I thought about the wisdom of it when I heard the address. Then I decided it would be stupid *not* to see it because of her. But I'm damned if I do or don't, aren't I? What sort of a fool wants to buy a house for his wife simply so he can ogle an old . . . interest of his, anyway? Is that the kind of man you think I am? Then I'm as insulted as you're obviously hurt now."

He stalked on, and before she could answer, added, "I'd never hurt you, Bren. Believe that. Take that house, or another. I don't care. Whatever you decide is fine. I only wanted you to be happy, set up like a gentlewoman deserves to be."

Brenna knew she had to choose that house now. If she didn't, it would look as though she was as afraid of Annabelle's influence as she was. Her crestfallen silence told him more than she knew.

"Damme, you females complicate simple matters," he'd muttered. "I don't want you forever wondering about my motives. The only one I had was for your pleasure. But I'll never be believed, will I?" His temper flared. "I take back what I said," he said angrily. "I wouldn't live there for any money. We'll find a place that puts that one to shame. You pick it. But make sure it's far away from any female I ever *looked* at!"

His lean cheeks had grown ruddy as his hair; his jaw clenched hard. Brenna smiled. His fury relieved her more than an abject apology could have done. "Oh," she said innocently, "then we have to move to the moon, do we?"

Their laughter healed the moment.

But hours had gone by, and now her fears crept back. He seemed himself again. But men forgot arguments sooner than women did. Did they forget past loves as easily? Could Rafe forget Annabelle? She couldn't. Especially not here.

Brenna glanced around the familiar room. She honestly didn't mind staying on here. The sporting prints on the walls, the general clutter, even the utilitarian furnishings, didn't bother her. She did mind the fact that this room reminded her so much of the nights they'd spent here before they married.

She remembered the conversations they'd had then, her brother, Rafe, and herself. How she'd admired Rafe from afar. It was too easy to recall the wistful sorrow she'd felt knowing she'd no chance to attract him. Because he'd been courting Annabelle. Those were the days when the mere mention of Annabelle's name was guaranteed to make his expression soften and his gaze go far away to some place she could only imagine.

Would it still? she wondered.

She was haunted by Annabelle tonight, even if Rafe might not be. She shivered, not because of the light gown she wore.

There was a folly, she thought sadly. She'd changed her warm gown and put on a dark rose-colored one because it was the only one she had that was almost red. It was a summer gown, low at the breast with little puffed sleeves, too scanty and light for such a chilly autumn evening. But it was a color he seemed to like. At least he had this afternoon. When it was worn by another woman. Now he didn't seem to notice. She moved closer to the fire.

"Chilly?" Rafe asked, looking up. "Want a glass of wine to warm you up?"

"Oh. Yes, thanks."

He rose, stretched, and walked to the sideboard. "Here you go," he said, pouring her a glass from a decanter there. "Red wine for red blood. It matches your gown too."

She smiled. "I didn't think you'd noticed."

He handed her the glass and sat by her side. "I notice," he said. He had, but not the color. Her gown was gauzy and sheer, the firelight bright. He could see how the ruddy light outlined her profile, all of it, from the tiny bump on her aquiline nose to the interesting state of the puckered nipples on her breasts. He ran a finger along her bared collarbone and bent his head so that his lips were at her ear. "I just don't usually comment on gowns," he said, scenting her perfume, letting his finger gently trace more of that fascinating profile. "That's more Drum's style. He can talk a female out of her gown easier than most men could strip one off."

She shivered again. This time from the sudden shock of heat she felt at his touch. "Cold?" he asked again, his mouth on her neck as his lips lingered there.

"It was foolish of me to wear this gown," she said breathlessly. Her body was tingling; she knew his touch for what it was, a preamble to lovemaking. She desperately wanted that for the joy of it, and tonight for reassurance as well. But she had to speak before her body spoke for her, because it was a different kind of reassurance she needed now. "It's for the summertime," she said, "but I saw how pretty Annabelle looked in red. I have no winter gown in that color, and I—I wanted to look pretty for you, Rafe."

"*Pretty?*" he chuckled, as his lips followed his finger on its journey. "God help me if all women looked so pretty."

He took her in his arms and laid her down on the settee. He followed, his mouth on hers. They kissed, they clung. She saw his hair burning copper in the firelight as his lips touched her breast. She raised her hand from his neck and stroked his hair, with wonder. "You're the one who looks best in red," she said on a quivering breath.

He raised his head and smiled. "Dinner be damned," he whispered. "A moment," he said, rising. He went to the door and locked it.

She watched him blow out the lamps and return to her. She didn't need more than the firelight to see how moved he was by her. If she didn't have the evidence of his kisses, the tight fit of his breeches made it clear. She was thrilled she could move him so easily. It only seemed fair, since he could so effortlessly capture her senses too. She eased off her gown as she watched him slide out of his own clothing before he joined her on the couch again. Skin to skin, they shuddered at their first touch. It was always a shock of pleasure, more so tonight. To make love outside their own bed was somehow dangerous and exciting.

She looked into his eyes and saw the heat in them

before he shuttered them and bent to pleasing her. But she was already pleased. To make love here would set the seal on this new love of theirs, she thought as she arched her neck and caught her breath as he entered her at last.

But for all it was, was it love? she wondered. Until his lips and his hands and his body brought her a different kind of wonder, and mercifully banished all thought as he took her to exultation.

Twenty-two

T hey sat and ate breakfast in easy silence, like an old married couple or dear old friends. Or the new lovers that they were, exhausted but content for the moment. Rafe read the paper, Brenna the post. She smiled at her mama's letter and chuckled at her brother's. Rafe looked up with interest.

"It's from Eric," she told him, handing it to him. "He's coming to visit, and instructs us to find him the most beautiful females in London—although not necessarily the most marriageable."

Rafe grinned, took the note, and soon was chuckling himself. "We can save ourselves the bother. We'll have to beat the females off him," he commented when he picked up the paper again. "Fellow talks as smooth as my brother does, but looks like a Viking. A lethal combination, at least for the ladies."

"Yes, and that may be why he hasn't married," she

sighed, "the way women keep flinging themselves at him! He never has a chance to really get to know one, or know if they care for him for himself and not those looks of his."

"Poor man," Rafe muttered. "You mean I've been luckier in my lack of looks?"

"Angling for *more* compliments?" Brenna asked archly.

His sudden smile showed he remembered how she'd praised his body during the night. "Yes," he said, with a significant glance at the footman stationed by the table. "Remember that—for later."

"Gladly," Brenna said, grinning. She sighed again, this time with happiness, and opened the next letter. It was written on expensive scented vellum. When she finished reading it she was frowning. She put it down, then picked it up again, holding it gingerly, by two fingers, as though it were some kind of bug.

"What's that you've got there?" he asked, looking up from the *Times* as though he'd heard her unspoken thought. "And why are you holding it like that? Afraid it's going to bite?"

"In a way," she said, handing it over to him. "It's an invitation—to Lady Annabelle's soiree."

She watched his face. It went blank. He scanned the lines and looked back at her.

"Want to go?" he asked, watching her reaction.

"I don't know. I don't know if I belong there," she admitted, trying not to admit what she was really worried about. "She is, after all, your friend."

He coughed. "*Friend?* Hardly that. Never that, actually."

"You wanted to marry her," Brenna said quietly.

He shrugged and picked up the paper again. He glanced at it, then lowered it, looking over the top of the page at her. "But I didn't know her well enough to consider myself a friend."

"Well, that's just foolish . . ." she began, and fell still, looking down at her porridge. When they'd become engaged, he hadn't known her well enough to call her more than a close acquaintance.

"It's up to you," he said. He fixed her with a thoughtful stare. "We don't have to live cheek by jowl with her. But she is fashionable, and we can't avoid her. Actually, it would be as good a way as any for you to meet the social world here in London. I'd thought to have my friends, the Sinclairs, the Ryders, the Wycoffs, or even Drum—he's a monster of fashion—introduce you to the people who matter. If that matters to you. To tell the truth, it doesn't interest me much. But I expect you'd like to know some of the other females here in town, to go to tea with and such. I'd thought we could give our own party when we move into a new house. Going to her *do* is an easy way to see which people you like enough to invite to your party. It's your decision."

He picked up the paper again, as though it really didn't matter to him. But he seldom spoke so long about their future social life; in fact, they'd never discussed it in any detail before. Brenna's hand went to her mouth, a fingernail to her lips . . . She realized what she was doing and hastily put her hand in her lap. She'd vowed to break her habit of nibbling on her nails so she could have lovely, graceful hands for him. Like Annabelle had. But when she was nervous she forgot. She was very nervous now.

"Don't bother to announce me," an amused voice said from the doorway. "I smell toast and eggs. They'll be expecting me."

Rafe looked up. "I should have told them not to make toast. Like putting fish out for the cat."

"Give you good morning too, my churlish friend," Drum said as he strolled into the room, dressed to a shade like a gentleman of fashion. "My lady," he said over Brenna's hand, "Am I welcome at your breakfast table?"

"Always," she said sincerely.

"As ever," Rafe added.

"I thought that though the honeymoon isn't over—may it never be," Drum said, "it's at least permissible to visit you in the mornings again. I used to run tame at my cousin Sinclair's house," he told Brenna as he strolled to the sideboard and inspected the dishes there, "and what must he do but marry and remove to the countryside? After that, I'd no choice. I banded with Rafe, who also found himself without a breakfast partner. We would forage together. It's a hard habit to break. I hate eating alone. The gents at my club are amusing in the evening, when seen through the bottom of a wineglass. It's much better to greet a new day with a friend. Ah, shirred eggs," he said with pleasure, lifting the top from a chafing dish. "That will do nicely. Along with the ham, a slice of that beef, and some toast, of course," he told the footman standing by the sideboard.

"And a rasher of bacon," Rafe commented. "But it's actually good you dropped in," he added as Drum sat at the table. "You'd be the best one to know. We've got an invitation to Annabelle's party, and Bren doesn't know if we should go."

Drum's azure eyes lit with interest, "Indeed?" he said after a look at Brenna's face. "But she did warn you of it when we met, didn't she?"

"Yes," Rafe said thoughtfully, "but when she heard I'd married I'd thought she'd change her mind."

"I think she'd heard about it before that," Drum commented, as he inspected the plate the footman brought him. He looked up to meet Rafe's cold blue stare. "That's not a criticism. If there's gossip in London, trust Annabelle to have heard it. She's the consummate lady of fashion, you know. I expect it was her way of teasing. She's expert at that, as you also should know."

Brenna couldn't see a flicker of change in Rafe's impassive expression. The two men were verbally fencing. They often did. But this time the subject was of utmost importance to her. She desperately wanted to know if it was to Rafe too.

"Yes, it's her way," Rafe said, "but what *you* should know is if Bren would enjoy herself if we go."

"I?" Drum said in a show of surprise. "But, dear boy, that's what *you* ought to know by now."

Rafe made an impatient gesture. "I know Bren, if that's what you mean. She's got tender feelings. Annabelle's always got some private rig running. So what I hoped you knew, since you're usually a downy one when it comes to a female's intentions, is if Bren would enjoy herself as Annabelle's guest."

"You mean, would Annabelle torment her in some sly fashion?" Drum asked meditatively. "Maybe. Maybe not."

"Well, I think," Brenna burst in, hardly believing her ears, "that *she*—meaning me—has some say in the matter."

"Whoever said you didn't?" Rafe asked, surprised.

"You were talking about me as though I weren't here," she answered, sounding wounded.

"Sorry," Rafe said quickly. "It's just our way, Drum and I. Many's the time we hashed things out together, some of them vital to our lives. Anyway, you said you didn't know what to do."

"Children, children," Drum said with a smile, "don't squabble at the table, please. Now, as to Annabelle and her intentions. I think it's a thing I could discover for you—on one condition."

"And that is?" Rafe asked tersely.

"If I can have a cup of that coffee—it smells heavenly," Drum said with longing.

"Drummond," Annabelle said as the tall, elegant nobleman bowed over her hand. "This *is* a surprise. Or is it?"

"A delightful one, I hope," Drum answered smoothly, "though your surprise both pleases and astonishes me."

She laughed, a trill of what sounded like such pure amusement the other gentlemen paying a morning call on her looked on with jealous interest. "Lud!" she said, fanning herself with one dainty white hand. "They don't exaggerate when they speak of your charm, my lord! I'm surprised because I've seen you at this soiree and that masquerade, at Vauxhall and the opera and wherever the fashionable assemble since the day I made my come-out. You've always had a bow for me but never a personal word. Now, what could have spurred your sudden interest, I wonder?"

"I had my eyes examined," he said promptly. "A few drops of ointment, and suddenly the world is clear to me."

"To me as well," she said with a much-less-amused smile.

"Is it?" he said. "I wonder . . ."

"As do I," she snapped.

"You don't have to. If I could have a few moments of your time, all would be explained."

"Explained? With no dissembling at all?" she asked, arching one exquisitely shaped eyebrow.

"Though it breaks my heart not to give due praise to your beauty," Drum said, "no, if you wish, none."

"Then stay on when the others leave," she said, as she abruptly turned from him. "I think we'll both find the interview fascinating."

Drum found the wait fascinating too. He sat in her morning salon and watched the three other men in the room make fools of themselves. Annabelle was gowned in old rose and gold lace; she was really one of the most beautiful women he knew. But even

Aphrodite didn't merit the treatment she got from the fools in her salon, Drum thought. Did men really think making spaniel eyes impressed a woman? If it did, then the weak-chinned young lordling hovering near her had the key to her heart. If long-winded speeches did it, then the foppish Lord Perry was ideal. And if glowering won the day, Sir Miles was her man—if she didn't mind fattish gents twice her age. Drum watched, bemused. She was lovely. She was clever. He'd also always thought she was cold, vain, and utterly spoiled. He couldn't blame her for that. Whether she was also vindictive was what he was here to discover.

When the visiting gentlemen straggled out of the parlor, they had as many jealous backward looks at Drum as they had adoring ones for Annabelle. Only because he had a private audience with her, not because he'd get anything else. The door stayed open. A footman stood outside it. A maid sat in a window seat. But servants weren't supposed to have ears.

"Simply put, because I gave my word to get right to the heart of the matter," Drum said before she could ask him, "I've come to discover why you invited my friends the Daltons to your party next week."

Her eyebrow went up. "Is it such a mystery? I often invite acquaintances. If one didn't, one would never have above a handful of guests. A wise man once said a person can only have as many true friends as fingers on one hand, you see."

"Still," Drum said, "one would think a newly wed pair are not the most enlivening guests. All that sighing and eyeing of each other is not very amusing, surely."

"I saw none of that the other day," Annabelle said with a pretty air of concentration. "In fact, the newly wed gentleman was only looking at me, as I recall."

Drum's slow smile was chilly. "I see. You've answered me."

"I have?" she asked, surprised. "Oh. You think I invited them so I could show the world how easily I could have had him? That is, if she hadn't stolen him from under my nose by means no lady would attempt? You think I bear a grudge? You think I'm spiteful enough to want to show her she's won nothing but his name?"

Drum looked solemn, and gravely as a bridegroom, answered, "I do."

"Do you? Well, but you'll never know, will you?" she said, her own smile slow and small. "Because I'll do nothing but be there, and be a gracious hostess. Surely there's no harm in that?"

"You honestly believe she staged that accidental incident in his hall? And that he still wants you?"

"You do not?" she asked.

"Then it's good that you invited them," Drum said. "So you can see how wrong you are. I give you good day, lady. And would wish that your intentions matched your appearance. You really are quite lovely, you know."

She looked up into that bony, clever face, her smile anything but lovely. "Am I? How strange you only

note it now, when your friend is involved. And he
still is, my lord. You may bet on it."

"I can't. Because it wouldn't be sportsmanlike. I
never take advantage of any superior knowledge I
have when making a wager," Drum said, and wished
he could be sure of it.

The two men didn't look happy. Rafe and Drum
looked up from their deep and whispered conference
as Brenna entered Rafe's study that night.

"What is it? Has anything bad happened?" she
asked quickly when she saw them exchange a worried look.

"No," Rafe said, "don't worry. We're just two
glum old lads. Come sit with us," he said, patting the
seat of the couch. "You'll brighten the night."

"Glum about what?" she asked as she sat beside
him.

"It's nonsense," Rafe said, picking up one of her
hands in his. "Only that maybe we ought to skip
Annabelle's stupid soiree. It's sure to be full of
bores . . . Well, well, look at this," he said with interest, looking at her fingertips, with their fragile, carefully shaped, longer fingernails.

"Just a beginning," she said, pleased and embarrassed. "But why not go? Has she rescinded her
invitation?"

"No," Rafe said, "just that it's not going to be
interesting. No need to trouble yourself getting all
togged out for it. We're going to have our own soiree
soon, aren't we? A bigger, better one too."

Brenna slipped her hand out of his. She looked down at her newly manicured fingernails.

"Damme, Bren," Rafe said, "I won't lie to you. Drum thinks Annabelle's still . . . hostile. No need to subject yourself to that, is there?"

"You think she'll be rude, say hurtful things, insult me?"

"She's too clever to be obvious," Drum said. "She'll do it with subtlety. It may be more hurtful that way. And there's new gossip."

"What are they saying?" Brenna asked.

"The usual, about the manner of your engagement. Your character. And some damnable new things. They're saying Rafe still longs for Annabelle and is moving in next door to her because of it."

"It wasn't next door!" Rafe said angrily. "And I mentioned the house to her because if we were going to see her in the street every day, I didn't want her thinking it was anything *but* chance!"

Drum nodded. "I don't doubt it. You were always a fellow who went straight to the point. And I don't see how you could have avoided it. But now they're also saying you're brokenhearted, and not the least of it's because Brenna's expecting your child rather prematurely—or at least, she told you she was. Your child," he added, casting his brilliant gaze down, "or another's."

Brenna gasped, "But I'm not even—"

Rafe's hands turned to fists. "If I only could face them!"

"Do," Drum urged. "That's the only thing to do with rumor. But not with your fists. By disregarding rumor and by letting them see your happiness. Face them. That's how you end it."

"I would, by God, I *have* done all my life, and it's never ended a thing for me," Rafe said harshly. "People will think what pleases them. Scandal always makes them happiest."

"So let it stand as a truth?" Drum asked. He leaned forward, his expression sober. "Make no mistake, my friend, it's not a trivial matter. Gossip's a powerful weapon. You think only a sword or a pistol can be lethal? They're merely more dramatic. Gossip can kill a reputation as effectively. Reputation is what our society is all about. Brenna can learn to turn her head when she hears the whispers. You can ignore it, go live in seclusion in the countryside, I suppose. Your children, when they go to school and face Society, are another matter. Rumor becomes legend if it's not stopped quickly."

"But if they consider the source?" Brenna said. "I mean to say, surely our friends can counter it?"

"Gossip's like free beer in a barracks, a thing swallowed without a care for who provides it," Rafe said bitterly.

"Exactly," Drum said eagerly. "An apt analogy. Because if you can make new gossip, the old will seem stale. The freshest is the tastiest. Go to the soiree looking as radiant, devoted, and blissful as you are together. Then the look on Annabelle's face will be enough to start a torrent of new gossip and divert it from you. Because she's only a spoiled lady, not an actress."

Rafe scowled.

Brenna saw, and worried. Was he afraid of hurting Annabelle's feelings? Or was it only because he'd dislike hurting any woman?

Drum shrugged. " 'Consider the source'? Yes, do. And you'll discover Annabelle and her mama. I've only gossip to prove that too. But I think this could be a way of laying the tattle about you to rest forever, whoever started it. If Brenna is willing to chance it."

"Do you want me to stay or go?" she asked Rafe.

"I want you to be easy in your mind," he said. "I must leave it to you."

Her breast rose and fell in a deep sigh. She lifted her head high. "In our family we never turn from a foe or run from a battle. If Annabelle is such a social lioness, I can't avoid her forever, can I? So if you *really* don't mind, Rafe, I think it's better that I go. I got a letter from Mama. My family's coming, you see. If it's going to be a crush as most London parties are, do you think we can get invitations for them too?"

"Doubtless," Drum said. "I'll see to it."

"Good," Brenna said. "I can face anything with them at my side."

"And with me there?" Rafe asked, his eyes searching her face.

"At my side?" she asked frankly. "Then yes."

They couldn't look away from what they saw in each other's eyes.

"Well," Drum said, rising and stretching his long frame, "time for me to leave. No, it really is," he added as Rafe protested. "If you don't mind my saying, visiting newlyweds is more gratifying in the mornings than at night, anyway. I'm off to a few places where I may find some gentle companionship myself. Give you good night. Look for me in the morning. Or don't. I'll likely be here anyway."

"Did we embarrass him?" Brenna asked when Drum had left.

"Embarrass Drum?" Rafe asked. "Embarrass a rock more easily. He only stopped in for a chat. He's a bachelor with rare taste. He really does have to visit quite a few places to find female companionship he approves of. He ought to marry, and would, I think, if he could find a female he could stay interested in above a month. Now, as to our night's entertainment—I have a few letters I have to write, and then . . ."

He leaned over, and inhaling the scent at her neck, whispered, "I think we could find some entertainment of our own. Unless, of course, you'd rather go to the theater, or the opera, or a ball?"

But since he punctuated each possibility with a light kiss along her neck, ending at her lips, Brenna couldn't answer for a while. When she did, it was only by putting her hand on his cheek and whispering, "Yes. I'll be upstairs."

When Rafe entered their bedchamber he found the lamps glowing low, his bride in his bed, her arms outstretched to him.

Poor Drum, he thought as he went to her. *Every man should have this*. But he didn't say it. Because her kiss put the thought from his mind and he had more important things to say and do. She was warm and welcoming and as needy as he was. He pulled away the coverlets and exposed her to his sight. She wore what he liked best, her own skin and a smile. She didn't shrink from his heated gaze anymore. She'd learned so quickly. So had he. She'd taught him much about the deeper joys to be found knowing what was needed and wanted, and being able to discover more. He filled his hands with her, slaked his thirst at her lips, and grew hungry even as he fed upon her desires, so sweetly expressed.

"Yes," she gasped, as he feasted on her. It was all she could say while they made love. It was enough for him. She did much more. She tried the things he'd let her know he liked. He'd thought a wife would be above some of them, but she'd insisted on knowing all his needs. He'd doubted his decision to show her. Not anymore.

Her lips were warm, her mouth hot, doing wondrous things to his body. But he wasn't selfish; he fought for control as he put his hands on her shoulders and drew her up. He kissed her lips, then lingered over her to reciprocate. And forgot himself in the sweetness of that, and what had to follow, lest he lose his mind and not just his control.

Too soon, and after too agonizingly long a time, he heard her gasp again. He looked down into her face and saw her rapture. Finding her release, he could at last allow his own, and reveled in it.

They lay entwined, letting their racing pulses slow.

He drowsed on the borders of consciousness, unwilling to relinquish his luxurious contentment to speak or sleep.

"Rafe?" she whispered.

"Hmmm?" he breathed.

"Do you really mind?" she asked. "Would you rather not go to Annabelle's party?"

Her voice was so clear he realized she'd emptied her mind of their lovemaking. It amazed him how women could do that so quickly, no matter how moved they'd been. He settled her closer to himself. "Don't be silly. It doesn't matter. As you say, it's inevitable. So why not now?"

He heard her unspoken question. "You're my wife," he said, trying to answer it.

Eventually he felt her relax in sleep. But he was wide awake now. He could see her in the dying firelight. Her raven hair was in glorious disarray, startling in contrast to the white of the pillow slip. Something about wild and witchy midnight hair always appealed to him. He smiled to think of how she'd scold herself in the morning for forgetting to tie her hair up when she tried to comb the snarls out. *Have to get her a maidservant,* he reminded himself. *She'll have to look smart for that damned party . . .*

He knew what else she'd wanted to ask and was glad he hadn't had to answer. He wasn't good with words. Or emotions either. He'd denied them too long to be comfortable with them.

How *would* he feel seeing Annabelle once again? he wondered. When she was dressed like an angel, dancing with every man in the room, knowing she was available to them and never to him anymore? When she would probably take pains to let him see what he'd passed up? How would he react if she was cruel to Brenna? What could he do? *Had he loved Annabelle?* His eyes went wide, though there was nothing to see but the shape of his bitter thoughts in the night.

He knew he'd vowed never to think of her when he lay next to Brenna, but tonight he couldn't help himself. It was Brenna who had brought the subject up, and now he couldn't let it go. His feelings about Annabelle confused him. He'd been heartsick, no sense denying it, when he'd seen her shock as he told her of his hasty engagement. When he'd learned he could have had her and had been cheated of the chance. *Had he been cheated?* How could he think so with his wife at his side?

Still . . . what road would he have taken if he could have taken one of his choosing?

There was no sense to this, he thought in disgust, turning so he cradled Brenna against himself. He locked a hand over her breast and closed his eyes. There was no sense to this kind of thinking at all. He'd never had a choice. His life had been plotted out for him since birth. He'd tried to fight it, taken risks and chances, plunging himself into jeopardy time and again. To no avail. The truth was, he'd been labeled and put in the proper slots all his life. He was a second son, a cuckoo in the nest to boot. It had made his pattern.

It was like that Puffing Billy steam engine all London had been agog to see a few years back, everyone standing amazed as it went round and round on its track all by itself. It was as if his life, too, had a clear track he had to follow and he'd been set in motion on it, and would travel it, whether he meant to or not, until his death.

He stroked Brenna's hair back from her face. She arched her sweetly shaped rear, tucking it closer into the curve of his body, pressing it into his abdomen. Sated as he was, he felt rising desire. His life had been prearranged, from birth and likely to his death. That was the way of it for him. Not all of it was bad, he thought as he felt his body stir against hers. But no—none of it had actually been his choice, had it?

Her bent his head and nuzzled her ear, in apology for his thoughts. She turned to him so quickly he realized she hadn't been sleeping. He kissed her. She answered his ardor with such desperation he wondered what she'd been thinking. Until he could no longer wonder because of the ecstasy she took him to.

Twenty-three

I come from a family of soldiers. I'm prepared for war. Or at least, I would be if I could decide which gown to wear, Brenna thought as she gazed at the gowns she'd strewn on her bed. She couldn't decide which to wear to Lady Annabelle's party.

The blue was lovely. But Annabelle's eyes were blue; it would look better on her. Brenna pensively fingered a lovely simple white gown. She looked good in white, but it was too virginal. Surely those who'd heard the gossip about her would snicker if she wore it. Gold—that gold tissue gown was regal and expensive looking. Too much so. It would make her look elegant, but might fuel more talk about her being greedy and grasping. Green was out of the question, she thought sadly, glancing at a pretty spring green gown. The lyrics about the courtesan in that old folk tune "Greensleeves" would surely occur to everyone if she went wafting into Annabelle's house wearing that!

She had to dress to fight rumor as well as to look her best. Mostly she wanted to look good enough to Rafe to make him forget his lady Annabelle. But for that, Brenna thought sadly, she needed a fairy godmother, not a dressmaker.

"What are you scowling about?" Rafe asked as he strolled into the room. He glanced at the gowns on their bed. "Oh. You have to get yourself a maid, Bren. They put clothing away for you. I'll ask Peck if you like. He'd find you one in a snap."

"Yes. Past time I hired a maid," Brenna answered, "but that's not why I'm frowning. I don't know what to wear to that party we're going to. Nothing I have seems right. I want to look just . . . splendid. After all, it will be like my debut in Society, won't it?"

"You'll look splendid whatever you wear." He locked his hands around her waist and pulled her back against himself. "If you're not happy with any of these, buy another. Your mama's coming. Take her with you and choose one you like."

"I wish I could," Brenna sighed, leaning back against the solid warmth of him, "but mama won't be here until the night before the party."

"Then enlist Drum. No, really. The man has an eye. I'd go with you, but much good it would do. My taste in female attire runs to the sort of things an opera dancer might wear. Drum has taste in these things. And he owes me a favor."

She laughed, "Poor Drum, he'd enjoy it that much? No need to go that far."

"Then take your brother."

"His taste in female finery is like yours. Besides, he's coming with my parents."

"Is he?" Rafe asked. "Then what's he doing downstairs?"

She spun around and yelped. "Eric's here? Oh, wonderful!"

She raced down the stair, into the hall, and threw herself into her brother's welcoming embrace.

"Such a greeting!" Eric laughed, hugging her hard. "Has that villain been mistreating you? Well, I'm here to settle him."

"You're welcome to try," Rafe said, from where he stood watching them.

"You're staying here?" Brenna asked, peering beyond his wide shoulder. "Where's Mama and Papa?"

"I'll stay if you'll have me, and they're not here," Eric said. "They're going by coach. I rode in. And Mama has the most wonderful surprise for you two—just wait."

"That's why they came so slowly?" Bren asked, "They could have sent it on."

"Not this gift," Eric said with a grin. "But you'll see. Now. Rafe, you wrote I must come to a party? I hope not tonight. I'm done in. I'm healthy as a horse now, mind. But I've been on the road since dawn."

"Not for a week," Rafe said.

"You wrote to ask Eric to come to the party too?" Brenna asked Rafe.

Rafe nodded. "I thought you'd like to have him with you. Your sister thinks we're going to visit the queen," he told Eric, "not just to a social do. But it's her first in London, and I want all to go smoothly for her."

"Will the lady Annabelle mind?" Brenna asked.

"Mind a chance to host a dashing bachelor? Not likely," Rafe said. He sounded so casual, Brenna's spirits rose. "Hostesses always need extra males to take pity on the wallflowers," he went on, dashing Brenna's hope that he didn't care if Annabelle was attracted to another male. "Now come, let's sit him down before he collapses in my hall again."

"Only offering me a seat?" Eric asked. "How about some dinner and a warm bed? That would go a long way to having me forgive you for inviting me to a party as a treat for the wallflowers."

After dinner they spent the night the way they'd done so many times before in the days before Brenna and Rafe had married—or even thought of it. They sat in the parlor and talked. Eric had news about Tidbury. Brenna hung on every bit of it. Rafe eventually stood, yawned, and rubbed the back of his neck.

"I think I'll leave you two for a while. Don't take it amiss," he said as the other two stopped talking. "It's good that you catch up on news of home. But I don't much care if Granny Tittle cut off her son without a cent, or if Squire made a fool of himself at the parson's party. I have letters to write, anyway. So if you'll excuse me for now?"

"More letters?" Brenna asked.

"Yes," he said. "All to make your 'debut' run

smooth. You'll see. Your mama's not the only one. I've got surprises in store too."

"He's a good man," Eric said quietly when Rafe had left the room. "Happy at last, Bren?"

She didn't answer right away, which was answer enough for him. He sat forward, waiting for her to say more. Her voice was rough and solemn when she did.

"I don't know," she said. "I don't and that's a fact. Oh, he's a good man, Eric, don't get that look in your eye. He'd never hurt me, intentionally. The problem is that I . . ." She paused, and went on doggedly, "The problem is I love him very much. He's everything I'd want in a husband and I don't doubt he'll make a good father too, someday. But before that day comes, I need to know if I'm doing the right thing by staying with him."

"What the devil are you talking about?" her brother demanded.

She was still another moment, debating whether to discuss it with him. If she didn't tell someone soon, she'd burst. If she discussed it with her parents, she'd hurt them more than help herself. Eric had protected her most of her life. If she couldn't talk about this with him, she couldn't speak about it to anyone. And she had to.

"I'm talking about the fact we both know," she finally said. "He married me because he had to. Not because he *actually* had to. It would be better if he had. If he'd made love to me the way they all thought he'd done, at least I'd know he wanted me

from the start." She looked at the fire instead of her
brother because of the way her cheeks were burning.

Eric frowned. "Has he given you any reason to
doubt him?" he asked, watching her carefully.

"No," she said, looking up at him, her eyes filled
with hurt, "but I've seen his face when he sees her.
I've seen it when her name is mentioned."

"A man can't help his face!"

"Nor his emotions. That's the point," she persisted. "If I didn't care for him so much, it wouldn't
matter. But you know I can't do anything lightly—
especially not live out the rest of my life that way. I
know he didn't love me when we married, but in my
vanity I suppose I thought I'd find a way to his
heart. Now I wonder if I ever will, or if it will always
be obligation and duty he thinks of when he thinks
of me."

"I've seen his eyes when he looks at you," Eric
said, grinning. "How can you say that?"

Her face grew warm; she looked away. "*That's* one
thing—you know very well love's another. Look,"
she said in exasperation, "the facts are that he loved
her. He married me. I wondered if he could forget
her. Now I see she hasn't forgotten him. It's not just
about my happiness. What about his? I can't imagine
any more bitter thing than to spend a life wanting
something you can't have. For him—or me."

"That's nonsense," Eric said. "Put it from your
mind. He's an honorable man. She's an unwed lady
of quality. You think she's so lost in love for him
she'll invite him to an affair and ruin her name? Or

that he'd do it? Then you don't think much of him,
do you?"

"I think everything of him!" she shot back. "*You*
think a minute. She must marry. She will. And soon
too, no doubt, and I doubt if there'll be love in it for
her either. She cared for that handsome Damon
Ryder, well, everyone in London knows that. Then
she set her sights on Rafe. Poor lady, I could almost
feel sorry for her. But I don't, because she was cruel
to me. You think she'll toss her heart over the moon
again? I think not. She'll wed, and well. You know
how that kind of marriage works in Society. Married
women are free to have affairs after they've given
their husbands an heir. Damon Ryder's utterly in
love with his wife—that's clear. But if Annabelle still
fancies Rafe, and he's still in love with her, and they
kept seeing each other—and in this small world of
ours, they will—once years have passed, who knows
what may happen?"

"There's nothing certain in this life but the end of
it," Eric scoffed. "Why trouble yourself with such
notions?"

"If you loved, you'd understand. You know the
gossip about me. I can bear it because it isn't true.
What if some of it becomes so? What if I did cheat
him of his lady, what if I *am* the only thing keeping
him from real happiness? I don't want to feel like a
villain for the rest of my life, Eric. I won't."

"Divorce is well nigh impossible," Eric said. His
head shot up. "You're not thinking of anything drastic? I tell you, Bren, this is absurd, all of it. Put it from
your mind. You want him to go down on one knee

and spout poetry at you? Rafe's a plain-spoken man, I doubt if he'd shower any woman with praise. His actions *are* his words. And if he's acted badly to you in any way, I'll eat my words."

"He hasn't, he wouldn't, and don't worry. I'm sad, but not mad. I don't intend to dispose of myself," she said firmly. "But if I come to see he still loves her, I *can* do something about it. I can remove myself permanently, and not remove myself from the world."

Eric stared at her as if she had run mad.

"I can pack up and go abroad," she explained. "I have done, and know I can do it again. I can go away, to some other country, and start a new life. That way he can get a divorce, even an annulment, without scandal on his head. Don't look so shocked. I can do it. I *have* done. When I picked up and went to India to tend to you, everyone was scandalized. Now I know why. That kind of independence not only gives a woman ideas, it shows her she can realize them. At least it showed me how wide the world is and how much a female can do, if she must. I won't be a hindrance to him. And now I know I don't have to be."

"You don't even have to consider such things!" Eric thundered. "What an absurd thing to say—to think!"

"Is it?" she shot back, "What about Mrs. McNeal, Mrs. Gray, Lieutenant Gumm?"

He was silent. She'd named good people who'd done bad things, wrecking their lives and others because of their loveless marriages.

"I don't want that for me—or Rafe," she said. "I suppose I am a 'modern, reckless female who doesn't know her place' like the gossips said when I picked up and crossed an ocean to follow my heart to you. But Rafe's my heart now. And if he can't give me his, if I must always know I'm second in his dreams—I promise you I'll do it again."

Eric shook his head. "You aren't a quitter, Bren. We don't run away. Father taught us better. You know that."

"You don't fight a losing battle, Eric. He taught us that too," she answered sadly.

Eric frowned. It was an unfamiliar expression for him, but he was obviously deeply troubled. She knew he knew her too well to argue what might be true.

"You're getting ahead of yourself—wait," he said. "Your decision either way will last a lifetime."

"I know!! It's a drastic and dreadful thing. The mere thought makes me shake, believe me," she said on a broken laugh. "But if that's the only way to make him happy, that's the only way I can really be happy. Or at least, be able to live with myself, no matter how unhappy it makes me. I love him too well to allow myself to be merely tolerated by him. Mama may say there's no Gypsy in me, but people aren't that wrong about these dark looks of mine. I find they do mean a passionate heart. And whether it came to me from Wales or Romany, I must follow it."

Now Eric snorted. "And you'll be able to know what to do after one party? Rash of you, Bren, to even plot such stuff now."

"Rash, but not unwise. I'll see the direction the wind's blowing. And so will you."

"Well, for myself, I intend to court the lady," Eric said, sitting back and stretching out his legs. "Don't goggle. I'd rather court a snake. But I want to see how fixed she is on Rafe. I'm not a monster of vanity, whatever you say, but I do know females. I should be able to at least interest her—if she's not lost in love for Rafe. I doubt she is. Not that Rafe's not attractive in his fashion. But I think, my dear sister, you're so fixed on him you can't see reality anymore. I just may be able to show it to you."

"How will that show me how he feels?"

"It won't," he said as bluntly as Rafe might have done. "But if you see it's all a game to her, at least you may realize that staying with him is in his best interest."

She nodded. "But if I can see I'm still second place in his eyes? If I'm right? Will you help me?"

"Bren," he said gently, "you don't ever have to ask me that."

Brenna's new maid arrived with the morning post. She was slender and small, hardly out of girlhood, brown as a fawn, with great pansy brown eyes that looked around the hall with wonder before they settled on Brenna's face.

She put her traveling bag down and curtsied. "If you please, ma'am, I'm Rebecca Forest. Your mother sent me to you. I came all the way from Tidbury. I hope I suit."

"Welcome, Rebecca," Brenna said happily. "I'm

sure you will." Trust her mama to see things were done right. This modest little maid would definitely suit her much more than an arrogant London lady's maid ever would. "Your first duty will be to accompany me to the dressmaker today."

But in the end, Rebecca accompanied Brenna and two of Rafe's best friends, Drum, and Gilly Ryder, to the dressmaker.

"We got the summons, and so here we are!" the fair Gilly announced when she and her husband came to the door soon after breakfast. "Ready to see you togged up fine as fivepence for any party you go to. Well, only me. Damon's off to his office, but he's letting me stay with you and Drum."

"Summons?" Brenna asked, looking up at Rafe, whose cheeks began to match his hair.

Before he could answer, Gilly spoke up. "Summons? More like orders."

"Is this why you were writing so many notes?" Brenna asked Rafe.

He nodded. "I thought you might like to know you weren't alone here."

"Exactly!" Gilly said with a sunny smile. "You're new to London, and we're old friends of Rafe's. Where else should we be? And it's a wonderful excuse for me to leave the house. This fellow," she said, beaming at her husband, "thinks I'm the first female since Eve to produce offspring. He worries like a cat with one mouse."

"That's 'with one kitten,'" Drum said. He'd breakfasted with Brenna and Rafe, and came ambling out of the morning room to see who was at the door.

"Still correcting me!" Gilly said cheerfully. "In your case, *mouse* is the better word. Anyway," she told Brenna, "Damon acts like I'm the first female in the world to litter. I know," she said, sending Drum a sparkling look, "not ladylike. Much I care. But he let me go when I said Drum would come with me," she went on. "I'm delighted. Rafe said Drum was going to help you choose a gown. Huh! I know a sight more about gowns than he does," she added on a giggle. "The outside of them, at least."

"Baggage," Drum chided her. "Marriage hasn't changed you, has it? I'd be offended, but it happens to be true."

"Nothing can change our Gilly," Damon Ryder said, "thank God! "

There was no way Brenna could tell this merry crew of elegant people that she didn't need them. Besides, she realized she did.

"Drum may know fashion, but I know Rafe," Gilly told Brenna, as they rode to the dressmaker in Drum's fine carriage. "Don't fret. We'll pick the best gown in the world, one that suits you and makes him proud too. The thing is to find something you feel comfortable in, something you can forget you have on. Because no matter how lovely the gown, it's the woman in it that matters most. Now, we'll look at gowns, and keep Drum from making advances to the females modeling them, and stay all day if we must to find the perfect one."

"The perfect one is the one Brenna wants," Drum said.

"I don't think that's so," Brenna said. "I have to look respectable."

There was a silence in the coach, until Drum said gently, "You are respectable."

"There's gossip," Brenna said, shaking her head. "You can't deny it."

"But that's exactly what we're here to do," he said sweetly.

They looked at a dozen gowns. They joked and laughed, and made Brenna feel at home even in the elegant salon. They liked a yellow gown, admired a pink one, and walked round and round the model in a gold and gray one. Brenna thought any of them would be fine, but when the model walked out wearing a long-sleeved crimson gown, she caught her breath. It was simple and sleek and cherry-ripe red. It had no ruffles, no overskirt, no panels or shirring, only a black design at the hem, and maroon ribbons at the sleeves and high waist. Its silken folds fell in a scarlet flow from under the breast to the tips of the model's slippers. The simplicity of the gown made it unusual; the color made it remarkable. And too daring and sensuous for her, of course.

"Is that what you fancy?" the observant Gilly asked her.

"Much that matters," Brenna said wistfully. "It would never do." But it was just what she'd always wished she dared wear.

"Try it on," Drum said. "The model has fair hair. That doesn't show us how you'd look in it."

Brenna protested, but short of insulting them, there was no way she could refuse. With the help of her new maid, she soon had the gown on. It took an imperious summons from Drum to get her to walk out of the dressing room. When she emerged from the back of the shop, there was a sudden silence. Rafe's friends stared.

"Yes," Drum finally said. "It's that one, and none other."

"Oh, don't you look a treat!" Gilly cried, clapping her hands.

The sound woke Brenna to reality. "It's very lovely," she agreed. "But I look too exotic in it." She wanted to say, "too erotic," but caught herself in time. She'd seen herself in the mirror. It was a beautiful frock. But it was a wanton's gown. It clung, accenting every one of her long, supple curves, the color making them look as though they'd been outlined by the devil's paintbrush. It suited her coloring, and her reputation. *Exotic?* she thought. She looked like a painting of a saint's temptation, the absolute confirmation of every bit of gossip about her. The woman she saw in the glass certainly would have stripped herself naked and posed in a bachelor's parlor in order to lure him from his ladylove. At the very least.

"Yes," Drum said again. "Exotic. Exquisite. There won't be a man there who'll doubt Rafe's reasons for choosing you. Wear it."

Gilly agreed. They made Brenna buy it, and

argued with her all the way back to her town house, because she'd insisted on buying the pink gown as well. She was certain Rafe would prefer she wear it.

"Try on the red one for him," was all Drum would say, as Gilly nodded wisely.

"We've achieved a gown," Drum told Rafe when he saw him. "Have her put it on and show you."

Rafe raised an eyebrow at Brenna.

"Later," she said.

When they were at last alone that night, Brenna knew she couldn't wait any longer. She had to try the gown on for Rafe's private viewing. She went into her dressing room and slipped it on. Taking a breath, she walked into their bedchamber. Rafe was stripping off his jacket when he turned to see. He froze where he stood. He looked at her long and hard.

"Take it off," he said tersely, at last.

"See?" she said too gaily, because although she knew he'd feel that way, she was still regretful. "I knew you'd hate it."

"I love it," he said, taking her into his arms. "I meant, take it off so we can make love without ruining it."

Later that night, Brenna lay awake as Rafe slept at her side. She couldn't sleep, though her body was limp. Pleasure could only banish her worries for a little while. She was very worried.

Rafe loved her body; that was clear. But she'd never doubted that. Keeping the company of soldiers had taught her men could easily separate the desires of their bodies from those of their hearts. So, thrilling as it was, his ardor was not reassuring.

Greedy, greedy wench, she thought miserably. What more did she want?

She had his name, his easy affection, his ever-willing body too. But all of it was as nothing without his heart. *Well, not really,* she admitted, looking down at the big, tanned hand that cupped her breast, even as he slept. It wasn't *nothing* without his heart.

But worry tainted all her pleasures now. How would the rest of her life be if she discovered it would always be Annabelle's body he really wanted? Annabelle whose company he preferred? Worse, Annabelle's image he yearned to see in his children one day?

How could she ever be happy, knowing she was the barrier between him and his utmost desire?

So she had to put on her new wanton's gown, go to that party, watch closely and listen even closer. And that way discover once and for all if she was always to be Rafe's second choice. Or if she really was his second chance at happiness.

Twenty-four

"Stay here? Oh my dear, I hardly think so. The house would burst at the seams," Rafe's mama said, looking around the salon moments after she arrived. She'd obviously summed up Rafe's town house at a glance. Her expression showed only the faintest disdain for its modest size. "Your father, brother, and I will be far better off in a hotel, I promise you."

Brenna thought she would be too, but made a token protest.

Rafe didn't. "If you'd let us know you were coming to London, we'd have made arrangements for you, or asked you to wait until we moved into a new house, which we will soon," he said. "As it is, Brenna's parents are due. They're staying with us. So, much as I'd like to argue with you, I can't. Might I ask what moved you to this sudden visit?"

"Why, we heard they were coming, and *so* wanted to meet them," the marchioness said as she pulled off her gloves. "It's been so long since we graced London, we quite liked the idea. Then, too, we heard there were to be many galas this Season. Perfect for Grant. He isn't getting any younger. It's time he took up residence here again."

"Again?" Rafe asked.

"I was here a few times in the past years," his brother said. "You were away every time."

"Yes, he's come to London time out of mind," the marquess said silkily, "and come home empty-handed as many times."

"Empty-handed?" Rafe asked, not understanding his parents' matching smiles.

"Without a wife," Grant said abruptly.

"So you can imagine how pleased we are that he's here on the hunt again," his mama said. "Seeing his younger brother sharing wedded bliss inspired him, perhaps."

"Perhaps it was the thought of his younger brother breeding before he did that encouraged him to such rashness," Rafe's father said dryly. "After all, now he can clearly see time waits for no man. Even if he is firstborn."

"Hardly," Grant said, with a forced laugh. "I've always known that if anything happened to me, Rafe would inherit the title. Rafe lived in the cannon's mouth so long you conveniently forgot it."

"We scarcely forgot," his father said. "Weren't you the one who always complained about how your mama pored over the reports from the front all those years? My dear boy, get your arguments in a row, if you please."

"Aren't they?" Grant asked. "You insisted on this journey, after all. And insisted on coming along this time too, though God knows why."

"You don't have to invoke the Lord's name," his father said, with a smile to show how little he meant his pious rebuke. "You should know too. It's the Season. Such a lot of things for your mama and me to do here now."

"Rather say, such a lot of things I have to accomplish in a short time, and you want to be sure I do," Grant said bitterly. "If I happened to fall victim to a fever or a footpad, or a bad tooth, it's Rafe—or any son he begets—who'll step into your shoes. That possibility is suddenly abundantly clear to you now, isn't it? So I see your need for my haste. But I remind you, *I'm* the one who'll pick a wife. Or not."

Brenna's hands closed into such tight fists she felt her newly grown fingernails dig into her palms. These three were still locked in a cruel knot, constantly snarling and biting at each other. Maybe they didn't realize how their comments could hurt Rafe. Or maybe they did, and didn't care. But she did, and though he kept his face expressionless, she knew Rafe did too.

"There'll be a number of eligible ladies at Lady Annabelle's party," she said quickly, to stop them before they uttered another hurtful thing. "Why, the lady herself is available, and just the loveliest woman in London, all say."

They turned their attention to her. But she had no

eyes for them. She saw Rafe's expression. She swallowed hard. "Though I don't know if we can get you an invitation at this late date," she murmured, shaken to her soul. Rafe's face was unreadable now. But she'd got a glimpse of some powerful emotion, and realized what she'd done. She'd only said it to divert them. She hadn't considered the implications of what she'd suggested. That he should lose Annabelle was bad enough. But dear God! What if she'd set the wheels in motion for his brother to marry her? What pain would that cause Rafe? And herself?

"The lady Annabelle?" the marchioness asked, her eyes brightening. "But isn't that the very woman *you* were courting, Rafe? Before that incident . . . before you met your lovely wife?"

"She is, the same," Rafe said tersely.

"And inviting you to her soirees now, is she? What a gallant female," his father said. "Do you know this paragon of forgiveness and discretion, Grant?"

"I've seen her, of course," Grant answered. "Only that. It would be hard not to. She's generally acknowledged to be the Toast of the Season. But I dislike being part of an admiring throng."

"I wonder how thronged she is now, my dear," his mama purred. "To my recollection, she's been the Toast for years. Fairly stale toast now, I should think."

"Fascinating," the marquess said, glancing at his sons. "I should hate to miss such a social event. Can you get us invitations, Raphael?"

Rafe nodded. "Your names will be enough to make you welcome. I'll send a note to Annabelle."

A silence fell over the room. Brenna didn't know what else to say; her tongue felt as heavy as her heart did now. They sat in the salon. The bright sunshine that flooded in through the windows couldn't dispel the edgy tension her visitors brought with them, or the anxiety that gripped her. She was grateful for the stir she heard at the door, and got up quickly, looking for any excuse to leave the room. She didn't need one.

"Good afternoon," a merry voice said. "Am I intruding?"

Eric stood in the doorway.

"Never," Rafe said. "Come in, Eric—meet my family."

After he made the introductions, his mama spoke up. "One would scarcely believe you were brother and sister!" she exclaimed as she stared at Eric.

"We're half siblings," Eric said, "though wholly devoted."

"Prettily said," the marquess commented. "It seems brothers and sisters make better siblings than brothers do. Our two also do not resemble each other much." His lips curled as he exchanged a glance with his wife.

Brenna shot a glance at Rafe. He didn't move a muscle when he heard his father's oblique taunt about the circumstances of his birth.

"Nor are they devoted to each other, I fear," the marquess added dryly.

Rafe stayed silent. Grant bowed as though acknowledging the comment.

"Oh, but we're a devoted family," Eric said, "with enough sentiment for everyone. In fact, I know my parents are anxious to meet you. Your presence was missed at the wedding, and much commented on. I trust you're fully recovered now, my lady?"

Devoted? Her brother, Brenna thought with an inward smile for Eric's polite barb, would fight the devil himself for his sister. She thought in that moment that her brother and Rafe's were examples of all that was different in their families.

Eric was tall, blond, and handsome. So was Grant. But there any resemblance ended. Eric bore himself with casual leonine grace; he was a man with great kindness, absolute confidence, and easy laughter. It showed. It attracted more than women; his male friends thought the world of him, and the men who had fought with him all said they'd have followed him into the fire if he'd asked them to. Some had.

Grant, on the other hand, was fair as ice, and about as warm as that too. He was lean and taut, his good looks compromised by his haughty expression. It was good he wasn't a soldier, Brenna thought, because she couldn't imagine any man would be at ease if he had to fight beside him. She wondered if females would yearn to be in his company either. And although it was clear his parents favored him, it seemed even they didn't get along with him.

"Thank you for asking," the marchioness told Eric. "I'm quite recovered." But she had the grace to look a little self-conscious.

"I'm relieved. It's good you're here today," Eric added. "My parents are arriving soon."

"Soon?" a familiar voice boomed from the hall. "Eric, you lie. We've arrived!"

Brenna looked beyond Eric. "Papa!" she yipped. "Mama." And without bothering to wonder what Rafe's parents would think of her manners, she rushed past her brother and out to the hall to greet her parents.

"How long have you been here? Oh, wicked Eric, you knew! You and your jokes," Brenna cried as she hugged her parents in turn. There was much laughter and many exclamations. They greeted each other as though they hadn't seen each other in a year, not just a month. But too soon, Brenna knew it was time to turn and face Rafe's family again.

Rafe did the introductions.

The marquess inclined his head; the colonel put out his hand. But Rafe's mama picked up a small gold quizzing glass to inspect Brenna's mama before she greeted her. Brenna's face grew hot because of how rude that was. Then she had to hide a grin. Because her mama stared back at the marchioness. She didn't appear one bit impressed, but instead, very curious. Then she smiled.

From the falseness of that smile, Brenna knew her mama had heard everything that had been said before her husband had made their presence known.

"My lord," Maura Ford said sweetly as she bobbed a bow to Rafe's father, "how good to meet you at last. My lady," she said, inclining her head in a bow to the marchioness. "But there was no need to introduce this fellow to me," she said, turning her attention to Grant. "Unlike Rafe, one can easily see whose son he is!"

There were gasps, Brenna didn't know whose, because she'd done it too. Rafe's eyes glittered; he went still as a standing stone. Maura Ford had managed to shake even Rafe's parents into a moment of shocked silence. They might hint about Rafe's parentage at every opportunity among themselves. But this was outright uncivil, coming from a relative stranger. What could her mama be thinking of? Brenna wondered, appalled.

Her mother seemed unaware of her slip. She went on to compound it. "Yes, your eldest is your spit and image," she told Rafe's father, "while it's clear Rafe takes after his celebrated ancestor," she added comfortably.

"His . . . ancestor?' the marquess asked carefully.

"Indeed, the illustrious founder of your line," Brenna's mama said. "Sir Griffith. The famous 'Griffin' of Arrow Court himself."

"Hardly," the marquess drawled, relaxing. "I imagine you say that because they were both warriors, in their fashion. But there's no way to know what our illustrious Griffin looked like."

Maura Ford laughed, the sound pure and silvery in the quiet room. "Oh, but there is! I don't know if my daughter told you, but my consuming passion is the study of ancestral bloodlines. Not that I'm one of those people who'll back you into a corner, reciting my own lineage chapter and verse! Though I could, of course. The entire study fascinates me. I had a letter in *The Gentleman's Magazine* on the topic once. Perhaps you saw it? Of course, I signed it 'M. Ford' since I was very sure a 'Maura,' no matter how learned, couldn't get her words into their hallowed pages!"

She laughed merrily. "I became interested in the subject after Brenna was born. Well, but anyone can see Eric's a replica of his papa, and Bren is obviously from my side. But the poor child was always being accused of being from some other even more foreign land. I proved it was all Wales, and met many fascinating relatives doing it. History is long, but blood does not lie. And Mother Nature's lazy and likes nothing so much as repeating a pattern. The long and short is that when Bren wrote to me about meeting your son, I set to researching your lines. I congratulate you, a commendable family. Almost as old as my own. There was a lot to read about. And so the moment I met Rafe I saw he belonged to your house—more than any of you, I might add. Because he's the absolute archetype, of course."

"Of course?" the marquess asked with a puzzled frown.

"Indeed," she said with surprise. "Surely it was apparent the minute he was born? I'm surprised you didn't name him 'Griffin.' But I suppose his pet name 'Rafe' is close enough. These things skip generations, but never entirely leave the line, do they?"

The marquess started to speak and stopped, his mouth partly open. His wife stared. Grant narrowed his eyes. Rafe stayed still. But Brenna realized Eric and her father were holding back laughter. She relaxed and slipped her hand into Rafe's cold one.

She'd trusted her mama all her life; she wouldn't stop now.

"My dear sir!" Maura Ford exclaimed. "Sir Griffith—the Griffin? You didn't know?"

"Obviously," the marquess said coldly, "not." He dropped each word like a stone. "What is it, my dear woman, that so amuses you?"

"Well, my dear sir," Brenna's mama said, stepping in front of her husband, whose eyes had kindled at the other man's tone of voice, "the name, for one thing. The heritage, for another. There are many red-haired people in your district, are there not? I could regale you for hours about the Saxons, Gaels, and Celts of similar coloring who settled there well before Hastings. Before the Romans or the Danes, in fact. But the name surely is the key?"

She puffed in exasperation at her audience's obvious confusion. "Gruffydd is a Welsh name, a variant form of Griffin," she said patiently, like a teacher with dim students. "That's your ancestor. And that's likely why he had the name, not because he fought like a griffin. They were very literal in the old days, you know, not schooled in the classics. I doubt they even knew how fierce a griffin was supposed to be. That's what first alerted me to it. The rest was simple. 'Griffin' also means the same thing as the Celtic 'Griffith' and the Greek 'Rufus.' And that is, of course, self-explanatory. There you are. There it is. You see?"

She stopped, looking pleased. When she saw everyone gaping at her, she added, much too sweetly, "They all mean 'red-haired.' And so, what with one name or the other, it's unmistakable. Your Griffin was likely the spit and image of your Rafe, of course."

"Of course . . ." the marchioness said after a moment's silence. She smiled, honestly for the first time, and exhaled a long sigh. "Of course," she said, raising her chin and looking at her husband triumphantly. "Yes, of course! As anyone *ought* to have known."

"I don't know if it's true," Rafe finally said out of the blue into the quiet of the night. Brenna held her breath. He didn't have to explain what he was talking about. It was obviously what everyone had been thinking about since her mama mentioned it. Rafe hadn't said a word on the subject since it had been brought up. No one had. His family had left hours before, bemused and uncharacteristically quiet. Her family was tucked into their own beds under this roof.

She and Rafe were in bed together. He lay staring up at the ceiling, his arms behind his head. For the first time since they were married, except for when she'd got her courses, he hadn't made a move to make love to her. But now, at last he was ready to speak to her.

He chuckled. "But I don't know if it's not. Which is the point, isn't it? God! What nerve your mama has! I thought your father was the fighter. It all may be humbug, but did you see their faces? Mama, looking like she'd swallowed a canary. Father, baf-

fled for the first time I can remember. Poor Grant—
his birth was the one thing he felt he had over me,
apart from being the elder. Your mama threw the cat
among the pigeons. No one's any the wiser than
they were yesterday. But the worm of doubt will eat
away at them now."

"But surely Mama proved it?" Brenna asked.

He snaked an arm around her and pulled her
close. "No," he said. "What's in a name, after all?
But now at least there's doubt. I don't think my
mama knows the answer herself. If she did, she'd
have proven something one way or the other by
now. I think she wondered what the baby would
look like and hoped that would tell her who
fathered it. When I appeared, red as that rogue she'd
dallied with, she thought she had her answer. She's
resourceful. She used her problem to her advantage.
She teased my father with possibilities, making him
desire her more for the desirability she'd had then,
instead of casting her off as he might have done. I
suppose that kind of cleverness is commendable.
Though it almost killed me and surely killed what
little sense of family they had."

"And so you'll never know?"

"No, but now at least I have a doubt. That's something." He laughed. "Was ever a man so delighted
not to be sure who his father was? The Griffin and I
may be related after all! I doubt it. But I have the lux-
ury of doubt now. What a gift. Thank you, Bren. Your
mama gave me more than she knew."

He kissed her.

"Is that for my mama?" she asked breathlessly.

"No," he said, dragging her closer, "that's for me. And you, I hope."

"Oh yes," she said, because that was all she could say when he kissed her again.

But she wished he'd answered, *Yes, that's for your mama—for giving me you too.*

Twenty-five

B renna stared at her reflection.
The gown was certainly *red*. Her figure was certainly lush looking in it. A tiny golden locket glowed at her breast, her only ornament. Her hair was brushed to a glossy sheen, pulled back from her face. There was a red ribbon woven through the knot of her hair at the back of her head. She tilted her head from side to side. The effect was severe and utterly exotic. She looked nothing like an English lady. Or remotely virtuous. She hesitated. There still was that blameless pink gown . . .

She saw her little fawn of a maid staring at her. *There is a gentle soul, and a virtuous one*, Brenna thought. She caught the girl's gaze in the mirror.

"Well, I'm dressed," she said to their reflections. "Do I look well? Honestly, now."

"Well?" Rebecca asked, amazed. "Oh, so much more than that, my lady!"

"No. How do I look, *really*? Don't worry about what I think. I must know."

Rebecca paused. She thought deeply. "I don't know the exact words, and I know they're important to you now, my lady," she said softly. "But as for how you look tonight?" She ducked her head, her cheeks showing a rosy blush. "You look—the way your husband's eyes do sometimes when he looks at you, when you don't notice. It's very . . . exciting, my lady. I don't think you could do better."

"Well, then. Then neither do I. I can only hope it's enough," Brenna murmured as she picked up her shawl and went out the door to meet her fate.

But she met her mama first. She saw her eyes grow round.

"I can change," Brenna said quickly. "I knew this gown was wrong, no matter what Rafe's friends said."

"Wrong?" her mama asked. "Oh no, my darling, it's exactly right. How shocking. How lovely. How clever."

"That's what Rafe said," Brenna sighed. "Eric and the earl of Drummond too. But they're men. Still, Gilly Dalton said the same. But I don't know . . ."

"*Know*," her mama said with determination. "Know you're beautiful in it. Know you *are* a good person, and don't care a jot about vile gossip. And let the world know it too."

"And let them think I stole Rafe?" Brenna asked sadly.

"Lud, child!" her mama exclaimed. "In that gown, he'll have to make sure no one steals you!"

"But it's the lady Annabelle he's going to see tonight," Brenna explained.

Her mother smiled. "So he will. It's time, I think. Don't you?"

Brenna nodded. It was. Her mama and friends were right. Better to face her future boldly than to slink into Annabelle's house as though she knew she was wrong. There was time enough for regrets. A lifetime, in fact.

It was a glittering party. It would be on everyone's lips the next day. Because *everyone* was there, or so everyone there was saying. The Wyldes' town house was large, but only a palace could comfortably hold the guests. They weren't looking for comfort. They were happy however crowded it was. That was the whole point of being there. It was *the* place to hear gossip, and start it, or spike it. London lived for gossip and it clearly lived here tonight.

Brenna stood at the entrance to the ballroom with Rafe. Her hand was on his arm, his hand over hers. Her parents were with her. Her brother stood behind her, with Drum. Rafe's other friends were in the crowd as well. Even his oldest friend, Ewen, the Viscount Sinclair, and his wife were here somewhere, up from the countryside just for the night. She stole a glance at Rafe and felt her heart swell. His parents and brother hadn't come. Just as well. He'd called on his true friends; he'd rallied the troops for her.

She stifled a smile when she saw his other hand go to his hair to smooth it. It must feel strange to him. She'd told him she preferred his hair a little longer. One night as they'd made love she'd mentioned that she'd like it longer, so she could feel silk, not bristles, under her fingers. She hadn't thought he'd paid attention. But he had. He'd stopped cropping it brutally short. It made a huge difference, and not just to its texture. It may have been pure fire when he was a child, as he claimed. But now it glinted like antique copper in the lamplight, actually enhancing his looks, bringing vivid life and color to his otherwise somewhat severely masculine face.

It wasn't a formal ball, so he was dressed in his usual neat, close-fitted clothes, a dark blue jacket, white linen, and cream breeches. She thought he was the most attractive man there.

So did her hostess.

The moment their names were announced, Annabelle looked up and through her usual throng of admirers. Her beautiful bluebell eyes riveted on Rafe. Then she spared a glance for Brenna. She stared—looking up and down Brenna's gown—and lingered pointedly on Brenna's flat abdomen. One of her sable eyebrows went up when she saw Brenna's eyes upon her. Her lips quirked in a tiny smile. Then she looked her fill at Rafe again.

Rafe looked back at her. *But what man would not?* Brenna thought. Annabelle's black hair was all curls, framing her face. Her gown showed her figure with equal charm. It was petal pink with an overskirt of golden rose, the color of clouds on an early summer's dawn. The cut was extremely low, but the innocent color took away any thought of improper intent on Annabelle's part. If a man thought her breasts very fine and her figure neat, he'd note it covertly, thinking it was something Annabelle never meant to show him. Then he'd look again.

Brenna's heart sank. Annabelle could have posed for the illustration of "Virtue" she'd seen in a Bible school book. And in her scarlet gown, Brenna could have been "Vice."

Annabelle kept her gaze on Rafe.

"A fine, handsome chap is our Rafe," Brenna heard Drum remark to Eric, low, "but not, I fear, worth *such* a look. I venture to say it may be because our Bren looks even better than she knows tonight."

Rafe didn't seem to hear him. "At last we're out of that hothouse of a hall," he told Brenna as they stepped into the ballroom. "It's not that much cooler here, but at least you can crook an elbow without stabbing someone. But here we are. So we might as well dance."

"Such a pretty invitation," Drum commented. "Well done, Rafe. Were I a female, I'd swoon with pleasure. How glad I am that I'm not. But how can I be equally happy? I know! My lady," he said to Brenna, on a bow, "please may I have the next dance, or will you sentence me to pine away for the rest of the night, alone?"

"Showing me up again?" Rafe laughed. "Well, I deserve it. But I have the right of first dance, for all my crudeness. And I am a surly fellow. Forgive me, Bren. Please, will you dance with me before every male in the house descends and tries to sweep you away?"

"See, you can flatter if you put your mind to it," Drum said with amusement.

"But he doesn't have to," Brenna said, looking up into Rafe's eyes. "Yes, I'd love to."

They danced. Brenna never would be sure, even afterward, what it was they danced. It wasn't a waltz, because she wished he had his hand on her waist to steady her. Even so, the touch of his hand on hers and the smile on his face upheld her. She stepped through the figures of the dance, her eyes on his. Which was good.

Because occasionally she looked around.

The other guests weren't staring at her, she thought as she spun her head back to face Rafe. They were goggling. And whispering together as they darted glances at her. She knew she was self-conscious about her gown. She knew they'd arrived late too. But only all the previous gossip could have spurred such interest in her tonight.

"Never mind them," Rafe said as they paced through the dance. "You look beautiful. That's half of it." He had to leave her to follow the form of the dance. When he returned, he added, "No question curiosity's the other half. It will fade. But your beauty won't."

Her eyes widened.

He grinned. "Yes, I can flatter. If it makes your color rise, good. It suits you."

Her color rose higher when she danced with Drum. He flattered her unmercifully. "Wonderful," he said as he danced with her. "I didn't know how you could blush. It's irresistible to make you do it. But I'd better not keep on or I'll be meeting Rafe at dawn—and not for breakfast. Now, there's another amusing thing. He's possessive as a bear about you. But who can blame him? Ah, more color. Good."

She danced with Drum, she danced with Damon Ryder, she danced with his elegant friends the lords Wycoff and Sinclair too. She began to enjoy herself. Until she looked around the room for Rafe—and saw Annabelle. She wasn't dancing. And she wasn't with Rafe. But she stood at the sidelines, talking animatedly to a man she obviously found fascinating. Eric.

Brenna's heart clenched. Much as she was glad it wasn't Rafe with Annabelle now, she hoped Eric didn't find her as lovely as Rafe did. *How awful if Eric found his heart in Annabelle's clutches too!* Eric was more than her brother, he was her friend and support. If he came to love Annabelle, he'd love with his whole heart. He'd be hurt and angry if his sister didn't share his affection for his wife. She'd lose brother and husband. Bad enough to wonder if Rafe still loved Annabelle. Worse if she were in the family where Rafe could always see her, and compare her, and want her. Brenna didn't for a minute doubt Eric could win any woman he wanted. She prayed he didn't want that one. For her own sake, and for his.

Annabelle fanned herself. Not because of the exertion of the dance, but because of her reaction to the man who had appeared beside her the minute her last partner bowed and left her. She craned her neck to look up into the tall, blond gentleman's admiring eyes. Eyes the color of twilight, hair the shade of honey in the comb. He had such wide shoulders she couldn't peer over them. And such a face!

"I've been watching you and waiting, my lady," he said in a deep, amused voice. "They were playing an intricate set. My war injury would have made my trying it a travesty. I waited for them to strike up a waltz. I think I could manage that. I think I'd move a mountain to try, whatever my injury, if you'd grant me one?"

"Such fun!" she said gaily. "Now, there's a reason to have a party. See what mysterious strangers appear when you do?"

"Mysterious? Do you think I'm a jewel thief? But I have an invitation. No need to have the footmen turf me out. All I'm out to steal is a certain lady's attention."

"You certainly have that," Annabelle said.

Another man approached to ask for the next dance. She turned to show him her back. She wasn't ready to leave this prospective partner yet. He was the most interesting thing that had happened in weeks—months. A stranger. Fascinating, and obviously fascinated with her. He made her forget the bitterness she'd felt when she'd seen Rafe come in with his slut. He made her remember how it had been at her first party, when she'd worried about how men reacted to her. When she'd thought that mattered. Before Gilly Dalton and then Rafe's harlot had taught her otherwise.

She'd grieved too long for Damon Ryder. She'd tried to heal her hurt with Rafe. And see how he'd wounded her in turn? Maybe this man could help her go beyond that. She'd spread tales about Rafe's wife; it didn't seem to matter. She had to look elsewhere for relief from this frustration and ache in her heart. She looked at this stranger. He was more attractive than any she'd seen in a long while. And he couldn't take his eyes from her.

She smiled. "You say you have an invitation, sir. But how could that be? It *is* my party. And I don't know you."

"Then here's your chance," he said in his velvety voice, offering her his hand.

She laughed again; her pulses raced. She'd noticed him the minute she'd seen him, a half hour past. How could she not? He stood half a head higher than most men in the room, and every female there was ogling him. He was well dressed and the best-looking man there, apart from Damon, of course. He'd danced with no one. Just kept watching her.

She was tempted to cast caution to the wind and just take his hand, because he offered it so confidently. Because his looks, his smile, his air of assurance, disarmed her. The only question was whether he was a moment's flirtation or a real catch. Was he wellborn, moneyed, appropriate for her? Or only some clever interloper, a hanger-on, a climber beneath her touch? She had a heart. But it had only led her to sorrow in the past; her head ruled it now.

"Can I dance with a stranger?" she said softly. "Perhaps once. But never again."

"Your pardon," he said. "I thought you'd heard it when I was announced. I'm Eric Ford, my lady, formerly Lieutenant Ford, late of His Majesty's Royal Dragoons."

He bowed and raised his eyes to hers again.

She put out her hand. She liked the feeling as his big hand closed over it. She was a small woman; most men made her feel vulnerable. But he was so big he made her feel vulnerable and yet protected at the same time. She liked that too. *A soldier? But a lieutenant, which is something. Ford . . .* She blinked. "Ford? Not a relation to Brenna Ford? Raphael Dalton's wife, as she's called now?"

"Her brother," he said, still holding her hand.

"Brother? You're joking, surely," she said, standing arrested, though the waltz was starting. "You're different as night and day."

"Half brother. We're only different in appearance. I've my father and my mother's looks. Both were fair. Brenna's got my stepmama's looks, and my father's warrior's heart."

"And another lady's love," Annabelle said angrily, snatching her hand from his. She breathed rapidly. "Is this some joke you two cooked up together?"

"No. I see no humor in it," he said.

"Nor do I," she spat. She took a deep breath, calming herself. At least on the surface. She felt the blood fizzing in her veins. Her heart pounded; her mind raced. She remembered the conversation she'd had with Brenna, every word that two-faced liar had said right here in this house. All that mock contrition, all those apologies and protests of innocence—with all that deception seething underneath. Because what did the slut do but promise to leave Rafe forever— and then leave the house, go back on her word, and snare him, marry him, steal him away forever. Now, to cap it, she'd sent her brother to court the woman she'd stolen him from!

Of course, Annabelle realized, the vicious, shameless creature wanted her triumph complete. Why else wear a gown that all but shouted, *Slattern*!? To boast about her conquest and show how she'd done it. Why else send her brother to beguile the hostess while she queened it at *her* ball? To make her victory complete.

Annabelle had planned to show Rafe what he'd missed tonight, by showing him the contrast between what he'd got and what he might have had. It would have been a slow, delicious revenge. Now she saw mists of red before her eyes. She'd been careful, secret and sly, spreading rumors, causing gossip. It hadn't hurt them a bit. In fact, they flourished. Vengeance had to be achieved. Instantly. She could think of nothing else. Rafe wanted her; she'd seen it in his eyes. Now she'd make sure Brenna and all the others saw it too.

"Dance? I think not," Annabelle said with a glittering smile. "I find I don't care to. Oh! Look there, your sister's abandoned her husband and is dancing with another. Why am I not surprised? I think I must offer him some consolation. Good evening, Lieutenant Ford." She spun on her heel.

"*Rafe!*" Annabelle cried as she hurried toward him. The waltz was playing, but the musicians kept their eyes on their hostess. This was her soiree; her every move was noted. She'd raised her voice loud enough to attract attention. The music slowed and wound to a halt, the musicians waiting for their next cue. Was it to be another set of country dances? Or time for dinner? Annabelle's mama stopped gossiping with the other matrons and looked at her daughter. Everyone did.

Rafe heard his name called, and looked away from the dance.

"Rafe!" Annabelle said again as she came up to him. "Where have you been all evening?"

"Here," he said abruptly. He'd been at the sidelines all night watching his wife when he wasn't dancing with her. "How are you, Annabelle?" he added belatedly. "It's a very good party. Beautiful gown."

"You like it?" she asked in a smaller voice, casting her glance down, holding out her skirt as if inspecting it. Her voice grew sad. "I don't know. It's so subtle. It isn't red as fire, or clinging. You don't think it's too girlish? I mean to say, is it attractive enough?"

Her smile was tentative. She was a tiny woman and a very lovely one, the petal pink of her gown making her look exquisitely fragile. In that moment she looked lost, vulnerable again, as she had when he'd first seen her. Rafe felt his conscience stab him. He was accountable for that. He, who'd only tried to ease her sorrow, had now added to it again.

His face showed his regret.

Brenna had left the dance to rejoin Rafe. When she saw him watching Annabelle with a lost, sad expres-

sion, she hesitated and hung back. He put out a hand
and drew her to his side. He frowned as he felt her
hand tremble in his.

"Lady Dalton," Annabelle said, "how good to see
you again. And in such a fine gown. I was just telling
Rafe how it quite puts mine to shame. And he
couldn't deny it."

Rafe saw tears in Annabelle's eyes. "No," he told
her, "it's just that I'm no man for words. I said your
gown's beautiful. It suits you, it does."

She raised her petal-soft gaze to his. "Does it,
Rafe? You think so? Then why haven't you asked me
to dance?"

He laughed, but not happily. "I'm a married man
now."

She laughed too, not merrily. "So you are a married
man, Rafe. But that doesn't mean you're a dead one."

He showed no expression. But there was something in the back of his eyes she couldn't name.

"I promised my wife this dance, lady," he said.

She put out her hand to him. The room went
absolutely still. She raised her chin to let him see the
dare, as well as the need, in her eyes. "It's my party,"
she said, her eyes entreating him. "Dance with me,
Rafe. You have the rest of your life to dance with
your wife."

Brenna went very still.

"You're right, I do," Rafe said.

Annabelle's lips began to curve in a tiny, tilted
smile.

But Rafe didn't take her proffered hand. He held
Brenna's as he sketched a bow to Annabelle. "I'm

sorry," he said with real sadness in his voice. "I have the rest of my life to dance with her, true. But it won't be long enough, not even if I lived two lifetimes, my lady."

Annabelle stood looking at him, her hand still extended.

"In fact," Rafe said abruptly, "if you'll excuse us? We came here to show how we appreciate your friendship. We enjoyed ourselves, and thank you for it. But we are newly wedded, after all, and have other things to do tonight. It's time for us to move on now. It really is."

He bowed again, and holding Brenna's hand tightly, turned and walked away from Annabelle, leaving her standing alone, her hand still reached out to him, in the midst of all the silent, watching company.

Twenty-six

S he wept. Brenna sat in the carriage as they drove home, and cried as though her heart were breaking.

Rafe raked a hand through his hair. "What did I say? What did I do now?" he asked her in frustration. "You didn't want to leave? I'm sorry. I thought you'd want to. I complimented her gown? How could I not? Damme it, Bren, could you answer me? You're weeping like a leaky bucket, and I don't know why!"

"I don't cry," she sobbed, "not like this. And I don't know why I am now." She dabbed at her eyes; her voice hitched. She waved him off when he drew near, knowing that if he took her in his arms to comfort her, she'd only bawl the more.

"I didn't cry when they told me my fiancé was gone, never to return," she cried, shaking her head.

"No, not even when I heard about my *second* fiancé's betrayal. Nor even when I heard Eric was wounded, and alone in a far-off land." She caught her breath and choked back another sob. "I went into my room each time, and when I was alone, *den* I wept," she said, her voice becoming nasal with her tears.

He didn't know whether to smile or weep for her himself. He offered her his handkerchief instead. "Blow your nose," he said.

She did. Then she drew a long, shuddering breath. "I *don't* weep like a bucket. At least, never in front of anyone. I grieve when I'm alone. But this! It's just that what you said—you made me so happy. Did you mean it?"

He stared at her.

"You didn't dance with her," Brenna said, turning a shining face to his. "You didn't act as though you loved her. Oh, Rafe, I was so sure you did. I was so sorry you had to marry me. You can't know—I even considered emigrating to rid you of me. If I saw you still longed for her, that is."

"Emigrating?' he asked, shocked.

She nodded. "Yes, if I had to. I've traveled far from home and braved the unknown before. I despaired at the thought of losing you, but it would be worse to lose you where I could see it every day. What kind of love is it that deprives someone of what they want the most? I couldn't. I *wouldn't*. Then, when I saw Annabelle tonight—when she enticed you—I knew I'd finally know what I should do. She meant to humiliate me, but she couldn't. You refused her. And

I could see it didn't bother you to do it. Or did it? Oh, Rafe, you do love me?"

"Of course I do," he said, putting out his arms for her.

But she didn't throw herself into his embrace. He knew he had to say more.

"Look," he said, "you know I'm not a man for words. Damme." He rubbed his forehead as though he could generate some by doing that. "But you need them now, don't you? Prettier ones than I can usually muster. Don't blame yourself. I should have said something sooner. Listen, Bren," he said, taking her hand in his, "I'll try to explain, though it's like asking a fish to sing, or something like that."

He thought he saw her lips quirk, and taking heart, went on. "I did love her. That's true. Or thought I did. But I never really loved a woman before you came along, so how was I to know?"

"She's very beautiful," Brenna said solemnly. "Who could blame you?"

"Yes. Yes, she is," he said eagerly. "There it is. Her looks. I think I saw in her an omen. Aye, that's it. Go on with that, you're on the track," he muttered aloud to himself. "I saw in her sort of a pale reflection, beforehand, of what I'd find in you. Does that make sense?"

Brenna's face was a study in puzzlement.

"She was a foreshadowing, that's all," Rafe said. "I always liked dark ladies. I never knew why. Now I do. It's because I was in some strange way looking for you. Do you see? Annabelle's dark—that attracted me. But so are you, and you're so much more. I can talk to you as well as to any man . . . Damme, there's no compliment," he groaned.

He sat forward. "What I mean to say is that what I found with you is what I was really looking for. Which is more than I ever expected or knew I needed. And I do need you. You bring me more than that beautiful face of yours, or that amazing body. It doesn't need a red gown, by the way, though I admit it nearly kills me to see you in it, and let you stay in it, that is. It's you, entirely. You suit me. You entice me just by sitting there. You fit me in every other way too. I like to talk to you as much as make love to you, and that's saying a lot."

He took in a breath. "That being the case, once I married you, why would I want her anymore? I feel sorry for her, that's all. I swear it. And I'm glad we went tonight so I could see it . . . as well as having you see it," he added hastily, grimacing at his clumsiness.

He didn't want her to realize that he himself hadn't known how much she meant to him until tonight, when Annabelle had tried to get him to hurt her. As if he ever would. He'd sooner cut off his arm, the way he hadn't let the surgeons do. He'd kept his arm through sheer will. Sheer luck had brought him his lady. He was lucky beyond his imaginings, literally. Annabelle had been a desire. Bren was everything he'd desired and more he hadn't even known he had. He saw it now, but that was a devil of a thing to say to her, wasn't it?

She hesitated, but her next question wasn't about that. "Still, the truth of it is, and there's no getting round it, though I wish there were ... that you thought you had to marry me, and that's the only reason why you did."

It was quiet in the coach. He thought very hard. It was, he knew, his final throw of the dice.

"Aye, that's true," he admitted, "but I didn't know I had to love you. God knows I do. She was like some bright star seen from afar. There's a clever lad," he muttered, "praising another to show your lady why you love her ... But I can," he said on sudden inspiration, "because that's just what she was, a star seen from afar—dazzling and distant. But stars are there to navigate by, and she led me to you! There it is," he said with relief.

She looked at him curiously.

He took her hand. "Bren, when I'm with you I feel like I've come home after a long and dangerous journey. And to a better home than I ever knew, at that. So when all's said, I needed her to find you. I'm grateful to her and glad of the unhappiness she caused me. I didn't know what joy she'd bring me, all unknowingly. And you're the greatest joy I've ever known. Never doubt it."

She smiled now, a real smile, if a watery one. He could see it in the shifting carriage lantern light. "That's the prettiest thing anyone ever said to me, I think."

He let out his breath. "Believe me, it's the prettiest thing *I* ever said. But I don't lie. You know that. Now. Once and for all, and then put it from your mind, because I can't promise I'll say it again. Not that I don't mean it, but it's hard for me. Thinking of the words as well as saying them. But know that I love you, and none other, and that's the way of it for me, now and forevermore. My word on it. So what do you say?"

She didn't. She threw herself into his arms. He kissed her. He thought, though he'd never say it, that he'd had better kisses of her. She tasted wet and salty, and since she was between laughter and tears, he kissed teeth as well as lips. But he relished the feel of her in his arms.

She put her head on his shoulder. They'd made a shambles of her hair, so he stroked strands of it back from her face.

"We probably caused such gossip," she said sadly.

"Yes. See what you've done? Now we'll be invited everywhere!"

She chuckled.

He turned his head, kissed her, and found this kiss much more satisfactory. Then much more than that. She was eager to show him how she loved him. He was anxious to show her how glad he was of that. Her skin was as silken as her gown, and he reveled in trying to discover where the margins between them actually were. But with that warm, willing body under his hands and her generous mouth under his, he almost forgot where they were. A jolt as the coach went over a broken paving stone almost rattled them off the seat, reminding him.

"Not here," he said with effort, drawing back. "We're almost home. We're almost somewhere else too. Peck is on the box. I'd like to see his face if we did that here . . . or even that. Stop it, Bren. Please.

No, much as I want to, we can't, not now. I'd never hear the end of it."

They sat in silence, holding hands.

When the coach arrived at their house, Bren entered the house, clutching her cape around her, a bemused, distant look on her face. Her hair was hastily pinned; her cheeks were very pink. Rafe was just as distracted. He said good night to Peck while watching Brenna mounting the stair. Never taking his eyes from his wife, he told her maid to go back to sleep, left word that they'd see Eric and the Fords in the morning, and without waiting for an answer, went straight up the stair after his wife.

They went into their bedchamber and locked the door.

They made love quickly, then slowly, and then lost track of time or the need for pacing it.

"Lord," Rafe finally said, as they lay back on their pillows again. "What a wife I have!"

He raised himself on an elbow and looked down into her face, his own very serious. He touched her cheek. "Bren?" he said. "Listen. Something else. Something I've been thinking. You've given me so much. This, of course," he said, stretching one warm hand over her belly. "Your trust, your patience. Your devotion and your loyalty too. And your family. I couldn't ask for a better. As to that, I'm grateful to you and your mama for making some peace for me with my own family. I'll have a measure of that from now on, I think. If only because they'll never again be sure that they aren't that, after all."

He looked troubled. "And all you've got is a

broken-down old soldier with few words, fewer social graces, and no looks to speak of. A poor bargain, I must say. How can I repay you? What can I give you in turn?"

"The most valuable thing you have," she said so promptly he wondered if there was a thing she'd been afraid to ask of him.

"Name it," he said as promptly, "and it's yours."

"Yourself," she said.

He was very generous.

America Loves Lindsey!
The Timeless Romances
of #1 Bestselling Author

Available wherever books are sold or please call 1-800-331-3761
to order.   JLA 0700

Captivating and sensual romances
by
Stephanie Laurens

"Her lush sensuality takes my breath away!"
—*Lisa Kleypas*